DEMON DEFEAT

PART TWO

Also by
M.J. Haag

Fairy Tale Retellings
(ALL IN THE SAME WORLD)

BEASTLY TALES

Depravity

Deceit

Devastation

TALES OF CINDER

Disowned (prequel) *

Defiant

Disdain

Damnation

RESURRECTION CHRONICLES
(hottie demons!)

Demon Ember

Demon Flames

Demon Ash

Demon Escape

Demon Deception

Demon Night

Demon Dawn

Demon Disgrace

Demon Design *

Demon Discord *

Demon Fall

Demon Kept *

Demon Blind *

Demon Defeat - 1

Demon Defeat - 2

* *novella*

Demon Defeat

A Resurrection Chronicles Novella

PART TWO

M.J. Haag

Shattered Glass
PUBLISHING

ISBN 978-1-63869-026-9 (eBook Edition)
ISBN 978-1-63869-032-0 (Paperback Edition)

Proofread by The Proof Posse (Jackie, Dawn, Heather, Mirjam, and Roxanne)
Cover design by Shattered Glass Publishing LLC
© Depositphotos.com

Version 2023.07.07

To fictional Katie…
…you will be missed.

To real life Katie…
…thanks for letting me use your name!

CHAPTER ONE

THE EVENTS OF THE LAST THREE MONTHS FELT MORE LIKE A DREAM than my reality. No one could have anticipated a plague that would claim millions and force the survivors to the coasts where we sheltered behind the protective mountain ranges. Or even dream of the unstoppable hellhounds created by an ancient curse.

While the plague and the hounds had ripped apart loved ones, those who survived almost destroyed what remained of the world with the bombs. In many ways, I'd given up.

However, since meeting Molev six weeks ago, so much had changed. He was saving lives, including my nephew's and the men and women who'd joined us on the recent supply run to Loveland. And that was the biggest change yet. Molev had given us all a reason to hope…and I still wasn't sure how I felt about it.

Truthfully, I preferred not to feel at all. It was safer that way. But Molev didn't care for that approach.

He wanted me to feel everything, especially when it came to

him, which was why I couldn't focus worth a shit on the task at hand.

My gaze slid to Molev again, taking in his slow prowl as he moved among the soldiers who'd joined our training session that morning.

"Andie, get your head straight," Roni said, giving me a hard shove to vent her frustration. It was better than another bite, but it still irritated me.

"Make up your mind," I snapped. "Am I supposed to care or not?"

"Care on your own time, not mine."

I stepped back from her, holding my hands up in surrender.

"You know what? You're right. I'm done. Pair up with someone who can focus."

I turned away from her and almost walked right into Molev's crossed arms.

"Where are you going?" he asked, studying me.

"I need a break to regroup."

"She's not focused," Roni said. "She's thinking of you instead of my teeth. Fix her, or I will, by breaking some skin."

Molev started to frown.

"No, you don't get to be mad at Roni for pointing out a very real problem," I said. "It's your damn fault I can't focus. I told you this morning that I needed some time to think, and you said no. Thinking wasn't good for me. Well, dying isn't good for me, either. So stand aside and let me sit in the dirt for fifteen minutes so I can wrap my head around some shit."

His eyes narrowed.

"If you growl at me again, I'm going to—"

He had the back of my head in his hand and his forehead pressed to mine before I could finish my empty threat.

"Talk to me," he said softly.

It was the same thing he'd said this morning when I tried to stay home.

"How can I talk to you when I don't know what's wrong? I need some time to process. To sort through my thoughts so that I *can* talk to you. I'm not trying to retreat; this is just how I work. You said you liked the way I think, so let me think."

His fingers moved in my hair, massaging my scalp lightly.

"Sit in the dirt where I can see you, Andie." He released me and strode away, scolding someone for not getting their arms up in time.

I scowled in Roni's direction but saw she was already working with another soldier. Finally free, I left the field and sat on the side. It took me ten minutes of just sitting there, watching everyone, to realize how adrift I felt.

My gaze tracked Molev, that stubbornly insistent man who was worming his way into my heart, while I thought about how hard he'd pushed himself on the supply run. He'd kept us safe. Alive. But at what cost? He moved fluidly now, his two-day-old injuries indiscernible if not for the visible stitches on the scarred, grey column of his neck.

The reality that Molev wasn't enough to stop what was happening was the cause of my internal emotional influx.

I hadn't ever thought that he alone was responsible for saving us. But I had thought we could find the answer to saving ourselves through him. However, Waurlyn's revelation regarding the trials the day before had shattered that fantasy. Knowing that the trials weren't working and that he was risking himself on so many levels to save us left me feeling helpless because I didn't know what to do next.

My goals had been so clear up until recently. In the beginning, when I'd left Irwin after the initial wave of the plague, I hadn't expected to come back alive. The goal back then had been clear: survive as long as possible to find one of the greys. After that, I'd focused on getting him back alive and then figuring out how to help those in charge find a peaceful way to work with Molev. The underlying goal for each step had been to find the cure.

But what if that wasn't possible? Where did that leave Molev other than within a nest of potentially hostile humans?

My gaze swept over the soldiers gathered. They all listened to Molev and responded well to his feedback. A few of them had been coming to these training sessions since almost the beginning. They smiled and joked with Molev. The others weren't as relaxed. But what if another incident happened, like at the hangar? Who would these people side with?

I knew nothing about creating vaccines other than what I saw in that initial room and heard in the doctor and Waurlyn's request for more testing. What would they want next if his blood wasn't working? And would he give it?

Hugging my knees to my chest, I rested my chin on them and continued to think.

Molev was still cooperating. Waurlyn had no reason to press for more than he was willing to give. Yet.

He chose that moment to glance in my direction. That easygoing fluidity he'd had in his movements ceased enough that I knew he didn't like what he was seeing.

"I'm sorry for getting upset," I said softly. "Everything that happened in the last few days was making my head a little too chaotic for me to think straight. But I've figured out what's bugging me and will be able to talk about it tonight."

He started walking toward me.

"Nope," I said, shaking my head. "This isn't me retreating or trying to buy time. We need to focus on this, for now, and talk things through tonight when the team's with us. They have good feedback, and I think we'll need it."

He didn't stop coming, though, so I stood and waited for him.

"I heard what you said to Roni," he said when he reached me. "You think I'm distracting you."

"Yes and no. Now, do you trust me enough to talk about this later?"

He didn't answer right away, which was answer enough.

"Would you trust me more if you sat on the ground and snuggled me in your lap in front of everyone for five minutes?"

He blinked at me, and I grinned a little.

"I thought showing everyone how much you mean to me was dangerous for you," he said after a moment. "Has that changed?"

"Nope, but I'd rather be a target for them than have your doubt."

He grunted. "Pair up with Roni."

I jogged back onto the field, aware that Molev was tailing me.

"Roni, we're a couple again," I called as I approached.

She hopped back from the guy she'd been grappling with and gave me a sour look.

"What do you sleep in at night?" she asked randomly.

"Why are you asking?" I asked as the guy chuckled and walked away to find someone else.

"I want to make sure you stay focused." She looked at Molev. "What does she wear?"

"A T-shirt."

Roni grinned at me. "First bite I give you, no T-shirt tonight. Second bite, no sleep bra, if you wear one. Third bite, no underwear. Are you focused now?"

"Extremely," I said, no longer annoyed with Roni. She had every right to be upset with me and ensure I wouldn't waste her time. Our daily training served a purpose, and it wasn't to get fit so we'd look good in a bathing suit. What we did now would keep us alive when we left to join Molev's people.

"So, what are you going to lose when I bite you?" I asked.

She grinned at me and lunged forward.

The following two hours progressed in a grueling blur until Molev called a break. I had faint bite marks up and down my arm when I collapsed to the ground beside Roni, but I wouldn't be sleeping next to Molev naked. Each bite I'd given her had earned an article back, and her arms were almost as decorated as mine.

"Have fun with panties only tonight," she said with a smirk.

"Day's not done."

A water bottle dropped in my lap, and I shaded my eyes to look up at Molev.

"We will run the courses for the rest of the day," he said.

Roni howled with laughter beside me.

"Was that decided before or after I lost my shirt and bra?" I asked.

Molev smirked slightly as he tossed Roni a bottle and walked away without answering. I shook my head and took a long drink. Sleeping next to Molev while only wearing underwear didn't bother me at all. I trusted him with my boundaries. I still didn't want to run the courses, though.

"So, are you better now?" Roni asked, watching me watch Molev.

"Sort of. Tonight will help."

"Hell yes, girl. About damn time you tap that."

I glanced at her. "Are thoughts of sex always running in the background of your mind?"

"Pretty much. Surprisingly, guys don't find that a turn-off. It's the wrestling before sex that usually sends them running."

"You saw me coming, didn't you?" Steve said from behind us.

Roni smirked, proving that she had, as I swiveled to look at him. He held out a snack bar to me and playfully threw Roni's at her back.

"It's not the wrestling that sends them running, Roni," he said. "It's the snoring."

She twisted and tried to grab his leg, but he jumped back to avoid it and jogged away while laughing. I almost asked what was going on between the two of them before I caught myself. Too much information that I didn't need. Getting closer to Molev was enough. I didn't need more.

The remainder of the day passed in a blur of exhausting activity. When it was finally time to go home, I half-collapsed onto my seat in the waiting vehicle. Molev sat beside me and wrapped an arm around my shoulders to pull me flush against his side.

"Tell me tomorrow's a rest day." Tipping my head back to look at him, I gave him my best sad face, pouty lip and all.

His gaze swept over my face, lingering on my mouth.

"We can rest tomorrow," he said, and his hold on me tightened as he looked away.

Since my minor meltdown this morning, he'd been watching me closely but not approaching. I knew he was trying to trust that I wasn't withdrawing from him, but I saw his doubt. Rather than bring it up, I let it be. Once we were home and in the privacy of our bedroom, we'd have the real talk we needed to have.

Leaning my head against his chest, I watched the turn to our house approach. The thought of a hot shower tempted me as much as dinner. Only timing would tell which one would win. Roland could move fast when he wanted the shower first, and Molev wouldn't let me sprint for the door after the way I'd acted this morning.

The vehicle stopped in front of the house, and Roland was jogging for the door before Molev climbed out. Katie hurried after him.

"How do they even have the energy?" I asked.

Molev grunted in reply, and I withheld my sigh.

"Can you stop them from showering?" I asked. "I'd rather get this talk done with so you can stop obsessing."

Molev's mossy green gaze flicked to me, and he started to frown.

"Yep, that's right. You're obsessing over something that's not happening…just like I was doing this morning. Do I think that means you don't like me anymore? No, I don't. I simply recognize that you have a lot going on in your head, and I'm going to do what I can to help you work through it until you're in a better place. See how that works?"

His fingers curled around the back of my head, and I struggled not to smirk at him.

"Are you teasing me, Andie?" he asked softly.

"Maybe." I shrugged slightly. "Better go stop those showers so you can find out after our group talk."

He blinked down at me then disappeared.

"Uh, what did you say to him?" Roni said, walking toward me.

I waved at the drivers as they left and motioned to her that I didn't know.

"Yeah, right," she said.

We walked into the house to the sound of Roland swearing somewhere inside and Steve laughing.

"What happened to the water?" Katie called from a bathroom.

"Group meeting first," I called back.

Roland appeared before she did. He had soap in his hair and a towel wrapped around his waist.

"Molev shut it off, didn't he?" he asked.

"Sorry," I said. "I didn't think you'd be at the soap stage already."

"Turn it back on, Molev," I called. The shower started spraying down the hall. "Hurry up and finish."

Everyone else gathered in the living room. Roland reappeared a few minutes after Molev joined us.

"All right, what's going on?" he asked.

I looked at Molev. "Are we good to talk openly?"

"Yes. No one has replaced the listening devices yet," he said.

My gaze swept over the others, noting their dried sweat and impatience.

"The vaccine trials aren't working. Molev's blood is changing the volunteers. Grey patches of skin. Pupils like his. They aren't surviving it."

"Shit," Brandon breathed.

"Yeah. The way I see things, we're still okay. But we won't be for long. Once they decide his blood isn't going to work, they'll go one of two ways. They'll ask for samples of something else from him, or they'll start messing with the hound corpses. Molev and I explained to Waurlyn why using the hound isn't an option, but we know what desperation does to people."

Sid swore this time.

"The current resource allocation indicates they still believe Molev is our best hope. We need to make sure they see him as more than a donor. And we need to plan like a vaccine won't be found."

Molev's hands settled on my shoulders.

"This is why I am relentless in your training," he said. "We will need to leave Irwin with or without Waurlyn's support. I've been away from my people for many days already."

"Six weeks," I said.

He grunted, his fingers smoothing over my shoulders.

"Okay. So, planning time," Roni said. "We saw what it's like out there. I think our best bet is still to leave in military vehicles. We know the Stryker can clear roadblocks and protect against the hounds, and our group is small enough to fit into one. It wouldn't be hard to take one."

Roni's answer was one I'd anticipated. Roland's wasn't.

"Rather than go that route, why not tell Waurlyn that Molev wants to check on his people? If his blood isn't working, she'd be more than willing to airlift us there on the off chance someone else's will."

I nodded. "Promising her access to the rest of Molev's people and dangling the carrot that different blood samples might produce different results could work. But, she'll know why he's interested in female volunteers once she sees they're all men."

"Then bring some of the volunteers with us on the first flight. A promise of more samples in return for a good faith show of half the volunteers," Roland said.

I twisted to look back at Molev. "What do you think?"

"It is a good plan. We will need to speak with Waurlyn again to ensure she is collecting the names of the volunteers."

"Agreed. On the off chance that this is a one-way flight, we need to be smart about who we select," I said.

"Hold up," Roland said. "Are we going to pull the same shit our government did and only accept people with specialized knowledge?"

"No," I said, facing the group again. "His people wouldn't need a cardiologist as much as they would need a handyman or a cheesemaker or a gardener. We aren't looking for higher education as much as we're looking for survival skills."

"We need humans who are willing to live with us," Molev said. "That is more important than what they can do."

"I agree, but if we have to choose between a friendly woman and a friendly woman who knows how to grow cucumbers indoors over winter, wouldn't it make sense to choose the second woman?"

He nodded once and glanced at Roland.

"Yeah, it does," Roland said, agreeing. "But you don't need two hundred farmers or cheesemakers. What you really need is an army of motivated people and a few with the skills you're looking for."

"I promise we'll diversify," I said.

"What kind of timeline are we looking at?" Roni asked.

"I think that will depend on Waurlyn and the trials once we talk to her," I said before glancing back at Molev. "We're going to need to wing whatever deadline we give her, but I don't think we should wait too long."

"No more than six weeks," he agreed. He looked at the others. "No training tomorrow. Rest. We will train even harder after."

Steve groaned, Roni grinned, and Katie closed herself in the guest bathroom.

Molev laced his fingers through mine and led me to our bedroom with the attached bathroom.

As soon as the door closed, I started tossing my clothes aside.

"Are you up for a co-ed shower and some more talking?" I asked, making my way to the shower. He didn't answer as I started the water, but when I glanced back, I found him undressed and waiting behind me. His gaze drifted down to my underwear, the only clothing I still wore.

"You said you trusted me with everything but retreating," I said. "The doubt you still have about that is going to cause problems. It would have today if you'd decided to be stubborn and insisted on talking out in the open about whatever was bugging me. So, how do I get you to trust that I'm not going to retreat?"

The water began to warm my hand, so I shook it off and removed my underwear.

Molev's hungry gaze swept over me.

"Are we going to be able to talk and shower, or is this too distracting?" I asked.

He closed the space between us and wrapped his arms around me. A moment later, the warm water sprayed my back and wet my hair. He tangled his fingers in the strands and tugged my head back, dipping his to lightly brush his lips against mine.

"I am not too distracted," he said. "You may speak."

"It's your turn, actually," I said, smoothing my hands over his chest. "You're supposed to tell me how I earn your trust, proving that I'm ready to start listening to my heart."

He stopped kissing my chin and pulled back to look me in the eyes.

"Tell me what I mean to you."

I made a face. "You're going right for the uncomfortable stuff, aren't you?"

He didn't react at all, just continued to wait expectantly.

"I'm not sure yet what you mean to me," I said. "It's not something I've let myself think about. Honestly, I haven't had the time. There's been a lot going on in the last six weeks. But I can tell you how I feel when I'm with you. Excited. Frustrated. Safe. Horny. Confused."

I trailed my hands over his pecs and started exploring his abs. "The frustration is mostly when you don't take care of yourself like I think you should. The confusion springs up during the quiet moments, like when I'm watching you talk to the other soldiers or when you're holding me at night. I'm having a hard time picturing our future. Some of that is still worrying that you're going to try to put me in a role I don't like. But mostly, it's because I'm struggling to imagine the community you're envisioning. Both of those things will get better once we're there, though."

He dipped his head and kissed me tenderly, one hand in my hair and the other cupping my jaw. It was sweet and conveyed a gentleness he rarely showed. I loved it, but I wanted that edge too. So I lowered my hand, brushing over his hip and down his thigh. When I came up again and brazenly cupped his scrotum, his fingers clenched in my hair.

I nipped his bottom lip.

He pulled back and stared down at me.

"Tell me you're mine," he said roughly.

"I'm not yours," I said. "I'm my own. But I'm willing to share if you're willing to play nice."

My hand gently massaged him then drifted up. My fingers struggled to encompass his girth as I slicked my palm up and down his engorged length.

His mouth crashed down on mine, and he kissed me with an intense hunger I'd never felt before. It robbed me of breath and stole all rational thought. I stroked him with one hand and clung to him with the other as he gave me what I'd been craving.

The hand cradling my jaw disappeared, and the heat of his

palm seared my breast a moment later. I groaned into his mouth, and my hand faltered in its work. He growled and nipped my lip as his hips jerked forward, thrusting into my hold. His hunger fed my own until all I could think about was how much I wanted the man.

He turned us, and the barely warmed wall hit my back before he tore his mouth from mine.

"Andie," he growled. "I don't share, and I'm struggling to be patient. Tell me what you want from me."

"Your trust," I said. "Let go. Give me a chance to show you I'm not going to run away."

He growled low but eased his fingers from my hair. I nudged him back. He reluctantly gave me room and allowed me to turn us so his shoulders blocked the shower spray. His compliance was a direct result of my hand still wrapped around his impressive size.

I looked down at it, the purple-grey hue dark against my skin.

"Andie," he said again. "Tell me you're mine."

"It's a good thing you're a patient man," I said. Before he could grab my hair again, I sank to my knees and looked up at him.

"I don't want to be owned, Molev. I want to be cherished for who I am."

Molev's eyes narrowed at me, but I wasn't worried. I had him right where I wanted him.

CHAPTER TWO

"You knew I wouldn't be okay doing anything in the tent," I said, stroking both my hands up his shaft to his swollen head. "Same applies here. No noise to give away what we're doing, okay?"

"What are we doing?" he asked.

"This."

I opened my mouth and licked what I was toying with. He hissed out a breath, and his hands cradled my head. My tongue circled the crown before I fit it into my mouth. Barely. He was huge, and I couldn't even grin as I sucked gently. He groaned softly, and his hands fisted into my hair.

Pulling back, I smiled up at him. "I like when you take control. Just a little."

His molten gaze held mine.

"Open," he said roughly.

I did and took him into my mouth. He thrust shallowly, and the snarled sound that erupted from him was everything. It lit up that fight or flight signal that somehow also tripped my libido.

On his next thrust, I pushed forward, willing him deeper. He made another angry sound and thrust again and again.

Then he was coming, flooding my mouth, so I had no choice but to swallow or choke on it. I did some of both as he continued to guide my movements with his fingers twisted in my hair.

I didn't get a chance to catch my breath after the last jet of his release. He dropped to his knees, kneeling with me, and kissed me ravenously. The shock of it distracted me from his hands until one wrapped around my thigh and nudged it to the side.

I pulled my mouth from his.

"Wait," I panted.

"No. It's my turn to taste you."

His fingers slicked between my folds, and he swallowed my moan with another kiss.

"Hey! Time's up," someone called, pounding on the bedroom door. "Hot water is shared in this house."

Molev snarled.

Loudly.

I covered his mouth with my hand and shook my head.

"Sorry," I called, reaching around him to turn off the water.

Molev's fingers feathered over my core, and I leaned back to watch him bring his fingers to his mouth and lick them.

His pupils dilated as he tasted me.

"More," he breathed a second before I was in his arms. In a blink, he had me on my back on the bed, my thighs held apart with his palms.

He knelt at the edge, staring between my legs like he'd found an all-you-can-eat meat buffet.

"Please be careful with your teeth," I said, embracing his hunger.

He grunted and leaned in, inhaling deeply. Then his tongue was on me. My hands covered my mouth for the initial sensation as I writhed underneath his ravenous onslaught. As soon as he figured out what I liked the most, I didn't stand a chance. The wave of my orgasm crashed and pummeled me like a rocky, windswept shore. It left me wrung out and oversensitive. When he continued licking, I swatted him away. He didn't go far, choosing to gently kiss my inner thigh and hip as his finger teased my opening.

"I can't," I panted. I was a one-and-done girl, needing at least an hour to recover.

"You can," he said, his finger penetrating me a few inches before retreating. Rather than the jarring shock of sensation I expected, it lit my hypersensitive nerve endings in a give-me-more way.

When he thrust again, I ground down on it.

"Yes," he said. "Like that."

He worked his finger into me, slowly building that need again. Once he was buried deep, he curled that thick digit and kissed next to my clit. My core clenched around him.

"So pretty," he said, kissing me on the other side.

I involuntarily clenched a second time and made a soft sound. He started moving his finger rhythmically.

"This is what I've dreamed of, Andie. Your taste on my lips and the sounds of your pleasure in my ears. Because of me. For me."

His tempo increased, and I struggled to focus. All those nerve endings were lighting up again, but never so much that I'd push him away. I teetered in that place in the middle, climbing higher as I clenched around him.

"Take the pillow, Andie," he said.

"Huh?" I lifted my head unsteadily and saw his wild gaze fixed on what he was doing to me.

"Place it over your face," he said roughly. He paused his rhythm, and I felt another finger ease into me.

I grabbed the pillow and flipped it onto my face just in time. His mouth closed over me again as he started moving faster. I squealed into the pillow and bucked. He held firm, flicking his tongue over my nub until the dam broke. My body bowed off the bed at the intensity of the orgasm that ripped through me. He eased up on the suction but didn't break his tempo until I collapsed onto the mattress again.

He removed his fingers and replaced them with his tongue, slowly thrusting into my core like he was kissing me. It helped soothe the strength of the aftershocks, so I didn't mind. I just lay there limp and let him do as he pleased.

Eventually, his mouth left me, and the pillow lifted off my face. I didn't open my eyes. I had no energy left for even that simple task.

A fingertip traced over my cheek and eyebrow.

"Did you like that, Andie?" he asked quietly.

"So much," I managed. "Tired."

His arms slipped around me.

"Sleep. You can eat later," he said.

MY STOMACH WOKE ME. I couldn't hear it rumbling but felt its demand for food, even in my sleep. However, my gnawing hunger faded to the background at the slow stroking of Molev's hand over my bare hip.

And thoughts of what we'd done before I'd fallen asleep drifted in. My hands gripping him... My mouth barely taking the tip of his massive shaft... The explosion in my mouth and his relentless hunger that followed.

Obviously, that hunger hadn't yet been appeased. The pressure and drag of his palm spoke his thoughts without words. But, no matter how enjoyable that was, we couldn't indulge in our baser desires whenever and however. We needed to have some measure of focus.

"What time is it?" I mumbled.

"Almost sunrise." His touch changed from the firm contact of his hand to the light sweep of his fingers. "Are you hungry for food?"

"Very. Will you let me out of this bed so I can feed myself, or will you consider that a retreat?"

My stomach growled more insistently, and he sighed.

"I can hear your hunger and wish I would have fed you last night so I could feast now."

I rolled toward him, dislodging his touch. His palm trailed over my stomach.

"Maybe next time you'll be better prepared. Is it someone else's turn to make breakfast?"

His gaze swept my face, and he shook his head.

"No, I will make it. Shower and get dressed. After, we will speak with Waurlyn."

When I arrived in the kitchen fifteen minutes later, he had a feast started. French toast—the regular kind—with maple syrup, a mountain of sausages in the oven, and an extra-large pan of scrambled eggs.

"Sit," he said.

I did and watched him move around the kitchen for a moment. He was so easy on the eyes that it was mind-numbing.

"How are we going to approach Waurlyn today?" I asked.

"At the hospital. I've already asked our neighbors to request that she meet us there."

I chuckled a little. "I meant, how are we going to ease into the topic of you wanting to return to your people? If we don't approach it carefully, she might have a knee-jerk reaction and try to keep you here."

"Waurlyn likes trades and needs hope. I will give her both."

"Is this one of those 'I need to trust you' tests? Because I do. I was just curious."

He glanced back at me, and something shifted in his gaze. He set aside the spatula and came to me, sliding his fingers into my hair.

"You distract me, Andie. I crave you in many ways. The taste of your pussy on my tongue. Your smile. Your humor. Your trust. I want all of you all at once. Forever. My need for that steals my breath and robs me of thought. And when you give me these little samples of what it will be like when you finally surrender everything to me, it solidifies my determination to do whatever is necessary to see my dream become my reality."

His words and the raw emotion behind them wrapped around me, pulling me back to that moment in the shower when I'd fallen to my knees for him. I'd enjoyed myself without reservation, and when I'd woken this morning, I'd told myself that was enough for now. But Molev's message was clear. It would never be enough for him. He would be waiting for more, accepting it gladly when I gave it freely, and goading for extra whenever I hesitated.

And I understood why.

He saw the world's uncertain outlook as a reason to grab everything by both hands and live fully. *My hesitation had to be killing him,* I thought.

"I hope it becomes a reality too. Just not today. You can't afford to be any more distracted than you already are. I'm sure your people are missing you. I would be."

He closed his eyes and rested his forehead against mine.

"I can see you will test my patience."

"I know you have lots of it," I said, patting his chest. "So I'm not too worried."

He grunted and eased away from me to turn the French toast. As he worked, he began to answer my original question.

"I intend to ask how many volunteer names she's collected so far and share our plan to interview them, keeping my desire to return focused on a slow integration to adjust resource management."

"Smart. She'll understand where you're coming from for sure."

"Yes. And by inviting the doctor to accompany us to collect more samples, I will alleviate Waurlyn's fear that I am abandoning the efforts to create a cure."

"You're doing more than alleviating her fears," I said. "You're creating a valid reason to maintain good relations between our two people." I exhaled gustily as I realized what that meant. "We won't need to live in fear of them trying to dissect you."

He chuckled. "That was not a fear I was living with."

"You should be," Katie said, shuffling into the kitchen. "Humans can be messed up. Is that French toast?"

He smiled at her and handed her a fixed plate. "There is meat in the oven, but it is still cooking."

"This is good," she said, coming to sit beside me.

The rest of the team slowly trickled in from their rooms in the following minutes with Roland appearing last.

"What are the plans today, boss?" he asked Molev.

"Relax. Keep Roni entertained so she doesn't start fighting with Steve again."

"I appreciate that you recognize it's not always my fault," Steve said around a mouthful. "Even though I'm the one who's always yelled at for it."

"I don't yell," Molev said. "I simply remind you not to hurt her."

"What about her hurting me?" Steve demanded.

"You don't have a vagina," Roni said with a smirk.

"That's sexism," Steve said, pushing away his plate dramatically only to snatch it up again when Roni tried to grab it.

"Welcome to the new world," she said. "I like the change in the pecking order."

Amused but trying to ignore it, I finished my breakfast and looked at Molev.

"Ready?" I asked him.

"Ready for what?" Roni asked. "Do we need to leave the house?"

I rolled my eyes at her. "No, we're heading to Waurlyn's like we discussed yesterday."

"We're not all going?" Steve asked.

"No. Mommy and Daddy want to talk without the kids along," Sid said.

The mutinous stare that Steve gave Sid was everything. I laughed, and Molev tugged me to his side, holding me close.

"I like this," he murmured in my ear.

Of course he did. I was feeling just like he wanted me to. While I didn't resent him for it, I wasn't exactly happy either. Regardless of our planning, we weren't all safe yet, and I knew where feeling attachment could lead. Katie was an example of it.

Shaking my head, I pulled away and went to the door to put on my jacket.

"Save some lunch for us," I called over my shoulder.

"Will do," Sid called back.

As soon as we were out the door, Molev had me in his arms.

"You've gotten better at this," I said. "You used to knock my feet out from under me."

He looked down at me as he started walking. "Is caring that difficult?"

"No. Caring is the easy part, Molev. It's losing the people you care about that's hard. I don't know how many more times I can go through that."

He brushed his lips against my temple.

"You won't lose me," he said softly.

I sighed and leaned into him. With this new plan, I was less afraid of that possibility.

Waurlyn was waiting for us at the hospital doors when we arrived. She smiled at us and waited for Molev to put me down.

"You have impeccable timing," she said. "I was going to contact you later today."

"About what?" I asked.

"The doctor would like to start another trial this afternoon. A male volunteer this time. Someone older." She watched Molev closely for his reaction to the news.

"Thank you for telling me. I would like to be there and speak to him before he receives the vaccine."

"Of course. He's already here for preliminary tests if you'd like to talk to him now."

"Before I do that, I wanted to discuss your progress on collecting the names of any females willing to live with my people," he said.

"Certainly. Let's go to the conference room so I can show you what I have so far."

Waurlyn wasn't Thomas. That much was clear when she reached the room and dimmed the lights to project spreadsheet data onto a screen. She had thousands of names, along with some valuable statistics.

"I understand that you want to interview the potential volunteers," she said. "Due to the number of people interested, we gathered some additional biographic data to help narrow your search. I did speak to Patrick and understand that race, marital status, and age don't matter to you. However, we'd already started gathering that data, so I decided to continue that course. And gender, of course. Since you didn't mention it at the gathering, I didn't exclude men from volunteering."

"That makes sense," I said. "Why upset them without reason? And who knows? Molev thinks Steve, Roland, Brandon, and Sid will be a good fit. Maybe we'll find others in the group, too."

"My thoughts exactly," Waurlyn said. "We continued collecting names daily as more survivors traveled to the evac site. I was going to ask if you'd allow us to take your picture. It would make explaining you to the newcomers a little easier."

"I think several pictures would be a good idea," I said. "Full body and face, and maybe one of him training all of us so they understand his current role as well as what he looks like."

"Establishing how he's already been accepted by others is smart," Waurlyn said with a nod. "How soon do you want to start interviewing?"

I glanced at Molev, deferring this part of the conversation to him.

"Considering the number of volunteers and the state of

unrest we witnessed when we were last there, it would be wise to move forward cautiously," he said.

"What do you have in mind?" she asked.

"The team explained the concept of a mixer to me," he said. "It would allow me to meet many people at once in a very short time. It would also allow me to observe how they behave around me in a group setting."

Waurlyn tapped the table for a moment. "I have several concerns with that approach. Mixers are usually social events where beverages and food are consumed. Due to our limited resources and rationing, I'm afraid providing anything along those lines in a social setting would give the impression that we are hoarding food while people are eating lighter than they would like. And that kind of display might encourage more people to sign up for that benefit alone rather than a real interest to cohabitate."

I knew she wasn't wrong. We'd witnessed the volatility of the crowd, and I didn't think it would take much to spark a riot.

"What if it was more like one of our training days but less intense and more instructional?" I asked.

Waurlyn was already nodding. "That could work. Introduce Molev, explain in a non-graphic way what it's like outside the barrier, and perhaps show them a few of the basic moves Molev's been teaching you to help save your lives. It's a win all around. They're learning something practical, and Molev can see firsthand if they're willing to work with one of his kind. And to be frank, anyone with aptitude who isn't interested in going with you could be trained to help replace the personnel we're losing.

"How soon can we start?" she asked.

"How soon can you get the first one hundred people here?" I asked.

"Tomorrow."

Molev grunted his agreement. "Start with the ones who volunteered first and work your way down. I will interview them all. Can we provide food and housing to each group for two days?"

"We should be able to manage that."

"Good. I will speak with the new trial volunteer now. What is his name?"

"Michael," she said, standing.

Michael, a middle-aged man of mixed descent, paused the treadmill when Molev entered the room.

"I saw you that first day at the evac site," he said, watching Molev warily. "You jumped onto that building like it was nothing."

"To me, it is nothing," Molev said. "Did they tell you what happened to the prior volunteers?"

Michael nodded. "They all died. Sara, the woman before me, lasted the longest but still begged for her death at the end. They've been honest about everything, but I appreciate that you're doing the same." He sighed. "Do you think there's any chance these vaccines will ever work on a human?"

"Yes," Molev said without hesitation.

"Then here's to hoping my shot's the winner. I wouldn't mind an increased vertical jump as a side effect."

The way the doctor looked down at her computer and Waurlyn's amused smile didn't comfort me.

"I will return later," Molev said, extending his hand to Michael. "Your contribution to finding a cure will not be forgotten."

Michael solemnly accepted Molev's handshake then returned to his run.

I hated the sadness I felt and waited until we were in the hallway with Waurlyn to voice my thoughts.

"They haven't isolated anything, have they?"

"Molev is something the team of medical professionals has never seen before. They are using human DNA as a codex to interpret his DNA and trying to isolate what is in an undead's saliva that is causing the mutation. It involves unraveling layers upon layers. Yes, they've isolated some things. But as you're well aware, they haven't yet identified the correct combination of what they are isolating in both Molev's and an undead's samples. It's a frustrating process costing us more than Michael's life. Three additional bases have gone dark since we last spoke."

"I would like to return to my people," Molev said without preamble.

I wanted to groan. Instead, I turned to look at Waurlyn, who'd stopped dead in the hallway to stare at Molev. He had the gall to smile at her, and it was the same 'isn't he funny smile' she'd used in the room.

I wasn't sure what to think.

"I believe it could help with many of the problems we face," he said. "Should we return to the conference room to discuss?"

She regained her composure as she nodded and led the way back to the room.

"The doctor said she would know more about me if she had other samples for comparison," Molev said when Waurlyn sat. "And Irwin and the safe zones are struggling to maintain the resources necessary to support the number of people here. If we interview and train until I find two hundred candidates, we could airlift those people and the research team to Whiteman. The research team could collect additional samples. Irwin would be responsible for fewer survivors. And by sending a smaller number to start, my people would have time to adjust their resource planning before the next round arrives. Spacing them out would also give the researchers time to analyze samples between collections."

The proposal wasn't horribly delivered, but I'd hoped for better after how smoothly the first part had gone. Unsure of Waurlyn's thoughts, I waited for some clue.

"The benefits are hard to ignore," she said. "But we're all aware that everyone I answer to will see the risk for what it is. That Molev is leaving and not returning."

"Then don't tell them," I said. "Not yet. Michael's trial might be the miracle we're all hoping for. And if it isn't, Molev still has thousands of people to meet and train. It will take weeks to weed through everyone and help train the personnel you need. Panicked bureaucrats will only slow the process down at this point. Give Molev more time to gain your trust. He hasn't broken his word yet, has he?"

"No. He hasn't," she agreed. "All right. Since this was a brainstorming idea only to help with the issues you noted, I'll hold off on disclosing the details of this request. Please notify me if you have any other ideas to help with resources or the vaccine." She stood. "If you'll excuse me, I'd like to discuss with the doctor the possibility of diverse samples and what they would mean for the research."

We followed her out the door and left, stopping to speak with a few soldiers who had questions for Molev about the training sessions. Once we were outside, he picked me up again. Instead of returning to the house, he brought me to the one next door to it, breaking the lock to enter.

"Pretty sure that's going to get us into trouble," I said.

His gaze swept the empty room as he stood in the opening.

He nudged the door shut behind him and strode farther into the house until he found a bedroom.

I swallowed hard, understanding what he had in mind.

"Molev, I don't think this is a good idea."

He placed me on my feet next to the bed and started removing my jacket.

"I'm serious. The lock's broken. Our neighbors probably saw you break it. How long until they come barging in to see why? I really don't want to be caught with my pants down, do you?"

"Finish undressing. I'll fix the door." He disappeared, and I crossed my arms.

"Molev, I don't care if you fix the door or not. I'm not ready for sex yet. I'm sorry if last night misled you into thinking I was. I just wanted to…I don't know. Do something fun and feel a little more connected. Baby steps, not jump straight into bed."

He reappeared, his vivid green gaze sweeping over my clothed body in silent judgment.

"We are not here to have sex, Andie. Although, I would welcome it if you wish to change your mind."

"Nope. No mind-changing. Why are we here then?"

"I want to taste you again. But this time, I want to hear each soft sigh and desperate groan as I draw pleasure from you again and again."

He had my attention.

"So, just oral?" I asked.

"Just my tongue loving your pussy."

I unzipped my pants.

"I guess I'll let you have your way this time."

CHAPTER THREE

HE WATCHED ME WITH HOODED EYES AS I REMOVED EACH ITEM OF clothing. When I stood naked in the cool room, my breasts briefly drew his attention.

"I like every detail about you, Andie. Your pretty sky-blue eyes. The sandy brown color of your hair. The shape of your body. The way you think. The way you resist. The way you defer to me."

The growing bulge in his pants jumped at that last part.

"What were you thinking just now?" I asked.

"I pictured you on the bed, your delicate legs spread wide in surrender."

I sat on the bed, reclining on my elbows and lifting my feet to the edge. His lips curled back in a silent snarl as I slowly let my knees fall as far to either side as they would go.

"Like this?" I asked.

"For now," he said, stalking closer.

His hands settled on my knees along my inner thighs.

"Tell me you want this," he said.

My insides flipped at the opportunity he was giving me to poke that inner beast and see just how much control he had.

"I want to feel those big, fat fingers moving inside me as you suck on my clit. I want to feel those waves of pleasure only you've managed to draw out of me more than once. And I want your tongue lapping me after I've come, Molev."

He growled, his hands squeezing my inner thighs and pressing them just a bit wider. I felt myself opening for him. He inhaled deeply as he dipped his head. Anticipation built inside of me, each of his soft exhales brushing across my sensitive core and driving my desire higher.

When his tongue finally lapped just left of my bundle of fun, I almost whimpered.

"I want to hear your sounds," he said. "All of them. No matter how soft or loud."

I gave in and moaned. He rewarded me with another long lick to the right.

He tormented me with indirect contact for several minutes before his lips closed over my sweet spot. I cried out and grabbed fistfuls of his hair, using it to direct his mouth. His chuckle vibrated through me, adding to the sensation. Seconds later, I found the edge I was looking for and tumbled over, my drawn-out moan echoing in the room as waves of pleasure washed over me.

"Good girl," Molev said as he left me.

I closed my eyes and drifted in a state of bliss until the bed dipped. Without warning, he flipped me so I straddled his legs with mine on the mattress on either side of his hips. I was about to ask him what he was doing when he bent his knees underneath my hips, lifting my ass into the air. I glanced over my shoulder at him.

"This is new," I said as he leaned forward and buried his face between my legs again.

His tongue thrust deep into my core, lapping at me just like he'd said. I groaned and wrapped my arms around his calves as my channel involuntarily clenched.

He brought me to another orgasm just like that, slow waves that pulsed through me. While I lay basking from the second one, he repositioned me again. But I squealed when his lips closed over my clit, and I pushed his face away.

"It's too much," I said.

He growled and nipped my fingers. As soon as I jerked them back, his tongue traced around my clit. Even that was too much.

"No, wait. Let me have a turn now."

He pulled back to look at my face, and I took that opportunity to slither from his hold. My legs, weak from the orgasms and the influx of exercise, shook as I folded them under me. But, the position protected the part he wanted to play with. Too bad it didn't do anything to calm the over-stimulated nerves.

"Turn?" he asked, gazing at me.

"Yes. Now I get to make you a puddle of happiness." I patted the bed beside me. "Pants off, big boy."

He was naked a second later, and his erection jutted toward me.

Eagerly, I shuffled forward and circled his girth with my hands, loving his reactions. The way he hissed out a pained breath at the same time he jerked in my hold distracted me from the realities of the outside world and kept me grounded in what was happening in that room. With him. Molev. The man of my unknown dreams.

I slid my palm up and down his veined shaft, memorizing

each delightful bump. He was bigger than anything I'd ever experienced before. At least double the size. But that didn't worry me. Molev had proven himself to be gentle, and I knew sex with him wouldn't be any different when the time was right.

Smiling in anticipation of that day, I kissed the tip, then licked his slit.

He made another pained sound.

"Too much?" I asked.

"Not enough." His rough words would have been enough to send a jolt to my core, but the way he fisted my hair and drew my mouth back to his shaft lit a fire in me. He was gentle but controlling, just the way I craved at that moment.

I opened my mouth, taking as much of him as I could, which wasn't a lot, and swirled my tongue over his head as I stroked his length.

He growled his appreciation and started slowly thrusting. I hummed and felt my core clench around nothing. His rhythm faltered for a second, giving me room to swirl my tongue again.

"Andie..." The low warning was all I got before he started thrusting as deep as he could.

This time, I was ready for the explosion and swallowed quickly so I wouldn't drown. He freed one of his hands from my hair and stroked my cheek.

"I wish you could see yourself as I see you right now," he said, looking down at me. "Your pretty lips wet and stretched over me. The moisture in your eyes." He grunted and started thrusting more earnestly. My eyes went wide in disbelief.

"I cannot decide which I like better. My mouth on you or yours on me."

He came again with as much force and quantity as the first time. As I did my best to keep up and breathe, I realized how far over my head I was.

"EARTH TO ANDIE," Brandon said. "Do you want another burger?"

I blinked him into focus and slowly shook my head, careful not to move in my seat. Everything down there still felt swollen and ready to go off at a moment's notice. I'd never felt perpetually on the edge of the big "O" like this before and didn't know what to do about it.

My gaze slid to Roni, who was scrutinizing me with narrowed eyes. She knew something was up. It didn't matter that we'd returned before lunch as we'd said. Or that my swollen lips and flushed face could have been due to a lot of kissing. Somehow, she knew. And I really wished I could have a ten-minute quiet conversation with her to figure out if there was a remedy for an overused fun zone. If anyone would know, I figured she would.

"You should eat another one," Molev said, his hand brushing over my shoulder.

I tore my gaze from Roni's and looked up at him. He still looked like he wanted to devour me. How many times had we gone down on each other? Four? Five? When was it enough?

"Can't," I said. "I'm full."

Next time he wanted to fool around, I'd insist on a shower. If I knew I could survive it, offering sex would be smarter, but I was pretty sure he'd break me and not because of his size. Molev was a monster and a machine.

Maybe thousands of years without sex did that to a guy. Maybe his libido would settle down once he started getting it on the regular. I shook my head, unsure I was willing to open that Pandora's box to find out.

"Something wrong?" Roni asked.

"Nothing," I said, eating a fry. "Any plans for the rest of the day?"

I really hoped they had plans. Part of me feared Molev would want to return to the house next door.

"I was going to go for a run if anyone wants to join me," Roni said.

I shook my head along with everyone else.

"I'll join you," Molev said.

Roni grinned like the Cheshire cat.

"Cool. Let's go."

I breathed a sigh of relief after they left and slinked off to the shower. My tender bits appreciated the cool water, and by the time I stepped out, wearing underwear wasn't such a chore. Feeling more human, I dressed again and went out to join the others out back.

Steve passed me a beer. "You've been pretty quiet. I take it that means the meeting with Waurlyn didn't go very well?"

I wanted to smack myself for forgetting about that and not updating them. My priorities were seriously messed up by Molev's detour earlier. Taking a large swallow of beer and clearing my throat, I thought back to this morning.

"They're doing another trial this afternoon. Molev and I met him. His name's Michael. Everyone was upfront with him about the previous results and the likelihood of success, which isn't good. But Waurlyn said they're learning more with each one, narrowing things down, so she hasn't given up hope that the blood will work eventually.

"Molev told her about his desire to go home in the bluntest way possible. It visibly shocked her, but once he explained why and how it might benefit the research, she seemed a little more receptive.

"Oh, and she thought having a mixer, or anything where

food and drink were provided in a social gathering way, would be problematic since the camps are rationing."

Sid looked down at his beer.

"Hey," I said. "We're earning this. Trust me. Since a mixer was out, we agreed to some light field training. That means all of us will be working with the volunteers, teaching them a few of the basic moves that Molev has taught us to stay alive. The first one hundred are showing up tomorrow."

"Wait," Katie said, leaning forward in her folding chair. "Are you saying we get to do the training instead of the fighting tomorrow?"

"Yep."

"Thank God!" She wilted in her chair and took a swig of her beer. "There isn't a part of me that doesn't hurt."

"Even your boobs?" Steve asked.

Roland smacked the back of his head.

"Even those," she said with a fierce blush. "I think it's from the climbing, and I won't mind a few days off of that."

"Does that mean another day of sleeping in?" Brandon asked.

"I'll find out when we go back to the hospital later. The volunteers are going to be given temporary housing after they arrive here so we can have two days with them. Waurlyn wants us to vet the rejected volunteers for any military aptitude."

"She's smart," Sid said. "She'll probably feed them well while they're here working hard. Big pay for hard work. It might sway a few to join her rather than Molev's group."

"Which is fine," I said. "Molev wants the people who want to be there. The ones who believe in what he's doing."

"And what is he doing?" Steve asked. "I mean, he's saying he's building a community, but we've seen what it's like out there. It was bad in the beginning, but it's even worse now. How is Whiteman going to be any safer than here?"

"It's the mountains and the fence keeping us safe here," I said. "And you saw how effective those both are. Molev thinks it's only a matter of time before we're no longer safe here. And you also saw how effective a fence and just one fey are against four hounds and hundreds of undead. Can you imagine that scenario with five hundred of them? Where would you rather be?"

"With Molev," Sid said. "Doesn't matter where as long as he's there."

The rest nodded, and Steve held up his hands. "I wasn't doubting his skills, just the living conditions. Excuse me for liking showers and food."

"Then we'll make sure to build a community that has both," I said. "Molev told me that he and his brothers go out for supply runs regularly. He won't let us starve."

Steve nodded and stared at his beer.

"What's really going through your head?" Roland asked him.

"That undead that looked us in the eyes," Steve said. "They're getting smarter, and I'm letting this place brainwash me into thinking it's safer."

"Stay focused on what you can control, not what you can't," I said.

He nodded, and we all looked at the sliding door at the sound of it opening. Roni and Molev came out to join us.

"How was the run?" I asked, looking at Roni.

"Necessary," she said, taking a seat. "What'd we miss?"

"We're training the first group of volunteers tomorrow instead of having a mixer," Sid said. "Andie's going to find out when they're arriving."

"Good." Roni glanced at Molev, who stood beside my chair. "What are we looking for tomorrow? I mean, there's the obvious–anyone too afraid of you or the assholes who dismiss or look down on you. But what are you really looking for?"

"People like you," he said, looking at all of us. "People willing to work together. Willing to listen to one another. People who understand loyalty and hardship. People who haven't given up hope and are willing to fight for a better future. Even if their way of fighting isn't with guns or training."

"I think I'm tearing up," Brandon said. "No one's ever said so many nice things about me."

Katie rolled her eyes at him.

"What moves do you want us to cover?" Roland asked.

"We should stick with basic blocking," Sid said. "There's seven of us. We can divide the volunteers into even groups to pair them off, each of us in charge of seven to eight pairs. Assess and rearrange based on skill. That way, Molev can move around, watching all of them. When he calls the first break, we can send the ones with the lowest skill to him."

"Why lowest?" Katie asked.

"Because Molev doesn't need fighters," I said, understanding Sid's thought process. "He just needs amiable people with the will to survive."

Molev grunted. "I like this plan."

"But what will the people we weed out first do with the rest of their time if they're with us for two days?" Steve asked.

"We can assess if they have any useful skills," I said.

"Based on the number of stitches Molev's received, it wouldn't hurt to have people who know how to sew," Roni said.

"If we get a few people who make the cut from this first group, maybe we could ask Waurlyn for some kind of internship with whatever skill-groups we need," Katie said. "It could be like a secondary test to ensure we're getting people who are actually willing to pitch in."

"Not a bad idea," Sid said.

"We can talk to Waurlyn about that," I said, "but I'm not sure what skills we need."

We discussed it as a group as we sipped our beverages. Steve came up with the most useful ideas based on games he played in the past. We needed people who knew how to build such as carpenters and engineers. We needed people who knew how to farm and/or grow food. We needed mechanics. In a world with people dependent on today's advancements, it made sense to have someone around to repair what broke. Above all, we needed problem solvers. Creative people who could think outside the box to come up with solutions.

"Do I look like Human Resource material to you?" Steve asked.

Roni snorted. "Do any of us look like elite soldiers ready to train the next generation? No. But we're still going to give our best to see that through. Don't be a baby about vetting people's personalities either."

Steve frowned into his empty beer.

"I didn't say I wouldn't do it. I just don't think I'm the best person for the job."

"There is no one better than the people here," I said. "Some of our personality quirks are as diverse as they come. Roni loves provoking people and is blatantly open about her body and what she wants. Katie's reserved but friendly to everyone and very smart. I distance myself from people and am thoughtful but a little blunt. Yet, we all get along. You've lived with us for weeks. You know what harmony and comradery look like.

That's what you're looking for. People who can support one another."

Molev's hand settled on the back of my neck. That was all it took for my core to clench and reawaken the part of me that had finally settled down. One core clench set off an echo of post-orgasm twitches again.

His fingers moved against my skin as he spoke.

"Andie is right. My brothers and I need more good people like you. If you meet a person who you would not welcome into this house now, we will mark them as unsuitable."

The others nodded, but I couldn't move. I was too afraid of sending off more wrong signals to my brain.

The faint sound of our doorbell broke up our impromptu gathering, and I sighed in relief as Molev released me. I stayed right where I was and let everyone else file inside first. Roni lingered, watching me with a smirk.

When Roland asked if we were coming in, she waved him inside.

"Problem?" she asked when he closed the door.

"Just enjoying the sun," I said.

"Bullshit. I heard you went back for sevenths on his passion pistol's scream cream." She took the chair beside me. "And I want the details."

"He told you that?" I asked, fighting not to show my shock.

"Hey, no getting mad at him. He needs to talk to someone about this stuff. Would you rather have him going to Steve for girl advice?"

I slouched lower in the chair and winced.

"I'm not spilling anything until you tell me what you two talked about."

"He said he went down on you until you pushed him away and offered to blow him instead. When he started talking numbers, it didn't take a genius to figure out what happened. I told him he needed to pace himself. That your baby maker needed to acclimate to his stamina."

"Acclimate?"

She grinned. "Gurl, I got the impression he would eat you out all day if you let him. You better set some boundaries, or you'll find yourself sitting on his face instead of that chair next group meeting. Anyway, I told him to ease into it and take breaks. Now tell me…how big is he? Was it amazing?"

I rubbed a hand over my face.

"You already know how big he is. You felt it, and you saw it. And has Molev ever been anything less than amazing?"

She gave a wistful sigh.

"I can't wait until we get to meet his people."

I snorted. "You're just thinking about getting laid. What are you going to do when you have a possessive man trying to tell you what to do, Roni? Based on what I know of Molev, I don't think his people are the love them and leave them type. Are you ready to settle down?"

She made a horrified face.

"Exactly," I said. "So be careful what you wish for."

The sliding door opened behind me.

"Waurlyn would like us to return to the hospital now," Molev said.

The beer I'd enjoyed helped make walking a little easier as I cautiously stood and followed Molev to the vehicle parked out front.

Molev was quiet on the ride to the hospital, spending most of his time frowning slightly as he studied his hands. I didn't ask what was wrong. We were on our way to watch someone die another potentially agonizing death. Which was precisely why I'd allowed Molev to distract us both so many times this morning.

Despite how tender I was, I didn't regret it. But I would definitely follow Roni's advice and set some boundaries before I opened that door again.

The driver stopped in front of the hospital doors and let us out. Molev matched his pace to my slower one as we made our way inside and met with Waurlyn.

"Thank you for sending for us," Molev said.

"Of course. The injection won't take long. They're trying a very small amount this time. The doctor doesn't anticipate seeing any reaction for the first twelve to twenty-four hours."

"I understand. I still want to be present."

"How long will the doctor wait before testing the infection on Michael?" I asked as we took the elevator down.

Waurlyn gave me a startled look. "We haven't injected any of the trial participants with the infection yet."

"But Sara..." I'd watched her vomit and saw the way her eyes changed. And how she'd bitten Molev. "I don't understand."

The doors opened, and we left the elevator.

"The infection is in Molev. His immunity to it is preventing the trial participants from fully turning. It's also preventing them from coming back once they die."

Molev was infected?

My stomach churned, and I started to feel a little lightheaded. How stupid was I? I'd just made out with a carrier of the infection.

"Are you all right?" Waurlyn asked when I stopped walking. "You look extremely pale."

Molev picked me up and hugged me close to his chest. "Where is the doctor?"

Hadn't Molev said that there were other fey and human couples already? If all the fey were immune and already sleeping with humans, I would be fine.

"I'm fine," I said. "It's fine. It's just been a really long day."

Both Waurlyn and Molev studied me for a long moment.

"You know yourself best," Waurlyn said finally. "If you say you're fine, then I believe you."

When she started walking again, I patted Molev's chest.

"Please put me down. This doesn't feel good," I said softly.

He did as I asked without comment, and we followed Waurlyn to the same lab as before. Michael was already in the glass room, eating an apple. He grinned when he saw us and held up the fruit.

"Can you believe this? I've been so hungry for one of these, and they managed to find one."

"Are you sure you wish to do this?" Molev asked.

Michael sobered and nodded. "I'd rather go out doing something useful than sitting around in a camp waiting for the food to run out."

The doctor prepared the injection as he finished his apple. Molev and I waited outside the room as he received the dose.

"The first batch of volunteers will arrive tonight," Waurlyn said beside us.

"Tonight?" I asked, surprised.

"Yes. This way, they'll be well-rested and ready at dawn. Also, evening departures and arrivals help give us more time to change over, allowing personnel to wash bedding between groups. We had a lice outbreak in one camp, and I'd like to prevent the same here."

The doctor emerged from Michael's room, joining us in the observation area as he lay down.

"Now we wait," she said.

CHAPTER FOUR

"THE FIRST TWENTY-FOUR HOURS ARE PRETTY QUIET," WAURLYN said. "However, you're welcome to stay if you'd like."

I glanced at Molev, who shook his head.

"I understand. Perhaps we can take those pictures you mentioned before you leave?" She turned to the doctor. "Please keep me informed of any changes."

The doctor nodded absently before we all left.

In the hallway, Waurlyn used a cell phone to take close-up and full-body pictures of Molev. Once she had them, she promised to keep us updated on Michael's progress and asked if there was anything we needed for the training the following day.

"Molev usually makes a bunch of sandwiches and has water ready for everyone," I said as she got into the elevator with us.

"I can arrange for easy-to-consume meals, or they can go to the mess hall," she said.

"Let's do the mess hall in the morning so they can have a little time to wake up, something easy to consume for lunch on the training field, and the mess hall again at the end of the day."

The doors opened.

"I'll see it's done," she said, getting out.

"Thank you for helping with this, Waurlyn," Molev said.

"Don't thank me prematurely. You have a long road ahead of you and may not find the volunteers you're looking for." She paused in the hallway to face him. "We haven't turned away anyone who has wanted to sign up. The mood of many of these people is grim. They're quiet when they sign up and equally quiet when they go to their respective spot in the field near the evac site."

"The evac site?" I asked.

"Even though we have signups posted at every camp, the ones who traveled to the evac site are staying there, not trusting that we'll search for them at their camps. Meanwhile, the lists at the camps barely have any names on them. It's helping the overcrowding at the camps but causing issues at the evac site. Again, there's no fighting. They understand that would have them immediately removed from the list. But sanitation is a problem, as is keeping them adequately fed."

"What happens to them when they leave here?" I asked.

"To prevent riots regarding the number being turned away, we will fly those not selected to the northernmost evac site. It will be too cold for them to stay there. We have buses already set up to drive them south where they can trickle back to their original camps."

"What happens to the people I accept as volunteers or those we identify as suitable trainees for you?" Molev asked.

"We'll move them to different housing on base."

"Won't that tax the resources here?" I asked.

"What better reason to get them to their final destination as quickly as possible?" she asked.

Although she'd met our initial request with shock, she seemed to be rolling with the idea pretty well now.

"Thank you," I said.

"Let's just hope we have a vaccine before the housing situation becomes overcrowded," she said. "Your volunteers will be at the field shortly after sunrise. Good luck."

We accepted a ride home, which I appreciated, and updated the rest of the team on the plans. Molev was quieter than usual, standing with his arms crossed as he listened to me explain everything. When I finished, he held out his hand to me.

I hesitated, and I felt no shame for it. My bits still felt too big to fit between my legs and would probably fall off if he even looked at them wrong.

Roni snorted and nudged me.

"Don't be a baby. Go set some boundaries."

I shook my head at her and took his hand. As soon as the bedroom door closed, he released me and sat on the bed.

"Did I hurt you?" he asked.

"No. Everything was fine. I'm just a little tender now."

He grunted and looked down at his hands. "Is that why you discouraged Roni?"

I tried to think back but couldn't come up with anything.

"I'm not sure how I discouraged Roni," I said.

"You told her to stop thinking about sex. You asked what she would do with a possessive man and if she was really ready to settle down.

"My brothers and I are fighting against hounds and the infected. But we also have to fight the fear and prejudice humans have. We are never not fighting, Andie.

"To have one person…a female waiting to welcome us without reservation… Why is that so horrible to want? Are you not also waiting for that one person who will accept you just as you are? Very few females will even look at us without cringing. Roni, Katie, and you? You are rare, Andie. Not many will be like you.

"Waurlyn is correct that I have a long road ahead of me. It will not be easy to find even half the volunteers I asked for. Don't rob me of the ones I already have."

His words fanned the emotions he was so insistently waking in me. I walked over to him and framed his face with my hands so I could get him to look at me.

"Roni isn't some timid little Miss. She flashed you, Molev. She propositioned you more times than I could count. Whether she's ready to settle down or not, she'll be very interested in your brothers. My warning wasn't to discourage her but to protect some poor, unsuspecting fey from getting his heart broken by her. Unless she's crazy in love with him, there's every chance she'll sleep with him and leave. I don't think that's the kind of example you want to set starting out with the volunteers, is it?"

"No."

"Okay, then."

His hands gripped my waist, and no matter how tender I was or how much that sudden heat in his gaze sparked my interest, I couldn't take any more of Molev. At least, not that day.

"We need to set some boundaries," I said.

"I know. I heard."

"Yeah, we'll get to the sex ones. First, we need to talk about couple privacy. Roni doesn't need to know about our sex life."

"She does. She cannot guide me if she doesn't know what happened."

"Guide you? How?"

"She explained why you pushed me away. That I needed to give you time to recover."

"I'll tell you that."

"Why should I trust you will when you chose not to the first time?"

I blinked at him like he tended to do at me when he didn't like what I had to say. His lips quirked in the corners.

"Okay. You make a very valid point," I said. "And it's not like you have anyone else to talk to when you have questions. How about this? If you have questions, ask me first. If you doubt what I'm saying or think I'm not answering fully or, hell, even if you want a second opinion, then ask Roni. But you may not talk to anyone else about what happens between us. Deal?"

"Do you believe these details will be used to harm you and control me if I tell any of the others?"

"No, I trust them not to say anything. I just don't want to make things uncomfortable for them. Not everyone is open about their sex life. Katie's discreet. Do you think she'll still want to go with us if she thinks your brothers will talk openly like you?"

He grunted. "I will ask you first and practice discretion when speaking with Roni."

"Thank you. As for the boundaries Roni mentioned… I'm sore from what we did. I don't regret it, but I'd rather not repeat it any time soon. I can feel everything when I walk or sit, and that's not a good thing. But I want to be clear that this isn't me retreating. I'm not challenging that rule. I simply can't physically keep up with what you'd like to do."

He grunted and held my hands, smoothing his thumbs over the backs of mine.

"How do I know this isn't a retreat, my clever Andie? I have waited too long to taste you and do not want to give that up."

"I'm not asking you to stop. I don't think any woman in her right mind would. But I am asking you for time. Tomorrow may be too soon. Maybe the day after would be okay. It will depend on how I feel."

He released my hands and pulled me to stand between his legs. I kept my hands on his face as he held me close.

"Will you continue to allow me to touch you? Will you still touch me?"

"This kind of touching? Absolutely," I said. "You touching me between the legs. Definitely a no for tonight."

"Can I touch you everywhere else?"

"Sure."

"Will you sleep beside me without clothes?"

"If you think it's safe enough, sure. If your sixth sense is still whispering we're not safe here, I'd be smarter to sleep clothed with my riot gear beside the bed."

"Will you shower with me?"

It didn't take a genius to figure out what he was really asking.

"I have no problem giving you a shower blow job every now and again. But I need to be really, really in the mood for that."

A slow, confident grin split his lips.

"You will be."

I returned his smile.

"Are there any other boundaries you would like to set?" he asked.

"No."

That grin grew bigger.

"I can see already you're going to be trouble," I said.

He chuckled and stood suddenly, lifting me high enough so he could reach my lips.

"I am going to be your everything."

His hot mouth claimed mine, robbing me of any retort and drawing me into a storm of sensation. By the time he pulled back, I was very much in the mood to shower with him. Sanity prevailed when I attempted to wrap my legs around his waist and winced.

He kissed my nose and eased me to my feet.

"Take your pants off, Andie."

"That's what got me into this state."

"Trust me."

Making a face, I stripped out of my pants.

"Better?" he asked.

"It's always better without pants."

"Then don't wear them."

I spent the rest of the evening lounging around in my underwear. Molev's hungry gaze followed me everywhere. Since I was ignoring it, so did everyone else. Except Roni.

I only caught a few of her mumbled phrases. "That's what you get for wearing out your new toy." "Your balls have to be so blue by now. Poor baby." "I really hope everyone is team fey tomorrow. I'm ready for my own vine."

But based on Molev's smirks, I was confident he heard them all.

After dinner, we played a few games and turned in early. As soon as the door was shut, Molev stripped out of his clothes and climbed under the covers completely naked.

"That's probably the opposite of what you should have done if you were trying to tell me it's okay to sleep naked."

"Take off your clothes, Andie. I know where not to touch."

Shaking my head but unwilling to test the determination in his eyes, I removed my shirt and bra. He didn't say anything about the underwear I'd left on when I joined him.

His palm skimmed over my skin as he pulled me close. The heat of his chest against my bare back branded me. I snuggled closer, feeling every inch of contact.

"Sleep, Andie. Tomorrow will come quickly."

It felt like I'd barely closed my eyes when a tingle between my legs and a gentle, hot tug on my nipple woke me. As I surfaced, the sensations became the realization that Molev had his mouth on my breast. He continued toying with that side until I tangled my fingers in his hair, then switched to the other, giving it just as much attention as the first.

"Good morning," I said when he lifted his head.

"It is. Did you like that?"

"I did."

"Can I kiss you some more?"

I glanced out the window, and he sighed.

"You are correct. The sun will rise soon. Take your shower. I will make you something to eat."

He got out of bed, giving me a full view of his impressive morning wood and offering me a hand up.

"Is the soreness easing?" he asked.

"A little," I said. Or maybe what he'd been doing a minute ago had been enough to distract me from it.

He kissed my forehead.

"It will be better tonight," he said. "I will have Roni and Steve give the demonstrations. All you will need to do is observe and give direction."

He grabbed his pants and pulled them on.

"Shower," he said with a nod.

Loving him more for his consideration and the space he was

allowing me, I took a quick shower and discovered things were almost back to normal. Sounds from the kitchen drifted into my room as I dressed.

By the time I opened the door, I could hear Steve begging for the first plate since he'd been the first one up.

"Okay. But you do clean up," Molev said.

"Fine by me."

Everyone was in a good mood as we quickly ate and discussed what Molev had planned for the day. Roni and Steve were willing to do the initial demonstrations, and Sid agreed to pair up with Molev again to do more advanced training after the midday break.

A pickup truck was waiting for us when we left.

"This is all we have today," the soldier said. "Sorry."

"Don't be," Roland said. "Riding in the back beats walking any day."

They gave us a lift to the training grounds where personnel were unloading coolers.

"We have water in these," one woman said, "and food in the ones we'll stack off to the side. If you need more of anything, just radio it in."

"Thank you," Molev said.

They'd no sooner left than the first wave of vehicles appeared with the volunteers. I took in the wild array of people, mentally categorizing. We had a fairly even split of men and women, ranging in age from sixteen to seventy. Some of them looked like they hadn't slept or eaten well in weeks, which wasn't a surprise. Desperation radiated from each one of them.

I glanced at the rest of my team and saw they were all watching as well. Molev caught my eye and nodded as the last group left their vehicle.

"Good morning!" I called loudly. "And welcome to Camp

Irwin. You're here because you showed interest in starting a new life away from the camps. If you feel you're in the wrong place, please return to the vehicles."

No one moved toward the vehicles, but several people were moving closer to the coolers.

"If I can have your undivided attention for five minutes, I'll give you a quick rundown of what to expect today." Everyone but one man focused on me. "This is Molev. He is one of the many men who emerged from the crater in Irving, Texas. He is not responsible for the hounds or the disease that the hounds have spread. However, he is immune. He's working with our doctors, who hope to create a cure. While they work, he has volunteered to teach some skills that will help keep us alive out there.

"Yes, out there…beyond the barrier where the rest of his people are. They know how to fight and kill the hounds. We"—I gestured to my team and myself—"are alive because of Molev. Since joining us, he has killed six hounds and thousands of infected. And he's only one man.

"It is possible to live outside the barrier with their help. That is why you are here. They are looking for human volunteers to help create a community where his people and our people can peacefully co-exist. We will not sugarcoat what you will face out there. If you have questions at any point, ask. You're probably not the only one with the question you have."

Roni stepped forward and took over speaking, as we'd discussed.

"As you know, volunteering doesn't mean you'll be selected. We are looking for people who are willing to work hard as individuals, together as a team, and resolve conflict peacefully. Today and tomorrow, we will ask you to participate in different activities. We do not expect perfection. But we are watching for the three things I mentioned.

"When your name is called, please come forward."

Steve unfolded his piece of paper and started calling off his fourteen names. "You are Team Steve for the first half of the day." He moved to the side with his people and started a quiet conversation with them. Just random stuff to break the ice and get to know them.

Katie went next. The volunteers started to relax a little. The guy who was eyeing the coolers was edging closer to them. He was underweight and probably still hungry despite the breakfast I knew he'd been given. Yet, I already knew he wouldn't be going with us to Whiteman. Rather than asking what was in the cooler, stating he was still hungry, or any other honest approach, he was simply hyper-focused on the coolers.

I caught the eye of one of the soldiers standing off to the side. He nodded and went to speak to the man, quietly leading him back to a truck. Likely, he would be fed another meal and sent to rest in the housing until the transport back.

After Roland finished calling his group, I went last and called off my names.

"You are Team Andie," I said. "We'll work together in this group until lunch. If you have any problems or questions before then, please ask me. That's why I'm here."

"Where did that guy by the coolers go?" a younger woman asked.

"Probably back to the mess hall for more food," I said. "He'll be fed and housed until it's time to return with the rest of the volunteers who are not selected."

"He got kicked out?" an older man asked.

"He did."

"Can you explain why?" an older woman asked.

The other groups grew quiet to listen.

"Like Roni said, we're looking for team players. There were times out in the field when I had to go a little hungry because I was on guard duty and couldn't eat. I understood that responsibility and was willing to make that sacrifice to keep the people with me safe. The man's actions were self-focused, not team-focused. We understand that you've been without quality food. But we need you to understand that there may be periods of time that you will be asked to do without, and we need to know you're okay with that. There were nights out in the field where we all managed maybe four hours of sleep at a time. It was necessary for survival."

"That is not the life I am asking you to live," Molev said suddenly. "But it is something you need to be willing to do. Once we reach my people, we will have the men and supplies to see you are safe and fed."

"But you may need to sacrifice both food and sleep to get there," Steve said.

"Did we answer your question?" I asked the woman.

She nodded.

"All right. Then let's get started. Whether you want to be selected or not, I highly recommend that you pay attention during the next few hours. What we are about to show you may save your life one day."

Everyone worked hard after Roni and Steve demonstrated the basic blocking moves. I paired up the people in my group based on size at first, then rearranged based on skill. The older woman only lasted twenty minutes before she looked at me and apologized.

"I'm not making excuses," she said, breathing hard. "But I'm out of shape and feel like I'm two seconds from a heart attack.

I'm willing to keep going, but I need a minute to catch my breath."

"Go ahead and sit for a minute. There's water in the coolers if you need it."

She nodded and sat off to the side, looking like she was on the verge of tears. I caught Molev's gaze as he watched her.

"Talk to her," I said softly.

He hadn't said anything since his interjection to our announcements, choosing instead to be a silent observer for now. Focused on the task at hand, most of the people barely noticed him as he moved around the groups. A few did, though. And not in a good way. Suspicion and fear reflected in their eyes. It wasn't reason enough to cut them from the list yet, though. Molev was new. Different. It took some of us several days to warm up to him.

The woman didn't move away when he sat next to her, but she did duck her head to try to hide the fact she was crying in earnest.

Letting Molev deal with her, I focused on my group and had her partner pair up against one of the better defenders.

We took more breaks and did more slow demonstrations to show technique as the morning progressed until there was a pretty clear group of people who couldn't fight at all and those who could or probably could.

Molev called for the lunch break and personally handed out the sandwiches. Katie followed behind with the bag of chips. I observed them eating while I nibbled on my own sandwich, watching for anyone who looked like they were coveting their neighbor's food. A few stood out, and I mentally crossed them off the list for Molev but kept a few of them as potential Waurlyn recruits.

After lunch, we reshuffled the teams. Sid and Roni took

twenty to the first course to train them there. Molev took four women, including the one who'd needed a break.

"How do you feel about walking a mile with me?" he asked them.

I watched them leave and focused on my own group.

By the time dinner rolled around, I was ready to go home and relax. While the day hadn't been exceptionally taxing physically, I was mentally exhausted and a little down. I had a list of names, and only six of them had made the cut for Molev's group. Waurlyn had thirty potential candidates. Every rejected name had a note next to it. Not one of them was rejected simply because they were a male.

But my impression of people wasn't the only one that mattered. We all had our own lists.

Brandon came over to stand by me as we watched them leave.

"Think we should eat in the mess hall with them tonight?" he asked.

"I wasn't planning to. I don't think they'll talk as freely with us there."

He nodded.

"Was there someone you wanted to keep an eye on?" I asked.

"The woman wearing the grey sweatshirt. She's quiet and has shied away from Molev every time he gets close. But she's good. She's a mix of Roni and Katie, I think."

I looked down at my notes. I'd written her off because of her aversion to Molev.

"We'll put her in Molev's group tomorrow and see how she does," I said.

The others joined us and shared their recommendations on the way to the house. Everything they said was close to what I'd noted, and we decided to put three women and one older man with Molev to start with the next day.

Once we were inside, we gathered in the kitchen as Brandon and Roland started dinner.

"So if they pan out, we have eight women and two men out of one hundred volunteers," Katie said. "At that rate, it would take us about eight weeks just to reach two hundred people. Are we being too picky?"

We all looked at Molev.

"No," he said. "You are doing well. Many things require patience. Choosing the right people is one of them. And if we were to rush it, Waurlyn would question why."

"Is she going to question why we're being so picky?" Steve asked.

"I doubt it since we're also being picky about who we recommend to her," I said. "But I'll give her our notes just in case."

Waurlyn knocked on our door thirty minutes later.

"Sorry to interrupt your meal. I wanted to check how everything went today and if there was anything we could do to make tomorrow run more smoothly."

We invited her to sit, and we shared our thoughts on how the day went along with our compiled notes.

"Thirty is good news. Hopefully, a few of them will accept our offer," she said, looking everything over. "And six is probably lower than you would have liked, but these were randomly selected. Hopefully, the next group will have more promise.

"If you don't need the full day tomorrow, you can dismiss them at midday. They can eat at the mess hall and then fly back. It would enable us to transport the next group before dark."

Molev agreed, and she left to coordinate what she would do with the thirty names we'd given her.

The others drifted off to do their own things, leaving me with Molev.

"Would you like to go for a walk?" he asked, holding out his hand to me.

The look in his eyes was enough to tell me he didn't plan to go far...

CHAPTER FIVE

I TIPPED MY HEAD BACK AND LOOKED UP AT THE NIGHT SKY AS WE walked next door. Although the tenderness between my legs had faded, that didn't mean I could handle as much as I had the day before, and I debated how much I was willing to give.

Molev's hand closed around mine.

"Do you still miss it?" he asked. "The sounds?"

"I guess I haven't thought about it much since we've been here," I said honestly. "You've kept us too busy for those kinds of thoughts."

He grunted and opened the door for me. My gaze swept the vacant room as he closed the door. I was still scrutinizing the space when Molev's hand tangled in my hair. The next thing I knew, he had my front pinned against the wall and was nibbling his way up the side of my neck. His teeth scraped my ear, sending a shock through me. My pulse jumped as I pressed my palms against the wall.

"Do you like this, Andie?" he asked, his voice rough.

"Probably more than I should." I couldn't hide the catch in my breathing, and he growled.

"When you answer like that, I want to do more. But I fear scaring you. I fear losing you. It makes me desperate like the people we saw today. But in a different way." He nipped my neck again. "Do you know what I want to do to you?"

I licked my lips, already anticipating his answer.

"Tell me," I said.

"I want to hold you down and taste your need for me. I want to fill my ears with your whimpers." His hand released my hair and gripped the back of my neck instead. "I want to sink deep inside of you and fill you with my seed. Your mouth is nice, but I crave feeling your pretty pussy wrapped around my cock."

My core clenched as he pressed the aforementioned weapon of destruction against my ass.

"Do you want that too, Andie?" he asked.

"You have no idea how badly I want to say yes, but I can't, Molev."

He growled and spun me around, picking me up and pinning my back to the wall while wrapping my legs around his waist.

"You can," he said angrily a second before his lips claimed mine.

I reveled in the turbulent kiss and returned it with a hunger of my own. He thrust against the cradle of my thighs, rubbing me in all the right places as one hand wedged between us and kneaded my breast.

When he pulled away to nibble a path down the column of my throat, I arched my neck to give him better access.

"Tell me you want what I want," he repeated. "Tell me you are mine."

"Being yours and being physically ready to be yours in every way are two different things," I said.

He pulled back to scowl at me, and I lightly kissed his chin. Then his jaw and his collarbone.

"Why do we need to rush? Can't you give us a chance to enjoy each new step?"

"I've waited thousands of lifetimes for you, Andie. Isn't that patience enough?"

"If you've already waited that long, what're a few more weeks?"

He growled and stepped back from the wall, cupping my ass with one hand as he carried me with him.

"What do you fear?" he asked as he made his way to the bedroom.

I cupped his face as he lowered me to the mattress. "I fear that sex won't be enough, Molev. Give me some time to figure out how to give you my heart too."

He inhaled deeply as he closed his eyes and touched his forehead to mine.

"I wish you could love me as readily as I love you."

No matter how much I tried not to, I internally shuffled about ten steps back.

"Love? You don't know me well enough to love me," I said.

"Do you truly believe there is anything that I might learn that would stop me from loving you? I know there isn't."

I turned my head away. It was a stupid mistake. One that I realized a second too late.

He growled. Not in that playful way or the frustrated one but in the way he'd growled on the Loveland mission. The way that struck a note of fear in me.

While that sensation was still vibrating its way up my spine, he grabbed my legs and tugged them hard enough that I fell back and slid partway off the bed. My pants disappeared, whisked away by deft hands that moved too quickly.

His palm settled over the base of my throat, his pinky just below my clavicle, while his thumb curved around the column. It wasn't a chokehold but the hinted threat of one. It didn't matter that I knew he wouldn't hurt me; I still felt fear.

"Molev, wait. I'm sorry. I didn't mean—"

His mouth covered mine, and he kissed me with the same pent-up frustration as before. I didn't even think of shying away from it. I knew better. Instead, I reached between us, stretching until I could rub my palm along his trapped, hard length.

He pulled back with another angry sound, but I chased him, claiming his lips before he could say anything else. My pursuit calmed him a little. Some of the tension left his hold on my neck, and the kiss gentled.

When he pulled back a second time to look down at me, I didn't chase him. I begged. Prettily.

"Please," I said softly. "I want to give you what you want. But you're asking me to do something I'm not good at. I'm going to make mistakes. I need your understanding and patience. I'm trying."

The next kiss he gave me was tender, and when he finished, he stroked my cheek as he considered me.

"Undress for me," he said.

I quickly removed my shirt and bra, tossing both aside.

"All of it," he said, hooking his finger in the waistband of my underwear.

"I was hoping you could help me with that part," I said.

His pupils dilated noticeably as he stood and removed the remaining garment. He trailed his fingers over my sternum and down my thigh, studying me.

"I have never felt as strongly about anyone or anything as I do with you, Andie. And it grows each day we are together."

His idle touch drifted to the V of my legs.

"Open for me. Let me see all of you."

I did, wondering what more there was to see after how thoroughly he'd gotten to know that area the day before.

"You've retreated enough for today," he said, slowly lowering himself. "I was going to limit myself and stop after you cried out three times, but I refuse to settle for less than you have already given me." He tore his gaze from my mound and looked at me. "No pushing me away tonight."

It was well after midnight when I let out my final shuddering wail and collapsed against his legs.

"My sweet Andie," Molev said, kissing the base of my right ass cheek then my left before spreading me wider to slowly stroke my core with three fingers.

"You took them so well. Your pussy will accept my cock with ease when you are ready."

When I was ready. That phrase was music to my ears and one I'd worked hard to earn.

His fingers slid from me, and I whimpered at the sudden emptiness.

"Shh," he soothed before his tongue dipped inside, lapping at me. I basked in his touch and drifted off for a few minutes. When I roused again, he was slipping my shirt on over my head.

"Come. You need rest. Dawn will come early."

FOR THE NEXT TWO WEEKS, the team fell into a routine. Molev woke everyone just before dawn for a quick breakfast before we reported to the volunteer training field to weed through the candidates. The morning of the first day was basic defense demonstrations and assessing personalities, followed by more advanced moves in the afternoon. Since Molev didn't want us to slack on training, we all participated in demonstrations. When the volunteers left that evening, we jogged back to our house. Molev insisted. On the second day, each of us paired off with the more advanced candidates and really got a workout until they left at midday. After that, Molev put us through some drills with any base personnel who showed up.

But no matter what our day was like, I ended up in the house next door with Molev every night. If I said I was too tired, he offered to carry me and promised I wouldn't need to do anything but make happy sounds. Lying there, blissed out of my mind wasn't a hardship, but it was exhausting. And it didn't take me long to figure out that we weren't done in his mind until I came the required six times. I learned to tell him what I needed to come faster so I could go to bed sooner.

He loved when I got bossy in bed, and I loved the results.

But the more time I spent with Molev between my legs at night, the more my thoughts began to wander during the day. After lunch, I would find myself watching Molev more than I watched the volunteers. Impatience crept in around dinner time next. I managed to hide it well the first few times it happened, but Roni eventually noticed. Of course she did.

By the end of the second week, she made me go for a run after dinner and quizzed me about the long looks I'd been giving him.

"You're a-dick-ted now, aren't you?" she accused. "I thought that might happen. I mean, you probably still feel him after he's done and gone." She made a humming wistful noise.

"We aren't having sex, Roni," I said.

"Why in the hell not?"

She and Molev still went for the occasional run after dinner, and I knew she was probably sharing information to help him.

She fully planned to live vicariously through me until we reached Whiteman and she could grab her own fey. Which was precisely why I couldn't give her the whole truth.

"He doesn't just want sex," I said. "He wants it all. My body and a permanent ribbon around my heart with his name on it. He wants forever."

She made a face and looked off into the darkness for a minute. "Times sure have changed. What happened to the men who just wanted a good one-night stand?"

"There might still be a few out there. Are you trying to tell me to find one of them?" I asked.

"Hell no. I'm on team Molev all the way. I think you're just not trying hard enough. Take a shower with him, drop a bar of soap, and fall backward when you try to pick it up. Once there's penetration, there's no going back."

I snorted. "You do realize that won't work because of the height difference, right? Things won't line up."

"Then put a step stool in the shower. Be a problem solver. My point is that you need to find a way to ride Thor's mighty hammer before the good widow Johnson decides to take it for a spin. Did you see the way he looked at her?"

"Her name is Alison, and Molev wasn't looking at her. He was looking at Lucas." He'd done more than look at the kid. That fierce, big grey fighter had sat down at the picnic table with the little boy and asked the kid to arm wrestle.

"Yeah, and that's why you're in trouble," she said. "The way he took to that kid punched me right in the ovaries. Every other woman there felt it too. Lucas doesn't have a dad, and his mom is scared out of her mind. Why else would she have volunteered to go to Whiteman?"

"She heard they could get a meal if they came here," I said. "I don't think she intends to go to Whiteman."

"Pfft. The people who sign up are fed and housed on base in exchange for reading books until it's time to leave. In what universe would she say no to that?"

I looked at the lit-up houses on the block over. Those were our people. They were already job shadowing anyone with skilled knowledge. Electricians. Carpenters. Cooks. And when they weren't shadowing, they were reading and learning on their own. We had fifty-three total so far. Each house had seven to ten people.

It was a good start, but not enough.

"And stop distracting me with side topics," Roni said. "Stay focused. We're talking about Molev's unattended sugar chute. If you don't step up and claim it, someone else will. Stop dragging your feet already."

Knowing she wasn't going to let up, I gave her another half-reason for my continued resistance to having sex with Molev.

"We don't know anything about how compatible humans and fey are genetically. That's part of the reason the trials aren't working like they thought they would."

Michael and another man had died, and the doctors still had nothing tangible to show for all the research they'd done. Waurlyn wasn't freaking out yet, claiming that they were making headway and the doctors were learning more with each test. But I knew it was a matter of time. So did Roni. Which was why we'd started gathering volunteers when we had. But we needed more volunteers and more time.

"But what happens if Molev and I are compatible enough? What do you think they would do if I got pregnant here, Roni?" I asked softly. My aging IUD's expiration date was nearly up and a valid reason to be wary.

"Is that what you're afraid of?" Roni asked. "That you'd get knocked up and they'd somehow find out and use you?"

"Not me," I said. "Whatever hybrid miracle we make."

"So use a fucking condom."

The answer was so Roni that I snorted. "Even if we did manage to find something to fit him, once I open that Pandora's box, we'd run out quickly. Do you know how many times he can go without stopping for recovery?"

"No, because you don't ever tell me anything good," she said irritably.

"It's because I don't know. I managed my sixth orgasm before he could come the ninth time," I said, purposely trying to distract her. "He never got soft, Roni. Not once. But my stomach is. I was bathed in it by the time I finally met his quota."

She howled her laughter for a good minute.

"This shit's starting to feel like Christmas," she said. "I cannot *wait* to open my present."

"You know what? I can't wait for it, too. I'm going to go on nice long runs with him and give him all sorts of helpful advice," I said.

"You're a good friend, Andie," she said with a grin. "But let's not worry about me yet. We have time. You don't. Your man just wants to get laid. You do, too, based on the way you keep eye-fucking him. Just give in already. You can't live your life in fear of what-ifs that might not ever happen. Do what you want when you want, and let the rest work itself out."

By the time we headed back toward our place, I saw Molev waiting at the door of our "sex house."

"Make naughty choices," Roni said when my pace started to slow.

I waved and let her continue home as I made my way to Molev. He didn't say anything until the door was shut behind us.

"Take your clothes off, Andie."

Liking when he was abrupt and dominant when we were alone, I immediately obeyed. His gaze raked over me once I was bare, lingering on my stomach before he picked me up and carried me to the bedroom. He positioned me on the mattress just as he liked but then sat beside me, his fingers trailing over my stomach.

"I heard what you said to Roni, and I am struggling not to be angry, Andie," he said, watching his hand instead of looking at me. "How many times must I prove myself to you?"

"Hold on. I wasn't the one who said you were interested in Alison. That was Roni. I know you love me."

As soon as I said it, I wanted to take the words back. Love wasn't something we'd talked about…mostly because I feared that openly acknowledging how he felt about me would require me to reciprocate, and I wasn't ready yet. I liked to take my time with the L-word. It wasn't one I tossed around on a whim. My family heard it all the time. Especially Zion and Nova. I knew how important it was for a child to hear words of love. Beyond my family, though, I didn't say it often. Okay, I didn't say it at all.

Molev's hand stilled on my stomach, just below my belly button.

"I do love you, Andie. That is why I am trying to be patient. But I am not talking about how I feel for you or Alison. Why do you still doubt that I will keep you safe?"

"I don't doubt that," I said, grabbing onto that topic like the lifeline it was. "I know you'll do everything in your power to protect me."

"Then why do you think I would not protect any child you might carry?"

It felt like a crater had opened up in the room, and I was falling in.

"Child?" I echoed while my mind raced.

His hand skimmed lower, feathering over my folds before a finger teased my opening.

"I can see you thinking, Andie. Save your guarded words and speak plainly. Why are you withholding yourself from me?"

"I'm not," I said, trying not to focus on the sensation of his slow penetration.

But Molev was impossible to ignore. He knew exactly what I liked and reached up to stroke his thumb over my trachea as he cupped my neck.

"I do want everything, Andie. If you refuse to give me your heart, give me your body." He stroked me twice then dipped his head to kiss my clit and flick it with his tongue. His thumb brushed a little harder against my skin, and I clenched around his finger.

"Each response tests my patience," he said, kissing my inner thigh as he continued his slow assault. "What will you do when I run out?"

I couldn't hide the quiver that ran through me or the way I clenched hard around him.

"I thought that might be the case," he said almost sadly.

He added a second finger, working it in carefully.

"We walk a fine line, Andie. You like when I use force. I can feel and see how much you enjoy it. It goads me. It tells me to prepare you with my fingers until you drip with your need then ease myself inside you even as you beg me to wait. I want to fill you with my seed while you try to push me away."

He exhaled heavily. "I want to dominate you in every way, Andie. But I fear that giving in to what you secretly want hands you the reason you need to reject me." He nipped my thigh hard enough to cause me to jerk but not enough to leave a mark.

"You are like your leaders right now. Your words and your actions do not match. I will ask you again, why do you continue to deny me, Andie?"

He moved his fingers more forcefully inside of me, driving me closer to my first orgasm.

I knew I couldn't chase the pleasure. If I did, I'd forget why I couldn't tell him the truth. No matter how badly he thought he wanted it, I knew he wouldn't accept it. People rarely did when I said I didn't want to have kids.

My desire to never procreate had nothing to do with some preemptive maternal instinct to protect any baby we create from experiments. I hadn't wanted kids before the earthquakes when the world was only shitty. I especially didn't want them now.

But I knew Molev did. Badly. The way he'd been with Lucas today proved it. Molev was great with kids. If he had his way, he would probably have me barefoot and pregnant for the rest of my life, which was a terrifying thought for so many reasons.

"Do you know that some people wait until they were married to have sex?" I said breathlessly. "Why are a few weeks that big of a deal?"

He growled and brushed his thumb over my folds while he started curling his fingers inside of me.

"Then marry me, Andie."

Those words were like a bucket of cold water splashed over me. All the good feelings he'd been evoking dried up.

"What?" I croaked.

The movement between my legs stilled, and the slight pressure on my throat increased.

"Mya explained marriage. It is a promise two people make to spend the rest of their lives with each other. Why does that promise scare you, Andie?"

"It doesn't. I just—"

He flipped me over on the mattress, his arm underneath me as he pinned me with his weight.

"I love the way you think. But sometimes you overthink things," he said, nipping my shoulders as he moved his fingers between my legs.

"Do you like this?" he asked.

I nodded hesitantly, the echo of his proposal still bouncing around in my head.

"Do you like when I care for you?" he asked.

"Yes."

He kissed my back and rested more of his torso on me. The heat of his skin and the feel of his hard length felt too good to ignore.

"Other than carrying you over my shoulder, what have I done that you have not liked?"

"I've liked it all," I admitted.

He stroked deep.

"Then imagine how I will feel inside of you." He arched into my ass as he continued to use his fingers to reignite the fire he'd briefly doused. "Are you thinking about it?"

How could I not?

I moaned and turned my head. He nipped the back of my neck.

"You are mine, Andie. Rings and words won't change what I already know. Accept it before I lose patience."

He twisted his fingers and pressed just right inside of me, setting off an explosion.

His weight lifted off me.

Panting and dazed from the ordeal, it took a moment to register that he wasn't touching me any longer. I rolled to my back and managed to lift my head to look for him. The room was empty.

When he didn't return by the time I caught my breath, I went to look for him. Instead of finding him, I found my clothes neatly folded on the back of the couch.

He had never left me before. Not like that.

Biting my lip, I dressed and returned to the house. He wasn't waiting for me there either. Understanding that I'd upset him, I decided he probably needed some time and went to bed alone.

Which was exactly how I woke the next morning.

Alone and worried.

"What did you do?" Roni asked when I emerged from the bedroom to find everyone else working together to make breakfast. Something Molev usually did for us.

"I don't know what you mean," I said.

"Do not play stupid with me," Roni said. "You went to the hookup house, came back alone, and he's still not here."

That had everyone's attention.

"Did you fight?" Katie asked.

"No," I said. "We better hurry. I didn't realize I slept so late. Someone should have woken me."

"We thought you were having cuddle time," Steve said.

"Why did he leave?" Sid asked. "He's never been gone this long."

"When he shows up again, you can ask him," I said. "We need to get going, or we'll be late for the new group."

"No one is buying your bullshit, Andie," Roni said. "But if you don't want to talk, that's fine. One way or another, we'll find out soon enough what's going on. The fact that we didn't have anyone pounding down our door means he's around here somewhere, and I'm sure he'll be happy to fill us in."

I grabbed a piece of toast.

"Sounds about right. I'll meet everyone outside."

CHAPTER SIX

Molev wasn't waiting by the vehicles, either. I knew I'd really let him down and understood it wasn't because we weren't having sex yet. Our physical relationship was only a small piece of what he wanted from me.

He worshipped my body, but he wanted my heart. And I'd frozen when he'd asked for a long-term promise.

It wasn't my first time freezing, either. But I doubted telling him that would give him any comfort.

Suppressing a sigh, I ate my toast and tried to think of a way to nicely tell Molev that I had no interest in marrying, ever, or having a child. Ever. No matter how nicely I said it, I doubted it would go over well. It never had in the past, which was precisely why I'd hoped to avoid the topic altogether.

Telling people I didn't want kids always resulted in shock and shame. Their shock and their attempts to make me feel shame for my choice.

Unfortunately, I doubted I would be able to put off the conversation with Molev for long. I'd known it was looming and that it would bite me hard sooner or later. I'd hoped it would be much later. As in "after there's a vaccine and all the undead are gone" kind of later. But it looked like our long overdue discussion couldn't be avoided any longer.

Considering Molev's attitude toward Lucas, I knew Molev wouldn't take the news well. The topic of having children had ended five of my relationships. My refusal to return an "I love you" had been the death of at least two. Looking back at all my failed relationships made me feel a lot older than twenty-six. In my defense, some of them had come and gone in three months.

Why did I end up with men who liked to move fast?

At least, now I felt more certain Molev wouldn't just leave.

Possibly.

Maybe?

The rest of the team joined me by the time I finished my toast.

"We can go," I said once they were seated.

The soldier driving my vehicle gave me a questioning look.

"He'll meet us there," I said, hoping it was true.

Molev wasn't at the training course, but several personnel were already there, setting up the water coolers.

"This is going to be a really awkward introduction," Roni mumbled as we gathered by the drop-off point.

"Just stick to the routine. We know what he's looking for," I said, taking the folder one of the personnel handed me.

I handed out the master list of names that someone had already divided into seven groups for us and started reading the demographics as we waited for the trucks to arrive. This batch had more women in it than men. Notably more. While I saw it as good news for Molev, I wondered what it meant. Was Waurlyn testing us? Were there simply fewer male volunteers? Was word spreading that we were taking mostly women?

The first truck rumbled down the road before I finished

reading. Looking up from the paper, I watched the volunteers get out and look around.

"Good morning, and welcome to Camp Irwin," I said loudly, calling everyone's attention to my typical welcome introduction.

"Andie?" a voice called from the back, interrupting me.

I paused, scanning for the speaker until the people parted and someone from my past came rushing forward.

Cory wrapped me in a bear hug when he reached me.

"Oh my God. Andie. I never thought I'd see you again."

I hugged him back, stunned since I'd never once considered I'd actually see a face I recognized in these volunteer groups. Fort Irwin and the evac site weren't anywhere near where either of us had lived.

"Uh, can we save this reunion for later?" Roni asked.

Cory immediately loosened his hold and looked over at Roni.

"Yeah. Sorry for interrupting. It's just…crazy. I never thought—" He looked at me, emotion lighting his gaze.

"I understand," I said. "It's good to see you. Let me get through the introductions first, and we can talk later."

He nodded and released me, backing up a few steps as he nodded at me to go ahead. His gaze shifted to something behind me a second before a set of hands settled on my shoulders.

"I am Molev, and this is Andie. You are here because you want a chance for a new life—a safer one—with my people. We will welcome those who know how to work well with others and want to see a diverse community thrive in a failing world. However, we have zero tolerance for theft of any kind."

Molev's grip on my shoulders took on new meaning with those words.

I reached back and patted his hand, hoping he wasn't openly glaring at Cory, and took over the welcoming speech. Molev didn't leave my side as we divided into groups, not even after Cory went off with Team Katie.

The morning stretched into the eventual midday, and Molev finally called for a break.

Typically, our team ate with the volunteers, just another chance to get to know them. But I hung back with Molev as the volunteers went for water and sandwiches from the coolers.

"You left," I said when there was no one around to hear. "Was it to punish me or because you needed some time to process?"

He crossed his arms and scowled at me. "I doubt you would find my absence a punishment."

"I'm sorry my reaction upset you to the point that you needed space."

"Will you tell me why you dislike the idea of marriage?" he asked.

"Whoa," Cory said, having approached without either of us noticing. He held up his hands when we glanced at him. "Didn't mean to interrupt *that* conversation. Hopefully, you can give him a better answer than you gave me," Cory said with a good-natured laugh, but I saw the lingering hurt in his gaze as he turned to walk away.

"Wait," Molev said. "Did you ask Andie to marry you as well?"

Cory paused. "It's old history," he said. "Nothing to worry about. I promise."

Molev grunted. "What reason did she give you?"

I couldn't believe he was asking my ex that. "I don't think this is the right place for—"

Cory answered over me. "Two years ago, she didn't want

kids. She told me that, once people get married, there's an inherent pressure to breed the next generation. She was dead set against mini-Andie's running around. She was even talking about having her tubes tied at the time but was having a hard time finding a doctor willing to do it."

"Explain tubes tied," Molev said.

"It's a surgery to prevent pregnancy forever," Cory said.

I turned and started walking, angry at both of them for judging my choices. I'd yet to meet a man who tried to see things from my point of view. Why should they? The idea of starting a family was easy for them. Find a good woman to have sex with. Watch her grow a baby for nine months. Be there when she gives birth. Then work hard to provide for the little wifey and rug rat.

Why did men think I was any more into changing poop diapers than they were? Or sleepless nights? Or giving up a carefree lifestyle?

Arms wrapped around me from behind and lifted me off the ground. I scowled up at Molev. He didn't look down at me as he started running away with me, though.

"Put me down," I said.

"Soon."

He ran faster, forcing me to tuck my face against his chest so I could breathe. When the rush of wind stopped, I lifted my head and saw he was letting us into the "sex house."

He put me down the moment the door closed behind us.

"You do not want children?" he asked, watching me closely.

"No. I don't." I crossed my arms and gave him that hard, angry stare he'd given me countless times.

"Is that the role the men before me have tried forcing you into?" he asked softly.

"It's one of the roles, yes."

He slowly pulled me into his arms and wrapped me in a hug.

"Will you tell me why you do not wish to have children?" he asked.

"Why? So you can tell me my reasons aren't valid?"

"No. So I can understand them."

I let out a long breath, unsure if it was smart to hope that Molev would be different.

"Life is filled with burdens," I said finally. "We have bills to pay. Jobs to complete in order to pay those bills. Health needs we have to take care of. Friendships to maintain. Those are all burdens that we can choose to prioritize however we please.

"It doesn't matter which way you want to spin it or how precious people think they are, kids are one of the biggest burdens life throws at us. But next level. For men, kids are typically a financial burden. For women, it's another story entirely.

"Kids take over our lives. We forgo careers and all our previous freedom to ensure the kids are cared for. Moms do all the leg work. Making appointments. Scheduling playdates. Taking time off work when the kids are sick. Figuring out what to feed them. When to feed them. How to entertain them. It all defaults to the moms. They're on duty twenty-four-seven because society says we're the primary caregivers by default. Dads are tagged in when the mom asks for help.

"*Asks*. As if the child wasn't co-created. I didn't want the responsibility of supporting another life before the world was filled with undead and hounds and failing resources. It would be doubly irresponsible to consider it now. I simply don't want the burden of having kids."

Molev's hand smoothed over my back.

"I have only seen one baby," he said. "He was very small

and fragile. He did not look like a burden to me. However, he was to the woman who kept him alive. He was starving because they ran out of food, and she understood that leaving with him would cause both their deaths. Having a baby with you would fill me with joy, but only if you are filled with joy as well, Andie."

I pulled back to look at Molev and saw understanding reflected in his gaze. But there was also sadness.

"I know you want kids, Molev," I said. "You'd be better off finding someone who is interested in the same."

He frowned at me and shook his head as his hand covered the back of my neck. "Nothing has changed. You are mine, Andie. If you do not wish for the burden of a child, then you will not be burdened. But you will be mine."

His hold on my neck tightened a moment before his mouth claimed mine in a searing kiss. When he finally released me, I was panting and more than ready to make up for the lost orgasms from the day before. However, Molev hadn't forgotten about the people we'd left behind.

"Tonight, you will surrender to me, Andie," he said, nipping the base of my throat. "Be ready."

He picked me up and ran back with me before the message sank in.

Tonight? Be ready?

I looked around for Roni after Molev put me down and strode away. I caught her eye and motioned for her to join me. It took her a minute to break away from the conversation, which was fine. It gave me time to move farther away from the people who were finished with their meals.

On her way over to me, I scanned the area for Molev and saw him talking to the personnel by the water coolers. Hoping he was distracted, I waited for Roni

"Did you two make up?" she asked.

"We didn't fight," I said. "How do I get my hands on condoms that will fit him?"

The grin that lit her face had me rolling my eyes.

"Just tell me," I said.

"I've been collecting them since Molev told me about the big boy waiting for me in Whiteman."

"I need a box."

She snorted.

"I have three goliath-sized condoms. I'll give you one."

"One?" I echoed, looking at Molev. "I don't think that'll be enough."

"Teach him the pullout method," she said with a shrug.

"That's like Russian roulette. I am not banking my future on pull-and-pray." Granted, I did have the IUD, but still. I wanted to wrap my uterus in all the "Do not enter tape" and add a padlock for good measure.

"Hey, I don't want to either, but it's not looking like we're going to have much of a choice. Like you said, they don't really make them in their size."

When I glanced at the coolers, Molev wasn't where he'd been. I spotted him coming our way.

Roni chuckled.

"I'll slip you what you need at dinner," she said. "But you have to promise to tell me everything." Then she jogged away, leaving me to face Molev alone.

He came up to me, grabbed the back of my neck, and kissed my forehead.

"Do you trust me?" he asked.

"Yes."

"Then stop overthinking this. I promise you will not be burdened with a child. Now, focus on your group. I think the woman with the long hair will be a good fit for our community."

Our community.

I nodded and let him lead me back to the group.

The afternoon passed in a blur of redundancy. I stood beside Katie as we said farewell to the volunteers for the evening then joined the others in our pre-workout stretches. Molev's pace on the way back was a little quicker than usual. Roni kept grinning at me whenever Katie begged him to slow down.

"You need to learn to run faster, Katie," Molev said when we were almost home. "Your speed might save your life."

She grumbled but kept up as we ran right to the front door.

Roni and Sid bolted for the showers, and Molev went to the kitchen to start dinner. We typically took turns on the days we didn't train hard.

Brandon looked at me and shrugged, choosing to sit at the island and watch Molev work. Not that he provided much of a show. He quickly assembled two dozen sandwiches, wrapped four of them, and strode toward me.

Roland tried hiding his smirk as Molev grabbed my hand and started pulling me toward the door.

"But…wait…I need—"

He threw me over his shoulder.

Steve laughed and opened the door. "You two have fun."

"Dammit, Molev," I said as he jogged across the yard and let us into the other house. "You know I hate this."

He didn't let up until he tossed me onto the bed. I bounced so hard my teeth clacked together.

"Why are you mad now?" I demanded as I settled.

He tugged his shirt off and threw it aside.

"This is not anger, Andie." His hands went to his pants. "This is impatience. I told you to be ready."

He shed his remaining clothes and reached for mine.

"Wait. Wait. I can do it," I said, scrambling away from him. He'd wrecked one pair of my undies already, and I didn't want to explain why I needed more clothes.

His hand closed around my ankle, and he yanked me to the edge of the bed. I squeaked at the force and stared up at him as his weight settled over me.

His hand gripped the back of my neck.

"Do you like these clothes, Andie?"

I nodded.

"Then remove them quickly."

"I will. Can I just get something from the house real fast before we start this?"

Anger flickered over his expression a second before his lips crashed against mine. He kissed me hungrily, devouring any thought of protest. And somehow, when he pulled back again, I wasn't wearing any pants.

"Remove the rest, Andie," he said.

I hesitated, trying to think of a way to get that condom from Roni.

He growled low, hooked a finger in my underwear, and pulled hard. The well-worm material gave way under his aggression and ripped free.

"Dammit, Molev!" I swallowed any additional lecture I had. While his mouth claimed mine, he gripped my thigh and started coaxing my legs apart.

I resisted, still fixated on getting the condom.

He bit my lip. Not hard enough to break the skin but enough to break through my one-track thinking. I jerked back to look up at him in surprise.

"No more waiting, Andie," he warned. "Yield to me."

"I will. I just want to get—"

He flipped me over and drew my hips to the edge of the mattress. I flailed, scrambling to pull myself back onto the bed because I knew, once we started, there wouldn't be any stopping until he was done with me.

A hand pressed down on the middle of my back, and another delved between my legs. His fingers stroked over my clit twice, immediately sending jolts of pleasure into my core. After weeks of his practiced touch, my body was ready and willing to respond.

"Wait," I panted.

"That is all I have done," he said. His legs nudged mine farther apart, and then I felt his tongue on me. I groaned and arched back against him.

"Molev, I just wanted to get a condom. It's a covering that's used to prevent pregnancy."

He grunted and thrust his tongue inside of me. He replaced it with two fingers a moment later.

"Yes," he said when I lifted my hips. "Like that."

He flipped me over again, replacing his two fingers with his mouth very briefly before returning with three. It was a stretch and something he typically didn't do until after my first orgasm.

His palm rested on my collarbones as his fingers circled my neck, and he stroked my core.

"Tell me you are mine," he said. "Tell me I can have all of you."

"You can. Just don't—"

He claimed my mouth with another fierce kiss. His fingers left me, replaced by something much larger.

My hands flew to his chest. Even as I kissed him, I pushed against him. He growled into my mouth and grabbed my knee, drawing it up to my side as he pressed into me.

I tore my mouth from his.

"Wait, I—"

He claimed my lips again as his fingers tightened on my throat. I tried wriggling away underneath him and pushed harder at his chest.

But I no longer wanted him to stop because of the condom.

I wasn't even thinking of that anymore. Excitement and need clawed at me. I wanted to resist him while he carefully took what he wanted. So I pushed and clawed at his chest while he held me by the throat and slowly worked his massive length inside of me. It burned and stretched.

A few times, I stilled, and his hold eased. His kiss turned tender and coaxing, peppering over my face and nipping at my chin. As soon as I adjusted to the intrusion, I started pushing at him again, and the aggression I craved returned.

"My Andie," Molev said when he was finally, achingly fully seated. "Do you like this?"

"Yes," I breathed.

"Will you tell me if I hurt you?"

"Yes."

He started to move at a slow and steady pace that stroked deep. He filled every inch of me and more. When I matched his rhythm, he began to move faster, angling his thrusts to hit that sweet spot inside.

I stopped pushing at him and wrapped my arms around his sides.

It only took seconds for me to find my first orgasm. He didn't slow. Not long after, I felt the hot wash of his release inside of me. I didn't pause to consider why that was a bad thing. I was too close to another orgasm.

He didn't stop.

He wrang his required orgasms out of me, incrementally

releasing in between until I was drenched and couldn't move underneath him.

Light kisses peppered my face.

"You are everything to me, Andie. Everything."

I WOKE with a groan and a wince. My insides felt like they'd been rearranged by a sledgehammer. Or menstrual cramps. I curled up and felt a wet squish come from between my legs.

Worry set in. I hadn't had my period in months, and when I had, it had been light.

Prying my eyes open, I looked around the room. I was still in the "sex house." The ceiling light was off, but I could see.

"Molev?" I called.

Silence answered me.

Gingerly, I sat up and threw back the covers. Thankfully, I wasn't hemorrhaging. At least, not blood. The copious amount of white coating my skin wasn't much better.

"Shit," I breathed, flopping back onto the sheets.

Rather than thinking about things I couldn't control, I focused on what I could and got out of bed to wash up. Then I stripped the bed and washed everything. My neatly folded clothes and a note waited on the living room couch.

HE SAID you could take today off. Personally, I think it's because he doesn't want you to see Cory. You absolutely should come to the field if you're not crippled. He told me he didn't stop until you passed out. He promised you still had a pulse and that he was really careful when he "took you forcefully the way you liked." Gurl, we definitely need to have a long talk about that one.

Anyway, he's blabbing care instructions at me while I write what I want.

Make sure to limp when you show up!

Roni

WALKING with a hitch in my step would be happening whether I wanted it to or not. Tugging on my jeans commando didn't help, no matter how careful I was.

No one witnessed my tentative return home or how I had to throw my jeans into the wash because I'd leaked the whole way.

I took another shower and tried to wash more thoroughly. The water helped soothe the sore parts, and I felt a little more human when I dressed and left the house again.

However, walking to the training grounds proved that I'd worked out more than my fun zone. My legs ached by the time I saw the volunteers moving in the distance.

I spotted Molev working with a group of women to the side and wondered if they had any idea what they were actually signing up for. Probably not. I had thought I'd known, but I hadn't. Not really. Last night had opened my eyes, though.

If Molev's brothers were anything like him, each female would find herself entangled with a fey. And bed sheets. And copious amounts of baby batter.

My core clenched at the thought, and I winced even as I felt a renewed spark of interest. But I was a twisted individual like that.

I made it a few more yards before Molev's head snapped in my direction.

"It's not okay to use a girl like you did and just leave her to wake up alone," I said softly, knowing he would hear me. "It makes her feel abandoned."

He left the group and jogged over.

"I did not abandon you. Did you not see Roni's note?" he asked.

"Oh, I saw it," I said. "Once I worked up the courage to leave the bedroom."

He blinked at me.

"It hurt to move," I explained.

He frowned.

"It kind of feels like my insides were rearranged. And I'm still dripping," I said.

The tips of his ears turned dark grey.

"Forgive me. You were making happy sounds. I thought I was watching closely for signs of discomfort, but I may have let my own pleasure blind me."

He closed the distance between us and gently cupped my neck where I knew I was lightly bruised.

"I will take more care tonight," he said.

"Tonight? You're going to kill me."

He jerked like he'd been shot.

"Everything okay over there?" Roni called.

"Everything is fine," Molev called back without looking at her.

He claimed my lips in an extremely gentle kiss then pressed his forehead to mine.

"You were sore when you first allowed me to taste you. The tenderness you feel today will pass, too. I will not forget myself tonight. I swear it. But I will have you again."

CHAPTER SEVEN

My thoughts raced. Regardless of his reassurances, my fear of eventual pregnancy remained. Yet, as I stared up at Molev's growing frown, I had to also acknowledge I couldn't take back what we'd done. He'd proven last night just how much he wanted me, and my insides clenched at the memory of the way he'd slowly dominated me.

Despite my concerns, I'd loved every second of what we'd done. And if not for his obvious desire for the whole white picket fence dream, I wouldn't have a second of hesitation.

But what were the chances I even had to worry about any of it? The vaccines were failing. Molev's blood alone was killing the volunteers. If that didn't scream incompatible, I don't know what did.

"Okay," I said. "I'm willing to try again. But if it hurts even a little and I tell you to stop, you need to respect my answer and give me more than twenty-four hours to recover."

His frown faded, and he pulled me into his arms.

"Did I truly hurt you that much?" he asked.

"You're big, Molev, and I did a lot of stretching to

accommodate. I heal slower than you do. How long would it take you to recover from a pulled muscle or a light abrasion? Double that for a human."

His lips pressed down on the crown of my head.

"Forgive me."

"I know you didn't do it on purpose."

"Then forgive me for wanting you so badly right now that I am considering running with you again, even knowing you are hurt. It would be better if you returned to the house and waited for me."

I pulled back and looked up at him.

"You had self-control enough not to behead the people who shot at you. I think you have enough self-control not to run away with me." I patted his chest. "I'm staying. A little bit of movement will help me loosen up for this evening."

"Hey," a familiar voice said from nearby. "Roni sent me over for Molev. She needs you for the next demonstration."

Molev's grip on me tightened briefly before he kissed the top of my head and turned to face Cory.

"Tell her I will return in a moment," he said.

Cory nodded and looked at me. "You okay? You look exhausted."

"I'm fine," I said, smothering my grin as Molev slipped an arm around my shoulders. "All the training is just catching up with me."

"I hear you. I had a hard time getting out of bed this morning. Might be due to the fact that it was an actual bed and not the ground, though." His gaze shifted back to Molev. "If you have time before we leave, I'd like to hear more about how you and your brothers coordinate supply runs. I'm hoping it's something some of us civilians can start doing on our own, too."

"I wouldn't recommend it," I said, even though he wasn't talking to me. "The military can barely manage it with their armored vehicles and weapons."

"That's exactly why I think we need to try," he said softly. "It won't be long before there isn't a military left to protect the barrier and gather food." He looked at Molev again. "You said that teaching us these basic defense skills might save our lives. A lot of these people think you're saying that because we *might* someday face an undead. I don't think that's what you mean at all. The undead are coming, and if some of us are lucky, what you're teaching us today might save us when they do." Cory tucked his hands into his pockets. "I'll let Roni know you're coming."

He left us, jogging back to his group, where Roni smirked in our direction.

No doubt, she'd meant to cause trouble, but based on the way Molev's hold on me had eased, Cory had changed Molev's opinion of him.

"He would make a good addition to our community," I said. "My problems with him were never because of who he was as a person. I just couldn't see myself settling down with him. Ever."

I tipped my head back to look up at Molev, and his mossy green eyes met mine.

"He would work hard and support unity. And more importantly, he would never become a reason for you to be jealous."

Molev exhaled heavily. "When I look at him, I wonder if he touched what I now touch and remembers the soft sounds you make when you sleep. Those thoughts make me want to send him far away from you."

"I heard he got engaged after we broke up," I said. "He hasn't said anything about a fiancé or wife, though. Like everyone, he's probably gone through hell since the earthquakes. Life experiences shape who we are, Molev. They change us. And sometimes, what was once important changes too."

Molev grunted.

"Go help Roni," I encouraged. "I'll take it easy until it's time for us to train together."

The rest of the morning passed quickly. Molev always seemed to know where I was and what I was doing, no matter what he was doing. I liked knowing he was paying attention to me.

When lunch rolled around, he joined me on a patch of dormant grass as we watched the vehicles leave with all the volunteers.

"How many do you think we'll get from this batch?" Steve asked, joining us.

Roni and Brandon followed with the cooler of sandwiches. They started passing them out as the rest came over. We all waited for Molev's answer.

"Twenty-six," he said. "If they all accept."

He would have spoken to the ones he wanted before they left, giving them lunch to think it over and make their decision. After that, Waurlyn's people would try to entice the ones they wanted into staying.

I took a bite of my sandwich as a vehicle with soldiers pulled up for the afternoon training.

"That's a decent number from one group," Roni said. "Will Waurlyn have housing for them?"

"She said she would make arrangements for whoever stayed," I said after I swallowed. "I'm not too worried."

"Hey, Molev," one of the soldiers called. "Waurlyn sent us to pick you up if you have time."

Molev and I shared a look. It had been days since the last trial ended. However, Waurlyn didn't typically summon us during training for trials or samples. She tended to wait until the evening for both so she didn't interrupt our day.

"I guess we won't know what's going on until we go," I said with a shrug.

"Want company?" Roni asked.

"Nah. If you don't hear from us in a few hours, you can start looking for us."

"You know we will," Brandon said.

We left them to eat lunch and made our way to the hospital where Waurlyn waited for us. Stress emanated from her.

"Thank you for coming on such short notice," she said briskly.

She led us down the hall to the conference room without hinting at why we were there.

"We need to talk," she said as soon as the door was closed behind us.

She took a seat at the table, but the energy radiating from her would have been better suited for pacing the length of the room.

"I've shared your ideas regarding additional samples and sending the volunteers you requested in increments to ensure your people can care for them. The response wasn't favorable. They liked the idea of additional samples but not losing you. They fear you're going to leave on your own as you've done several times already, which is why they would like me to take you into custody."

"Please tell me you're smart enough not to try that," I said.

She gave me a sharp, frustrated look. "Of course I am. However, disregarding their orders isn't going to help our cause. If I'm unwilling to listen, they will bring someone here who is dumb enough to try. And then where will we be?

"We need to mitigate this situation before things escalate."

"What do you propose?" I asked.

"I was hoping you would have some ideas. Something more than samples to offer them to convince them you're not trying to leave. That you're truly trying to help us."

I couldn't believe what I was hearing. It didn't matter that Waurlyn was only the messenger. I still couldn't believe that the people above her weren't yet satisfied with everything that Molev had already done to help us.

"Do they even understand what the word volunteer means?" I asked. "No one forced him to come here. Why do they think they have any right to force him to stay?"

"I understand. Please believe me. I really do. But desperation knows no reason. I tried for hours. Do you know what their answer was? They told me to use your family as a means to get you to help me convince him, Andie. I am so far in a corner that I can't see the hope that brought me here, and I know they can't either."

The threat to send my niece and nephew back here didn't sit well.

"All of this just because he wants to see his family again? How is he being unreasonable?" I asked. "It's been two months since he left them."

"Exactly. We have no idea if they're still alive," she said calmly.

While I knew those weren't her words, I still resented that she said them.

"Then try to contact Whiteman," I said. "Don't use your secret coded relays. Just send out a message on all channels and ask people to keep spreading the message. There were still people out there when we were in the field. Survivors who are digging in deep. They're listening to the radio."

"We have tried," she said. "Either Molev's people aren't listening, or they're on the wrong channels. Either way, the lack of response doesn't give a lot of people confidence that they're still where Molev said they were."

Heart sinking, I glanced at Molev. I hadn't really considered something might have happened to them. I didn't doubt they were still alive; I'd seen what one fey could do. But looking at how many bases had been evacuated, it made sense that his people may have had to move too.

"What do you think?" I asked Molev.

He considered the table for a long silent moment.

"I think Waurlyn is correct that we need to do something before the situation escalates. You have proven yourself as someone I can trust," Molev said, looking up at her. "Not fully but enough that I do not wish to deal with whomever your people might send to replace you if I do not comply. So I will, for the last time, give more than your people are willing to give."

He leaned forward, resting his forearms on the table.

"There is another reason to return to Whiteman," he said. "A young woman is there. She was bitten, died, and came back. But not infected. She is the same as she was. I saw the scar myself and have no reason to doubt what I was told."

Waurlyn leaned back in her chair, looking sick to her stomach.

"An immune human? How?"

Molev shook his head slowly. "I cannot say for certain."

"Why didn't you share this information sooner?" she asked.

"You've acknowledged the desperation of your people," he said. "Although they would believe otherwise, they cannot do as they please with me. But this woman is human. She does not have my strength or speed…only the one thing your people want above all else."

"And you don't trust us not to hurt her," Waurlyn said with an understanding nod. She sighed. "I don't know what to do with this. You're right. A lot of people are desperate. I'm desperate too, but being here changed how I see things.

"I know you're truly helping us. I see how bad things are getting. We're losing more people every day. Getting supplies to feed the people we have is becoming increasingly impossible. Based on the reports, or rather the lack of them, the infected are migrating away from the Midwest to the coasts. I'm not just facing the pressure of the higher-ups. I know our clock is ticking, and we're running out of time to help the people in this building come up with the solutions we need."

"Allow me to help with supplies again."

She shook her head. "Too dangerous. You were too—"

"It was dangerous because I did things your way. Try doing them my way," he said.

"What's your way?"

"Tell me where you want to go. I will secure the location alone. Your people can then airlift the supplies out safely while I maintain the perimeter like I did in Loveland. The infected and the hounds aren't interested in me. They're interested in humans. The larger the group, the more infected the group draws."

My stomach dropped as I realized what we'd done by hiding behind the mountains. A nice big pocket of humans. Was that why Molev's gut was telling him we needed to get the volunteers and get out? How long would it take the infected and hounds to realize what they wanted was on this side of the barrier? Maybe they already had. It would explain why the watchtower outside of Loveland in the middle of nowhere had been attacked.

"How many people are in the camps on the east coast?" I asked.

"A fair amount," she said, letting her understanding show. "Similar to the west coast, but their camps are closer together and more severely overcrowded. Or at least they were. With the number of bases we've lost in between, we're no longer receiving regular updates."

"But you *are* still receiving updates from the east coast?" I asked.

"The last one was weeks ago. We believe the loss of bases in the central states is preventing communication."

"What are you thinking, Andie?" Molev asked.

"That we need to listen to your intuition," I said before meeting Waurlyn's steady gaze. "Weeks ago, he said it didn't feel safe here. That's why he wanted to go to Loveland and see what was happening out there. And look how it turned out. If he hadn't gone…if he hadn't been there, we wouldn't have found the infected inside the barrier, and the hounds in Loveland would have made their way in. If we want any chance of saving the people who are left, we need to start listening."

"Okay," Waurlyn said.

I could see her mind racing and waited for her to say something.

She nodded after a moment. "Sharing the news of the immune woman will work for us. Whether they believe it or not, I'll insist on establishing communication with your group. That will give us time to continue working on the vaccine. And if you're still willing to leave for supplies, that will enable you to gauge what's happening outside the barrier for yourself. Do you agree?"

"Yes," Molev said. "But I would like one more thing. The three of us need to start planning how we will move the volunteers I've selected from here to Whiteman. We need to save as many as possible."

A heavy silence settled over us, and I watched Waurlyn look down at the table briefly. She understood what Molev was asking her to do and why now. But would it be enough to gain her cooperation, or would she toe the line those above her had drawn.

"How soon do you think we'll need to leave?" Waurlyn asked, looking up again.

"Sooner than either of us would like," Molev said.

She tapped her fingers on the table, deep in thought.

I glanced at Molev. We were still four weeks away from our original six-week mark goal. Was he moving up the timeline, or did he simply want to be prepared? After today's high number of accepted volunteers, I suspected it was the former option.

"Any emergency evacuation of the personnel from here would be nearly impossible with most of the aircraft allocated to supply retrieval and transport to the sanctuaries," she said. "However, if you're leaving on supply runs and I request more airlift support for that, no one will deny me. Irwin likely wouldn't be the waypoint, though. That would mean moving the personnel from here to a primary waypoint."

"Like Gypsum was?" I asked.

"Exactly," she said. "Somewhere inside the barrier with enough room to accommodate everyone. But any waypoint would question housing unnecessary personnel. So they need to be necessary. We can train your volunteers and ensure they all have a purpose. The team working on the vaccine will be the hardest to move."

It sounded like Waurlyn was committing to us completely

with those words. Her body language and calm demeanor made it hard to say for sure, though.

"Your people will be unable to choose between food and a cure when supplies are running low," Molev said. "To have both, I believe they will be willing to allow the team to come to me to obtain their samples."

Waurlyn smiled slightly. "You're a smart man, Molev. I hope I'm not misplacing my trust."

She stood, a clear signal that we were done for now.

"I have messages to send and a lot of moving pieces to arrange. Continue with your normal routine for now. I'll let you know when I have a supply location set. Will you want your team to go with you to the waypoint, or will you want them to stay and continue evaluating volunteers?"

Molev and I shared a look. We needed more people if we were going to leave for good.

"I should stay," I said. "At least for now."

"For now," he said with a slow nod.

"Good," Waurlyn said. "We'll talk soon."

Soon. It was something people said instead of eventually. So I told Molev we should return to the training course.

A decent number of soldiers had joined the team on the field. Too many to have any kind of confidential conversation. Nodding to Roni to indicate everything was fine, I joined in with what I could.

A vehicle showed up a few hours later, and the driver jogged over to Molev.

"Waurlyn's made the arrangements. Everything is in place to fly you out just after dark."

"After dark?" I asked. "Tonight?"

The man nodded.

"Waurlyn wanted to get him in place tonight so he can leave

whenever he's ready."

Or because removing him would be the best way to ensure no one would try taking him into custody. Especially if he was in the middle of rounding up food.

The soldier looked at Molev. "Thank you for your service, and be careful out there. I'll be back to pick you up at dusk."

He started walking away, and Brandon, who had been nearby, jogged over.

"What's going on?"

"Andie will explain tonight," Molev said, picking me up. "Continue training."

Then he was running with me. He went straight to the house next door.

"Molev, we don't have time for this," I said, batting away his hand when he reached for my shirt. "We need to—"

The hand on the back of my head held me in place for his aggressive kiss. I immediately stopped resisting. It served no purpose. Molev would have whatever he wanted, one way or another. And right now, he wanted me as willing and as desperate as he was.

I was too sore, though.

Or so I thought.

Once I gave in, he gentled and did all the right things to rekindle that hunger I had for him. Just the right amounts of aggression balanced with hot, tender looks and feathering kisses.

And when I lay panting beneath him, he eased into me with controlled caution, watching for any hint of discomfort. I felt a little, but nothing that lasted with his thumb stroking my throat.

"You are mine, Andie," he said. "Protect yourself when I'm gone. If anything happens to you, I will not hold back. Do you understand?"

I nodded and clung to him as his rhythm intensified.

"Mine," he said again as I peaked, and he joined me.

He didn't let up until it was almost dusk, and I once again doubted my legs would be able to support me. I listened to him move around the room as I lay on the bed, waiting for my pulse to die down. A damp cloth gently swiped between my legs.

"One day, I will be able to take my time with you," he said.

"That's not a day I'm looking forward to," I said. "I like being able to walk afterward."

He chuckled and tenderly kissed my knee.

"You will be fine. Come. Stand. We don't have much time left."

I took the cloth from him and finished cleaning myself once I was on my wobbly legs. He had me dressed and in his arms again in short order.

Sid opened the door to our house for us when we approached. Spread out between the kitchen and the living room, the rest of the team waited.

"What's going on?" Roni asked. "Why are you leaving?"

"To keep the peace here, I will leave to clear the infected from the barrier and secure more supplies. Continue evaluating the volunteers. Waurlyn knows Irwin won't be safe forever and will start sending the people you select to join me. Take care of each other. Take care of Andie." He paused and pressed his forehead to mine. "Remember what I said."

Outside, an engine rumbled.

"Train hard," he said. "We will see each other again soon."

Then I was on my own feet, staring at an empty doorway. Outside, the engine rumbled again.

"We're going to need a lot more explanation than that," Sid said

"And I have one, but I need a shower first."

"Go," Roni said. "Food will be ready when you're done."

It was a quick shower but a long dinner with a lot of conversation. Everyone was on board with the new plan and nervous about Molev's intuition that things were going to go downhill fast outside the barrier.

We went to bed early, and Katie had to shake my shoulder to get me out of bed the next morning. Once again, it hurt to move, but I powered through it.

The next day was easier. So was the following one.

We sorted through the volunteers and trained hard, often well past dark. Waurlyn kept me involved in decisions and updates, especially regarding Molev's progress.

A week passed quickly. Our volunteer numbers increased by increments. Waurlyn slowly moved thirty of the ones who'd been with us the longest to the waypoint for one reason or another, making room for the forty-five we added.

At the start of the second week, Waurlyn sent for me just after I gave the welcome speech to the fresh group of volunteers.

"We might have a problem," she said as soon as we were in the conference room. "Since the latest trial failed, the research team has been running more tests on the hound corpses. They're running a comparison between the three source samples: Hound, Undead, and Molev. They believe they've identified the infection and the piece that is stopping the hounds and undead from dying."

My stomach dropped. "They're working on a way to kill them that doesn't involve Molev?"

"Worse, Andie. They're splitting the research team. Half will continue working on isolating the source of the infection. The other half will start working on isolating what makes them immortal."

I couldn't believe what I was hearing. "The infected and hellhounds aren't immortal. They're decaying. Dead. What are they thinking?"

"It's easy to pretend things are not as bad as they are when they've hidden away on an island. They aren't facing the hardships and realities we're facing. Which is why I think we need to move up the timeline. The team isolating the infection will need more samples soon. I need you to be ready to join Molev by the end of the week."

"We could be ready in fifteen minutes if needed," I said. "How many volunteers can you move this week, and how many can we take with us when we leave?"

"I'll start moving what we have. Molev is securing locations daily so no one will question reallocating personnel to help with the influx of supplies. Having that many people in one place so close to the barrier does concern me, though."

I agreed. After Molev's warning, I wasn't sure it was smart either.

"What bases are the closest to the barrier?" I asked. We looked over the map together and found a base in New Mexico that would work. It was running on a skeleton crew due to the difficulty to reach without an aircraft, which kept it isolated.

"They're due for supplies soon. I'll move up the timeline and throw in some personnel. Yours and some additional soldiers to keep the commander there quiet."

"Do you have a way to let Molev know what's happening?" I asked.

"I do. Be ready, Andie, and keep quiet. With Molev gone, you're a person of interest. A safety net for his return."

"And you'll be kicking the hornet's nest by sending me away."

CHAPTER EIGHT

FIVE DAYS LATER, I WOKE WITH A SLIGHT HEADACHE THAT I couldn't shake.

"What's going on with you?" Roni asked when I collapsed on the ground after the volunteers left for lunch.

"I feel like I drank too much last night."

"You didn't drink," she said.

"Exactly. I must be coming down with a bug or something."

"Or maybe you're just low on vitamin D. I bet Molev's dreaming of when he gets to give you another dose."

I shook my head and sat up. "I would say you have a one-track mind, but we both know you're too focused on the day-to-day to accuse you of that."

She flashed me a smile. "Speaking of…if you approve of the names we've checked, that'll put us at two-twenty-seven total. Exactly two hundred women, counting us."

"I approve," I said without looking. "How many are currently in housing?"

"Just the ones from the last group. Waurlyn wanted to give them a few days before moving them."

"Okay. Let her people know this is it for now. Groups are temporarily suspended while we take a few days to rest."

We both knew we wouldn't be resting. We would be making final preparations.

That evening, Waurlyn's knock on our door wasn't unexpected.

"How is everyone?" she asked politely as she took off her coat.

"Good," I said. "The new volunteers are settled and understand they might be temporarily reassigned to help with supply redistribution. How are things on your end?"

"A little rocky. The team responsible for the mortality cure requested to start their first trial tomorrow. The serum is derived from hound DNA."

Brandon swore under his breath, and Katie sat with a thump.

"How can they be so stupid?" Steve asked.

"They don't view it that way. It's a carefully calculated risk versus reward. They believe they've isolated what they needed. And they've tested different methods to expunge infected cells and are reasonably confident that, if the trial fails, they will be able to reset the room."

"You mean they're fairly sure they'll be able to kill the person they inject," I said.

"Yes."

"When do they want to do that?" I asked.

"Tomorrow afternoon," she said. "And since, in the delegation's eyes, I've managed Molev well, they've agreed that I should head off any potential conflicts of interest by flying out to confer with him tomorrow before the test takes place."

"Do you honestly think he's going to be okay with this?" I asked.

"I know he won't be, but I think he was expecting this all along and is the reason behind all of the work we've been doing. It's been leading up to this. Are you ready?"

"So we leave tomorrow, then?" Roni asked, leaning forward. "It's been nice here, but I'm glad we're finally moving."

Waurlyn gave Roni a small smile.

"Yes. Everything changes tomorrow. Many people are eager to learn more about Molev's people, which I hope to use to pacify the delegation once what we've done is discovered. Here are the radio frequencies and times," Waurlyn said, handing me a folder. "Communicate regularly to preserve the trust Molev has won."

"What about you?" I asked. "Are they going to replace you when they find out what we've done?"

"Very possibly," she said. "But that's a risk Molev understood when he asked me."

Molev hadn't been the only one to understand the risk. Waurlyn had, too, when she agreed. So, I felt a smidge of guilt that we had no intentions of returning—something we still hadn't acknowledged—when I accepted the papers.

We all knew we were playing a dangerous game. The power players trying to control Molev... The scientists meddling with things they didn't fully understand... Even Waurlyn.

Playing both sides rarely worked out for anyone. Yet, she was taking the risk anyway because of the potential benefit. The scientist who accompanied us could continue working on a vaccine. If they found it, the game would be that much less dangerous. Hopefully.

"Thank you for this," I said. "We'll communicate on schedule even if there is nothing new to report."

"We need a vaccine, Andie. Without it, no one stands a chance. Not even the people who go with you. You heard what

Molev said. The undead are attracted to large gatherings of humans. If the barriers fall and we all turn, your group will be the largest remaining group of humans, and the undead will come after you in force. Five hundred fey won't stand a chance against millions of infected humans."

I understood then that Waurlyn had seen our plan from the beginning and understood we weren't coming back. And she'd put all her money on who she thought would be the winning team.

"We won't let that happen," I said. "We *will* find a vaccine before it gets to that point."

"I hope so."

After she left, we spent the evening checking gear and weapons. I hadn't exaggerated when I'd told her we could leave within minutes. We had very little to pack.

We slept as late as possible the next morning and ate a quiet breakfast together before leaving to check on the last group of accepted volunteers. We found them packing up, having already received orders from Waurlyn's people that they would be moving out. The women were nervous, which I could understand. They hadn't volunteered to fight. They'd asked to be taken to a better, safer place. Instead, we were asking them to do something potentially dangerous. I just hoped that, in the end, what we were doing would pay off, and they would find the haven we were all promised.

A large truck showed up within the hour to shuttle us all to the landing pad near the hospital. Two large aircraft waited. The researchers were moving crated supplies into a nearby storage cube. I saw the doctor directing her team of twelve.

Waurlyn stood off to the side, speaking to Thomas. She looked just as put together as ever with her smart business suit and folder of papers. His gaze flicked over the chaos and landed on me as I disembarked with the rest. I maintained eye contact as we waited for our orders.

"The general doesn't look too happy," Roni noted.

"Has he ever?" Steve asked.

"He didn't get to where he is by being a stupid man," I said softly. "He sees us—me—as leverage and won't like the idea of us leaving, no matter what the reason. But he's in no position to override Waurlyn's orders."

Waurlyn caught his stare and waved me over.

"In your own words, what is the mission?" Waurlyn asked when I reached them, confirming that Thomas wasn't a fool.

"Try to convince Molev we aren't making a mistake that will end the failing scraps of humanity in complete egotistical arrogance," I said without hesitation.

Thomas's gaze narrowed on me.

"Whether I agree with it or not, I understand the mission. Just like you understand that Molev's trust in what we're doing here is hanging on by a thread. Don't mess this up, Thomas. We can't afford another mistake." I looked at Waurlyn. "Where do you want us?"

"The far aircraft," she said. "I'll be joining you in a few moments to rehearse what we'd like you to say."

I nodded sullenly and returned to the group.

"We're over there," I said, gesturing toward the far aircraft. We took our places while the scientists went in the other one along with the majority of the volunteers.

Waurlyn was the last one onto the aircraft. The door shut behind her as she took her seat and gave me a long look.

"After the way he previously interrogated me, any other response would have been inappropriate," I said.

She exhaled and closed her eyes as the engines started. It

took a few minutes to connect the cargo carriers, and then we left Fort Irwin behind.

We reached the base by midday. I wasn't quite sure what to expect when we landed. However, the overstaffed, crowded landing pad wasn't it. People moved about, carrying supplies and reloading another container nearby.

"The aircraft will take supplies to the evac site before returning for us," Waurlyn said, claiming my attention. "Molev's this way."

The team and I followed her to two waiting vehicles that took us to a building on the far side of the base. The scent of food teased my nose when we opened the door, and my stomach growled.

Molev looked up from his plate of food, and his gaze locked with mine as we entered. I doubted he saw the other people with me. He was on his feet a second later, closing the distance between us.

It was hard to admit to myself how much I missed him in the weeks we'd been apart.

"Molev," Waurlyn said. "I know you were looking forward to seeing Andie, but if I could have a moment of your time before you take her away, it's really important."

He glanced at her then back at me.

"You need to hear what she has to say," I said. I could see the resentment and anger growing in his gaze. Rather than let him think I was trying to put him off, I grabbed a handful of his long hair and tugged him down to my level.

"A quick hello kiss isn't going to hurt anything, though," I said softly.

His lips curved at the corners, and before I knew what he intended, he had me in his arms, flush against his chest, with his strong hand gripping the back of my head as his lips claimed mine in a powerful kiss.

I wrapped my legs around his waist and gave back as good as I got. The kiss scorched through me, making me ache for the feel of him again.

Someone cleared his throat.

"I'm sorry to break apart your reunion," Roland said, "but the faster you listen to Waurlyn, the faster you can take Andie somewhere else. I'm not sure Roni can handle much more of this display."

"Shut your face, Roland," Roni said. "I'm two seconds from making some popcorn."

Molev kissed my forehead then set his to mine.

"I missed you," he said.

"I missed you too."

I could see his small smile before he released me.

Roni was grinning like a fool when I faced her.

Molev kept his arm around my shoulders as he addressed Waurlyn.

"It is good to see you."

"Thank you for your service, Molev. Your efforts are not going unnoticed."

"Is that why you're here? To thank me?"

She smiled slightly. "I wish it were. Have a seat."

I scanned the mess hall, noting all the personnel present. Why a public meeting?

We sat at the dining table, and Waurlyn passed the papers across the surface. When she flipped open the folder, there was a picture of a very muscular-looking man.

"The vaccines based on your blood samples have continued to fail, and the research team has been given permission to try alternative methods. Despite my objections, they will inject this person with a serum that, by all accounts, should prevent his death when exposed to the infection. At least, that's what they are hoping it will do. However, the serum is derived from the hound's genetic material, so I doubt that'll be the outcome."

Molev slowly shook his head. "They are fools."

"They understand that you might feel that way, which is why they've sent us to speak with you. We need a vaccine, Molev. As I pointed out to Andie, we will not survive without it. Please don't abandon the remaining people to their fates."

"I won't." He considered her for a long moment. "This is why you're here? To tell me they are disregarding my warning?"

She nodded.

"You should stay here for the night and return in the morning," he said.

"Why?" she asked.

"My instincts are telling me something will go wrong soon. Perhaps it's the tests they will run in Irwin. Perhaps it's something else." He shrugged slightly. "I cannot protect you if you leave."

Waurlyn's careful mask slipped away to reveal her true emotion. Gratitude showed through.

"I want you to remember this, Molev," she said. "You will not be able to save everyone. It's something I acknowledged the moment I came here to take over for Thomas. I knew I would not be able to save the lives of every remaining person. There will be losses. Don't lose focus on the big picture. We are here to save as many as we can. And because of that, I have to go back. I have to make sure that they are taking every precaution. We don't want to unleash something even more monstrous than what we are already facing."

"I understand," he said.

"Good. I wish I was here to tell you that you've earned a few days of rest, but the resources you've secured over the last two weeks have proven what a valuable asset you are to have in the field. If you're willing, I would like you to continue doing what you're doing. I have identified additional resources. However, it would require a larger relocation."

Molev grunted.

"I'd like you to go to a temporary forward operating base and continue the necessary supply operations from there. And because the doctor and I still believe you're the key to discovering the vaccine, I've determined that half of the research team will accompany you, along with enough equipment for them to run the necessary tests.

"I will start transitioning personnel if you agree."

And now I understood why she had wanted to have the discussion in the open. She'd played her part well, publicly persuading Molev to not only continue to support us but to keep working to bring in supplies. No one would question a mass relocation if it meant more food for the survivors.

Molev agreed for anyone listening in the cafeteria.

"Thank you for your cooperation," she said. "Can you be ready to move in an hour?"

"Yes," he said.

"Then I will make arrangements. I know this is a lot to ask, but please wait here." Her gaze flicked between me and Molev, and I knew she was telling him not to run off with me.

"We'll stay here," I said.

Molev watched her walk away. After weeks of getting to know him, I was able to read him well enough to see his suspicion. I threaded my fingers through his to gain his attention.

There was so much I wanted to tell him, but I knew it wasn't the time or the place. So I settled for leaning against his arm and resting my head on his shoulder. My stomach growled again.

"You need to eat," he said.

The team and I went to help ourselves to the midday meal, and we caught Molev up on the volunteer training we'd been doing.

"So that's five women total with kids and three teens," Katie said.

"Waurlyn held them back as long as possible," I said, "but with the personnel and supply shortages, they left with the last group."

"They aren't here," Molev said, that suspicion returning.

"The supplies are being distributed to several reallocation points. The evac site is one, and there's another farther north," I said. "They're probably at one of those. Don't worry. Waurlyn won't forget what they volunteered for."

Molev wrapped his arm around my waist, and his fingers found their way under my shirt to play over my skin.

"Thank you for finding so many," he said to the team. "Our community will thrive because of everyone here."

Roni sighed heavily. "I'm looking forward to the day when I get to bask in someone's praise."

Molev chuckled, and Steve rolled his eyes. "I'm going to regret not packing a spray bottle for you."

Waurlyn returned as Steve was pantomiming spraying Roni like a misbehaving cat.

"Everything is set," she said. "I stopped the aircraft before they left. They'll deliver you and some initial supplies to the new base before returning here for supplies for the evac site."

She walked us to our transport and waved farewell as we joined the volunteers.

"Good luck," she said.

"I think you're going to need that more than we will," I said.

Everyone inside the aircraft was quiet as we lifted off. Mostly because they were trying not to stare at Molev. Although they'd seen his picture, they hadn't had a chance to meet him in person like the earlier volunteers had. I held his hand and smiled whenever I caught anyone's gaze. The light inside the aircraft was beginning to fade by the time we reached the remote base in eastern New Mexico, well outside of the barrier.

After disconnecting the cargo containers, we landed and met the base's commander. He was pretty easy to read and openly curious about Molev.

"Didn't think I'd ever see any of you up close stationed out here," he said, holding out his hand. "I've heard good things. My name's Rick."

They shook hands.

"I'm Molev."

"Some of your personnel are already here and ready to get to work. Let me know if you need anything, Molev. I'll do my best to support you and stay out of the way. Thank you for your help."

"Can you have someone show us to our quarters for the night so we can stow our gear?" I asked before Molev could say anything else. I wasn't sure what Waurlyn had told Rick and wanted to let Molev know what was going on before we spoke to anyone else.

"Of course," Rick said, waving a soldier over.

The man led the way, and we passed several familiar faces. The volunteers nodded hello but didn't stop to talk.

Unfortunately, the quarters we were shown weren't what I had hoped for. Nothing private. The rows of bunks had Roni laughing.

"What are you gonna do now?" she asked.

"Talk to you," Molev said. "There is much you do not know."

His seriousness cut through her playful mood. We all moved closer as she crossed her arms.

"What's going on?" she asked.

"The infected are changing. They are growing smarter. The number of humans living at that border base were attracting the attention of the infected in the beginning until they realized I was there."

"Were you leaving body piles?" Sid asked.

"No. I moved all the undead away from the base. The infected still understood I was there and avoided the area. I scouted farther to the north and found them accumulating in larger numbers. I shared this information with the base commander, and he shared it with his people."

"Does Waurlyn know?" Roni asked.

"I don't think so," I said. "She didn't mention anything to me, and she's been open about everything else."

"Based on what she said earlier, I believe she knows and is prioritizing," Molev said. "Supplies are necessary as is a vaccine. Whether or not the infected attack the barrier, neither of those priorities change."

I thought of what Waurlyn had said to Molev and nodded.

"She understands what's at Whiteman—a potential cure," I said. "Between the serum and the infected gathering, it's enough of a reason to move up the timeline and send you home."

Molev grunted.

"This base is hard to access without air transport," I said. "It's why Waurlyn and I picked it. We should be fine here while we wait for the rest of our people to join us."

"How long will that take?" Roland asked.

"Waurlyn didn't share that part with me," I said. "Just that she was going to reallocate resources to help Molev obtain supplies. I don't know what she told Rick, but I'm guessing he's going to expect you to want to go somewhere and scout soon."

"Do you have a map?" Molev asked.

"No, but I'm betting Rick does."

Molev stared at me for a long moment. "This is not the reunion I hoped for."

Roni chuckled. "We'll give you some alone time later," she said. "Let's figure out how far we need to escort our ragtag group once they all get here and what kind of transportation we'll have."

We left our assigned bunkhouse and asked the nearest soldier for directions to the Commander. When we found him, he was in the middle of facilitating the relocation of the researchers' cargo container. The doctor noticed our approach first.

"Molev, if you have a moment, could I collect a few samples? I have some tests I'd like to run as soon as—"

"No more injections," Molev said. "Not out here."

She nodded quickly. "Of course. I hope you understand the team and I were aware the research hasn't progressed to the point where we are ready for trials. Each one was done under orders and duress. There's still so much more we don't know about your genetic makeup, which is why I'd like the samples."

He glanced at me.

"I think it'll be fine as long as they don't inject anyone."

He motioned for her to go ahead and looked at Rick.

"Do you have a map that I can look at? I would like to familiarize myself with the locations Waurlyn has provided."

Molev was really good at saying just enough without giving anything away.

"I'll take you to my little slice of map heaven as soon as the good doctor is done sticking you," Rick said with a smile.

It didn't take her long to finish up.

"I'm going to hang out with the research team and keep an eye on things," Katie said.

"I'll tag along with her," Brandon said.

The two of them followed the doctor while the rest of us accompanied Rick to one of the few permanent buildings on the plateau. He opened the door to a large conference room littered with maps and powered-down computers.

"Here we go," he said, moving to a map on the center of the table. "I've already taken the liberty of marking the locations. We're here. The personnel you've trained are coming from here and here. I'm guessing you'll see some of them tomorrow. But Waurlyn said supplies are dangerously low and emphasized getting you in the field as soon as possible. So, I can have you at a drop point here"–he pointed to a new spot–"an hour after dawn."

Molev and I studied the map. We were on a plateau in New Mexico east-southeast of Santa Fe. Our goal, Whiteman, was in Missouri, almost one thousand miles away as the crow flew. In between, three locations were marked. Amarillo, Texas; Wichita, Kansas; and Kansas City.

Kansas City would bring us the closest to our goal.

"Weren't the biggest cities bombed?" I asked.

"Waurlyn said the distribution center is just outside of the blast zone. It's funny that one caught your eye first. She said it's likely to have the biggest payoff but the highest risk too. Vance would have been an ideal refueling location, but it was evacuated a few weeks ago. The fuel's still there. Not sure we can get to it, though."

"We can," Molev said. "Was everything left behind in the evacuation? Vehicles? Food?"

"It was an air evac, so yeah. That doesn't mean it's still there, though."

"There were a lot of people out there still looking for supplies," I said to Molev. "Remember the gunshots when you were out of it in the MRAP? Those were from raiders. If they saw the evacuation, they might have tried to go in."

Molev considered the map.

"The infected are drawn to large gatherings of humans. I saw it at the last base. The barrier is at risk because the humans on the other side have already drawn the attention of the infected. Once the volunteers arrive, I want to move quickly so we don't draw the infected here."

"Understood," Rick said. "Waurlyn promised adequate air support to move everyone. I'll make sure my people are ready to refuel and get you off the ground as soon as they arrive."

Molev grunted, still looking at the map.

I could see it in his eyes.

We were so close to home now.

CHAPTER NINE

QUIET TIME TOGETHER WASN'T REALISTIC. NOT WHEN WE RETURNED to the bunks and found several of them occupied. I patted Molev's arm.

"We can still cuddle," I said softly.

Roni overheard and snorted.

Molev's gaze flicked to her before he picked me up and left. We ended up on the roof of the commander's building. Molev sat with me in his lap, and we watched the sunset together as he held me.

"What are you thinking?" I asked.

"I'm thinking of my brothers, wondering what I've missed since leaving them. Hoping they are well and some of the females have changed how they think."

"How did they think?" I asked. I wasn't sure if he still meant their fear of them or something else.

"That we're too different to love."

I twisted to look up at him. "If they haven't, we'll help them change their minds."

He dipped his head and kissed me tenderly.

"I feared you would have changed how you think," he said, studying me.

"And how do I think?" I asked with a slight grin.

"Too much and too often."

I elbowed him. It was like elbowing stone. He wrapped me tighter in his arms.

"You doubt the wisdom of opening your heart when so many are dying every day. You doubt my ability to keep you alive. You doubt that I will honor who you are and will try to force you to become someone you choose not to be."

"Hmm. Sounds like you were listening."

"I was. I will always listen to you."

"I'm going to remind you that you said that."

"Listening to what you say does not mean doing as you say."

I laughed lightly. "No, it doesn't. Are you nervous about what comes next?"

"With you? Never."

"I meant out there."

He was quiet for a long time, his breath teasing the top of my head.

"Yes," he said finally. "Those who have volunteered aren't fighters. They do not know how to survive out here. I will need to keep them alive. But I am only one man, and there will be many females."

I nodded slowly.

"Remember what Waurlyn said. Don't lose focus on the bigger picture. If you die when we're out there, we'll all die. You can't sacrifice yourself to save one life when you have two hundred more counting on you."

He grunted and kissed the top of my head.

We talked on the roof for another hour before he returned me to the bunk and told me to rest.

"What about you?" I asked.

"I will return later."

"You're going to check the perimeter, aren't you?"

He grunted and kissed me. "Warm the bed for me."

Roni snorted from her bunk, and I rolled my eyes.

"Hurry back," I said softly.

No one spoke as I claimed a bunk and pulled a blanket over me without removing any of my clothes or layers. The time for comfort was gone.

Molev woke me sometime later when he curled around me. I settled into his warmth and drifted off again. The next time I woke, I was alone, and it was light outside.

Roni sat on the bunk across from me with a cup of coffee in her hands.

"You going to be able to walk today?" she asked, waiting for me to sit up before handing over the cup.

"Nothing happened. Too many people around."

"I wouldn't have let that stop me."

"Thanks for the warning," Katie said above me.

I grinned into my cup and took a tentative sip.

"Anything happening out there?" I asked.

Roni shook her head. "I know where the mess hall is. The researchers barely slept. And Molev's watching over everything. Everyone else is waiting for our people to show up."

I stood and stretched, rolling the stiffness from my shoulders and missing the softer bed back at the base.

"I'm betting we'll see them later today."

The three of us had just finished our late breakfast when

someone ran into the mess with news that a fleet of aircraft was approaching.

Katie took our trays while Roni and I went outside to watch the spectacle. Rick was yelling at people to move the few vehicles they had on the plateau. Molev stood nearby, watching the approach of the line of aircraft making its way toward the base. Spaced so far apart, the seventh one was barely visible in the distance.

The whomp-whomp-whomp of their double rotors grew louder, and I couldn't hear what Molev said to Rick. When Rick nodded and jogged away, Molev turned and saw us. He came over, his body language conveying urgency.

"Get your things. We will leave in these once they are all refueled," he said.

"I'll get your stuff," Roni said. "Send Katie when you see her."

She hurried away, and I stayed with Molev to watch the first one land.

"What's going on?" Katie asked, joining us as the blades slowed.

"Refuel," someone yelled as the door to the aircraft opened and people poured out.

While a group of soldiers directed them to the bathrooms, another group moved a fueler into place. Everyone hustled. The next aircraft drew closer. I scanned the space available.

"Are they all going to fit?" I asked over the chaos.

"No. Once this one is done refueling and everyone is back on board, they'll move to the next plateau to wait for the others to refuel," Molev said.

The neighboring plateau was a good distance away and not as steep as ours.

"Is it safe?" I asked.

"For now," he said. "If there is trouble, they will contact Rick."

The landing area fit three easily. It might have fit four, but before that one reached us, the first one was refueled and reloaded. I stood with Molev and watched as each aircraft refueled and made room for the next.

The rest of the team joined us with their gear and waited.

I noticed that each aircraft also had four armed soldiers. Familiar faces from our training groups. Rather than feel a sense of relief, I worried. What did it mean that Waurlyn sent people she knew would work well with Molev and his people? Sure, she'd already acknowledged we had no intention of returning, but did she think that meant we would hold the transport hostage? I doubted that very much. Which left two other possible scenarios.

The first was that she'd given the soldiers and pilots orders to stay at Whiteman so we could return when we were ready. Doing that would not only ensure she had access to Molev's people but the scientists she sent with us. And it would be a huge goodwill gesture.

However, giving up seven cargo-ready aircraft in the midst of a supply shortage seemed just as unlikely as us holding the soldiers hostage.

Which meant the final scenario was the most likely. She'd listened to Molev and his warning that something was going to happen and was sending these people with us because she doubted there would be anything for them to return to.

I looked at Molev.

"Are we rushing to get to Vance because you're homesick, because you're worried Waurlyn or someone else will change their minds, or because something's telling you we need to hurry?"

Molev looked at me and blinked. That was it. Just that slow blink.

It wasn't reassuring. Doubly so when he wrapped his arm around me and pressed a kiss to my temple.

"Focus on what we can control," he said against my ear. "We have about thirty people able to help secure Vance if I include females. It was a large base. How would you secure it?"

I looked at the sky. We still had several hours before midday.

"Are we planning on overnighting at Vance or only refueling?" I asked. "I'm asking because we need to make sure we're not arriving at our final destination at dusk."

"Rick believes we should be able to make it to Whiteman before nightfall if we refuel."

"Okay. Then, if the gates are still secure, land everything at once. You'll be able to handle anything the sound draws out during the day. Those who are able can guard the people who will help with refueling. Everyone else can stay put and wait for departure."

He grunted.

"How do you think we should secure the base?" I asked.

"I like your idea," he said.

"Did you have a different one?"

"No. But having you say it means you will accept remaining safely in the aircraft where I want you."

Roni snorted nearby. "Fell right into that one, Andie."

"Pretty sure we're all stuck in the tin deathtraps," Steve grumbled.

Roni went quiet, and I didn't need to turn around to know she was pouting. Although, quietly seething was probably a better word for her version of it.

"If staying inside keeps you focused while you clear the immediate area, then that's fine. But my answer changes if the gates aren't secure. There are too many places for infected to be hiding inside the base for us to be on the ground this long." I nodded toward the aircraft still refueling. "You'll need help."

He grunted and said, "I will communicate the plan to Rick." His gaze swept over all of us. "I will be in the first aircraft to land. I want the rest of you to split up and join the others. Keep yourselves alive. Keep your cargo alive. No risks."

His gaze locked with mine on the last part, and I nodded, hiding my surprise. After being apart for so long, I wouldn't have thought he would be willing to separate again. Yet, it made sense. We all knew the plan, where we were really going, and why. And none of us would panic under pressure. We knew how to protect ourselves. We understood how the infected worked and how to work together to keep them back.

"Then I guess it's time for some of us to start hitching a ride," Steve said, shouldering his pack. "See you all in a few hours."

Katie and Sid did the same.

Molev walked me to the second to last aircraft and kissed me sweetly.

"No risks," he repeated.

"I'll be an angel," I said.

He grunted and waited until I was inside before walking away. People I'd met over the course of the last few weeks watched me with varying expressions.

"We're on the home stretch," I said, holding on to the nearby straps. "Another refuel, and then we should arrive at Whiteman, our final destination for the day, before dusk."

I could see the tension leave half of them, and I offered a small smile to reassure the rest. Did I think everything would go as smoothly as I'd just made it sound? Hell no. Things never went smoothly in the field. But spending the next four hours worrying about it wouldn't do anyone any good.

The sound of the engine wound up, and the increasing thump of the blades drowned out the possibility of conversation. I looked through the window as we lifted off and watched Molev's aircraft lead the way with the cargo cube suspended underneath.

The soldier next to me leaned in to ask about the plan for landing in Vance.

"Won't know until we see the state of the base," I said in his ear, knowing no one else would hear me.

He nodded and started to check over a weapon that had probably been checked several times already. I set my hand on his arm, and when I had his attention, I shook my head slightly.

"Sleep."

He nodded and tipped his head back, closing his eyes. The other three with weapons did the same. I offered one more smile to everyone who was quietly observing me then followed suit even though I'd only been awake a few hours.

I found that place again, the one between sleep and awake, where I drifted for the remainder of the flight. When the soldier next to me nudged my arm, I opened my eyes and glanced out the window at the approaching base.

The bird's eye view showed the interior fence that had sectioned off a few buildings and the nearest airstrip. The scaled-down size of the defensible area would work to our advantage if there was a compromise in the fence.

With the distance between aircraft, I had a good view of Molev's aircraft swinging around the larger outer perimeter base before heading toward the airfield. We weren't far behind.

I checked my weapons and shoved the helmet on my head. One of the soldiers was motioning for everyone to stay put while the other two went to the door. We touched down a few minutes later.

As soon as I knew I would be heard, I started talking.

"The plan is to remain in the aircraft with the doors shut as we refuel." I pointed to the two male volunteers in our group. "If that door does open, I need both of you to close it behind us. Do not open it for any reason if we leave. Trust in Molev. He will keep you safe."

The sounds faded further, and I moved to watch out the window.

The base was quiet. The other side of the distant fence was also empty. He'd told us that the infected were migrating west toward the barrier, but I hadn't fully believed that would leave the interior so quiet.

Molev was standing on top of the cargo cube he'd disconnected, just watching and waiting as the final aircraft touched down.

As soon as it cut the engines, he went to his aircraft and opened the door. Several personnel emerged and pointed to a nearby building and tanker. Molev nodded and started in that direction at a jog. Though he was moving away from me, I could see the way he was scanning for infected.

"No infected in sight," I said to everyone else. "That doesn't mean they aren't there, though. Sit tight while Molev does a sweep and moves the tanker closer."

"Will we be able to get out here?" someone asked.

"Not if we can help it," I said.

"The base has been deserted for a few weeks, and the infected like to hide now," another soldier said. "It's safer if we stay put."

Molev reached the tanker and started it up. Nothing moved as he drove it toward us.

"This doesn't feel right," the soldier next to me said softly. "Where are they?"

I didn't answer. Like him, I wasn't sure if I believed what I was seeing.

Molev parked the tanker nearby and got out to talk to the men waiting. Under his close supervision, they got to work, getting everything into position to refuel. And then they just stopped and looked at each other. One went over to knock on the tank while another ran around to the other side of it.

The second Molev looked at me through the window and nodded, I understood what he wanted.

"They're having problems fueling," I said, looking at the two men. "As soon as we leave, close the door and don't open it, no matter what happens. In here, the infected can't get you. Out there, they can. It's that simple.

"Don't forget your training."

One woman looked close to throwing up. The rest looked pale or stunned as the door opened, and the five of us jumped out. Once my feet hit the dirt, I was scanning for infected. Everything was quiet.

"Andie," Molev called.

"Stay here," I said to the soldiers as I jogged over to him. "The fuel is gone. They know where the rest is kept and will drive the tanker there."

My gaze flicked over the fence and the nearby buildings.

"Even if this is a trap to split us up, we need that fuel to get out of here," I said. "So, put Sid and a few others on that roof with a radio, keep one for yourself, and go with the tanker. They'll radio if they see anything. The rest of us can stand guard."

He exhaled heavily and nodded.

"Sid!" I called. If the sound of us landing hadn't brought

anything out to greet us, my voice wouldn't either. But if it did, I preferred to have it happen when Molev was around.

Sid joined us a minute later. I found a set of radios and two other soldiers with decent long-range proficiency. As soon as Molev had them deposited on the roof, someone started the engine on the tanker.

The rest of the team joined me and a few other personnel as we watched them drive off.

"Guess I was so used to keeping our fueler's tank full that I never thought this one would be empty," Roland said.

"Same," Roni agreed.

"Let's just hope they can fill it quickly," I said, watching it disappear behind a building. The sound of its engine faded.

After that, we were quiet, watching and listening. The light breeze couldn't even muster up any sounds.

I waited to hear the sound of the engine approaching, but it never came. Instead, Molev and two other men came jogging around the corner almost twenty minutes later.

Molev lifted a hand to show everything was okay.

"Was anyone reassured by that?" Roni mumbled. "Because I sure as fuck wasn't. Why are they running and not driving?"

"It was empty," one of the men said when they got near. "The reservoir and the fueler. We ran out of gas just before we reached the reservoir. Looks like someone emptied it all."

Molev held my gaze for a beat.

"We need to get a message to Rick and find out what's close," I said. "Maybe there's an airport or something nearby that we can check."

I glanced at the aircraft behind me before facing Molev again. "Since we don't know how long it will take to find the necessary fuel, we need to find somewhere else for everyone to wait. Something easier to defend if we have to spend the night here."

"We passed some barracks not far from here that should work," one of the men said.

I watched Molev, waiting for his answer.

Finally, he nodded. "I'll take Roland, Brandon, and four others with me. Wait here until we return."

Roni, Steve, Katie, and I watched them leave.

"I don't miss this," Katie said.

"What part?" Roni asked. "The nights spent guarding? The shitty food? Cuz I know it's not the company you have a problem with."

Katie smiled slightly. "The constantly being on edge."

"Same," Steve said. "But I hear Molev's settlement isn't like that. I'll hang in there if you do."

Sid's waving from the top of the roof caught my attention.

He gestured to the right, the opposite direction Molev had gone, then held up a single finger.

"We better check it out," Roni said softly. "Steve, you're with me. Let the rest know what's going on."

While they moved off to the right, I went to the others by the aircraft and gave them a quick update. Roni and Steve were back before I finished and joined me by the others.

"Just one infected. He was moving slow like he was recently turned. Civilian. But get this, he was wearing what looked like a ball cap that had a bullet lodged in the front. I think someone tried a headshot that was stopped by the plating tucked into the cap."

"Weird," Katie said. "Why would someone not want to be killed if they were going to turn?"

"Maybe it wasn't for that," Steve said. "The guy was wearing a backpack full of food and ammo."

"A raider," I said. "It would explain the empty fueler and reservoir."

"Why would they want all that fuel?" Katie asked.

I shook my head slowly, wondering the same. It didn't stay good forever, and I hadn't seen a non-military plane in ages.

"Heat source?" Steve asked.

"If only the dead could talk and tell us," one of the soldiers said.

"Don't even say that," Katie said with a shudder. "It's bad enough the dead can run now. If they start talking, I'm out."

Steve and a few of the others chuckled.

My gaze slid over the buildings, searching for infected, but I wasn't sure we'd see any more. The base had been locked up weeks ago. There were no soldiers to become infected and return to the place they knew. And if the one infected we'd seen had been left for true-dead by a raiding party, the locked front gate would have meant one of two things. They'd either locked a mess of infected inside, or they'd locked it to keep the place clear.

Since we hadn't been swarmed yet, my guess was the latter.

However, that didn't make me feel any safer. Humans desperate for supplies were just as dangerous as infected.

I doubted they would return soon, though. It would draw the attention of whatever infected were still in the area. That gave us a few days before we had to worry about them. Not that I thought we'd linger that long. There were too many of us gathered in one spot for us to be safe based on Molev's observations about attracting infected attention.

The sun descended another inch toward the horizon before Molev and his group returned.

"Find anything?" I asked.

"No infected, but someone's been here. We found a stash of canned goods in a closet," one of the soldiers said.

"That fits our theory," Steve said. "Roni and I brought down a lone infected that we think was part of a raid group."

Molev grunted. "We should move them quickly. We left a guard at the door."

Tension was high when the volunteers finally emerged from the aircraft. I gave my sister-in-law a reassuring smile and returned Cory's nod. No one made any extra noise as they worked together to unpack whatever supplies we'd brought with us. The researchers didn't say a word about the storage cube we left behind either.

The dorm-style housing didn't relieve the high tension, despite the reinforced bars over the lower-level windows. They all understood the danger we were in.

Just like back at Irwin, they divided up and shared rooms. A guard took position at each floor's exit, and one remained just inside the door of the main entrance.

Once it was secure, Molev took my hand. "We will return soon."

Roland shook his head in humor.

"Soon isn't a measure of time you should use when you're alone with Andie, my friend."

Roni chuckled, which I could see confused Molev.

"Let's go," I said before he could tell me to explain.

It felt good to be in his arms with the cold wind battering my face as he ran impossibly fast to the building with the radio. As soon as he reached it, he put me down and hugged me close.

"I know," I said before he could say anything. "Stay behind you. Stay close. No risks."

He pulled back enough to capture my chin and hold my gaze.

"I love you, Andie."

It was so unexpected and out of place for the situation that I wasn't prepared. Panic slipped into my gaze before I could stop it.

He frowned, and the hand pressing against my back pressed harder, molding me to him.

"Don't," he said, his voice low with warning.

CHAPTER TEN

"I'M NOT THE ONE MAKING DECLARATIONS OF LOVE JUST BEFORE going into an abandoned building like he thinks we're going to die. Pardon me if I'm feeling a little freaked out."

He huffed a partial laugh, his intensity easing.

"I did not confess my love because I think we will die."

"Okay, well, I'm going to pretend I didn't hear it then and wait for you to say it again at a less life-threatening time, okay? My poor human heart can only take so much." I captured the hand holding my chin and threaded my fingers through his so he wouldn't think it was a retreat. "Ready?"

He pressed a kiss to my temple and led the way inside.

Nothing popped out or crept up on us as we navigated the hallway. Like the watchtower's radio, this one also had a battery backup that turned on with a switch. The second it did, static and faint words filled the room.

"I'm broadcasting this message on all frequencies for twenty-four hours. The western barrier has been compromised. I repeat, the western barrier has been compromised. I'm relaying the message word for word as it was broadcast. End message." There was a long pause, and it started again. "Begin message. This message needs to make it to the east coast. I repeat, this message needs to make it to the east coast. I'm broadcasting this message on all frequencies for twenty-four hours. The western barrier has been compromised. I repeat, the western barrier has been compromised."

I hit the button to broadcast.

"Message received," I said. "How badly was the barrier compromised? Do you know the location?"

I released the button and waited.

"You're breaking up. Repeat."

I did and waited a second time with growing impatience.

"Don't know," the man finally replied. "I'm in the mountains north of Colorado and heard planes heading north a while ago. Not sure if that means they're heading north to help or fleeing the south.

"I'm going to switch to the next channel and repeat the message. Make sure to try them all until you get someone."

"We will. Thanks."

Once there was nothing but static, we changed the channel to the one Rick said they'd be monitoring.

"We just got a message that the western barrier was compromised. Anyone there?"

"We're here," Rick said. "It's not looking good. They're evacuating anyone they can. It's a good thing you left when you did. Our base is now a new safe zone. Is Vance secure?"

"It's secure for the moment, but all the fuel's gone. Where's the closest refuel?"

"The nearest military one is Whiteman. The rest were either cleaned out or marked inaccessible. Not sure about private airports."

"Your base won't be safe for long, Rick," Molev said.

"We know. Waurlyn already warned us that large groups of humans are the problem. She's spreading out the safe zones and redistributing the numbers so there's no more than two hundred in any one place.

"She told me to tell you that time's up. We need that cure and your people's help to stop the tsunami that's going to be coming."

"Understood," I said. "We'll contact you again at the assigned times."

I switched off the radio and turned to face Molev, leaning back on the desk.

"We were that close," I said, holding up my thumb and finger only an inch apart. "If Waurlyn hadn't come to us when she had, we would have been there."

Molev wrapped his arms around me and set his chin on my head.

"I know."

"There's no one out there who can help us. We are the help."

"I know."

I pulled back enough to give him a partial glare.

"If you tell me to focus on what we can control…"

His lips twitched a little.

"I know."

"Real funny," I muttered, resting my forehead on his sternum as my mind raced. "Okay. We need to work with what we have, right? If we can't fly to Whiteman, we piece together a convoy. Every base that was emergency evacuated left equipment behind. We just need enough to transport almost two hundred and fifty people."

I lifted my head and looked around the room for a spare set of radios. The neat row of charging banks had several. I went to check the batteries and found a pair that was still working.

"Take this. I'll lock the door behind you and use the radio if anything happens here."

"Why am I leaving you?"

I smiled at his calm question, liking the fact that he didn't tell me no and trusted I had a good reason.

"I'm going to repeat the message like he asked. There are other people out there who need to know what's happening. And you need to scout this base and take inventory of the food, vehicles, weapons, and fuel that was left behind. We both know you can move faster alone. And the sooner we leave, the sooner we can reach Whiteman. We need that cure before the infected reach the coast and turn around for everyone they've missed."

He grunted and looked down at the radio in his hand for a second before his gaze swept the room. I removed my sidearm and set it on the desk. Then I turned the chair so I'd have my back to the wall while working the radio and watching the door.

"I'll be fine," I said. "But my life isn't the only one depending on you now. We brought these people here with a promise. We need to deliver. Go."

He took my hand and led me to the door where he tested the lock first before leaving.

"Lock it," he said as soon as he was on the other side. Once I did, the knob rattled as he tested it from his side. "I will return soon."

Then he was gone.

I returned to the radio and started repeating the message on the next channel. No one answered, but I refused to believe it was because no one was listening. After five minutes, I went to the next. Then the next. Eventually, my throat ran dry, and I stopped to look around for water. There wasn't any. I glanced at the door then picked up the hand radio.

"How's everything looking out there?" I asked.

"All clear," Sid answered.

"Do you need me?" Molev asked next.

"Everything is fine here," I said. "But if you happen to see a bottle of water, I wouldn't mind a delivery."

"Same," Sid said.

"I will be there soon," Molev answered.

I smiled at the exchange, knowing that Molev would stop what he was doing to find enough water for everyone. The fact that he cared for his people was evident in everything he did and said. And he considered us all his people now.

Turning back to the radio, I continued repeating the message at five-minute intervals until someone knocked on the door.

"What's the password?" I called, already getting up.

"You never set one," Molev answered.

Grinning, I unlocked the door and let him in.

"Hearing your voice is enough of a password." I closed the door behind him and accepted the bottle. "How's the search going?"

"Not well. The vehicles that remain inside this fence have no fuel. Even if they did, there are not enough of them to carry everyone."

"What about food and weapons?"

He shook his head. "Very little food remains and no weapons other than the ones that came with us."

"Well, that sucks."

His pupils expanded, and he took a step toward me. I quickly held up my hand.

"Stop right there. I can see exactly where your mind went. And we both know that this isn't the time or place for that." I closed the distance between us and set my free hand on his chest. "Once we're home, we can do all the things we've been missing since we've been apart."

He studied me, and I knew he was trying to discern my sincerity.

"So much suspicion," I said, lifting on my toes and offering my lips.

He gave me a chaste kiss that morphed and evolved into a heart-pounding need within minutes. I grabbed his shoulders, forgetting about the water bottle I held. It fell to the floor with a crash, and I jerked away from him. Panting, I slowly shook my head.

"See? This is why we need to wait. We get too caught up. It's dangerous. Maybe not for you, but it definitely is for me."

He cupped the back of my head and rested his forehead against mine.

When he didn't say anything, I began to get nervous.

"Are you okay?" I asked softly.

"I am tired of the games and wish we were already home."

I pulled back enough to look him in the eyes.

"You think I'm playing games with you?"

"The games I've played to meet you, to find more people like you, to get those people here." He gently smoothed back my hair, his gaze gaining intensity instead of softening. "I'm tired, Andie."

Understanding, I wrapped my arms around his waist and hugged him close.

"It hasn't been easy. But don't give up now."

His hold on me tightened.

"With you by my side, I will never give up."

I smiled and pressed a kiss to his T-shirt-covered pec. Then I nipped his clearly defined nipple. He jerked in my arms, and I grinned as I looked up at him.

"That's so you know this isn't me retreating and a promise that your patience will be rewarded later."

He growled, the sound vibrating from his chest through mine.

"Focus," I said, patting his chest. "We need to brainstorm how we're getting these people out of here, not how to get me out of my pants."

"Removing your pants would be much faster and easier."

"No doubt about that," I said, trying to ignore the throb his hungry look was creating. "Did you check the family housing outside the fence?"

"Not yet."

"I think I remember one of the soldiers mentioning a school and a hotel on base too. I'm sure everything outside the fence was already cleaned out by base personnel, but it doesn't hurt to check. While you're looking, keep checking the tanks of any vehicles you pass. If the raiders left a stash of food in the closet, that means there had to be a reason for them to want to come back here."

He grunted, kissed my forehead, and started for the door.

"Lock it behind me."

I hurried to do as he said then returned to the radio with my water.

The light outside the window began to fade before Molev knocked on the door again.

This time, he wasn't alone. I wrote down the message for my replacement and handed it over along with the notes about what channels I'd already tried.

"He said to broadcast it for the next twenty-four hours," I said. "As long as we're here, we might as well keep repeating it."

The woman nodded and sat down in the chair. I gave her the

hand radio with a warning to watch the battery and call before it ran out.

Molev carried me back to the housing where I ate a cold MRE while sitting on the floor in a free corner of the room where Roni, Katie, Sid, and Roland were already sleeping.

"Did you find anything?" I asked Molev quietly.

"There was a semi-truck parked in front of the school. The back is partially loaded with some food and supplies."

"Was there gas in the tank?"

"It sounded like there was some, but the key was missing."

"That's frustrating. But we can siphon the diesel out of that and use it in one of the armored vehicles."

"Think bigger," Roland said from his bunk. "Use the diesel to fill a tanker. Take the tanker out and start siphoning what's left on the roads. Fill a tanker. Then we can drive whatever we want out of here."

"Sorry for waking you," I said, keeping my voice soft.

"Wasn't sleeping yet," Roland said.

I looked at Molev. "I like his idea but not the attention it might draw. Landing here was bad enough."

Molev grunted and leaned his head against the wall. Since I wasn't sure if he was thinking or resting, I stayed quiet and finished my meal. The sun slowly set as we sat there. Brandon came in just before it was completely dark and nudged Molev.

"You're up, my friend," he said. Then he went over and woke Roni and Katie as well. "Thanks for keeping it warm for me. Come on over here, Andie. I'll let you have the wall."

I glanced at Molev. The overly large fey who'd been territorial more times than I could count in the past nodded.

"Rest," he said. "Roni will wake you in four hours to take over for them."

I SAT ON THE ROOF, watching the sunrise in my peripheral as I scanned for movement along my section of the fence. The night had been quiet. Terrifyingly so. If nothing was moving here, it truly meant that the majority of the infected had migrated to the coast already.

How long would it take them to make their way through the mountains and to the camps along the coast? With seven of their aircraft here, would they have enough time to evacuate everyone? I felt a surge of guilt and relief that we'd made it out and that Rachel was with us. Not that I'd gotten any time to speak to my sister-in-law yet.

She was safe. For now.

We needed to get out of Vance, though. My mind had been running through scenarios since I'd taken my position on the roof. Fuel was a big problem, and I wasn't sure a single filled-fueler would be enough. We'd likely empty it by filling the vehicles here. Then we'd run out in the field. No, we'd need to fill everything here and then fill the fueler again.

Whatever diesel was left in that truck needed to be used wisely. And idling on the road while Molev checked one car at a time wasn't wise. The smarter bet would be to check all nearby fueling stations. However, if they were easy to access, they were likely already dry, too.

A thump on the roof nearby drew me out of my thoughts.

"I don't like quiet nights like this," I said. "It's like the calm before the storm."

I turned my head to look at Molev.

"Vance is a few miles south of Enid. It makes more sense to scout there for a fueling station rather than wasting the fuel in the truck by driving around backroads, looking for more diesel sitting in someone else's abandoned gas tank. I think Enid is our best bet for finding fuel. The raiders would have avoided any gas stations there because of the risk. We have no idea how much of Enid is still standing or how many infected are there."

Molev grunted and helped me to my feet. He waited while I shook out my legs then jumped to the ground with me safely in his arms.

"I will scout Enid and return before midday."

He threaded his fingers through my hair at the back of my head and tightened his hold. It sent that half-fear, half-excitement jolt through me that I loved.

"You will be here when I return."

"I've survived too much to be careless now. Go. I'll be here when you get back."

He exhaled heavily and pressed his forehead to mine.

"Did you sleep at all?" I asked softly.

"No."

"Fey or human, we can only run on fumes for so long. You're going to need to sleep soon, or when we need you the most, you're going to fail."

He opened his eyes with his forehead still pressed against mine. This close, that danger warning in my head went crazy, and my pulse stumbled.

"I will never fail you, Andie."

Why did he have to say things that made me want to climb him like a pole at a strip club?

"Do you want to leave right away, or do you want to find a bed with me and snuggle for a bit?" I asked against my better judgment because I knew where snuggling would lead.

I knew he understood what I was saying when he used his hold on my hair to tip my head back and kiss me hungrily.

"You tempt me, Andie," he said when his lips lifted from

mine. "But a bit of you will not be enough. I want all of you for hours."

And I wanted him the same. But I didn't say it. Instead, I nodded and focused on calming my rapid pulse.

"Go then. Find the fuel we need to get out of here."

He kissed me hungrily again then disappeared.

I quietly made my way back to the housing and paused to talk to the soldier by the door.

"Molev left to scout Enid for fuel. When was the last change over?"

"Ten minutes ago," he said.

"I want more eyes on the roofs while he's gone. One trained with one untrained. I'll be back with your new watch buddy. Teach her everything you can."

Over the next hour, I slowly emptied the housing of people, giving everyone a task. While I hoped Molev would find exactly what we needed, I knew we also needed to prepare for a longer stay, just in case. So I sent out two teams to search the buildings within the interior fence for anything useful. Roni's team found a cache of clean clothes in the laundry. She'd wisely picked out stuff that would fit Molev and left it in the bathroom of the housing for his return.

Other than that, they found a bit more food left behind here and there. Nothing major.

I assigned another group to take inventory of what we had and estimate how long the supplies would last us. The answer wasn't good.

"We need to look outside the fence," Roland said. "Roni and I will head up the teams."

"We know the infected like to hide. Only take people you trust to have your back."

They nodded and left to gather their teams.

Exhaustion pulled at me, and I looked at my watch. Almost midday. Just a little longer. I went to the entrance of the housing and waited there along with the two guards.

Molev appeared almost thirty minutes later. Gore spattered his shirt and face.

"I found several of the gas stations. They all had fuel in their underground tanks."

"Looks like you found a few infected too. How hard is it going to be to get the fueler to the gas stations?"

"Not difficult. The roads are undamaged, and there are ways around the vehicles left behind."

"There are some clean clothes waiting for you in the bathroom. Why don't you shower while we talk?"

I followed him into the barracks, and he didn't even hesitate to strip down in front of me once we were alone in the bathroom. The state of his hard length drew my attention, and if not for the ick he needed to wash away, I would have reached for him.

Instead, I motioned for him to get into the shower. "How many infected did you run into?"

"A few larger groups," he said. "But I drew them to me on purpose to see how many were still there."

"Do you think you got them all?"

"After the second group, they stopped coming to check the sounds I made. So I started a vehicle and drove it down the street. That worked twice before they stopped coming toward that sound."

"Hmm. You thinned the herd, which is good, and you set a pattern. If we go in there with the fueler, we might not draw their attention. And if we do, you'll need to deal with them. So, once you're done here, I want you to sleep for a few hours before we make a move."

The water shut off, and Molev stepped out, clean and devastatingly handsome. Unfortunately, my appreciative gaze didn't stay appropriately fixed on his face. It drifted south, down the hard plains of his chiseled abs to that cut V that made my mouth water.

Before I knew what I had planned, I wrapped my hand around his hard length and sank to my knees.

"Andie," he growled as he fisted my hair.

"I know," I said with a smirk before I placed my mouth over him.

He hissed out a breath, and his knuckles pressed against my scalp as his grip tightened in my hair.

"Open wider and take more." The demand and strain behind those words had me eagerly complying. I couldn't fit much, but he groaned in appreciation for every bit I did take. He began a slow thrust in and out of my mouth, his girth sliding against my wet lips.

I hummed.

He grunted and picked up speed.

I chuckled.

He groaned and used his hold to change the angle.

"Yes," he groaned. "Like that."

I increased suction, and it was all over for him. He came with a harsh sound that rang in my ears as I swallowed convulsively. Then, he pulled me off of him and kissed me ravenously.

The intensity of what we were doing robbed me of all sense until I heard, "Damn, gurl, why are your clothes still on?"

I jerked away from Molev, which caused him to growl, and looked at Roni, who was standing in the hallway—the same one we were now somehow in—along with six other people. Her smirk grew as heat ignited in my cheeks. I wasn't particularly shy, but public sex wasn't really my thing. And the way I'd just been kissing Molev with my legs wrapped around his naked waist while I ground down on his hard length had crossed a line. Especially in front of Rachel, who was staring at me in shock.

I scrambled out of Molev's hold and turned to face everyone.

"I'm sorry about that. It won't happen again."

A hand settled on my shoulder. Probably a warning because the big idiot thought I was retreating from him again.

"The fey aren't shy about nudity, but they do respect that we like our privacy. He was caught up in the moment and didn't hear anyone in the hall when he left the bathroom."

"I apologize," Molev said, catching on quickly.

"Don't apologize," Roni said. "Continue. This is the most action I've had in months."

"Are they all built like that?" I heard one of the women whisper.

"Yes," Molev said. "My brothers are very similar to my build."

"Damn," someone else whispered.

"Andie, could I speak to you privately for a moment?" Rachel asked finally.

"Of course." I turned to Molev, making sure to stay positioned so I blocked their view of his important bits. "Your clean clothes are in the bathroom. Get some sleep. I'll find you later."

As soon as the door shut behind him, I left with Rachel. We walked toward the interior fence. My eyes continually scanned as I waited for her to say whatever was on her mind.

"I'm not judging you," Rachel said. "Molev seems really

decent and like he really cares about you. I just want to know you're happy and maybe listen to your story."

I glanced at her and exhaled heavily. "It's a weird one."

She gestured around us. "Look at where we are. It'll be fine."

So I talked, and we patrolled. She asked the occasional question but, for the most part, just listened. And by the time I was done spilling everything, I felt lighter. Especially when she paused and pulled me into her arms to hug me.

"I hope you let go of all the past hurt and bad examples and let yourself love him, Andie. You deserve to love and be loved in return. And he seems worth the risk."

She released me and held my hand.

"You aren't your parents. You aren't the type to scream at someone or throw things at them, and neither is he. You know that, right?"

CHAPTER ELEVEN

I STARED AT HER FOR A LONG MOMENT BEFORE NODDING. SHE smiled at me and indicated the housing.

"Ready to go back?" she asked.

I found Molev passed out in a twin bed. I could have wedged myself against him. Instead, I sat on the floor and watched him sleep for a while and thought about what Rachel said. My parents had been a shit example of a relationship. But I'd also had so many good examples in my life. My brother and sister-in-law were amazing together. The fear of ending up like my parents, though, made me hesitate every damn time.

Did I love Molev?

I stared at him, trying to find the courage to admit the answer to myself.

My back started to hurt, and my ass went numb long before he opened his eyes and looked at me.

"Come here," he said.

I shook my head and smiled slightly.

"The way we're both feeling, we'll probably lose what's left of the day in selfish gratification instead of doing what we need to do to ensure the safety of everyone here."

He grunted and sat up.

"Did you get enough sleep?" I asked, looking at my watch. It'd only been about two hours.

"Enough for now," he said.

He stood and pulled me to my feet.

"Are you angry that your sister-in-law saw us kissing?"

"No. I was maybe a little embarrassed, but that's gone now too. Just…let's not do that again in the future, okay? It'll make the women here more nervous to meet your brothers."

Molev grunted and hugged me close.

"I know you drive well, but I want you to stay here when I leave. I will take Brandon with me."

"Isn't the safest place for me to be with you?" I asked.

"It is, but we lead together. You are my voice when I am away."

I tipped my head to look up at him.

"Then go. I'm going to leave Roni in charge and get a few hours of sleep myself. Hurry back."

"I'll tell Roni. Rest."

He tucked me into the bed, and I closed my eyes.

The next time I opened them, Rachel was shaking my shoulder, and a vivid orange light painted the opposite wall.

"Molev said it's time to wake up."

"They're back?"

"For an hour now. They've moved the vehicles we have to the airstrip and already made plans to go out again tomorrow."

She didn't look excited, though. She looked worried.

"What's wrong?"

"They ran into a lot of infected. Brandon and Molev were trying to be low-key about it, but the fueler and Molev were disgusting when they returned. Steve and Roni made them spill everything, saying ignorance wouldn't keep us alive."

"What'd they say?"

"They were swarmed at the first gas station. Brandon was safe enough inside the truck, but Molev had to work fast to keep the infected from wrecking it. Then, once he thought he had them cleared, he found some hiding under it, clinging to whatever they could like they were going to hitch a ride back here."

I nodded. "Yeah, they're smart like that. You said first gas station. Did they have to go to a second?"

"They did, but not for gas. Brandon had Molev clear out the food from both. They came back with boxes tied on the roof of the cab and around the tanker. So we have food and fuel now."

"That's good. We'll need it. Did I miss anything else?"

She shook her head, and we left the room to find Molev. He was speaking to a group of soldiers and gesturing to the roof and fence. When he saw me, he stopped and focused only on my approach.

"Everything okay?" I asked.

"I think we will not have another calm night," he said with blunt honesty.

"I kind of figured that would be the case and had the volunteers pairing up with people who had more experience as lookouts today. We can use them to add to the number of people on the roofs."

"Good. Did you eat?"

"Not yet."

"Go eat. Find me before the sun sets."

I returned to the housing. Instead of eating, though, I coordinated securing the building. We moved furniture and mattresses into the second-story hall, and I explained how the people standing guard would need to use them to barricade the stairwell in case of an emergency. After that, I braced my heart and went to talk to the handful of moms and kids. I explained the sounds they might hear, including moans, roars, and gunshots, and how, no matter what, they couldn't make a sound.

Molev found me silently crying in the bathroom after that.

"I never want to have kids," I said softly, crying against his chest. "They would never be safe enough."

Molev didn't argue or try to tell me all the wonderful things kids would bring—things I already knew because of my niece and nephew—he just held me and stroked my hair until I stopped crying.

"You did well, Andie. They will be safer because of you."

I snorted. "I traumatized them, Molev. No matter how nice I was about it, I stripped away a layer of innocence they should have been able to keep for years yet."

He didn't say anything more and just held me until I pulled away on my own.

"Sorry."

"Never be sorry for your compassion, Andie. Too few humans have enough of it."

He threaded his fingers through mine and led me out of the housing and into the early dusk.

"I want you on the roof with me," he said. "We have lights around the perimeter of the fence, radios with every lookout, and night vision in each direction."

"So you're expecting a lot of trouble then."

"My gut is telling me this night will be long." He picked me up and jumped up to the nearest roof. I settled into position as he stood over me, his eyes seeing more than I could ever dream of seeing.

We heard the first moan an hour after dark. Molev left as silently as he came. When he returned, he was bloody.

"A single infected," he said. "I will check the fence."

He didn't return. Occasionally, I'd hear a moan, or the radio would softly crackle to life to report a sighting in some direction. Otherwise, the night seemed fairly calm in comparison to some of the nights I'd spent in the field.

Someone came to relieve me around three in the morning, and I returned to the housing to check on things there. The second–top–story hadn't needed to be blocked, and the kids were out cold in their beds with their moms wrapped around them. I stared at them for several long moments and wondered if we were all idiots.

Rubbing a hand down my face, I turned away and claimed the bed Molev had last used.

I roused slightly when Molev slid in behind me and wrapped his arms around me but quickly sank into sleep again.

The sun was up, and Molev was still holding me when I woke for good. I tiredly checked my watch and noted I'd managed four and a half hours of sleep. It was enough.

Carefully easing from his hold, I left the room and found a woman in the hall outside our door. She motioned for me to stay silent and pointed toward the guards at the other end of the hall. I went to them, and they repeated the keep quiet sign and motioned down the stairs.

Once I was outside, I found Sid, who looked ready to drop.

"Molev went inside about an hour ago," he said. "The body piles from last night seem to be keeping everything away for now. I told everyone to keep quiet so he can sleep as long as possible. Lookouts are on the roofs." He handed me the radio and went inside to get the rest he desperately needed.

I climbed the nearest ladder and took a position with the

lookout there, using binoculars to find the body piles. The number of beheaded infected stunned me. Based on what I'd heard last night, I would have guessed Molev had to deal with a few dozen. What I saw as I checked every section of the fence over the course of the next few hours was ten times that.

Katie found me as I was coming down from a roof to the south.

"We saw movement in the north," she said.

"Why didn't you radio it in?" I asked.

"It watched us for a bit then left."

We both knew what that meant.

"I'll go wake him," I said.

Molev opened his eyes and sat up the moment I touched his shoulder.

"They spotted one that was watching and left," I said.

He grunted and stood, stretching so that joints popped and cracked.

"MRE," Steve said, poking his head in to toss two bags to Molev. "No red sauce. Eat and hydrate before you leave."

Steve winked at me, causing Molev to make a sound between a grunt and a growl, then left.

"He enjoys antagonizing people," I said, looking at Molev. "It's his way of showing affection."

"Does he antagonize you?" Molev asked.

I grinned widely. "He hasn't figured out how to yet."

"But I will!" Steve called from farther down the hall.

I sat with Molev, updating him on everything as he quickly wolfed down his food.

"Incoming!" someone yelled outside.

Molev disappeared, leaving open wrappers and a half-consumed water bottle in his wake.

"I've got this," a woman said, coming into the room. "Do what you need to do."

I ran out of the room, calling a reminder to the guards to be ready to block the hallway.

"Report," I barked to the nearest soldier, channeling my inner Patrick.

"A group of twenty or more infected approaching from the north," he said.

I grabbed his radio.

"Stay focused on your locations. Infected use decoys and distractions to find a way in."

"I have a single watcher in the south," someone said. "Stationary. Almost didn't see it."

"Stay low and unseen," I said. "Molev will check it out when he's done. Report anything unusual."

"Molev's cleared the group to the north," someone else said. "He's heading back now."

The infected ate away the daylight hours, testing our alertness. If Molev was visible, they didn't show themselves. As soon as he was absent for more than an hour, though, they'd send another group to the fence.

"How are we going to get more fuel this way?" Brandon asked.

"How is Molev going to get any sleep?" Katie asked, her worried gaze lifting to where Molev stood on the roof, prominently illuminated by the last rays of the day's light.

Roni crossed her arms, looking angry and thoughtful. None of us liked the situation we were in. Pinned down and unable to do what we needed to do. And the longer we stayed in one spot, the more the risk increased.

"Do they know it's him because he's so much bigger than us or because they can see it's him?" Roni asked. Then she uncrossed her arms and started toward the housing. "I'm going to find out," she called over her shoulder.

Steve shook his head. "I think she's losing it."

"Get to your posts," I said. "Radio if you need anything. Rest while you can. We know the routine."

Everyone nodded and split up. I climbed the ladder to join Molev on the roof.

"Were you listening?" I asked.

He grunted but didn't look away from his scan of the distant buildings.

"We need to figure out a way to get that fuel tomorrow. The longer we stay, the more we'll draw," I said.

He grunted again.

"Don't lose focus of the bigger picture," I said.

"Tomorrow, you come with me. Steve and the others are able to lead here."

I wrapped my arms around Molev from behind.

"No."

He didn't say anything. Neither did I. I just held him for a few more minutes then settled on the roof with the binoculars.

That night passed much like the one before. Not a lot of sound, but once Molev left, he didn't return to the roof. In the morning, there were more body piles. Only these were spread out along the outer fence and harder to see.

"I think he's marking his territory," Steve said when he joined me on the roof to take over. "I mean, pissing everywhere would be easier but probably not as effective with the infected."

I shook my head slightly, amused by him, as I handed over the radio.

Finding Molev wasn't hard. Now that the sun was up, I spotted him easily standing on a distant roof.

"Andie!" Roni called before I could go to Molev and tell him to come inside for something to eat.

She waved me over to the housing building, adding, "You need to see this!"

I started jogging at the urgency in her voice and watched her disappear inside before I reached the door. The guards nodded to me as I went in.

"First door on the right," one said helpfully.

I found Roni grinning at a homemade fey look alike abomination. She and the three other women with her had done more than just stuff some Molev-sized clothes. They'd sewn a replica of his head from a grey pillowcase, added button eyes, pointed ears, all the facial features, and even black bootlaces for his hair.

But that wasn't all.

If his slightly realistic face wasn't creepy enough, they'd ensured he had the same build. From the breadth of his shoulder to the thickness of his thighs.

My gaze stopped there. Or more specifically, at the enormous arm-sized bulge prominently displayed on the inside of his right pant leg.

"Realistic as fuck, right?" Roni said, nudging me.

"You have issues," I said with a head shake.

"He doesn't just stand there," one of the women said. "We can discreetly change his position too."

She walked around behind him and moved something. The Molev scarecrow folded down into a squat, braced by a tripod-looking thing coming out of his ass.

"Let's get this on the roof and see if it does the trick," Roni said. "If it does, Molev gets a little sleep, and we can send him out for more fuel."

It took almost twenty minutes and two guys plus Roni to get

fake-Molev onto the roof. I called Molev down from his spot, and we watched them from the ground as they worked fake Molev into a squat and then stood him up. They did it in a way that looked natural enough, like they were helping a friend stand, not positioning a dummy. Would it be enough, though?

I looked at the dried blood caking my Molev and hoped so.

"Come on. Let's get you showered, fed, and in bed. Hopefully, the infected won't catch on to the switch."

I left him alone to shower and waited in our room with food. He ate then pulled me into his arms. We both crashed pretty hard. At least, that's how it felt when I finally woke.

His arm tightened around me when I lifted my hand to check the time.

"Five hours," I said. "Were you here the whole time?"

"Yes."

"Good. The dummy works then."

He grunted.

"We should go take him down and see what happens," I said. "If the infected start coming at us again, then we'll know it was keeping them away."

He reluctantly released me.

We ate again in the room then went outside to see how things had gone. The roofs had their usual lookouts in addition to the Molev dummy standing prominently visible against the midday overcast sky.

"We were about to wake you," Roni said, spotting us and jogging over. "We've had a few sightings of watchers, but a group just started creeping closer from the west."

"Perfect timing," I said, looking at Molev.

"Yes. I will help them believe that it is me," he said with a glance at the dummy. "Make him disappear." Then he vanished, himself.

Roni waved to the lookouts lying against the roof at the feet of the fake Molev, and they knocked the stand out from under him, sending him tumbling down off the roof.

I glanced at Roni, and she shrugged. "He's down."

"Molev said the infected only fell for his tricks a few times. So we'll probably only have one more chance to use the dummy again. Someone will need to head out with the fueler on their own while Molev secretly follows so the infected think the dummy on the roof is still him."

"Agreed. Who do you want behind the wheel, and when do they leave?"

"Brandon knows what to expect already. I'll talk to him and see if he's willing to do it again first thing in the morning. He'll need someone to ride shotgun."

"I'm up for it," Roni said.

"Okay. Then, you can talk to Brandon. If he's not up for it, check with Roland."

"On it, boss." She jogged over to the Molev dummy sprawled on the ground, picked it up, wrapped her arm around its waist, and companionably walked it back to the housing.

I made my way to the western lookout and climbed the ladder, staying low as I joined the soldiers there.

"Any movement?" I asked.

One of the soldiers snorted.

"Not anymore. He's already made a new pile of them."

He handed me the binoculars, and I saw the pile for myself. But no Molev.

"Where'd he go?" I asked.

"He went south."

It made sense that he would do a circuit to see what else is moving out there. Hopefully, everything would be clear, and he would be receptive to leaving the following day.

I returned the binoculars and left the roof to do rounds.

When I ensured everyone was okay and changing shifts as needed, I went to the communications room to see if we'd heard from Rick. His base was still secure, but news from the west wasn't good. The infected and the hounds were sweeping through the mountains. The watchtowers had all fallen. Thanks to Molev's information about the hounds and the scientists' examination of corpses, the border operating bases were able to keep the hounds at bay so far.

Through Rick, Waurlyn reiterated our need to hurry, though. Once supplies and ammunition ran low, those bases would fall.

I stared at a map on the wall, studying the route between Vance and Whiteman as my mind raced. We had two hundred-plus people to move and one fueler to get us there. The armored vehicles would be safer but not effective, I realized. They weren't fuel-efficient, and we would need too many of them to move everyone. I thought of the semi and frowned. It was bigger, but we wouldn't be able to take the ditch to get around obstructions.

We had two Strykers, which could help keep the road clear. And Molev, of course. But we would likely need him to spend his time and energy keeping infected from swarming like he had on our trip into Loveland.

Leaving the communications room, I went back to housing and grabbed a few more hours of sleep. Roni woke me at dusk with an elbow to my side and a moody, "Get out of my bed, princess."

Katie, who was snuggled behind me, groaned when I left her. Roni was quick to take my place and wrap a soothing arm around her.

Outside, I saw everyone had been working hard. Mobile floodlights surrounded the housing, connected to a waiting generator surrounded by gas cans. The sight was both a comfort and a concern.

I saw Molev—the real one, not the fake one with the exaggerated pants python—on one of the roofs and went to join him. His gaze briefly flicked to me when I topped the ladder.

"How's it been?" I asked when I stood behind him.

"Quiet. I have been clearing outside the fence to keep the number of infected low. They are starting to avoid the area."

"That's good."

He grunted and crossed his arms, his expression almost angry.

"What's not good about it?" I asked.

"I saw a watcher with changed eyes. When it spotted me, it disappeared."

"Okay. Yeah, that's not good. What's your gut telling you?"

"There will be trouble tonight."

That explained the lights and the knives already strapped to his thighs. I took his radio from him.

"I want personnel who can use the Mark 19s in the Strykers now. Move one to the north and one to the south."

"Need a replacement on Roof 3," someone said.

"Heading to Roof 3," someone else said.

Three additional people responded, moving to the Strykers and asking for replacements for their various positions.

"We need a vest that will fit Molev," I said when they quieted.

"On it," someone said.

I looked at Molev. "I'll make sure the doctor is ready. Same rules as Loveland. I will stay out of the way as long as you're making smart choices. Close wounds immediately and rehydrate frequently."

He gave me a single, grave nod.

"Where do you want the doctor?" I asked.

"The housing roof is flat. I will see her there."

I left him on the roof and found the doctor and her team in their room-turned-partial-lab.

"I need you on the roof with a full medic kit."

She frowned at me in confusion.

"Molev thinks a hound's going to attack tonight. He'll be wearing a vest, which will help, but he'll still need patching. Last time the medic used mostly glue and tried to conserve the actual stitches for the deeper wounds. Dress warm. It'll be a long night."

She nodded slowly and looked around the room for a moment before springing into action. I watched her inventory a kit she had against one wall. She added several syringes and vials to it as well. Once she was bundled, I led the way outside.

Someone already had a ladder against the building.

"I'll take that up," I said. "You climb."

A moan echoed distantly.

The doctor glanced at me then nimbly scurried up the ladder. I wasn't far behind.

After leaving her with the kit, I made several more trips, setting her up with a camp chair, blanket, and hand warmers along with a table to hold her things.

"Pull the ladder up when you're by yourself," I said. "Molev can get up here without it."

The words had barely left my mouth when my radio crackled to life.

"Eyes to the north."

CHAPTER TWELVE

WAITING GAVE TENSION AND FEAR TIME TO TAKE OVER, AND BOTH led to mistakes. As the minutes ticked by and turned to hours, I began to wonder if that was exactly what the hound was hoping for.

However, Molev was good at waiting, too.

He crouched on the roof, listening to updates. The hound wasn't approaching. It was letting infected gather around it. Each howl drew more to it.

"Wouldn't it be better to kill it now, before too many gather?" I asked softly from the ground.

Molev stood, fluidly jumping off the roof to land beside me.

"They howl to call more of their kind. I wanted to know if another waited nearby."

"You don't think there is?"

"No. I believe it will try to use the infected to surround us."

"Then my question still stands. Shouldn't you kill it before that happens?"

He exhaled and cupped the back of my head.

"There are already too many infected gathered for me to

leave you unprotected. We will wait and see what it does next."

I shook my head. "I would rather be the hunter than the prey. Let's bait it in."

Molev tilted his head as he studied me.

"How would you bait it in?"

"Kill the lights to the north. Have the personnel there retreat very loudly while you get into position. Most predators are opportunistic, right? If it believes the lights failed and people are running scared, I think it'll come at us head-on. And if the hound and the infected are in one area, we can focus the majority of our forces there."

He remained quiet for a long moment.

"Some of the infected are starting to move," a voice said over Molev's radio. "To the east."

Molev brought the radio to his mouth.

"It's time for us to hunt. Anyone with a weapon, move to the north now. Leave lookouts to the south. Turn off the northern lights in two minutes and make a lot of panic sounds as you retreat to higher ground. Shoot the infected. I will deal with the hound."

He pressed a kiss to my forehead.

"Stay with the doctor. If anything happens to me, get the doctor to Mya. She's the cure."

I nodded, and then he was gone. I called up to the doctor for the roof ladder and made it to the top just as the distant northern lights went out.

The howl that pierced the night sent a shard of fear through my middle. How many of these things had Molev faced now? Nine? Ten? I'd lost count but couldn't stop myself from wondering if this was one too many for his current lifetime.

"Talk to me," the doctor said. "What's happening? Why did we turn off the lights?"

"Molev is going to try to deal with the hound before it can try coordinating an attack."

"They do that?"

"Yeah. They're pretty smart, and they've been starting to use the infected to help them. Molev said there are too many infected out there with the hound already."

She huddled deeper in her blanket and watched the north with me.

A smattering of gunfire broke out a second before I heard Molev's roar.

"Was that the hound?" the doctor asked.

"No. That was Molev."

The doctor slowly turned her head to look at me. The complete shock almost made me smile.

"Yeah," I said. "You and everyone in charge have been viewing him as something he's not. He's not human. He's not here for us to use or control. And he's so much more than his differences."

"I won't forget that," the doctor said.

The gunshots didn't slow down, and I started to pace the roof. I wanted to ask for an update, but I also didn't want to distract anyone. When I heard a howl cut short and turn into a snarl, I knew things were escalating.

A shot rang out much closer.

"Infected inside the fence," someone yelled over the radio.

I grabbed our radio. "Barricade the hallways now!"

I couldn't hear anything from the building below us over the growing sound of gunfire and ran to the roof's edge to look down at the two guards stationed at the main entrance.

"I want you up here, covering the entrance," I shouted.

The doctor had the ladder over the edge a moment later. I covered them as they climbed and got into position.

An infected turned the corner of the building a few beats later. One of the soldiers fired.

I left them and went to the other side of the building.

Infected were everywhere.

"Ladders up," I said over the radio. "Don't knock them down, or the infected will use them."

One of the infected below stopped running and looked up at me. Then it cocked its head.

"You want me?" I said, narrowing my gaze. "How are you going to get me?"

Its head tipped forward, and I knew it was looking around. That sign of higher intelligence should have terrified me, but I didn't let it. Instead, I watched, studying it as it searched for a way to reach the roof.

"That's right," I said. "No ladders. What are you going to do now?"

It went to a bar-covered window and used that to climb upward. It wasn't tall enough to reach the next window ledge, though, so it jumped. Its fingers brushed the sill but didn't grab on fast enough. I watched it fall to the ground. The impact should have stunned it. Instead of lying there for a moment to catch its breath, it stood and went right back to climbing up the window.

Another infected saw it, stopped running, and joined it at the window. When the first one was as high as it could go, the second one started to climb, grabbed the first one's foot, and placed it on its decaying shoulder.

"Fuck," I breathed as the second one leveraged the other one upward.

I waited until it had a firm hold on the second-story window sill.

"Hey, shithead," I called.

When it tipped its head back, I put a bullet between its eyes. When it fell, it didn't get up again. The second one looked up at me and moaned. I steadied my hand and shot again. It wasn't as clean, but it did the job, and the second infected went down too.

"They collaborate?" the doctor asked from nearby.

Her expression was a mix of curiosity and fear.

"That's what it looked like to me. Help me watch the other windows."

Molev roared again, and the hound's snarls turned positively feral.

Yelling broke out to the north, and I almost didn't hear the doctor's "Over here!"

The hound went quiet as I ran across the roof to find another infected trying to use the barred window. Only, this time, it was aiming for an outcropping on the building.

I shot it quickly and stayed there to ensure another one didn't try the same thing.

"Hound's down," someone said over the radio.

"We need backup on Roof 5. They're using each other like ladders," came Katie's disembodied voice.

Molev roared again.

"Does anyone have eyes on Molev?" I asked.

"He's helping us now," Katie said.

"How injured is he?"

The beat of silence didn't bode well.

"The vest is shredded and looks wet, but I can't see beneath it. He just said he's fine and will come to you soon."

"Knock them down, and get your ass over here now, Molev," I said, knowing he could hear me. "You have one minute. The rest of you work together to watch the roofs and keep them down until Molev is patched up and can clear them himself."

I looked over my shoulder at the doctor.

"Get ready. Stop the bleeding and close the worst of it. He won't give you much time."

When I focused on the window below again, another infected was quietly climbing it. When it heard me move, it looked up. Its faintly luminescent red eyes met mine as I pulled the trigger. A hole appeared in the marred expanse of its forehead, and then it fell back like a stone.

"We all need to take a side," I called over my shoulder.

Another shot rang out.

"Has it been a minute yet?" I called.

"I see him," one of the soldiers called.

I heard Molev land a second later.

"Andie, help her," he said, his voice full of command.

I pivoted, already moving in his direction before my sweeping glance registered why the doctor needed help and with what. Molev's vest was completely shredded and wet, as Katie had stated. But so were his arms, which was why he wasn't helping the doctor, who was trying to cut away the vest.

Together, we had it off in seconds, exposing the gashes on his chest. The bap-bap-bap of gunfire faded to background noise as I took in each injury. The hound had fought him hard. Claw marks criss crossed over Molev's chest. Those, though, weren't nearly as deep as the ones on his arms.

The doctor tossed a towel at me. "Put pressure on his arm. Stop the bleeding."

I copied what she was doing on his other arm until she grabbed for the sutures.

...bap-bap-bap...

My gaze met Molev's.

"How are you doing?" I asked.

"I will heal."

Something louder went off distantly.

"Do you want me to start giving you vague answers when you ask me important questions?" I demanded.

He pulled his lips back at me.

"That's right. Now give me a straight answer. What hurts the most, and what do you need?"

"The opening on my right arm hurts the most. I think one of his claws is still in there. I need water."

"Okay," I said as the doctor and I hurried to switch places.

While she started examining his arm, I grabbed one of the bottles we'd brought up and opened it for him. He watched me, his eyes showing that savage edge he usually hid from us just below the surface as I tipped the water to his lips. He drank greedily and ignored the doctor as she prodded his arm for the claw.

"Found it," she said.

A burst of closer gunfire almost drowned out her words.

I tossed the empty bottle aside and watched her pick up a long tweezer thing.

"I know you can feel what I'm doing, so I'll try to be as gentle as possible, but it's in deep," she said in a rush.

"I don't need gentle," Molev said. "I need fast."

He didn't look away from me as she dug into his arm. I held his gaze, willing myself not to flinch as fresh blood bubbled out.

"I saw a can of Spam in that closet," I said. "I told them to save it for you. If you're good, I'll make it for breakfast."

"What do I have to do to be good?" he asked.

"Stay alive."

He grunted at the same time the doctor made a triumphant noise and held up a claw.

"You were right," she said, setting it aside. She put pressure on the wound.

"Andie, get some gloves on. I'm going to apply glue, and you're going to pinch the skin together."

I grabbed some gloves and learned really quickly how to work with the doctor to glue Molev back together. I snipped threads and opened packets, moving quickly and as much in unison with her as I could manage.

When he stood several minutes later, he had a few sets of amputated glove fingertips hanging from various wounds.

"Stay on the roof until I return for you," he said.

He disappeared between one blink and the next.

I got on the radio and warned everyone he was moving again so that he wouldn't get shot, then went to check the sides of the building.

It took an hour for the all-clear to come over the radio. And another after that for a team to clear the housing and reorganize to continue searching the building. The infrared helped find a few trying to hide.

I saw Molev again as the sun rose. He was coated with dried blood and moving much slower than usual as he spoke to several soldiers.

"Set watches for the interior fence. We have no way of knowing how many might be hiding in the outskirts," Molev said. "And keep guards on the main housing door at all times."

"On it," the one man said.

Molev's gaze shifted to me at my approach.

"You're tired and dirty. Time for you to clean up," I said.

He shook his head. "I will only be covered with blood again when I leave. Is Brandon ready?"

I tilted my head at him like he'd done to me the day before. We both knew we needed to leave Vance as soon as possible. However, he'd lost too much blood and needed time to recover before he threw himself into another fight. But I knew saying that would only make him more stubborn about pushing forward. He'd sacrifice himself for us—for me—without hesitation.

So I went with a different approach.

"You just acknowledged that we have no idea what's lingering between the fences. Do you still think it's wise to leave now?"

He slow-blinked at me, and I could see his sheer exhaustion.

"I think it would be wiser for you to shower, eat, and sleep while we keep watch for a while. That way, you'll be close when we need you."

He grunted and, without any further argument, started toward the housing. I trailed behind, looking at his arms and the bits of glove still clinging to a few places. Some of them had fallen off. Mostly from the wounds that had opened up again.

"You shower," I said when I was inside. "I'm going to get the doctor. Stay put until I'm back."

The doctor looked up from what she was working on in her room when I entered.

"He's back and showering. Can you look at him again?"

"Of course."

She grabbed her kit and followed me to our room. I left her there to wait while I went to get Molev. He was just shutting off the water when I entered.

"How are you feeling?" I asked.

"Nothing hurts more than anything else."

He stepped out, unabashedly giving me a view. For the first time ever, he wasn't even half-mast in my presence.

"Are you tired?" I asked.

He hesitated a moment. "Yes. Why are you asking?"

I shrugged lightly. "Maybe I just wanted an honest answer from you like you always pry out of me."

His lips curved slightly, and he took a towel from the shelf. I stole it from him and started gently drying him off.

"The doctor is waiting in our room. I want her to check you over before you go to bed, okay?"

He grunted and let me wrap the towel around his waist when I was done.

While the doctor checked his wounds and removed any lingering bits of glove, I found him the promised can of Spam and another MRE. The doctor was taking a blood sample when I entered.

"Don't you think he needs every bit he has?" I asked.

"That's why I'm taking it," she said. "I need to check his counts and compare them to the numbers we have. If it's low, then I'm going to want to check again later to ensure it's going up." She removed the syringe and met Molev's gaze. "Seeing the severity of your wounds last night and the amount of blood you lost concerns me. There's so much we still don't know about you. I can close your wounds, but I have no idea how else I can help you." She set her hand on his forearm. "Everyone has a tipping point, Molev. We can't afford for you to reach yours out here where we're dependent on you alone. Take care of yourself until we fully understand how to take care of you as well."

She gave him a final arm pat and left with all her things.

I closed the door behind her. "Did she do more than take your blood?"

"She closed a few of the wounds again and said the others looked like they were healing well."

"Good." I handed him his Spam and opened the MRE.

He ate quickly then lay down.

"I want you to sleep six hours," I said. "If you're still sleeping, then I'll wake you up in the best way possible."

"What is that?" he asked, not moving as I covered him with a blanket.

"With my mouth on the part of you that really likes to be kissed."

The blanket over his hips jumped.

"Yep," I said, lightly patting his chest. "That's the part. Now get some sleep."

A woman was leaning against the wall when I left and shut the door behind me.

"I'll keep everyone quiet," she said.

"Thanks."

Outside, guards were watching the interior fence from the ground along with the lookouts on the roofs.

"If there's anything even remotely off, radio it in," I said over my radio. Then I went to the communications room to send a message to Rick, warning him that not all the hounds were on the coast.

The first shift change came quickly, and I readily left Sid in charge to get some sleep of my own. Not wanting to disturb Molev, I took the bed opposite his. He was still sleeping when I woke and checked my watch a few hours later.

Almost seven hours had passed since I'd covered him. Well past the time that earned him his prize. Yet, I hesitated to wake him up, no matter how much he'd like it.

My gaze drifted to the shut door then back to Molev's sleep-relaxed face.

I had no problem reminding him what he was fighting for. In fact, I was very eager for the rush of pleasure I knew we'd both find together. I just hated cutting into the sleep he obviously needed. And maybe there was a little bit of concern that we'd make too much noise.

Screw it, I thought, quietly getting out of bed.

Molev's breathing remained slow and even as I eased the blanket to the side and loosened the towel at his waist. However, the second I ran my fingers over his undisturbed length, his breathing hitched, and he started to harden.

Grinning, I leaned in to press a kiss to his flesh.

His hips bucked, and he was instantly ready.

I chuckled softly and closed my mouth over him.

"Andie," he rasped. He fisted his hands in my hair and thrust between my lips before catching himself.

I pulled back and met his ravenous gaze.

"I don't need gentle," I said, repeating his words from the night before. "I want fast."

He growled, and a second later, I was pinned under him, and he was kissing me hungrily. I kissed him back with equal passion, carefully touching his face and ears, places I knew weren't bitten or scratched up.

He pulled back and looked down at me.

"I need you, Andie."

"Take what you need," I said.

He did that silent snarl thing again, and a thrill shot through me. I grabbed his hair and gave it a tug.

"More," I said.

The next snarl had sound as he made quick work of removing my pants. The feel of his fingers stroking through my folds had my eyes rolling back in my head. The sensation tripled when he set his hand on the base of my throat and thrust a finger inside of me.

"Yes," I breathed.

He lightly bit my shoulder then claimed my mouth again as he quickly prepared me. I barely adjusted to the feel of his fingers when he replaced them with his swollen head.

"Tell me if there's pain," he growled in my ear a second before he thrust into me.

The sudden invasion barely registered before he was withdrawing and thrusting in again, this time to the hilt. I tilted my hips as he withdrew so he hit even deeper the next time.

The sound of our panting breaths and the slight creak of the bed filled the room for the next several minutes. When I started to involuntarily clench around him, the world fell away. Only Molev existed as he pushed me over the edge of my release. He swallowed any sounds I made and followed me a few seconds later.

He didn't slow when he finished, though. No, he kept that brutal pace, demanding an encore from my oversensitive nerve endings a few moments later.

I screeched into his mouth.

He still didn't stop.

Limp underneath him, I felt him release a second time before he rolled us so I lay on top of him.

His hand found its way under my shirt and stroked my sweaty lower back while I caught my breath.

"I shouldn't be on you," I said when I realized what he'd done. "You're going to pop your glue."

"If you try to leave, you will cause more damage," he rumbled, slowly thrusting into me.

"Does this mean we're not done yet?" I asked.

"Not even close. Have you caught your breath?"

"Yep."

He didn't ease up for an hour, and I didn't try to talk him out of it. After everything he'd done for us, I was willing to give a little back. It didn't hurt that he loved giving me one orgasm after another, no matter how much I resisted.

And we both discovered that, the more he restrained me, the

faster I found my release.

"You feed my need to dominate you, Andie, and make it that much harder to leave you," he said when he finally withdrew from me.

"My vagina thanks you for leaving, though. I'm pretty sure I'm going to be walking with a hitch the way it is."

He gently stroked his finger over my swollen and cum-soaked fun zone. "It will be recovered tomorrow."

His fingers stilled for a moment then left my folds to trace my inner thighs.

"Do you feel well? Does your head hurt?" he asked.

I snorted. "Is this your way of asking if we can go again? The answer is no, we can't. My head doesn't hurt, but my vagina is on strike."

He grunted and leaned in to tenderly kiss my lips.

"I love you, Andie."

I cringed and knew he'd felt it when he pulled back to look at me.

"I had shitty parents," I said. "They'd say they loved each other in one breath then say and do awful things in the next. It's not that I don't believe in love or hearing the words, I'm just not over the past trauma associated with them."

The hint of frustration that had been in his gaze immediately vanished, and he pressed another kiss to my lips.

"Thank you for explaining."

Then he got up and held out his hand. "Will you shower with me?"

"Sure."

The woman was missing from the hallways when we emerged. In fact, the whole floor was pretty quiet. I tried not to think about why as we closed ourselves in the bathroom and showered together.

Once we were both dressed again, we went to find the doctor.

She took another blood sample and checked his wounds.

"You're healing remarkably fast," she said. "I'm very interested to see what the differences are in these samples."

She turned away, already lost in her own thoughts.

We grabbed a bag of snack food that Molev and Brandon had brought back and went to check how things were going outside.

"It's been quiet," Roland said. "One of the new lookouts swore they saw a body in the pile outside the fence move, but we've been watching it, and nothing's happened yet."

"Show me," Molev said.

I let him go off with Roland and continued checking in with everyone. The next shift change happened just before dark, and after that, we all settled in for a long night.

However, it passed quietly enough that I convinced Molev to rest for a few more hours with me just before dawn.

Roni woke us at first light.

"Everything's been quiet," she said. "I think we should go."

Molev pressed a kiss to my temple, and I glanced at his wounds, which were mending but still there.

"If we wait for me to fully heal, the infected will regroup," he said.

"Fine. Let's put the dummy up like we'd planned. Are you both rested enough?" I asked.

"Yep," Roni said as Molev nodded.

"Okay."

I didn't have Molev's intuition for sensing trouble, but something was telling me that things wouldn't stay as quiet as they were now once he left.

Once we were both dressed, we went to find the doctor.

She took another blood sample and checked his wound.

"[illegible] healing [illegible] rapidly, too," she said. "I'm very interested to see what the differences are in these samples."

She turned away, already lost in her own thoughts.

We grabbed a bite of food [illegible] and [illegible]

[illegible]

[illegible]

[illegible] have been watching it and nothing [illegible]

"Show me," I [illegible]

[illegible] and [illegible] up to wall [illegible]

[illegible]

[illegible]

[illegible] to test for all [illegible] with [illegible]

[illegible]

"[illegible]," I said. "I think [illegible] said [illegible]

[illegible] passed [illegible] to my [illegible] which were [illegible] still [illegible]

[illegible] wait for [illegible] to fully heal [illegible] infected [illegible]

[illegible] to put [illegible] And [illegible]

[illegible]

"Okay."

[illegible]

[illegible]

CHAPTER THIRTEEN

THE SOUND OF THE TRUCK RUMBLING OUT OF THE GATE DREW THE attention of a few infected hiding in the distant trees. Once the truck passed their location, they tumbled from their cover and ran after it.

"A few are staying in the trees," Sid said on his belly next to me as he looked through his scope.

My gaze swept over the other roofs within the interior fence. Each one had a pair of lookouts, and we had extra people patrolling below, just like we'd done the day before while Molev rested. The only difference was the dummy. I'd wanted to save using the dummy for when Molev was gone.

"Stand up fake-Molev," I said over the radio. The soldiers on roof 3 changed fake-Molev from squatting to standing.

"The infected are paying attention," Sid said. "They retreated farther into the trees."

"Good. We'll reposition him on another roof in an hour," I said to him. "Hopefully, it'll be enough to keep them away."

I stayed with Sid for a few more minutes before making rounds, focusing on the watching infected rather than wondering how Brandon, Roni, and Molev were doing. Time passed quickly that way. So quickly that I was surprised when I heard "Truck incoming" on the radio.

"Please tell me it's ours," I said back.

It took a few beats for the response. "It's ours."

A weight lifted off my shoulders.

"Remove fake Molev from the roof," I said over the radio.

Then I scurried down the ladder and jogged to the interior gate where we already had extra soldiers waiting. The truck appeared before Molev did. It had totes strapped to it again, and my stomach rumbled, reminding me I'd forgotten to eat.

Molev cleared the fence out of nowhere and opened the gate for the truck.

Roni drove it through with a grin on her face.

"Things went well?" I asked.

"We have fuel and more food," Molev said.

"Good. Go clean up. I have fresh clothes waiting for you in the bathroom. I'll handle this."

He jogged off, and I followed Roni as she drove the fueler around to the airstrip and parked it next to the other vehicles we'd gathered there.

She and Brandon were all grins as they got out.

"We hit the jackpot on this last gas station. They had a meat case with cheese and everything. It's all vacuum sealed and still looks good."

"Looks like you ran into trouble," I said with a nod toward the fueler's exterior.

"Nothing Molev couldn't handle," Roni said. "He worked fast." The leer she gave me at the end let me know my time with Molev yesterday hadn't gone unnoticed.

"Bring the food in, and come to our room. Team meeting."

Molev was already out of the shower and waiting in our room with a towel wrapped around his waist.

"You might want to put some pants on," I said. "Roni will be here in a few minutes. We need to have a planning meeting before they rest."

His heated gaze never left mine as he pulled on the shorts he'd tossed on the bed.

"Knock-knock," Katie called before walking through the open door. "I was told there's a team meeting."

"Yep."

Our core group slowly trickled in, and I pulled out the map I had from Rick that showed the locations of all the FOBs between Vance and Whiteman.

"We need to plan how we're going to get to Whiteman. We know it's not going to be as simple as driving straight through. With the roadblocks, rerouting, and refueling, we'll be lucky if we can manage a hundred miles a day." I opened the map and pointed to the FOB outside of Wichita. "This is the closest FOB between us and Whiteman. It's just over one hundred miles away, and we know it's defensible and big enough to house everyone overnight. And it's remote enough that we shouldn't draw unwanted attention while we're there."

"Defensible and it might have more fuel," Sid said. "We're going to need it."

I nodded, glad I wasn't the only one who was seeing the problem we faced.

"We should be able to reach it within four to six hours. How much fuel we use is going to depend on so many factors. Idle time...backtracking...you name it. We'll have a better idea of how much fuel we're going to need and how far we can push after we reach it."

"Have we given any thought to using civilian vehicles

instead of military ones?" Steve asked. "They'll be more fuel efficient."

"They would, but they'd also be less likely to make it through roadblocks."

"How many vehicles are we looking at? Twenty-five? Thirty? That's a long convoy for Molev to protect," Katie said.

"Is one fueler going to be enough?" Roni asked.

Three hours later, we all agreed on the plan. While the others left to spread the word and start preparations, I hung back with Molev.

"How are you feeling?" I asked.

"Tired," he admitted.

"Then, sleep. We'll wake you up if the dummy stops working."

THE ABSENCE of Molev's arm around my middle woke me, and I opened my eyes in time to see him tug a clean shirt on in the dim light.

"Did you sleep enough?" I asked.

"I did. Rest. I will check the fences."

I sat up and shook my head.

"Nope. If you're up and moving around, so am I. There's plenty for me to do."

He didn't argue with me, and we left the room together. The guard at the end of the hall nodded to us as we passed.

Outside, Molev gave me a quick kiss then disappeared. I paused for a moment and looked up at the stars in the clear sky. Perspective hit me hard. Our daily struggles, no matter how intense, changed nothing in the grand scheme of things in our universe.

That insignificance didn't make me feel less important. Instead, it wrapped me in a blanket of comfort knowing that the mistakes I made ultimately didn't matter. Trying and enjoying the time I had while living to the best of my ability were all that did matter.

Feeling settled by that knowledge, I went to check on the preparations. The rest of the team had ensured everything was packed and ready. Even the research equipment was already safely repacked in another vehicle.

All we needed was the light of day.

I checked my watch then went to a roof to wait as Molev made rounds and removed any infected he found in the area. When the sun started to lighten the sky, he returned to shower and change again.

By the time the sun's first rays crested the horizon, everyone was in place and ready. The rumble of the engines echoed around the base as I looked around one last time and got into an MRAP in the center of the line.

As each vehicle pulled forward, they checked in over the handhelds they'd been given.

A few infected rushed toward us as we made our way out of Vance, but not as many as we'd anticipated, which I took as a good sign. Molev handled them quickly and sprinted alongside the convoy.

We learned fast that the radios were absolutely essential. Molev had no problem keeping an eye on things when we drove the straightaways. Turning and curvy roads were a different story, especially in wooded areas. But the new drivers learned to use the vehicles as a weapon if Molev wasn't right there. They also learned the importance of wiper fluid.

More roadblocks littered the roads than the last time we'd passed through the area, and the Strykers had to clear a fair share for the rest of the convoy. However, only a few infected poured from those traps.

I felt both relief and worry at the indication of how many infected had moved to the coasts.

Despite the reduced number of them, it still took the anticipated four hours to reach the intended Wichita FOB.

The base's closed gate was a welcome sight. The convoy rolled to a stop while Molev jumped over the gate and went inside.

The first body thrown over the wall made me smile, which my co-pilot noticed.

"Isn't that a bad thing?" she asked.

"Not really. The infected are just a part of life now. But the fact that they're in there means we're more likely to find fuel and food that might have been left behind."

"Ah."

She'd been pretty quiet the whole trip but had quickly caught on to a lot.

"Make sure you stick to the places that have been cleared," I said. "And even then, it's better to be with someone who's armed. Oh, and sleep fully dressed if you haven't been. You never know when you need to get up and run for your life."

She gave a deprecating laugh. "What do you think life was like in the camps?"

I glanced at her. She read as easygoing most of the time, which was why I asked if she wanted to be my co-pilot. But at the moment, a deeper bitterness was showing through.

"The idea of facing an infected is terrifying," she said. "But so was the idea of being raped in my sleep."

"I'm sorry you had to face that."

She shrugged. "And I'm sorry you had to face what you

faced out here to be this good at surviving. We've all had hardships. It's the hope of those ending that keeps us going."

I faced forward as the vehicle in front of me pulled ahead and slowly followed.

"I haven't seen the place we're going, but I trust Molev," I said. "He says it's safe. He says it's a place where we can sleep without our boots on."

"I noticed there are a lot of women in the group. It was something I noticed when I was selected, actually. A lot of us are wondering why we were really selected. Tell me I didn't trade one hell for another."

"I can't," I said. "Getting there might be a level of hell we won't survive. But if you're asking me to reassure you that you won't be raped by Molev's kind, that I can do. They're not human so try not to compare them to human men."

I parked next to another vehicle and shut off the engine.

"I heard you in the room with him," she said as I grabbed my water bottle for a quick drink. "Seemed like you were enjoying yourself."

I flashed a smile at her. "If his brothers are anything like him and you're lucky enough to attract the attention of one of them, you'll enjoy yourself too. Now, stay put until we give the all clear."

She nodded and watched me get out.

The rest of the team was already gathering with the soldiers and dividing into groups to clear the base. I went to check on Molev, who was drinking some water.

"How's the glue holding up?" I asked.

"Well," he said.

"Good. I'll go get—"

He whipped his head to the left and disappeared, leaving me alone by the vehicles.

"Incoming," I shouted.

The groups with weapons quickly returned to the vehicles. I scrambled toward Roni's. Back-to-back with the fueler to my left, we scanned the area for movement and listened.

The first infected appeared around the side of a building to our right.

"Got it," Roni said, aiming.

The sound of her shot already drowned out a scrape of gravel from my left. I looked toward the fueler at the same time something closed around my ankle.

I aimed at the infected's head. It pulled hard. My bullet pinged against the fueler as I fell. Not that I focused on saving myself from that. The gravel bit into my back and knocked the wind out of me. My head bounced. All I could think of was kicking the infected off of me. The flat of my boot connected with its head again and again.

My ears rang. The high-pitched hum almost drowned out Roni's garbled, under-water-sounding yell. It didn't dampen the roar, however.

Molev appeared on the tanker above us, a savage grey creature with a rage-twisted expression as he dove for the infected biting my leg.

He separated its body from its head then scooped me up and deposited me on top of the tanker. A second later, Roni joined me.

"Stay here," he ordered then left.

Roni kept her weapon up, her gaze scanning the area around us.

"Pull up your pant leg, and tell me if there's a bite," she said without looking at me.

My hands were steady as I checked. "Skin discoloration with teeth indents. There's blood, but the material isn't ripped. I think it's an abrasion from trying to get free. No idea if that counts as a bite or not. Make some space. If I start throwing up, try not to shoot the tanker. I already did that."

She glanced at me but didn't otherwise move as I noted the time on my watch.

"No one's that detached," she said.

"I'll start panicking if I throw up." I tugged the pant leg down again. "I really hope this means we'll find food and fuel here."

It took another five minutes for Molev to hunt down the rest of the infected who'd tried to ambush us.

He'd just landed on the tanker between Roni and me when someone called out for him.

"We have a problem," the person added.

Molev glanced at Roni then picked me up.

"Were you bitten?" he asked softly.

"Yes, but it's hard to tell if it's an actual bite or if it's from the pressure. My pants didn't rip. Not sure if that makes a difference." I glanced at my watch. "We'll know one way or another in a few minutes."

His hold on me tightened, and he jumped down. Farther down the line, I saw Roland and Steve standing side by side with their weapons trained on someone sitting against a tire.

I knew what had happened.

"Put me down," I said softly.

As soon as he did, I hurried forward with him at my side.

The soldier was holding his neck when I stepped around Roland and Steve. I was pretty sure his name was Murphy, but I wasn't positive. I'd chosen not to learn their names for the very reason in front of me.

"I'm sorry this happened," I said, hunkering down beside him.

"Me too," he said, wincing. He removed his hand from his bleeding neck to hold his stomach as he looked up at Molev. "I saw you. You were trying to be everywhere at once. This isn't on you. Shit happens. If it's okay with you, I'd rather take a bullet and keep my head where it's at. But not here. Those kids inside are terrified enough. Help me up, and we'll go somewhere else."

Molev helped the soldier to his feet and looped an arm around his waist.

Sid kept up with them as they walked away, and I looked at Roland.

"Six more minutes," I said.

His carefully blank expression shattered, and although he tried to pull it back together, he wasn't quite successful.

"I'm going to stand over there with my back to the building," I said.

He nodded and watched me as I walked away. That area between the ankle and calf was really starting to hurt like a bitch. Each step sent a more insistent twang straight to the bone.

"I'm betting it was dentures," I said when I faced Roland again. "I think I'm going to ask Molev to check."

Roland slowly shook his head, and I grinned a little.

"I get your MRE tonight if I'm right."

"Deal," he said right away.

A shot rang out. Neither of us jumped at the sound.

It took Molev another minute to return with Sid. When he did, he knelt in front of me and lifted my pant leg to inspect the skin. His gaze lingered on the perfect twin crescents bruising my skin.

"How do you feel?" he asked.

"Angry," I said. "A truck isn't like having a wall to my back. I should have been looking under and over as well."

He pulled me into his arms, hugging me close.

"You shouldn't have had to look at all," he said roughly.

I wrapped my arms around his waist, uncaring about the drying blood on him.

"What's the point of keeping me alive if I'm not willing to pitch in and try?" I asked. "It can't be your sole responsibility. None of this can. We're a team, remember? You were doing your part, and I was doing mine. Only, I messed up. Don't turn the blame on this. Be mad at me, and tell me you expect better of me because you believe in me and know I *can* do better."

He captured the back of my head as he drew away, holding my gaze. He studied me for a silent moment then pressed his forehead to mine.

"Do better, Andie," he said. "This life isn't worth living without you."

I closed my eyes and nodded.

His lips brushed over my cheek then my forehead. I basked in the sensation, focusing on that rather than the ache in my leg. His hold left the back of my head, and he scooped me into his arms.

"Start clearing the buildings," he said. "Watch closely for infected. No more mistakes."

He strode away with me, heading for the showers. I didn't fight him as he stripped me down and inspected every inch of me. I returned the favor when he shed his clothes and stepped into the spray of water. He washed quickly and held out his hand.

I was an idiot and went to him, dazed by his pectoral display and perfect abs.

The second my skin made contact with the frigid spray of water he stood in like it was no big deal, my brain short-circuited. All my composure and careful logic evaporated, and I screeched like a banshee.

Molev chuckled and pulled me into his arms even as I tried to scramble backward.

"Take your punishment and remember it well," he said in my ear. "Next time, you will be more alert."

He briskly scrubbed a hand over my torso, the only source of warmth, as I trembled and tried to regain control. It wasn't easy. The water felt two degrees from freezing.

My torture was done quickly, thankfully. As soon as I was thoroughly rinsed, he shut off the water and held me close. I didn't hesitate to wrap myself around him, legs around his waist and everything. Anything for more of his delicious heat.

His hands kneaded my ass as he held me. It helped warm me. Or maybe it was the knowledge that each movement brought his fingers closer to my core. I pressed my lips to his collarbone and shifted myself so my folds would be more accessible to his touch.

He growled and petted me where I'd wanted him to.

"I need you, Andie," he said, lifting me higher and bringing me down so I slicked against his hard length. "Tell me you need me."

"I do," I breathed, riding his ridges. "More than I thought possible."

He leaned in and nipped my shoulder as he repositioned himself at my entrance. When his gaze met mine, I could see the simmering rage there.

"Is this part of the punishment too?" I asked. My core clenched around nothing at the thought.

His gaze searched mine as his pupils slowly expanded.

"I have little control already, Andie. Playing with me now is dangerous."

My breath hitched. "Who said I'm playing?"

He bared his teeth at me and slowly forced me down on his hard length. He'd never taken me without at least one orgasm to make way. The stretch burned, a reminder that I was alive and me. But for how long?

I pressed down, forcing myself to take him. He snarled in my ear and thrust home. Panting at the sensation of mixed pleasure and pain, I dropped my forehead to his shoulder and tried to catch my breath. He didn't wait for me to adjust. He lifted me, withdrawing to the tip, then slammed in again. I gasped and clutched at him.

He hesitated, and I lifted myself to prove that I didn't want hesitation.

The second snarl resonated in my chest a moment before my back hit the cold wall, and he started a punishing pace that stimulated my core in just the right way. Head against the wall, I relaxed and let him take both of us to the place we wanted to be.

My orgasm ripped a drawn-out wail from me, and he bathed my insides with his release shortly after the echo faded. I continued to grind down on him, despite my languid exhaustion. Neither of us was close to being finished with the other.

The ache in my leg was nothing but a distant memory by the time I heard the water turn on again.

"You need to wash," Molev said, holding me in his arms.

He nudged my leg to the side, and the spray of the shower hit me squarely. Rather than steal my breath, it felt amazing on my abused flesh. Molev's fingers gently rinsed me. Then the water shut off.

I tipped my face when his lips brushed my forehead,

welcoming his gentle affection now that we'd worked all our frustration out. He kissed me tenderly as he walked.

"I found some towels and clothes for you," Katie said. "Everything's fine out here, so take your time."

"Sorry, Katie," I murmured, not opening my eyes.

"Don't worry about it. I'm just glad you're still you."

I smiled slightly. "Me too."

I heard the door close as Molev tried to stand me up. My legs didn't want to hold for the first few seconds, but they eventually figured out what to do. A towel rubbed down my arms and back. Heat enveloped my breast.

Letting out a content sigh, I threaded my fingers in Molev's hair and looked down at him as he sucked my nipple.

"I wasn't sure you knew to do that," I said with a smirk.

"Other parts always distracted me," he said, switching to the opposite side.

He didn't try to do anything more than dry me and kiss me. After, he lovingly dressed me before quickly drying and dressing himself.

Hand in hand, we left the showers.

The rest of the team was there, grinning like idiots. The doctor was there, too, looking far less amused.

"No dentures," Roland said with a smirk.

The doctor's concerned gaze swept over me. "Were you bitten?"

"Yes and no," I said. "An infected tried biting me, but my pants saved me. He never broke through the material."

"I'd like to look at it if you're willing."

"Sure." I looked at Molev. "Go do what you need to do. I'll find you when I'm done."

He frowned slightly and grabbed the back of my head.

"Ooh, we're going to get a show," Roni said.

"You act like you haven't been out here listening for the last hour," Steve said.

"That was the teaser. This is the real deal," she insisted. "Give her tongue, Molev."

His frown deepened as he stared at me, and I patted his chest. "This is why privacy is important."

He grunted and released me.

He stayed behind with the others while I left with the doctor. My gaze swept over the base, noting the guards and lookouts. We already had people on the roofs and on the vehicles in addition to a few patrolling the area on foot.

Satisfied the team had covered everything, I nodded to the guards at the entrance to the main bunkhouse and went inside. Several of the bunks were already occupied with sleeping personnel. I needed to get Molev in here to sleep soon, too, or he'd skip it entirely.

"Over here," the doctor said softly. She gestured to an empty bunk that had her medic kit on top.

I sat down and pulled up my pant leg without her asking and rested my foot on the bed. She gently prodded the area above my ankle with a gloved hand.

"You're very lucky," she said softly when she finished her examination.

"I am," I agreed. "If I were you, I'd ditch the scrubs and go with something heavier like denim or canvas. I'm proof that a little bit of resistance can be the difference between life and death."

She continued to stare at my growing bruise even as I tugged my pant leg back into place.

CHAPTER FOURTEEN

MOLEV STOOD ON THE ROOF, LOOKING OUT OVER THE BASE, WITH Roni by his side. The way he had his arms crossed as she talked to him had me wondering what she was saying that was putting him in a bad mood. Or maybe it was a lingering bad mood from my close call. Although I'd done my best to help him let it go, I knew very well it would have taken hours in that shower to completely reassure him. Maybe not even then.

"Did you eat yet?" I asked softly from my place on the ground, still yards away.

He unfolded his arms, said something to Roni, and jumped down.

"Hey, handsome," I said when he closed the distance between us. "Still angry at me?"

He cupped the back of my head and tenderly stroked my cheek.

"I was never angry at you, Andie. I am mad the fuel was taken and that we are not already home where you will be safe. I am mad your people did not listen to me sooner. I am mad—"

I threaded my fingers through his hair and pulled him down

for a kiss. It went from sweet to molten in a heartbeat, and I loved it. But I didn't want him to think I was starting something else. It was way too soon for another round with him.

Loosening my hold on his hair, I started easing up on the passion. He took my cue and pulled back to look at me.

"We can't change the past," I said. "All we can do is work on the present and make the best choices we can for a better future."

He grunted.

"Now, are you hungry, or do you have more you need to do?"

"I will eat with you."

"Eat and rest," I said. "You're not getting enough sleep. Especially when you're running for so long during the day."

He let me lead him to the mess hall where the majority of our people were gathered. They'd already sorted through whatever food had been left behind and had a big pot of something on the stove.

"Roland mentioned that you're a protein-based eater," one of the women said to Molev. "We found some canned meat that we set aside for you." She produced two large cans of corned beef hash. "Will these work? There's more if you want them."

"These will be fine," I said. "Thanks for thinking of him."

"Of course. Thank you for everything you're doing to keep us safe." When she said it, she wasn't just talking to him but to me too.

I nodded, accepted a bowl of the stew they were simmering, and took a spot at a table with Molev. We ate a quick meal with their quiet conversation floating around us. Guards stood inside the door, watching everything, even in here.

"It won't be like this once we reach my people," Molev said, watching my gaze.

"Haven't I proven that I trust you yet?" I asked.

The corners of his mouth tilted a little as he nodded and finished his meal. As soon as I was done, we left, and I led him to the bunks, where we lay down with the others.

"Keep those eyes closed until dusk," I said, running my fingers over his eyelids.

He captured my hand and kissed the tips of my fingers.

"Sleep," he said softly.

I WAS ALONE when I checked my watch and saw it was just after midnight. Swearing softly, I threw back the blanket and left the bunkroom. The guards stationed outside the door pointed me in Molev's direction.

Silence enveloped me as I moved forward, my gaze searching the rooftops. I spotted his barely visible shape crouched low on the roofline. His grey tones blended with the night sky, making him almost indiscernible with his dark shirt and pants.

"Did you sleep until dusk as I asked?"

He pivoted and rose to his full height at the sound of my voice.

"I'm worried about you," I said. "I don't want you to go until you drop."

He crossed the roof and jumped down.

I loved the way his steady gaze never left my face as he approached. It made me feel like I was the only thing that mattered in this world.

Sure, he'd said as much, but words and actions didn't always match in life. It was a lesson I'd learned early. But with Molev? He was different. He didn't manipulate, choosing to be straightforward instead. Even in the beginning, when he'd withheld information, he'd told me that was what he was doing.

He pulled me into his arms when he was close enough, and I readily returned his hug.

"I miss sleeping next to you," I said.

"I miss it too. Roni and Steve think we have enough fuel with what we found here to make it to Iola, Kansas. They believe an armory there will be defensible and have more fuel."

I could hear the undertones in his words, though.

"Why don't you want to go there?"

"My gut is telling me we should go to Parsons."

The place where we started.

I tipped my head back to look him in the eye. "Then we listen to your gut."

"We found a hound there the last time," he said.

"Did you kill it?"

"We did."

"Well then, it's not there anymore. And the chance there's another one there is just as high as one being at any location we pick. I am curious what we'll find there, though. Maybe an easy place to fuel up." I pulled completely out of his arms and took his hand. "How far would it be from Parsons to your people? If we reach Parsons by midday, could we reach your people by nightfall?"

Molev looked out over the buildings, considering my questions.

"If I were traveling alone, yes. But not with vehicles that must use the roads."

"Okay. Then I'm going to go look at our atlas and see if there are any likely places near Parsons where we can hole up overnight."

I placed a quick kiss on his cheek and tried to leave. His fingers tightened around mine and he swung me back toward him like we were dancing. I landed against his chest with an "oof" and looked up at him.

"Take a guard with you."

"I'll compromise with you and have a guard escort me and check the room before returning to their position."

He grunted, kissed my forehead, and released me.

"I like my method better but will accept yours."

I grinned at him. "That's so big of you. Thank you."

He actually inclined his head at me.

"Yes, I am big."

"Big and adorable," I said, waving and walking away.

I did as I promised, and once the guard agreed that no infected lurked in the small space, I spread the maps out on the table. It took hours to study the route and locations near Parsons and compare them to Rick's notes. My back started to hurt from my pronounced slump, and I stretched my arms over my head.

Nothing stood out to explain why Molev's gut was telling him to go to Parsons. There weren't any bases along the way or noted surpluses of supplies. Nothing to warrant a veer toward Parsons instead of heading in a more northerly direction to Iola, Kansas.

While I didn't doubt Molev's intuition, it did worry me to head toward an area without a secure location waiting. If there were only twelve of us or even forty of us, I wouldn't be as concerned. Rotating guard shifts and sharing beds usually meant plenty of room for everyone. Over two hundred people was a different story, though.

The doorknob rattled and startled me.

"If you're alive, you better say something," I said.

"I am alive. Did you eat?" Molev asked through the door.

I hurried to unlock it as I glanced at the time. Still two hours until sunrise.

"No, I didn't eat," I said. "I'm still trying to figure out what we're going to do once we hit Parsons. Where do we house everyone overnight? Where are we going to get more fuel so we won't run out before we get to Whiteman?" I sighed. "I trust your gut; I just hate unanswered questions."

He tilted his head as he studied me. "Take your clothes off?"

"What?"

His lips started to curve. "I will help you forget the questions you need answered."

I crossed my arms, trying really hard not to let my surprise show.

"Your solutions only offer short-term amnesia. I'd prefer actual answers."

He took a step closer to me, and I quickly held up a hand.

"However, I'm willing to forego any answers in this case and exercise some blind faith."

He laughed. The low sound wrapped around me and had me smiling in return. Not wanting him to think it was an invitation, I gathered the maps and waited for him to open the door.

The rest of the team was already gathered at a table in the mess hall, and several women were moving around in the kitchen area.

"So what's the plan, boss?" Roni asked, looking at Molev.

"We're headed for Parsons at first light," he said.

"At least, it's a route we know," she said.

"Any particular part of Parsons?" Brandon asked.

"Where my people first met yours," Molev said.

THE CONVOY ENTERED the fenced-in corral with little trouble. A few infected sprinted out from the houses, but not nearly as many as we'd originally attracted. Molev ended them as soon as he spotted them.

I knew right when we'd reached the point we'd first sighted his people. The decaying body piles gave it away. The woman next to me turned away from them and focused on me.

"I'm really glad the windows are up," she said. "I don't think the weather's cold enough to keep them from smelling."

"Probably not," I agreed.

"Molev's calling for a stop," a voice said over the radio.

"Here?" the woman asked, sounding panicked.

"He never does anything without a reason," I said calmly. "Sometimes it's hard to see the reason, but it's always there. Breathe. Calm down, and focus on what's moving around us. And, yes, you even need to look at the bodies. I wouldn't put it past an infected to hide in that mess."

She swallowed hard and went back to watching like she was supposed to be doing.

Molev appeared beside my window.

"Wait here," he said. "I will return quickly."

"Do you have a radio?" I asked through the glass.

He shook his head.

"Get one, and hurry back."

He disappeared, and down the line, engines went quiet.

"He's never just left us before," the woman said.

"I know. But he's worked really hard to build our trust for a reason. If he wanted us to die, he could have just let the hound have us the first night, right?"

She didn't say anything else after that. Minutes ticked by. More infected collected outside the fence.

"Molev, we're fine, but we need to start clearing the infected," I said over the radio, watching one try to climb the fence.

"I understand," he said back.

"Sid? Roland? Are you two able?" I asked.

"On it," Sid said.

"I'll take the back," another voice said.

Their shots rang out, one after another.

"Careful," Katie said. "I see Molev coming from the northwest."

"I am to the east," Molev said over the radio. "Welcome him, Katie. Tell him I am with you."

The woman next to me made the sound I wanted to make. Another fey?

"Stay here," I said, opening my door and using it to climb to the top of the cab. From there, I had a good view of Katie doing the same. She waved both arms at the fey, who was slowing. He wore the same style of leather pants that Molev favored and a tight-fitting T-shirt, but his hair was much shorter, barely brushing his ears.

"Hi!" Katie called. "We're friends of Molev's. He said to welcome you and to say he's with us."

The fey's pace increased, and he vaulted over the fence to land lightly on the cab next to Katie. She stumbled back a step, and he wrapped an arm around her, catching her fall K-drama style.

"There are over two hundred people with us," I said without yelling. "I don't suppose you brought some friends, did you?"

His head turned toward me. Katie said something I couldn't hear, winning back his attention, and he carefully righted her.

"Her name's Katie, and she's shy," I said. "What's your name?"

I could see him saying something to her but couldn't hear it. When she nodded and stepped away from him, he turned toward me and started leap-frogging from one truck to the next until he stood next to me.

"My name is Ben."

The very human name surprised me a little. All the names Molev had mentioned to me had sounded different. Unique.

"I'm Andie, Molev's friend."

"Where is he?" he asked the question but never looked away from me.

"I'm guessing Molev will be here any second. I think he was looking for you."

Ben grunted. "I have been looking for him since he left."

His gaze flicked to the vehicle behind mine. I turned to look and saw Steve smile and wave. The woman next to him did the same.

"Is she married?" Ben asked, once again fully focused on me.

"All of the women with us are single. A few have kids with them, which is why we're trying to get to your community as soon as possible. We already ran into one hound that gave Molev a few dozen more scars before he killed it. That's why I asked if you had friends with you."

"It is only me."

"Two fey are better than one," I said.

His smile was huge.

"Is Ben short for something?" I asked, curious.

"I will ask Hannah."

"Hannah?" I asked, starting to get the picture. "Did she give you the name?"

"Yes. She said it is the most human name she knows. I wanted a human one so females will be less afraid of me."

"I don't think your name has anything to do with their fears. And their fears are their problem to fix, not yours."

The words were barely out of my mouth when Molev jumped on top of the cab with us.

"Ben," he said a second before he hugged him with three solid thumps on his back.

I internally winced on Ben's behalf.

"I found females," Molev said. "Nice ones who want to live with us."

The fey's smile grew even larger, prominently displaying his very pointed canines. He grabbed Molev by the shoulders.

"Will you allow me to meet all of them before we return?"

Molev chuckled. "You may speak to as many as you wish."

"Maybe we should hold off the introductions until we're somewhere safer," I said.

Molev glanced over at me and nodded.

"Ben, this is Andie. She is my wife."

It felt like the world fractured beneath my feet, and I was free-falling into hell.

"Wife?" I echoed.

Molev's gaze locked with mine. His head tipped almost imperceptibly to the right, and the joy started to fade from his eyes.

"No," I snapped. "You don't get to get mad at me for having a panic attack when you spring stuff on me like that. You're going to be understanding that I need time to process and not push me about retreating, or I'm going to push you off this damn truck."

"She sounds like Mya when she's angry with Drav," Ben

said. "Mom says the baby hormones are making her extra moody."

Molev's attention ripped from mine.

"Baby?"

"Yes. Cassie had Mya take a test. We cannot hear the heart like Angel's baby, but Cassie promises it is there. It makes Mya sick and sleepy. Mom said that is normal."

Ben's gaze flicked to me. "Are you growing Molev's baby?"

I turned my back on them both and climbed down off the top of the truck. My co-pilot watched me closely as I took my seat and closed the door.

"This one seems more chatty than Molev," she said.

"Yeah."

She reached over and patted my hand.

"You okay to drive?"

"Yeah."

Molev and Ben left the top of our vehicle, and Molev's voice crackled over the radio.

"Ben will lead the convoy. I will watch the tail."

I took a calming breath as I started the engine and focused on thinking logically instead of emotionally. Panic did no good. If I listened to what it was whispering—to pull back, to retreat—I'd make matters worse for myself. And that was the last thing I wanted. Matters, as they stood, were bad enough.

Or were they? Had Molev been viewing me as his wife since we'd started sleeping together, or was he doing it to try to stake a claim on me? The answer to that would define his intentions.

I realized how I was thinking and mentally shook my head at myself. Molev hated when he ran into people who weren't up front with their intentions. He preferred his method of just being straightforward. Or, if he had to hold something back, he was pretty honest about it.

Why would he change who he was now?

He wouldn't. That meant he'd likely viewed me as a wife for a while.

Another jolt of panic and denial shot through me, and I admitted to myself that I had a real issue with being a wife. Why? Because taking on that role changed a person. So many societal expectations went with it. What if I didn't want to be the primary cook or clean-up crew? What if I didn't want to be the one responsible for doing laundry?

The convoy started forward.

In past relationships, whenever I'd started questioning the validity of today's continued unspoken gender norms, I'd been the problem. Some men had tried making it sound like I was just being lazy. Some tried pulling the "Well, I make more money" card. As if a higher income entitled them to cast their "cherished" partner into a servant role. Because that was how I saw it. When two people were both working an equal number of hours outside the home, why would one be more responsible for maintaining the home than the other?

I realized my thoughts were spiraling with resentment and took another slow breath.

Now wasn't the time. When we stopped for the night, I would talk to Molev. Until then, these thoughts were only a distraction I couldn't afford. Relaxing my shoulders, I focused on scanning the homes I could see outside my window.

"I think I see a watcher," the woman next to me said.

"Radio it," I said. "We don't want anything following."

"I see it," came Molev's immediate reply to her message.

We made it through the fenced-in area and cleared the other side of town without any other sightings. Ben led us to the highway. Whenever he spotted a trap, he would run ahead and start clearing it while Molev stayed with the convoy. Having two fey and few infected in the area really helped us put some miles on, but I knew we couldn't push through. Too many miles still separated us from Whiteman.

"We need to find a place to stop for the night," I said over the radio.

Molev sprinted past us, leaving his position at the tail. A few minutes later, his voice came over the radio.

"There is a farm ahead. We will stop soon."

The place they'd found was off the highway by a few miles. Enough that no one would see the lights on or hear us. We circled the vehicles around the property and waited for Molev and Ben to clear the house and the barn. Once they said it was clear, the second team went in to double-check. More or less as human bait to draw out any that might have hidden from the fey.

While everyone unloaded and stood in line for the bathroom, Katie asked Roni and me to stand guard so she could use the side of the barn.

"I'll pee my pants if I have to wait in that line," she said, motioning us to turn around.

Roni smirked and rolled her eyes. "Stop guzzling water while we're traveling. Wait until we stop."

"I wasn't drinking," Katie said just before she started relieving herself with a sigh.

Ben chose that moment to run around the side of the barn. Roni and I immediately stepped together to shield Katie. She made a panicked sound behind us.

"Could you turn around for a second, Ben?" I asked. "Katie would rather you not see this."

He immediately pivoted.

"I wasn't trying to look at your pussy, Katie," he said quickly. "I just wanted to make sure you are safe."

"You saw?" she screeched.

"It's not okay to look without permission, Ben," Roni said as Katie started mumbling to herself. "To even things up, you should probably pull down your pants and let us see your goods."

"Okay," he said at the same time I said, "No, don't."

Either he didn't hear me, or he didn't care because he spun and had his pants down a second later. His size was almost comparable to Molev. Almost but not quite. It still exceeded human expectations, though.

"Damn!" Roni said. "You are a gift to women everywhere. You see that, Katie? Please tell me you'll stop clutching your pearls long enough to hit that."

Ben's hands crept toward his hard length like he wanted to shield it.

"Hitting it will be uncomfortable," Ben said hesitantly, "but I will try to enjoy it."

"Oh my God," Katie breathed behind us. Based on the rapid rasp of material, she was pulling up her pants.

"I think it would be in your best interest to put that away now," I said. "Showing a woman that before she's ready might kill any interest she has in you."

He had his impressiveness tucked away again in seconds, not that his pants did anything to hide it.

"Just like our Molev doll," Roni said under her breath.

"I didn't kill your interest in me, did I, Katie?" Ben asked.

"Uh…" Katie said, giving me a nervous look.

"Hey, why just Katie?" Roni asked, her tone void of any lingering wonder.

I glanced at Roni's closely cropped hair and vest.

"She's a woman," I said quickly. "Her name is Roni."

Ben's gaze shifted to Roni. "I thought you were a man. Do

you have interest in me?"

"Not anymore," Roni said with a disgruntled look. "Katie, walk your man somewhere else so we can have some privacy."

"On it," she said. When she stepped around us, Ben only had eyes for her flushed face.

"You are beautiful, Katie," he said when she got close. "What is your favorite color?"

Roni snorted and glared after the pair as they walked away.

"When I meet the guy Molev said, I'm flashing my tits before saying my name."

"If Ben is the norm, you better flash before your fey sees any other female. They seem to have a love-at-first-sight thing going on."

"I'm riding into Molev's hometown Godiva style then," Roni said, dropping her pants.

I laughed and scanned the area until we switched places.

"You mind if I borrow Molev for a few minutes?" she asked when I finished.

"You going to try to molest him again?"

"Hell no. My pride can only take so much rejection in one day. He and I need to come up with a strategy once we arrive. I've seen too many dangling carrots to miss out on the promised land. My itch needs scratching bad."

"You're not going to rape anyone, are you, Roni?" I asked, walking toward the house with her.

"Pfft. He'll be willing. I'll flash my tits, spread my legs, and brace for impact." She rubbed her hands together. "It's going to be so good."

"What if he wants to...I don't know...get to know you first?"

She jerked as if I'd slapped her. "Shut your hateful face now."

"Dramatic much?" I asked.

"You don't understand, Andie. I've seen what you're getting on the regular. I've heard how amazing it is. It's okay for me to be jealous as fuck and needy. Let me have my dreams."

"Fine. You're right. If you're lucky, your dream fey will trip while he's whisking you away to his sex dungeon and accidentally impale you, sending you into an instant orgasmic spiral. Better?"

"And here we thought you were an unemotional robot incapable of relating to us," she said, grinning at me. "You get me."

Her gaze caught on Molev near the house, and she started waving at him.

"I need to talk to you, big guy. It's urgent."

The second he headed in our direction, I said goodbye and veered toward the front door. I had no reason to listen to any more of Roni's sex requests.

Inside, a group was working together to make a late lunch for everyone from the supplies we'd taken from the FOB. Rachel, my sister-in-law, was one of them and waved me over when she saw me.

"There aren't a lot of beds here," she said. "So I told the moms with their kids to take them."

"Makes sense," I said. "Did anyone have a problem with it?"

"No. Just wanted you to know so Molev didn't try claiming one with you. Not that he doesn't deserve the downtime and some decent rest," she added quickly.

"Don't worry about it. He'll be fine."

"Do you think we'll reach Whiteman tomorrow?" she asked.

The work in the kitchen slowed as they all waited for my answer.

"If luck's on our side, we should," I said.

CHAPTER FIFTEEN

"I see our destination ahead, folks," Roni said over the radio. She was in the lead vehicle, something she'd worked out with Molev, and I really hoped she still had her shirt on.

We'd kept the fact that we were headed toward Tolerance, Molev's home, instead of Whiteman from everyone but the core team. While I didn't think the end destination would matter, I hadn't wanted anyone to panic over the fact we weren't going to a so-called secure base.

"Ben just ran ahead and disappeared over the wall," she added. "We're almost home, people."

I could hear the excitement in her voice and shared it to a degree. Yes, we'd made it to Molev's home, but I knew we weren't truly safe. A tsunami of infected and hounds would be headed our way as soon as they finished with the coasts. And then what? We didn't have a cure to stop people from turning, and the method we had to kill the hounds was dangerous, especially if we were fighting off infected at the same time.

We needed more than a cure. We needed a miracle.

"Thanks for letting me ride with you," Rachel said. "This beats riding in the back."

She'd been pretty quiet the whole ride.

"I wasn't trying to ignore you," I said.

She chuckled. "I know that. You were being smart about who you assigned as a lookout and rotated. Plus, I had experience with kids and could help with the moms. Those poor kids. Terrified and bored isn't working for them."

Rachel got quiet again and stared off at nothing for a moment. That was the exact reason I hadn't assigned her as a lookout. She hadn't been the only one, though. So many of these women were dealing with some level of grief or trauma. I didn't hold it against any of them. They hadn't signed up to be guards or lookouts. They'd signed up for a better life. And now, hopefully, they'd have the chance.

"Get ready, ladies," Roni said over the radio. "We're getting a welcoming committee, and half of them forgot their shirts."

"Molev, you better block Roni's door, or she's going to scare a lot of people," Steve said.

"I like that you're all close," Rachel said. "It's like a family."

"I guess so," I said. "A slightly annoying one."

She laughed. "Aren't all families just a little annoying sometimes? But you know you can count on them, and that's what really matters."

"Very true," I said as a fey appeared beside my window. He smiled and nodded at me as I slowed to a stop.

"Um, you know I love your brother, right?" Rachel said.

"I do," I said as I slowed. I glanced her way and saw she was looking out her window at the group of bare-chested fey running alongside us.

"Looking isn't cheating, right?" she asked.

I chuckled and rolled to a stop just behind the vehicle in

front of us. "I'd be really worried about your mental health if you weren't looking."

She glanced at me with her cheeks flushed. "I miss him."

"I know. And I'll be sure to tell him all about how you were blushing like crazy today when we see him again. How many pull-ups was he up to again? Seven?"

She grinned. "Last letter from him, he said he was up to twelve."

"You're going to pounce on him like Roni's probably pouncing on some fey right now."

The words were barely out of my mouth when the radio crackled.

"Steve, I'm going to kill you," Roni said.

"We better get out there," I said.

As soon as the door opened, I was bombarded with a chorus of "Can I carry you?"

"Can I have everyone's attention for a minute?" I called loudly.

Every fey head swiveled in my direction. There had to be fifty, at least.

"There are over two hundred people who are going to need a lift over that wall, along with a lot of supplies. To keep things organized and moving quickly, I will ask that all fey willing to help carry humans and supplies over the wall wait by the wall."

The swarm of fey surrounding the vehicles shifted to the wall, giving us all room to get out and start unpacking. While Rachel dealt with organizing our vehicle's unloading, I jogged ahead to check on Roni.

Molev was just jumping back from her door when I arrived.

She got out, her booted feet landing with a thud, and scowled at me.

"He actually stopped me from getting out, Andie."

The fey by the wall were all watching us closely.

"First impressions are important, Roni," I said. "Let Molev talk to his people. He's been gone for a long time. After that, I promise he'll introduce you." I looked at him. "Right?"

A big fey—they were all big, but this one was close to Molev's size and had the same long flowing hair—jumped over the wall and landed not far away.

He and Molev stared at each other for a long moment. Then they came together in that same bone-crushing man hug Molev had used on Ben.

"Fine," Roni said softly. "I'll be patient and enjoy the scenery for now. But if I miss out, I'm coming after you."

I glanced at her and saw she was staring at Molev's back. Hopefully, whatever we needed to do to get settled wouldn't take too long.

"I was beginning to worry," the new guy said when he pulled back from Molev.

"I have been away longer than this. What caused your worry?"

The new fey's gaze shifted to me. "We have time to talk about those matters later. I want to meet the female that kept you away."

"I don't have that much power, and he's not that single-minded or shallow," I said, holding out my hand. "I'm Andie."

The fey grunted and took my hand.

"I'm Drav. Welcome to Tolerance. Mya will want to meet you."

"And I'm very interested in meeting Mya. I've heard a bit about her. But before we can, we need to get these people inside. They've been through hell to get here."

While Molev moved off to speak to the fey gathered, the team and I coordinated the volunteers and started unloading supplies. A few of them had bags of personal items, but not much. A young man named Garrett showed up and said he'd be happy to escort the newcomers to their temporary accommodations until they could find a permanent place for everyone.

Bit by bit and person by person, everything went over the wall.

Molev and I were the last ones over, and rather than clearing it in one go, like I knew he could, he landed on top of the wall. I looked out over the cluster of houses in the connected subdivisions.

"This is home now, Andie," he said.

Something in his tone sent a shiver through me and had my core clenching.

"When did I become your wife in your mind?" I asked, turning my head to look at him.

"The moment you gave yourself to me."

It eased a little bit of the tension inside of me because that had been after I'd explained my stance on roles and kids.

"Okay. Then take me to your leader's wife."

He chuckled and jumped down.

"You are the leader's wife."

Disbelief rippled through me as I stared up at him. I'd guessed Molev was higher up–but at the top? Since when did leaders go out on their own to learn more about their perceived enemies? Never, that's when.

The beginning hints of a frown crept into his expression.

"You're thinking too much."

"Doubtful," I said.

He grunted and started jogging down the street with me in his arms.

Knowing he was the leader didn't really change anything in

the moment. And, not knowing in the past had protected him. Yet, I still sort of wished he wasn't the person in charge. Leadership had set responsibility. Instead of arriving and passing the burden of finding a solution to our world's problems to someone else, he and I—

I stopped my thoughts right there and turned my face into his chest. When had we become a team in my head?

"You're thinking too much," he said again as he slowed.

"Probably," I said. "But there's a lot to think about."

He grunted and set me on my feet in front of a normal-looking house. Normal in that it had curtains and intact windows and doors and no blood smears or overgrown grass.

"Whose house is this?" I asked.

"This is Drav and Mya's home." Molev took me by the hand and led me to the front door. Drav, the fey I'd met earlier, opened it before we reached it.

"It's about damn time," a woman said from behind Drav a second before he was nudged aside and a brunette was hugging Molev. He glanced at me and patted her shoulder awkwardly, which I found a little endearing.

"You must be Mya," I said. "I'm Andie."

Mya pulled back and looked at me. Her gaze swept over me, assessing me in one sweep, but not exactly in a judgmental way. She was taking me in like I took people in. Noting details.

"Does he belong to you?" she asked.

"That's what he says," I answered.

She grinned a little. "Yeah, they're like that." She held out her hand to me. "It's good to meet you." I thought I was going in for a handshake. Instead, she pulled me inside the house. "Please tell me you have a ticket to exit this train to crazy town."

I followed her to a normal living room. The house in Fort

Irwin had been safe, but not homey. This place had all the touches that made a house a home. Extra pillows on the sofa. Throw blankets. A cup on the side table. Books in random places. It felt lived in.

"I'm not sure what you mean," I said, bringing my attention back to Mya.

"Take your coat off. Sit." She waved me toward the sofa she already occupied. "Before I get into the woes of Tolerance and surrounding communities, tell me where you're from. How many more humans are out there? What's the world like now?"

"Communities? As in there are more than one like this?" I asked, taking off my jacket, which Molev took from me.

"Yeah. This is Tolerance. We made this place when the people over at Whiteman were trying to use the fey like slaves. Then, when Whiteman fell, we helped the survivors build Tenacity to the north. Same setup with a secure automobile wall around houses in a decent-sized subdivision. But that's where the help stopped. Too many people there still wanted to use the fey without giving the fey what they were due."

"And what are they due?" I asked.

"The same considerations and rights that we have. Sleep. Help when needed. A simple thank you. But some of the people there weren't really ready to allow those things. Those people are gone now." Mya glanced at Molev. "The ones spreading the hate and causing all the trouble went too far. They beat someone to the point he couldn't walk and stole his food. They continued bullying and stealing until they were caught on camera. Hard evidence to kick them out for good. The fey are welcome to come and go in Tenacity as they please now."

Molev grunted.

"Because of that, Matt and June, they're the two heading up things over there, decided some restructuring was needed.

Fewer people crammed into houses and more opportunity for fey cohabitation had us all looking for a third location. Which we found. The wall is going up over there as we speak."

"That sounds amazing," I said. "Are there enough fey to keep the infected away from all of them?"

Her gaze swept over me, and I saw a flicker of judgment this time.

"It's not only the fey's responsibility to keep the infected away," she said. "We need to share it."

I glanced at Molev, who was quietly standing next to Drav. They were both watching us with a look of expectation.

"If you're the leader, why aren't you doing the talking?" I asked Molev.

"They prefer a more laid-back approach now that we're in the picture," Mya said.

"As in we're the leaders?" I managed to ask it without showing a hint of the shock or panic I felt.

"Think of us more as liaisons. We're not responsible for all of humanity. We just need to stand up for the rights on both sides. Voices of reason that they listen to when making decisions."

I gave a dry laugh.

"Not responsible for all of humanity? You're wrong. You want to know how many of us are left? Probably not many. The mountains and the barrier we created using them had kept the infected out until about a week ago. The west fell. The infected are in, drawn to the west by the number of survivors hiding there.

"Once they all turn, that wave of infected will be drawn to the next largest gathering of humans. I'm pretty sure that will be your three communities since Waurlyn, the leader at Fort Irwin, took Molev's warning seriously and started breaking up the camps into smaller groups.

"The survivors are counting on us to find a cure for the infection. So yeah, we kind of are responsible for all of humanity now. Molev said you're immune. We have researchers with us who'd like to study your blood."

Drav growled and stepped forward.

"I know," I said. "No one wants to be a lab rat. Molev's been giving them samples of his blood since we arrived on the west coast months ago. But all their attempts at a cure have failed. If we had months more, maybe they could keep trying with Molev's blood. But we don't. We have another week or two at most before that tide of newly turned infected heads this way. We need your help."

"It's fine," Mya said. "I think I should be able to safely give some blood, but it might not be necessary."

The conversation Drav and Ben had on the top of the truck echoed in my head.

"How far along are you?" I asked, my gaze flicking to her midsection.

"Hard to say. I'm guessing it happened a few weeks after the quakes. Cassie, our resident doctor-in-the-making, thinks I just finished the first trimester."

I glanced at Drav. He was staring at Mya with complete love and devotion in his gaze. Molev watched Mya with equal intensity but an unreadable expression.

"So babies are possible between our two species?" I asked, pushing back the panic by telling myself I had an IUD. I'd be fine.

"Yep. There are a few others who are pregnant too. But that's not the best part. I'm not the only one immune."

"Are you saying that the key to immunity is getting pregnant?" I asked, feeling a little sick. The idea of being forced to have kids made a cold sweat break out between my shoulder blades. I wanted to run. Hide.

Molev took a step toward me, and my head snapped in his direction. Whatever he saw on my face had him hesitating.

"Uh, no," Mya said. "Another woman was bitten and took a test. She's not pregnant, but she's obviously immune too. Our theory was that sleeping with the fey was the key. But I think we proved it." She stood. "Come on. There's something you need to see."

Drav helped her into her jacket, and Molev did the same for me. Only he stopped me from following them out the door and pressed his forehead to mine.

"Nothing has changed," he said. "I will not force a role on you that you do not want. But I won't give you up, Andie. You're mine. Forever. No matter what happens. Do you understand?"

"I think we have bigger issues to deal with at the moment, don't you? Sleeping with a fey for immunity is definitely going to motivate the women who've just arrived. But what about the rest of the people in the world? We still need a cure."

He grunted and let me pass.

Mya was waiting for me outside and gestured for me to walk with her. We started down the road at a leisurely pace with Molev and Drav trailing behind us. Other people were walking around. A few faces were familiar mixed in with some unfamiliar ones. And a lot of fey. They stood off to the side, watching everything.

"Drav let my mom know about the people you brought when you first got here," Mya said, noting my attention. "She and Garrett are working together to get everyone settled somewhere here for now. There's more room over at Unity, our new settlement, but we need to give Ryan, my brother, some notice so he can get the houses and supplies ready. Until then, everyone will be safe, warm, and fed."

"That's what Molev promised them," I said. One of the women stopped walking and waved a fey over from the side. I heard her introduce herself and ask if he had time to give her a tour of Tolerance.

"Oh, I like her," Mya said softly.

"Why is that?"

"No hesitation toward the fey. That's rare."

"Maybe it was with the people here, but it won't be with the people who arrived with us," I said. "Almost every one has met and spoken to Molev. They understand what he's trying to do and how important it is for us to find a way to live together peacefully. That's why they're here."

She paused and glanced over her shoulder at Molev.

"And just like that, you're forgiven for abandoning us when we needed you most, Molev." She said it playfully, but I could see that weariness creep in again.

"Has it been bad?" I asked.

"It hasn't been easy," she said, moving again. "We found livestock, which really helped boost morale. But people are still afraid and desperate."

"Not a good combination," I said.

"No. It's not. But we're managing. We're working together to find ways to support each other. We started doing classes a few weeks ago to share knowledge and skills. Bakers. Crafters. Cooks. We even have a knitting group."

"Oh, you're really going to like who and what we brought with us then."

"Why's that?" she asked.

"Since selecting the volunteers, they've been working hard to learn a skill. Anything that they wanted. Some learned what they set out to learn; some didn't. But we brought books to help us fill in the gaps. Farming. Engineering. Electrical. Plumbing. Chemistry."

"Wow. That's impressive."

We turned down another street.

"We tried to think of everything we'd need before we left. Molev said not to worry about supplies, that his people could find those, so my team and I focused on skills." I glanced at her. "I know the fey are particularly interested in females, but we have a few trustworthy, good men with us too."

"Don't worry. The fey won't discriminate against who they take in. As long as the person can accept the fey for who and what they are and don't cause problems, they're welcome here."

I mentally cringed.

"Um, there's one person in my group who may require a bit of leniency in the causing problems department. She's been really looking forward to coming here."

"Roni is already with Brog," Molev said from behind me. "He will ensure she behaves."

I made a choked sound. "You just left her with him?"

"Don't worry," Mya said. "All the fey understand boundaries and would never force anything."

"I'm not worried about Roni. I'm worried about Brog. She's very straightforward and may not stop to ask about his boundaries."

Mya laughed. "I definitely want to meet her. Don't worry about Brog. He's a big sweetheart and won't offend easily."

I wasn't sure Mya and I were on the same page, but she turned to walk up the sidewalk leading to one of the houses.

She knocked twice and let herself in.

"We're here to see the baby," she said softly. "Anyone awake?"

"We're awake," a male voice called from further in the house.

I followed Mya's lead and kicked off my shoes and removed my jacket. She walked into the living room where several fey were gathered around a petite blonde woman who was openly nursing a newborn baby while conversing with a rather broad-shouldered fey.

"You're strong. Stand your ground, and you'll get everything you want. I promise."

He exhaled heavily and nodded.

"Now, pay up," the blonde said.

I watched the big fey bend down and tenderly kiss the baby's forehead.

"Thank you for your payment," she said when he straightened. "And don't worry, Brog. You've got this."

"Brog?" I echoed, looking at the fey and then back at Molev. "He's the one?"

Molev nodded once, and I looked back at the broad fey.

"Where's Roni?" I asked the fey who was now watching me.

"She is at home."

"You left her?" I mentally cringed.

"Briefly. I will return now."

I watched him hurry out the door and wondered what had happened. Roni had been dreaming of an endless sex fest that would leave her on the edge of broken. How long had it been since I last saw her? An hour? Two, tops? Nowhere near long enough for Roni's dreams to become a reality. Had they not hit it off? Was Brog not interested?

"Andie," Mya said, gaining my attention. "This is Angel and her still-nameless baby. And that's her husband, Shax, and the newest group of spectators."

"Hey, it's good for them," Angel said. "I'm normalizing

what they're going to see a lot of in the next year or so. I always hated the idea of smothering my baby with a blanket just to appease someone else's offended sensibilities. A baby has rights, too." She looked down at the suckling infant. "The right to look at her mama while she's eating. Right, my little snack cake?"

The baby pulled back and gave a very newborn squawk.

"Burping time," Angel said. "Who's up?"

Every fey in the room looked somewhere else with growing panic.

"Me," Mya said, hurrying forward. "I get to burp the baby."

"You can't keep rescuing them," Angel said, handing over the swaddled infant.

"Says you." She kissed the baby's head then settled it on her shoulder. When she did, I saw it clearly. The grey spot near the baby's ear.

"They need to man up and hold her at some point," Angel said.

"We don't want to hurt her," a big fey watching the baby said.

Mya started patting the baby's back. Its eyes opened, and it looked right at me. One very human blue eye and one very fey eye.

I could feel Angel's gaze on me as I watched.

"So she doesn't have a name yet?" I asked.

"Not yet," Angel said. "Shax and I are still talking it over. She's special and needs a special name, you know?"

I pulled my gaze from the baby to look at Angel.

"My mom named me Andromeda. She wanted me to grow up to be something great. Until a few months ago, I was a barista. My brother Apollo was meant to be something great, too. A power player, you know? He got a lot closer than me.

He's a heart surgeon. But he did that because of our grandpa, not because of the mantle my parents tried forcing him to wear. Give her a name like Daisy, and let her be a kid."

Angel's slow smile assured me I hadn't crossed a line.

"I like how you think, Andie. She'll have enough pressure on her the way it is. I heard some researchers came with you."

"News travels fast here," I said.

"You have no idea," Angel said.

"How old's the baby?" I asked.

"I had her yesterday. I was a bit over five months when the earthquakes happened."

"So a human baby with fey traits." I glanced at Molev. "She looks like Sarah, the woman in the trials."

He nodded gravely, his gaze not shifting from the tiny infant in Mya's arms. A very healthy-looking baby except for the differences. But for how long?

CHAPTER SIXTEEN

"CAN MOLEV HOLD HER?" I ASKED.

Mya chuckled, and Angel's face lit up at the suggestion. Unlike the other fey in the room, Molev didn't panic when Mya approached him. His gaze shifted from the infant who was barely bigger than his hand to Mya.

"How do I hold her without hurting her?" he asked.

"Cross your arm over your stomach."

He did it all wrong, and she looked at me. "Can you help?"

Between the two of us, we had the baby draped over his forearm and secured against his body in no time.

"How does that feel?" Mya asked.

"I have never been more unsure of anything in my life," Molev said. "Too loose and I will drop her. Too tight and I will hurt her."

"You're doing great," Mya said. "Now just walk around with her."

I saw the chink in his armor when he lifted his gaze from the baby to look at Mya.

"No," he said.

He was starting to panic, but I doubted it was for the same reason I was now worried.

"Do you see now how wanting a baby and having one are two different things?" I asked.

He frowned at me and looked at the baby, then Angel.

"I have complete faith that you won't drop her," she said. "Go ahead. Walk."

He took one tentative step then another, making his way around the table in the dining area.

"See?" she said, looking at Shax. "Nothing to it, babe. Have Mya and Andie help you next so we don't have to have someone spend the night again."

Shax grunted, acknowledging her, but not looking away from the baby and Molev.

"So you've seen someone else like snack cake there?" Mya asked, drawing my attention.

I glanced at her and wondered how much to say in front of everyone.

"Yeah. At Fort Irwin. Sarah was a volunteer in the trials," I said, keeping it vague.

When I didn't say more, Mya nodded. "So now that you've seen the baby, what conclusion have you drawn?"

More than I wanted to think about, truthfully, but I focused on the conclusion she had likely hoped I would draw and the reason behind this field trip.

"Molev mentioned that you have grey spots. How many other women have them?" I asked.

"Every single woman who's been sleeping with a fey more than a few weeks," Mya said. "Eden, the other woman who was bitten, has them as well. At first, I thought my spots were due to the time I spent in their caves. But once I started getting sick again up here and saw more spots, I started to wonder if it was the same sickness coming back or something else. Then, when I found out I was pregnant, I thought the spots were because of that. Now, I think it has nothing to do with pregnancy and everything to do with unprotected sex with Drav."

"That does seem the most likely explanation. I think the researchers will learn more if they can take samples from everyone," I said.

Mya started to frown.

"I've watched the doctor take several samples from Molev," I said. "She took a little more than normal because of his size, but she was careful to monitor his counts too. She isn't some mad scientist who's going to strap people down. She *is* super driven to find a cure, but not at the cost of someone else's life."

"So you want to tell her everything?" Mya asked.

I glanced at Molev, who was still pacing with the baby. Only now, he was watching me.

"I see no reason not to at this point. Those researchers are the only means we have to find a way to end this for good. All of this..." I gestured to the house and the baby. "It's just a lie you're telling yourselves so you don't have to acknowledge the truth."

"And what's the truth?" Mya asked, maintaining her calm just like me.

"That we're already outnumbered and living on borrowed time.

"I've seen Molev kill hundreds of infected. He can easily wipe out a group of twenty before they reach me. But what happens when it's him trying to protect me from one thousand at one time? Because those are the numbers that we're going to be facing. No matter how strong the fey are or how fast they are, we *will* be overwhelmed. And that's just dealing with the infected."

Everyone in the room was watching me now.

"So the doctor and her researchers aren't just looking for a cure then," Mya said. "They're looking for a way to stop the infected and the hounds."

"That's what we need them to find," I said. "Without that, I don't see how we have any hope."

Mya glanced at Drav, the baby, then at Angel.

"Sorry for the heavy conversation," Mya said.

"Don't worry about it," Angel said. "It's the world we live in. I'd rather have the truth than hide from it. Where are the researchers now?"

"They are speaking with Kerr and Cassie at Eitri's," Drav said. "Eitri has a large, empty basement the researchers can use to set up their equipment."

"Well, if they're willing to make a house call," Angel said, "I'm willing to let them take a sample from me and a really tiny one from Daisy."

"Daisy?" Mya asked with a growing smile. "Is that her name?"

"I think so," Angel said, looking at Shax. "A pretty, delicate flower that grows in the heat of summer. It feels peaceful. I like it."

"Daisy," Shax said with a nod. "I like it too." His eyes shifted to the baby.

"Time to give Daisy back," Mya said, going to Molev. She removed the baby from his arm and headed toward Shax. The big guy only hesitated for a moment before he positioned his arm like Molev had.

"My Daisy," Shax said, "I will protect you with my life."

"I think my ovaries are melting," Angel said, watching him lean in to press a kiss to the baby's head.

"Come on, guys," Mya said. "Show's over. Time to let Mama and Papa have some quiet alone time."

All the fey who'd been silently listening to everything started for the door. Their farewells included, "Thank you for allowing us to see your breasts," and "Your nipples are very pretty." Angel treated each comment casually, responding with a "You're welcome," or a "Thank you."

I put my jacket on again and followed Mya out the door.

"So what's going to stop the researchers from using what they find to kill the people we love?" Mya asked once we reached the street.

"We will," I said.

She snorted. "Now, who's telling themselves a lie?"

"I don't believe I'm being self-deluded. I've been outside these walls, Mya. I've seen what's left of civilization between here and the barrier. And it's not much. Any form of organized society was on the other side of that barrier. The one that just fell. So who do you think will go after the fey? Everyone who was left was evacuated and scattered into smaller camps. They'll be defenseless by now with whatever trained personnel relocated to try to stop the main body of infected. How long will they last, picked off little by little? How long until the east coast falls and we're all that's left to care about who lives or dies?"

Mya sighed and looked up at the sky.

"We already got the message that the east coast has fallen," she said.

"When?" I asked.

"Several weeks ago."

I stopped walking and looked at Molev, who was silently following.

"We're screwed," I said, realizing what the old message meant. "There's not enough time."

His arm snaked out wicked fast, and he had me by the back of my head and against his chest a second later.

"You will not die," he said, setting his forehead to mine. "I waited lifetimes to find you. I will not lose you now."

"Then we can't hesitate with this. We need the researchers gathering samples and testing around the clock."

He kissed me and held my hand as we walked the rest of the way to Eitri's house.

My stomach growled as Mya knocked, a reminder that we'd arrived well after lunch but hadn't yet eaten. Molev heard and tucked me to his side.

"Eitri will have food for you," he said.

"I'd settle for something to drink and a hot shower," I said.

"Careful about where you shower," Mya said. "They don't view nudity the same as we do."

"Yeah, I'm getting that picture," I said.

The door opened, and a confused-looking fey stood there.

"Eitri, we need to speak with the researchers," Drav said.

The fey stepped aside and let us into the chaos that was his home. Packing containers sat all over the place in various states. Some open. Some with packing peanuts littering the floor around it. Some overturned.

"Everything okay in here?" I asked.

"Everything is fine," the doctor said, appearing in an open doorway. She already had her lab coat on and was tapping away at a data pad. "How can I help you?"

"This is the immune woman," I said, gaining all of the doctor's attention. "But there's a twist to this immunity thing. She's pregnant. More women are immune, and a woman who was already pregnant with a human baby before sleeping with one of the fey gave birth to a baby that has similar mutations to what you saw in the trial subjects."

The doctor stared at me for a moment.

"I need to examine the baby."

"The mother, Angel, has agreed to allow you to do a house call and take a small blood sample." I hesitated for a second. "What are the chances the baby will be all right?"

"When was the baby born?" the doctor asked.

"Yesterday," Mya said. "Why are you concerned about the baby?"

"None of our trials were successful," the doctor said. "However, rather than speculate, I'd like to do an examination first."

She turned back to the door and called, "Kerr. Cassie. I know how you can help."

A redhead and a fey appeared from downstairs a moment later.

"Cassie, I need blood samples from every woman having intercourse with a fey," the doctor said. "I need an approximate duration and frequency noted with each sample."

"When they started having sex and how often?" Cassie asked.

"Exactly."

"I can do that," Cassie said. "I think it'll be easier to have everyone come here if you're okay with it."

The doctor nodded and looked at Kerr.

"I need a semen sample, please." The doctor held out a plastic cup with a lid on it to Kerr.

Cassie looked at the cup, then Kerr, and started to grin. After taking the cup on Kerr's behalf, she asked Eitri, "Can you have everyone spread the word that we need to see the women having sex with fey as soon as possible?"

He grunted and left, which was probably a good thing

because the doctor produced two more cups and gave them to Drav and Molev.

"While they're providing samples, Cassie can do the blood draws for both of you."

I sat at the table and rolled up my sleeve for Cassie as Kerr, Molev, and Drav all shared looks and glanced at their cups.

"I know you're not hesitating because you're shy," Mya said, watching them.

"They're probably wondering if we'll help fill the cup," Cassie said.

Mya and Cassie shared smiles as the doctor looked up from her data pad.

"I would prefer uncontaminated samples," she said.

"Don't worry," Mya said. "They'll figure it out. They're smart."

Drav grunted and headed into the bathroom first while I estimated how long ago Molev and I first started having sex. Frequency was noted as sporadic.

Cassie wasn't great at drawing blood, but she wasn't the worst I'd had. Drav emerged with his topped-off cup just as Mya took my place. She yelped a little for her draw and paled, but she survived the process as well. Drav was helping her to her feet when Kerr left the bathroom with his cup. Molev gave me a long, measuring look before disappearing inside.

I inwardly smirked and watched the doctor add the samples to the tray. When it was Cassie's turn, the doctor gave her pointers on how to draw blood.

"If any of their partners show up, please ask them for a sample as well. Bring Molev's down when he's finished. I'm going to pack a kit and ask directions to Angel's house." The doctor disappeared.

"I think our work here is done," Mya said. "Let us know if you guys need anything."

She started for the door and paused. "What happened during the trials?"

"The researchers were trying to create a vaccine using Molev's blood. However, the results weren't good. His blood doesn't just contain immunity but the infection as well. So it changed the volunteers, giving them grey spots first before they turned infected. It took three days, on average, from start to finish."

Mya stared at me before facing Drav. "I need a nap."

Cassie looked at me as she and Drav left.

"There was no easy way to say that," I said.

"No, there wasn't. I think that's why so many people lie. It's easier than the truth, but lies rarely do any good."

"I'm Andie, by the way," I said, realizing I'd never actually introduced myself. "If you don't need us for anything else, I wouldn't mind leaving and getting something to eat."

"Nice to meet you, Andie. I think we're fine for now. Go get some rest. From what I've heard, the last few weeks haven't been easy on you."

"Nothing's been easy for any of us since the earthquakes."

She nodded and walked us to the door. I'd just gotten my jacket on when someone knocked.

"That'll be my first patient," she said, opening the door to a fey carrying a woman.

"Heard you need my blood and Solin's sperm. What kind of science experiments are we up to these days?" the woman asked.

"Welcome back," the fey said to Molev, who was standing just behind me. "This is my wife, Brooke. She's pregnant."

Molev's hands settled on my shoulders.

"Congratulations, Solin. Care for her well."

The fey nodded at the same time the woman said, "Oh, he does. Trust me."

We let the pair pass then hurried out the door as Brooke started asking questions about whether help was allowed when filling the cup.

"News really travels fast here," I commented.

"So do we." Molev knocked my feet out from under me and caught me in his arms.

I scowled up at him. "You could just ask."

He grunted and started running with me. The house that he turned toward was like any other. Only, inside, it reminded me more of the house on base. All the homey touches were missing.

He knocked the door shut with his foot, put me down, and started peeling clothes off of me. The impatience in his moves stopped all the background thoughts in my head. Molev became my complete focus.

He caught my face between his hands.

"How hungry are you, Andie?" he asked.

I knew what answer he wanted from me and considered denying him. But the heat in his gaze and the urgency of his movements had my core clenching and agreeing with him that I wasn't *that* hungry.

"It can wait," I said.

"Good, because I can't."

Squatting, he pulled my pants and underwear down in one tug. Hands on my ass, he pulled me forward and slicked his tongue through my folds. I tipped as he fell backward. Fast reaction time saved me from face-planting on the floor as he kept my thighs pinned to his ears. His tongue speared deep as I straightened, and his hands lifted me just enough so I could ride his face as he devoured me.

My orgasm ripped through me within minutes. It barely settled when he stood with me and pinned me against the wall. I tasted myself when he claimed my lips for a searing kiss.

"Tell me to slow down," he panted when he finally broke away.

"No retreating," I said, grabbing his hair and pulling him back down for more.

He groaned into my mouth. A second later, he was positioned at my entrance. I wriggled, trying to escape him. He tore his lips from mine and looked at me. My steady gaze held his.

"I don't want to think or give," I said. "It's okay if it hurts just a little."

He silently snarled, and his fingers curled around my neck.

"I will never let you go, Andie."

"Good thing I don't want you to. I'm glad you love taking what I pretend I'm unwilling to give. Now make it good."

He chuckled low, released my throat, and tangled his fingers in my hair. Slowly, he pressed me down to my knees. Then, with his free hand, he pried my mouth open.

"Take me, Andie. As much as you can."

It was the hottest blow job of my life with his hands in my hair, controlling every aspect of how he used my mouth. All while watching me closely. If my eyes watered, he eased up. He never went too deep or blocked my air for too long. And when he came, he praised me for each swallow. And he kissed me afterward. That was the best part.

"Now that I've fed you, you're mine," he said, carrying me to the bedroom.

Time blurred. I lost count of the number of positions and orgasms. He stopped once, disappearing while I caught my breath, and reappeared with a glass of water.

While I drank, he kissed my thighs and folds. We showered together. The water felt good on the thunder down under. Then he fell to his knees and ate me out like a starving man again.

I passed out after that.

When I came to, he was slowly fucking me on the bed. His hand was on my throat the way I liked—barely-there pressure while his thumb stroked my skin.

I clenched around him hard, taking in what he was doing to me without my knowledge.

"Did I go too far?" he asked softly, watching me closely. "Should I have waited?"

"No."

That orgasm dragged out until it felt like it was never going to end. His sudden release pushed me off the edge I hadn't realized I'd been standing on, and I disintegrated into a million pieces underneath him.

"My pretty, beautiful, Andie. All the remaining moments in our lives will never be enough."

He kissed my eyelids and my brow, bringing me back to myself.

"Now we have to be done," I said. "I don't think I'll be able to walk tomorrow."

"You will. Sleep, my Andie. Sunrise will come soon."

He left the bed and returned with a cloth. I felt no shame, lying there as he cleaned me up. I'd earned every moment of his tender care. Eyes closed, enjoying the cool feel of the cloth, I drifted to sleep.

Sweat and the need to kick off the covers woke me. But it wasn't covers that I needed to remove. There weren't any on me. Only Molev's front pressed against my back and the weight of his arm over my waist. His hand was anchored over my stomach, keeping me from moving as he slept behind me.

I lightly tapped his arm.

"I have to pee," I said. "Don't get up."

He released me, and I rolled away from him. My legs twinged and ached. Walking to the bathroom was the worst. Sitting wasn't easy. Standing again had me rethinking my life choices. I used a washcloth to gingerly clean myself and swore I would never provoke Molev to that level again.

However, when I returned and saw Molev awake and on his back with his meat mallet standing proud, I knew I was in trouble. The man dripped with sexiness...and his need for another round.

"I think you broke me," I said.

"I should check."

He disappeared from the bed. Hands gripped my waist from behind. And the next thing I knew, my back was pinned to the mattress with my knees pressed into my chest. His tongue carefully swept over my clit, nothing else.

"It looks tender," he said. "I will be very careful."

He was and had me crying out in minutes.

"Come," he said, drawing me into his arms. He led me to the shower where he washed me. I returned the favor by washing him until he groaned his release against my stomach. He kissed my forehead and turned off the water once I was clean again.

"Soon, we will be able to spend the day touching each other as we please. But not today. Kerr is growing impatient waiting for us."

"What do you mean? Why is he waiting?"

"He didn't say."

"When did you talk to him?"

"He spoke to me when I was checking your pussy. He's in the living room."

I turned in Molev's arms and looked up at him while he was drying me off.

"Are you saying he was talking to you from the living room while you were eating me out in the bedroom?"

Molev blinked at me.

"Oh, yeah, you know you're in trouble for that one," I said. "Kerr is too. You don't just let yourself in someone's house. You wait to be let in."

Molev took me by the shoulders.

"What are privacy and modesty other than lies we tell ourselves?" he asked with a hint of a smile. "Do you think Kerr is ignorant of what I'm doing to you if he stands on the sidewalk instead of in the living room? We hear well, Andie. Many fey will know the way you sound when I bring you pleasure. You have volume. And do not dare suppress yourself. Be who you are. Do not force yourself into a role that you do not want."

I stared up at him, processing what he was saying. I didn't like that he was right. Back at Irwin, the team had known what we were doing in the other house. The only difference was they didn't have super hearing to listen to it. But what did it matter if someone heard us going at it?

It only mattered if I made it matter. And there were too many other things for us to worry about than that.

"Okay," I said. "You're right."

He kissed me on the mouth and handed me the towel.

"Kerr says an ice pack will help with your tenderness. I will return quickly."

He walked out the door, fully naked.

I shook my head that he thought I was just going to wait here and pulled on a clean Molev-sized shirt. Skipping everything else, I went out to see what was up with the early morning visit.

Kerr was in the kitchen with Molev, speaking softly while my man bent over in front of him to look through the freezer, displaying all his goods.

I almost died at Kerr's revolted expression.

"I need to visit Roni today," I said to myself.

She would love hearing what I'd just witnessed. And then she'd run to tell Steve just to watch him turn inside out.

CHAPTER SEVENTEEN

MOLEV FOUND WHAT HE WAS LOOKING FOR AND STRAIGHTENED.

"Any update on the testing?" I asked Kerr as Molev wrapped the ice pack in a soft cloth.

"Yes. Daisy is perfectly healthy. No signs of her cells succumbing to the infection."

Immense relief flooded me. And not just for the baby. For all of us women sleeping with the fey. While not letting myself dwell on it, the moment I saw the baby, I'd understood there was a very real possibility that I could end up evolving into an infected like Sarah had.

"The doctor has been looking at the rest of the samples all night," Kerr said. "She confirmed that every female having sex with a fey is immune, like Daisy, and has asked for new volunteers that she can monitor. Females who have not had intercourse with a fey but who are willing to start so the transition can be studied."

While Kerr explained, Molev set the wrapped ice pack on a soft chair and led me to it. I sat gingerly. The cool lump was a little uncomfortable at first but started doing its job quickly.

"The samples from the existing females are too similar to ours," Kerr continued. "The doctor believes that, by analyzing the change as it happens, she will find the answers we need."

I considered the big picture for a moment.

"We need to approach this carefully. Yes, we need the cure, but we need to think about after the cure, too, when we recruit for this." I glanced at both fey. "We told the people with us that we were bringing them here to improve relations...that the people outside of this community were suspicious of the fey and their intentions. How is it going to sound to them if we start asking people to have sex with the fey in the name of science without proof? While we can speak to our people and let them know what's going on and what we need, I'm afraid that might make them feel singled out and start them questioning why we really brought them here."

I thought of Roni and wished we wouldn't have shipped her off with Brog already. She would have been an ideal choice for this assignment.

"Instead of only targeting the women we brought, we should spread the word to everyone. News travels fast here, right? Then we let the people know everything. Daisy's birth. The variation in her eyes. The confirmed immunity in her and the other women with fey partners. Rather than making it about sex, impress the significance of what the researchers believe that immunity means. That a cure is possible. For everyone. Then let it be known that the doctor is looking for volunteers so we can pinpoint what she was missing in her previous trials.

"By spreading the word to everyone, the newcomers will feel included in the community rather than that we're trying to use them right from the start. The existing community will hopefully begin to understand what the fey are trying to do—

which is to save everyone—and we might get more volunteers that way too."

Kerr and Molev both nodded their agreement.

"Will we have any trouble finding fey volunteers?" I asked.

Kerr and Molev shared a look.

"Any female who is willing to do this will have her pick of fey," Molev said.

"Okay. Then, rather than having the fey speak to the women, I think it should come from another woman. Let me get dressed and—"

Molev's hands on my shoulders kept me sitting.

"Ask Emily to spread the word in Tenacity," Molev said to Kerr. "See if Mya is willing to speak with the females here. We will start speaking to the females who arrived with us after Andie has eaten."

My mind drifted back to how he'd "fed" me last night, and I winced as I clenched around nothing. Molev could only be partly responsible for my current condition. I'd absolutely played a part in it as well.

However, once Kerr left, Molev told me to stay where I was, got himself ready, and made me a real breakfast. While I watched him move around the kitchen, what Kerr had revealed sunk in.

"I'm immune too, then, aren't I?" I said.

Molev grunted. "You have a grey mark on your inner thigh."

I looked. The spot was light and no bigger than my thumbnail. If I hadn't been looking for it, I would have thought it was a bruise from the night before.

"It changes nothing," Molev said, handing me a plate of waffles.

"It changes everything," I said. "It means we have a better

chance of surviving this. Even if it's still minuscule, it's bigger than it was before."

We ate, and when I stood again, I felt like I could walk without a limp.

After dressing, we left the house and went to Mya's parents' home. They were hosting a few of the women. But more importantly, Julie knew where the rest were being housed.

The women weren't ignorant of the situation with the researchers or life in Tolerance. It turned out the fey liked to talk, and the women we'd brought with us had been more than willing to listen. Through them, Molev and I learned that over twenty-five human-fey couples already existed, and over half of them were newly expecting. We also heard that one of those couples was a throuple. No one batted an eye at it. In fact, the news that the researchers had proven the immunity of the women in those relationships only made that woman's relationship status make more sense.

But more than that, I was surprised to hear a few of the women admit they were already interested in a certain fey when we brought up the researchers' request for volunteers. The only thing holding the women back was the uncertainty of whether or not the attraction was reciprocated yet. They assured us that, if it was, they wouldn't mind being monitored if something happened.

We sent those women to Eitri's house for initial blood work and left with a list of homes to visit. It took until lunch to meet with everyone and explain what was happening and what was needed, and why.

A young woman was waiting for us at our house when we returned.

"Emily," Molev said when he saw her. "Were you able to speak to the females in Tenacity?"

She smiled at him. "Molev, you are a sight for sore eyes." She looked at me. "I'm Emily. It's nice to meet you, Andie. I've heard a bit about you through the fey grapevine. Welcome to Tolerance. If you two have a few minutes, I can let you know how things went in Tenacity."

I liked Emily's open personality. She immediately felt like one of those rare people who said what they meant without any hidden agendas.

"Come in," Molev said, opening the door for us both. "Have you eaten?"

"I haven't yet. I came straight from Tenacity."

"Join us," he said.

She and I hung our jackets as he moved to the kitchen and started pulling out supplies from the refrigerator. Supplies I didn't recall from the day before.

"Where did all of that come from?" I asked as we sat to watch him.

"Kerr brought it over this morning," Emily said. "Heard you busted him for interrupting fun-time. He was super grateful you didn't yell at him or tell Cassie. But Cassie already knows about it, so I'm sure he's getting an earful. Speaking of earful… you're going to be in trouble too, Molev. Mya heard about your four-to-one hound fight and isn't happy you risked yourself like that."

I could only stare at Emily for several beats.

"How do you know all of that?" I looked at Molev. "I was with you. When did you have time to share that story?"

"Your team has been great about making friends with the fey here and sharing stories. So, of course, when the fey heard a break in last night's sex-a-thon, they came to pester Molev for more details."

I closed my eyes and rubbed my forehead. "They really were listening all night?"

"Oh. Sorry. Seriously, though, don't even worry about it," she said. "I live with Hannah and Merdon, and that girl is loud. Then again, I know he does stuff on purpose to make her scream like that. He said he had to listen to too many of her bad screams in the past, and the good screams are payment for that. I use headphones to block it out, but honestly, I don't mind. I'm just glad she's finally happy. It's hard to find, you know?

"Anyway, as you're learning, the fey hear everything. They'll talk about anything. And news travels quickly because of it. Which is why Eden and I didn't have any trouble convincing a few volunteers to come over from Tolerance. Proven immunity is a tempting carrot to dangle. They should already be getting set up over at Eitri's."

"Thank you, Emily," Molev said, handing us both plates of food. "What else have I missed since I've been gone?"

Emily was a talker but not an over-talker. She outlined everything that had happened since Molev left. The couples who'd gotten together. The breach at Whiteman. Then the breach at Tolerance. How the infected were getting smarter but the humans still couldn't figure out how to let go of prejudices. Finding cattle. Finding people. The classes to teach skills the people needed in order for the communities to thrive independently. How some people had to be kicked out. The arrival of about one hundred more fey, the remaining men Molev had left behind to guard the caves. Plans to meet up with other survivors out there who were looking for safety after hearing the eastern border had fallen. The progress on the third community. Seeing a hound in daylight.

And Adam.

The man who'd been bitten and kept alive to study.

"The fey know not to talk about it in front of June," Emily said. "She's still grieving. And Tor is absolutely amazing about supporting her, but it's still emotionally hard for her to know Adam is alive and suffering. Well, not suffering. The fey are really good about taking care of him. Before Roni came, Brog would go over and play the video games he knew Adam liked where Adam could watch. They said his eyes are changing color. Turning red. He doesn't do anything. He just sits there and watches everything."

I glanced at Molev. "The doctor will want to see him."

"No humans have been allowed in," Emily said. "Drav said it's too dangerous."

"We cannot risk the doctor or the researchers," Molev said.

"Then we won't," I said. "Emily mentioned cameras earlier. Maybe we can hook something up so the doctor can study him remotely, and Kerr could take any samples she might need."

Molev grunted.

"I'll take that as a yes. We can grab the cameras from Tenacity when we go there to talk to Matt about that radio he has. We need to send a message to Rick, if possible, and find out how things are there."

Molev took my empty plate to the sink.

"I'll leave you two to it then," Emily said, standing. "If you need anything, let me know. I'm happy to help."

We left the house together, and I watched her walk off in the direction of Eitri's home. She planned to check on the volunteers there to ensure everything was going smoothly and to just be there for the women who were jumping into uncertain relationships.

As I watched her, I realized what Molev had encouraged by standing back and letting others speak and make decisions. He wasn't the leader of these communities. He was *a* leader. One person that people could go to for help and answers, but not the only person.

I laced my fingers through his.

"You're pretty smart. You know that?" I said.

He smiled slightly at me and swung me up into his arms.

"I want to return to the house with you," he said.

"But you won't. Because you know I need more time, and we have a lot to do." I rested my head against his shoulder, and he just held me for a moment.

"I love you, Andie," he said softly. "You are the only light in my dark world."

Quelling my instant need to hide from that level of confession, I met his gaze and tried to give something back instead.

"You have very pretty eyes, Molev. I think I could look at them every morning for the rest of my life and never get tired of seeing them."

His smile widened, and he pressed a passionate kiss to my mouth before taking off at a run. He jumped the wall with me and started for Tenacity. It was a healthy distance away, but at his speed, it didn't take long until I spotted their wall. People walked the top of it. Mostly humans with a fey or two mixed in.

The streets of Tenacity were busier than Tolerance with more people gathered by a large pole shed.

A man spotted us and came jogging over as Molev set me down.

"Heard you were back, Molev. Welcome to Tenacity. June, Tenacity's new co-leader, should be around here somewhere. Let me introduce you."

"Matt Davis," Molev said, "this is Andie, my—"

"Partner," I said before he could claim me as his wife again. I shook Matt's hand. "We heard a lot about what's been happening here from Emily and wanted to return the favor with news from the outside if you have time."

Matt nodded and waved for us to follow him. When he spotted a fey, he called, "Can you find Tor and June for me?"

The fey ran off as we followed Matt to a house. It was more lived-in than Molev's, with hints of clutter here and there, but definitely not as cozy as Mya and Drav's place. On a side table, I spotted the radio.

"Have a seat," he said, gesturing to the sofa.

I withdrew the folder from my jacket as I sat and handed it over to him.

"This is the information your predecessor failed to pass to you. Frequencies and when to use them to contact the rest of the bases."

He took the folder and opened it to stare down at the information.

"I can't even imagine how things might have gone if I'd had this from the beginning," he said. "I've heard a little about what it was like out there for you. The barrier that was keeping the infected back. Camps of survivors. How you managed to leave just before it all fell."

He ran a hand through his hair.

"I have to admit…I'm both relieved and disappointed it fell. I don't want us to be the last of humankind. But I also don't want to worry about something interfering with the coexistence we've finally managed."

I heard the underlying warning in his words.

"Molev believes that the infected are drawn to humans. The larger the group, the stronger the draw. Right now, anyone who might care about what's happening here is too busy trying to stay alive. And even if they do survive, we all have bigger problems. Once the infected are done chasing the humans on the coasts, we'll be next. And we won't survive the numbers headed our way."

Matt glanced down at the papers. "I know you're not telling me to give up. You wouldn't have come all the way here and handed me these papers if that were the case."

"The researchers with us are working on a cure for the plague. And the team we left behind was working on an easier way to stop the hellhounds. The infected pose a threat because of their numbers and the hounds because of their indestructibility. We need the answers to both if we want to win. We need to get word back to Fort Irwin that there is a group of immune humans here and hope there's someone left to update us with their progress."

He stared down at the paper for another minute before nodding. "All right. I'll make it happen and let you know if we get an answer."

"Thank you," I said just as his front door swung open.

A young Asian woman came in, followed closely by a fey. Molev turned to nod at the man.

"Tor," he said.

"Molev." The big fey grinned and set his hands on the woman's shoulders. "This is my June."

"Hi, June," I said, standing. "I'm Andie."

"Hello. Heard you were looking for us," she said, glancing at Matt.

"I am. Andie just provided us with the means to communicate with the outside world–if there's anything left of it."

"What do you mean?" she said.

"That barrier message was as bad as we thought," he said.

"A wave of infected will be heading our way soon," Molev said, looking at Tor. "We need to prepare."

Tor's easygoing stance hardened as he nodded.

"How big of a wave?" June asked.

"Probably hundreds of thousands," I said. "And all at once. We saw a hound gathering the infected together and using them to coordinate an attack."

"And I saw an infected hiding a hound and using livestock as bait in an attempt to draw us out," June said, reaching back for Tor. "They're getting a lot smarter. How can we prepare for hundreds of thousands?"

"Higher walls?" Matt suggested.

"That won't keep them out forever," June said. "Not with those numbers."

"We don't need to keep them out forever. We just need to buy the researchers enough time to find the miracle we need," I said. "And higher walls could help with that."

Matt and June shared a look.

"It's not going to be easy," June said. "We humans were next to useless when it came to helping lift cars into place. And that was with Unity's main wall, which was on the ground. A third layer's going to be impossible for us."

"My brothers and I will add onto the walls," Molev said.

"We'll provide whatever help we can," Matt said.

"I have a roster of who's living where," June said. "I'll use that to get a new shift schedule together and send it over to Mya and Drav. Unless the two of you want it."

"Since we're not sure what you're talking about, stick with Mya and Drav."

"We'll create a work schedule for the walls in all three places," she said. "Even though another layer will require more fey power than human, there are still ways for us to help. So I'll ensure we have the right number of humans and fey in eight-hour shifts. This way everyone, including the fey, gets a break."

"We understand," Molev said. "Divide my brothers and me equally between all three locations, but add an extra shift for us each day. We will need to gather the materials we need for building as well."

"Mya's not going to like putting that much of the workload on you," June said. "But I'll assign groups to go out for cars with a fey escort. If I assign ninety per location, that leaves thirty-four fey who could assist with gathering supplies."

I glanced at him. "Three hundred and two fey? Why did you ask for five hundred females, then?"

"Your people love to give less than they promise."

"You continue to impress me," I said, shaking my head slightly while doing my best to hide my concern. They had almost half the numbers I'd believed. Just over three hundred fey to hold off hundreds of thousands of infected? How could we hope to survive?

Molev was watching me too closely again, so I stood. "We'll leave you to the scheduling then. Send whatever you come up with to Drav and Mya. Molev and I will stay focused on helping the researchers."

"If you require anything, send word," Molev said, taking my hand.

He didn't try to pick me up as soon as we left the house. Instead, he let me walk to the wall and think in silence.

"I'm worried all of this won't be enough," I said. "Part of me wants a plan B. Something to fall back on if the walls are breached or if the vaccine doesn't work. But the logical part of me knows there will be nowhere to go that would be safe forever if we don't find a solution."

"Have faith, Andie. We will find a way. We did not come this far, and get this close to having a life we never dreamed possible, to lose it now."

He swung me up into his arms and cleared the wall. This time, I buried my face in his chest and just let myself be held by him.

Someone called Molev's name the moment we landed inside Tolerance's wall.

"Go," I said. "I wanted to check on Roni and the rest of the team anyway."

He gave me a long look then nodded.

I found Steve and Brandon easily enough. They were staying with a group of human women we'd "trained." Sid, Roland, and Katie were staying with Ben.

"Good," Roland said when he answered the door and saw it was me. "You can talk to them."

"Them?" I asked as I entered.

"Ben and Katie. Sid and I can't do it anymore."

I was about to ask for a better explanation when I heard Ben say, "Katie, would you like me to rub your breasts?"

Katie's response was slightly muffled. "Please go away, Ben."

"The awkwardness continues to escalate," Roland said. "First, it was offers to make her something to eat. But when she said she wasn't feeling well, it switched to him trying to physically comfort her. Hugs. Back rubs. Now, boob rubs." He waved his hand. "Katie hasn't come out of her room since breakfast."

"I don't know how to help her," Ben said, appearing from the hallway to the right.

"Sometimes, people just need some space and some quiet time," I said. "Molev had to figure that out too. Why don't you go find him and ask him how he knows when I need quiet time?"

Ben nodded and left without another word.

"How?" Roland said. "I've been trying to get him to leave her alone since this morning."

"That's why it didn't work. He doesn't want to leave her alone. He wants her attention. He's going to Molev to figure out how to give her what she needs while still getting what he needs." I slipped off my jacket and headed down the hall.

"He's gone, Katie," I called.

The closed door swung open, and Katie peered out. A second later, she burst into tears and threw her arms around me.

"Whoa," I said, hugging her in return. "This isn't like you. What's going on? Did he actually try to touch your boobs?"

She gave a warbly laugh. "No, he just keeps talking about them. I think this is my mental twig snapping. Ben's been extremely sweet and kind. I've just never been so…"

"Pursued?" I guessed.

"Exactly. It's non-stop, and I just need a minute to be alone and hear my own thoughts instead of 'Katie, are you hungry?' 'Katie, do you want a drink?' 'Katie, can I rub your feet?' 'Katie, do you need another blanket?' Katie. Katie. Katie." She pulled back and looked at me, her eyes red and a little wild. "I feel like I'm going insane."

"You look like it too," I said. "Want to get out of here for a bit while he's away and check on Roni with me?"

"Yes. God, yes." She stepped around me and hurried for the door, waving to Roland and Sid, who were both in the kitchen.

"Thanks for trying, guys," she called.

I hustled to get my jacket on and follow her out the door.

"Which way?" she asked, obviously on a mission to get off the streets as soon as possible.

I led her to the house that Molev had pointed out earlier and knocked on the door.

A disheveled fey with a major hard-on answered.

"Um, did we come at a bad time?" I asked.

"No. Roni is inside." He strode out the door without a backward glance.

"Brog?" Roni called. "Don't you dare leave!"

"Hey, Roni. He's already gone," I said, stepping inside.

"Dammit." The word was filled with enough frustration that Katie hesitated on the step.

"It's Roni or Ben," I said. "Pick your poison."

She sighed and reluctantly entered.

The house was big with a very cozy sectional couch in the center of the living room. Beyond that, I spotted Roni in a crop top that barely brushed the bottom of her boobs and a thong, clearly showing off her recent grooming efforts. She was holding a casserole dish in her oven-mitted hands.

"Your timing is shit," she said angrily, plopping the dish on top of the stove. "I almost had him that time."

CHAPTER EIGHTEEN

"PROBLEMS IN PARADISE?" I ASKED, INTRIGUED.

"Uh, do you want us to go?" Katie asked from behind me.

"No, I want your help. He's not giving up the goods. It's been twenty-four hours, and he's run out of this house at least six times rather than just having sex with me." I heard a hint of hurt at the end just before she crossed her arms and glared at the door. "I don't quit, and he's an idiot if he thinks I will."

"How about you put some pants on, and we'll trade notes," Katie said. "Ben won't leave me alone."

Roni looked even angrier. "I know. Half the fey here heard about the 'sex with a human study,' and every single one of them is begging to pop a nut with any willing female in the name of science. Except Brog. I'm here. I'm willing—damn, am I willing—and nothing."

"Pants?" Katie asked again.

Roni gave her a death glare.

"Just go cover up so you two can compare notes," I said. "Shaking what your mama gave you while taking that out of the oven obviously wasn't working anyway."

She snorted. "Says you. I'm positive I felt a finger brush a cheek. And I'm not talking about the ones I use to smile."

"Please," Katie begged. "No more."

Roni sighed and stalked off to the bedroom.

"Don't be too hard on her," I said. "She's figured out how to keep a fey at bay."

"You're right. Enduring the unsolicited view of her crotch crater in exchange for some peace is worth it."

"I heard that!" Roni yelled from the bedroom.

Katie grinned at me.

I shook my head and started checking kitchen drawers for a fork. Whatever Roni had made smelled amazing. She reappeared just as I stabbed into the cheesy top.

"Might as well help yourself," she said. "I doubt I'll see him again until you two leave."

I sat back and ate as Katie and Roni shared their stories.

Katie related how Ben had been nice enough to offer her a place to stay and smart enough to extend the invite to Sid and Roland when she'd hesitated. But from the moment she'd set foot in his house, he'd been suffocating her with attention.

Meanwhile, the second Brog had carried Roni over the threshold, she'd ripped off her clothes and told him to plow her like a ten-year fallow field filled with rocks. He'd run. When he'd returned, she'd offered him head, thinking it would help "loosen him up a little." He'd run again. Each outrageous attempt at seducing him had ended the same.

"Last night, I almost had him," she said. "He fell asleep on the couch after we'd wrestled a bit."

"You wrestled him?" I asked.

"Well, it wasn't like he was holding still so I could mount him. I had to try something. Anyway, he fell asleep during our standoff, and that string on his pants was already loose from our scuffle. It wasn't a problem to open my present. He's as big as Molev said. I was two seconds from stuffing my mouth and dying a happy woman when he woke up. They move fast. He cleared the couch and was out the door with his dick slapping his abs before I knew he'd even moved."

Katie covered her mouth with her hand.

"You see the difference here, right?" I asked her. "Roni, you need to lose your interest in him. Complete reversal."

"Don't even go where you're going," Katie said when I glanced at her again. "I am not pursuing Ben. That will bite me in the butt fast."

"Or if you're lucky, he'll bite you on the butt fast," Roni said with a smirk.

"I think you're right," I said to Katie, ignoring Roni. "Any hint of acceptance from you will be the green light Ben's hoping for. Rather than that, why don't you sit down and talk to him about why you're not interested? Tell him about Ted and that you need more time."

Katie looked down at her hands for a long while. Roni reached out and clasped her arm.

"It's okay to be hurt," Roni said.

Katie nodded without looking up at us.

"The fey are actually super in tune with all the emotional stuff that comes with relationships," Roni said with a final pat. "On the way to the house, Brog was going on about how he wanted to know my heart and my mind. Of course, I set him straight real quick that I was a body-only kind of girl."

"Roni," I said. "You shot your own foot. I warned you that these guys don't do casual. That's probably why he's avoiding you now."

"No shit, Sherlock. I know that. I just need to break him down. The man's been vagina-celibate for thousands of years, and I dumped all the lotion and conditioner out the first time I heard him beating off last night. Either he uses his dick-stroyer to crack my vagina-vault wide open or he gets no relief. Just like me."

"I think you were dropped on your head as a baby," Katie said. "Who talks like that?"

"Horny people talk like that, Katie," Roni said. "I'm two seconds from running naked in the streets and leg-humping the first bulging quad I find."

"I feel like I need to get that spray bottle Steve mentioned ready," I said. "You're worse than a cat in heat."

"You do you," Roni said. "Meanwhile, let Molev know his end of the bargain is not fulfilled. He'll be getting a visit from me if this keeps up."

"Why don't you try getting to know Brog like he obviously wants to get to know you?" Katie asked. "He might need a little reassurance that you're not planning to love him and leave him."

"Whoa. Did you just slap a wedding dress and tiara on me?" Roni asked. "I still have two more years to rock my twenties and have no plans to settle down any time soon."

"Which is probably why Brog's avoiding you," I said. "I'm with Katie. If you want him to give, you can't just take. You have to give a little too. Besides, haven't you been bragging that he's the biggest ever? Do you think you'll be happy with anything smaller after your vagina-vault's been cracked by him?"

Roni frowned. "You're making a valid point. If I plan to sample, I should work my way up to Brog, not backward."

"That's not what I was suggesting," I said.

Roni shrugged and helped herself to some casserole.

A knock on the door had us all freezing.

"It's your house," Katie whispered to Roni. "You should answer it."

She rolled her eyes and strolled to the door. Molev and Ben stood there. Molev's gaze found mine.

"Come," he said.

The terse command had Roni glancing at me.

"Did you two fight?" she asked.

"No. I'm guessing he heard you twist my words into that not-what-I-suggested idea, and he's mad that his matchmaking might be falling apart."

"Ha!" she barked, facing Molev. "Your skills at matching suck. Brog was supposed to jump on me. Instead, he's running away. Andie's right. I need to play the field first."

"Not what I said," I stressed, standing.

She shrugged again. "I was promised a lay when I got here." She looked at the fey behind Molev. "Do you want to have some mind-blowing sex in the name of science?"

Ben's gaze shifted to Katie.

"Oh," Roni said. "You're hers?"

"Yes," he said at the same time Katie emphatically said, "No!"

I went to Molev and crossed my arms. "No scowling at me for this one. You know Roni. She does what she wants. Changing her mind isn't my fault. If Brog wants to keep her, he knows what he has to do."

Molev slowly dipped his head. "He does," he agreed.

He held out his hand, and I threaded my fingers through his.

"Good luck, ladies," I called. "I'm here if you need me."

"Wait," Katie yelled.

I didn't get a chance to wait for her. Molev tugged me into his arms and left with me.

"Did you talk to Ben?" I asked.

"I did."

"Did you explain she needs more time because she's grieving for Ted?"

He grunted.

"You know the only thing I was trying to dissuade Roni from was raping Brog in his sleep, right?"

He sighed. "I know. Brog knows that Roni plans to have sex and leave him. He is trying to win her heart."

"If he wants to do that, he needs to impress the hell out of her. Feats of strength. Show her something only he can give her."

Molev grunted again.

"So where are we going?" I asked.

"Home. I've spoken to Drav, and he sent the fey needed to Tenacity and Unity and the rest to retrieve the supplies we'll need. It will take them a few hours to return. I will help my brothers after that."

Understanding what he intended, I internally cringed at the same time my pulse sped in anticipation.

"I will take care," he said, kissing my temple tenderly.

THE SCREECH of metal followed by a crash pulled me from my sleep. I rolled over and felt the opposite side of the bed. Molev's place wasn't even warm. Sighing, I debated between going back to sleep and checking the time.

I checked the time.

It was just before midnight. I'd fallen asleep way too early after Molev finished with me.

Carefully rolling to my side, I sat up. Nothing ached too badly, so I stood. My legs were sore like I'd been climbing the rope course again. After a long hot shower, I started stretching and rubbing my thighs. Faint clanks and other metal sounds continued from outside, prodding me to dress and investigate.

The section of wall not far from the house was a bevy of activity. Fey worked together to hoist and weld cars into place, filling gaps with other metal objects. They were meticulous with how they placed pieces so it wasn't dependent on the welds to stay upright.

They'd already finished a decent section, moving the lights so they shone down outside the wall from the top of the new third layer. I scanned the fey for Molev's familiar shape and spotted him holding a car in place.

"Hey, handsome," I said. "I heard something fall. Was anyone squished?"

A nearby fey chuckled.

"No one was hurt, Andie," he said.

"Someone might be if you guys wake up any sleeping babies. Why don't you all take a break and wait until morning to keep going?"

The fey shook his head. "Molev said we need to complete this as soon as possible. We're running out of time."

I watched Molev. Although I was sure he could hear my conversation with the fey, along with every other fey present, he wasn't watching me. He was focused on the car he was trying to position.

That level of focus spoke to the urgency he felt. It had to be another gut feeling.

"Do you know if Drav is awake?" I asked the fey.

"If he is not, he will wake when you knock. Mya sleeps well and won't notice."

I nodded and made my way to Drav and Mya's house. I

knocked softly, just in case Mya was sleeping. It took a minute for Drav to answer.

"Sorry for stopping by so late. Matt mentioned he communicates with Tolerance over the radio you have. Would you mind if I check in with Matt?"

Drav led me to the radio they had in the kitchen, and I waited a few minutes for Matt to answer.

"Molev's working on the wall here like a madman," I said. "I'm guessing it's his intuition saying we need to hurry. It's never wrong. Have you heard anything from the bases?"

"Nothing. Every channel is quiet," Matt said. "We haven't stopped trying. June, myself, and a few other volunteers are taking shifts so we're continuously broadcasting."

Did that mean more bases had fallen or that we were too far into the dead zone to reach anyone?

"Let's change up our message. Instead of just trying to reach the bases, we need to reach out to anyone listening. We warn them what's coming and find out what's going on through anyone willing to communicate."

"It'll be tough getting answers," he said. "People are scared and afraid to communicate."

"We win their trust. Tell them, as of last week, Vance Airforce base was clear of infected but cleaned out of supplies. There are aircraft in the field, but they have no fuel. The infected in the area are watching it, and it should be avoided. Give them the location of the Wichita base. Let them know that's been cleaned out too. The road between the two locations had very little movement, but Vance was attacked by a hound that's now dead. Be specific. Say a fey killed it."

"Is that smart?" Matt asked.

"Would you believe anything else managed to kill one of those?"

"I wouldn't, but that's because I've seen what they can do."

"So have I. I'm betting there are more people out there who have too. Once we share what we know, ask if anyone out there has any updates on other locations regarding infected or hellhound movement. Give them a channel to listen to, and let them know you and your people will be listening around the clock. It will help anyone who's listening know they aren't alone and maybe give them enough hope to communicate."

"All right. We'll change up the message now."

"How's progress on your wall?" I asked.

"Good," he said. "About an eighth of it has a third layer. They're going to need to head out in the morning to look for more supplies. At this rate, they think they'll be done in five or six days."

"We have the same timeline," Drav said behind me.

"Same here," I said to Matt. "Let us know if you need anything."

"Will do."

I returned the radio to its original position and faced Drav.

"Sorry again for the interruption. Molev's urgency to finish this wall means we don't have much time. He hasn't been wrong yet. And getting any kind of update from out there will help us if we know what's actually coming our way."

Drav smiled. "Molev is the oldest of us because he listened to his instincts. I will send someone to you if Matt receives a reply from the new message."

"Thanks."

Rather than return to the empty house, I headed to Eitri's to check on the research team. I knocked softly again but didn't need to wait as long.

"Hi, Eitri," I said. "Is anyone awake?"

"Yes. Many are. They run tests and nap while waiting for results."

I followed him downstairs and found the doctor studying an image on a monitor. It wasn't the only monitor on. The amount of light flooding the basement had me looking around. When I'd first arrived at Tolerance, I'd noticed all the solar panels and had asked about the on-the-grid electric. There wasn't any in the subdivision. Not anymore. Only the solar panels on each house.

"It's incredible, isn't it?" the doctor asked.

"Yeah. I'd heard they added the solar panels to the homes on their own. I wouldn't have thought they had the battery banks big enough to supply this much power," I said.

"Oh. That. Yes, we needed to make some modifications. The woman who was studying electrical knew how to help us. It was a very smart move to ask them to learn useful skills. But I was actually talking about this," she said, tapping the monitor.

"What is that?" I asked.

"Infected blood. It's a sample from Adam. Now look at this one."

She switched the view to something that looked the same but different. Adam's sample had been bigger blobs of darkness. At least, that's how it had looked to me. The new view was of one and lighter red smaller blobs.

"Do you see the difference?"

"One's bigger and darker, and one's smaller and redder."

"Look again," she said.

She switched back to the dark view and zoomed in so close that I saw an extreme magnification of the edge of one of the blobs. It quivered so slightly it was almost imperceptible.

"Now you see it? I thought it was vibrations from the table or something. But look at this." She switched the view to another line. It didn't move. "That's my blood. I haven't had any sexual contact with a fey." She switched views again. "This sample is Eden's. She's the female with the longest history of sexual contact without pregnancy. I've compared hers to Mya's and Angel's and baby Daisy's. None of them have that vibration that Adam's blood has."

She tore her gaze from the screen and looked at me.

"I haven't determined what's causing it. Yet. But I think that it's a piece to the infection puzzle."

"Have you found anything in their samples from Mya, Angel, and the baby to help create a vaccine?" I asked.

"Ah, that's interesting too."

She showed me more slides, pointing out differences she only seemed to see. Then a slide of semen. Through all the science talk, I understood that she was learning a lot from the couples who'd volunteered to have sex.

"We've isolated the proteins that hold the cure to the infection and now understand the method in which the body can safely absorb it, and that is the key. Injections won't work. I have a single female volunteer who is strictly ingesting semen —no vaginal contact—whose samples are showing promise. If you know of any men who would be willing to consume semen, please let me know. I would be very interested in monitoring a male test subject to see if gender plays any role in immunity as well before we even attempt to start up another round of trials."

"I'll talk to Molev and see what we can do," I said. "Meanwhile, Matt Davis over in Tenacity has people on the radio around the clock, trying to make contact with Irwin. Hopefully, they're having as much luck there as you are here because we need more than a cure. The east coast fell weeks ago. We'll be the biggest gathering of humans between the two coasts. Even if we can't turn, we'll never survive what's coming if we can't find a way to stop them."

She nodded, looking troubled, and as soon as she looked at her screen again, I knew I'd lost her.

Making my way back upstairs, I considered what the doctor had shared with me. They'd found the cure but weren't sure how to administer it safely or if it would work on men. I doubted it would be easy to find a guy willing to down some fey semen, but only curing a select number of women able to have sex wasn't an option. We needed a way to mass produce the cure to save everyone who was left.

We needed more time.

I walked around town, paying attention to the homes.

We needed a plan for when the wave hit. Obviously, evacuating was out. But just sitting inside the houses and hoping the infected wouldn't find their way in wasn't a good idea either.

The subdivision was huge. The sprawling wall encompassing it would be hard to defend against the kind of numbers we'd likely see. While adding the third level would make it a decent line of defense, the survivors needed a second line of defense if that wall was breached. Something easier to protect against an insurmountable number of infected if the outer wall was breached.

No, not if. When.

How long would it take hundreds of thousands of infected to crash against that wall and trample over one another until they reached the top? Mere minutes?

I paused at the open space where they'd constructed a shelter for the livestock and watched them sleep.

What we needed was something smaller built in the center. Something big enough to house everyone for a number of days until…until what? Until the fey killed them all? How long could they fight before they dropped? Molev's stamina was inhuman, but he had limits. I'd seen him after that night in Loveland. He'd been spent. Hiding away in some bunker-like fortress wouldn't save us. We'd eventually starve, or the infected would find a way in.

We needed a better answer than walls to keep the infected out.

We needed a damn way to stop them in their tracks.

Restless, I turned toward Roni's place and knocked softly on her door. Brog answered it a few minutes later. He looked tired and a little harassed.

"Is Roni awake?" I asked.

"She has been quiet for a while, but I am not sure."

"Want me to check?"

He stepped aside to let me in and pointed me in the direction of the bedroom.

I opened the door quietly and peeked inside the dark room.

Something caught my shoulders and yanked me forward into nothingness. Training kicked in as my feet left the ground. The second my back hit the carpet, I used my momentum to flip Roni. The lights turned on as she sailed over me. She growled and disappeared.

Panting, I looked around and saw Brog had her wrapped in his arms, pinning her back to his chest and arms at her sides. She was completely naked and scowling at me.

I shifted my attention to Brog as I stood.

"I take it she's done this before?" I asked.

"Yes."

"Get dressed, Roni," I said. "Meet me by the front door in five. We'll go for a run."

"Fine," she said, elbowing Brog, who immediately released her and moved closer to me.

We left the bedroom and returned to the entry.

"Her independence and drive have been an asset," I said. "They've kept her alive until now. She thinks hooking up with someone means giving those up. She's not wrong. Women have to give up a lot when they commit themselves to a man. You need to show her what she'll be getting in exchange. Roni's an amazing person. Vibrant and full of life. Don't dim that."

"I won't," he said.

Roni emerged with an attitude and full gear.

"I'm going to need more than a run," she said.

"I'll do my best. But I'm a little sore. Molev really laid into me before dinner."

She scowled at me, and I smirked.

It wasn't until we were outside that I understood how much I'd changed over the course of the last few weeks. I wasn't the type who normally goaded someone else. I usually held my distance and observed. However, Molev hadn't just forced me to stop retreating from him. I wasn't retreating from anyone now.

Realizing that scared me in a way and comforted me in another. I'd learned early on to hold myself back. Getting close meant getting hurt. Yet, I couldn't return to the person I'd been. Especially not now with everything I faced. I would rather be hurt than spend my last days alone.

I jogged beside Roni, feeling the ache in my legs slowly ease as the exercise warmed them.

"What is the point of this?" Roni asked angrily. "If you're not going to fuck me, then let someone else."

I glanced back and saw Brog trailing us. I hadn't even heard him.

"He's clam-jamming me," Roni said with an angry scowl. "Every fey I've asked to eat me until I see stars says no. Because Brog just stands there behind me like some lost boy shadow and stares at them."

"Have you tried masturbating? Loudly?" I asked.

She gave me a disgusted look. "Of course I did. My kitty cat's been on every pillow in his house."

"No sleepovers at Roni's. Got it," I said.

"We know they have a heightened sense of smell. I wanted him dreaming of me…if he manages to sleep."

I sighed and shook my head.

"What's Molev's favorite food?" I asked her.

She gave me a confused glance before answering, "Spam. Although I did see the way he ate those hot dogs. I'd love to see him devour a footlong." She grinned.

"What's his favorite drink?"

"Water. He's lame like that."

"How much sleep does he need?"

"Five hours to be fully recharged but he can go thirty-six hours with a thirty-minute nap and be just fine."

"Tell me something about him that you think I don't know," I said.

She glanced at me curiously. "His favorite color is green. He'd stop and just look at the sky sometimes when it was completely cloudless. Always when it was cloudless. So I thought he was doing it because he liked the color and asked. He said he liked looking at the sky because it was so vast, but his favorite color was green."

"Do you regret getting to know Molev so well that you were willing to follow him here?"

She started to frown.

"No. Of course not." Her frown turned into outright anger. "Well, maybe. I could have gotten laid if I'd stayed in Irwin."

"You know that's a lie. You'd probably be dead if you were there."

"Fine. Whatever. I get your point, and you're annoying. Are you warmed up enough for me to take it out on you?"

"Not even close, but I'm betting Brog is. Have you tried your non-sex moves on him yet?"

CHAPTER NINETEEN

Roni stopped running and looked at me.

"I heard they have their own training grounds here," I said. "I wandered around a bit and didn't find it yet."

"I will take you there," Brog said from behind us.

Roni stared at his ass the entire time he led the way. Their training setup was interesting. They had a weird mountain of melted plastic dicks at one end. A stuffed dummy hung from a post off to one side. And a huge circle of packed dirt waited to the other side. For spectators, a few stumps waited by each area.

I took a seat on a log and waved around us. "Pick your poison, Roni."

"As tempting as that fist is sticking out of penile peak over there, I think I'd rather vent some of this steam the old way."

I glanced at Brog, who was watching Roni. Tension radiated off of him. So did a bit of hopeless infatuation. He wouldn't win Roni over with devotion, though.

"You up for this, Brog?" I asked.

He nodded once.

"All right, Roni. Show him what you've got," I said. "And I

mean your fighting skills. You've already shown him enough of the rest. And be nice."

"Screw nice," she said before launching herself at him.

Roni was a fighter. I didn't like sparring with her because she had wicked moves that could concuss a person. But she was smart about who she sparred with and held back based on skill. I'd seen her use her moves on others, though. I thought I'd understood the extent of her abilities, but seeing the way she went after Brog, I realized I'd been mistaken.

She did this low-ground pivot thing that hooked a leg behind Brog's. His knees went out, and as he folded forward, she flipped behind him and hooked an arm around his neck.

Had he been human, I would have felt worried.

"She's not made of glass, Brog. The sooner you embrace that, the happier you'll make her."

"Shut it," Roni yelled as she grabbed her forearm to add pressure to her chokehold.

Brog moved with human speed, reaching back to grab her jacket and using that to flip her over his head so she lost her leverage. She landed with a thump but immediately sprang up and struck out at him. He didn't block the first hit, but did the second.

They began moving together after that. Fluidly.

Minutes passed as he allowed Roni to attack before he countered.

The crack of his palm connecting with her ass echoed in the night. Roni froze. Just...seized up. A slow red crept into her face.

I could see the flicker of concern in Brog's gaze.

"Hold your ground," I said softly for his ears only. "Wait."

Roni inhaled deeply, and her unfocused gaze zeroed in on him.

"Again," she said.

"Don't ease up," I said just as softly.

They fought a few more minutes again before he found an opening to deliver another resounding spank to her other cheek. She froze again, only this time, I heard her hiss of pain.

"That hurt?" I called.

"You want one?" she asked in a partial snarl.

"And interrupt your good time again? Never. Focus. The object is to not let him touch your ass now."

She swore under her breath, and I was sure she was thinking about getting her guns so she could shoot Brog. But then he said the magic words.

"Would you like me to show you how I did that?"

Since they started, he'd only ever moved at human speed, keeping things as fair as he was able.

"Yes," she said. "Show me."

I watched them for a while longer before I knew I wasn't needed anymore. Roni was no longer seeing Brog as a mammoth dick attached to a moving body. His ability to teach her new skills had opened her eyes to his other values.

Neither seemed to notice when I quietly left the training grounds.

Back at the house, the clock by the stove showed it was a little after three as I shrugged out of my jacket and set my boots by the door. I wasn't sure how long Molev would work and wasn't tired yet, so I went to start something for breakfast.

He returned as the sun started to rise.

"Run out of supplies?" I asked.

"Yes. Some of my brothers left to find more."

"Hungry for some breakfast? I made a roast for you."

He grunted and came over to wrap his arms around me.

"I hunger for you, Andie."

I snorted. "Well, sex alone won't sustain you. Sit down. You eat, and I'll talk."

I told him about my talk with Matt, which he already knew about, thanks to Drav. He knew some of what the doctor had told me but not all of it.

"She wants human males to…"

I grinned at his inability to finish. "It's not like you'd need to ask any of your brothers to accept blow jobs from men. All the doctor needs is more cup donations like you've already given and a human guy willing to do a shot without throwing up. I'm betting we'll find a few who are willing to set aside their aversion for a chance at immunity."

"What if it does not make them immune? What if they have the same reaction the men in the trials had?"

"I don't think that will happen. We saw the trial results. Both the men and Sarah reacted the same way to the shot. There's no reason to think it would be different using this method. The doctor said the method of absorption seems to be a big piece of the puzzle."

He grunted and continued eating while I told him about Roni's frustration.

"Hopefully, she calms down a little after their training," I said.

"They will be fine. Brog has patience."

"Well, Roni has none."

Molev finished his breakfast and washed his plate. When it was back in the cupboard, he held out his hand to me.

"Are you tired?" I asked.

He slowly shook his head. My heart skipped a beat as I took his hand.

"I think you're tired," I said. "Maybe this time, you should let me do all the work."

Hours later, I collapsed on his chest, a boneless pile of sweaty woman who'd almost forgotten her own name with that last orgasm.

Molev's hand stroked down my back and pressed against the base of my spine, holding me in place so he could continue to thrust up into me. He came a few minutes later, washing my insides with another shot of anti-zombie serum.

"I can't move," I said softly against his skin. "You're going to need to wash me, feed, and clothe me for the rest of my life."

"Gladly." He kissed the top of my head and stood with me.

Still impaled, I didn't slip down his slick skin. He walked us to the shower before he lifted me off and let me stand. My legs wobbled.

"How many times would it take before it stopped doing this?" I asked, flicking his hard length.

"Do you want to find out?"

"Nope. I don't. I think I would break. Besides, I'm sure there are more supplies for you by now. I'd rather not have people waiting in our living room again while you have your way with me."

He smoothed his hands over my wet shoulders, a caress and a massage that had me leaning into him.

"Although, staying with you all day wouldn't be the worst thing."

He chuckled and leaned in to kiss my forehead. "I hope to experience that soon."

"Because we're trapped inside, surrounded by infected, or because we figure out how to stop them?"

He grunted and pulled me into his arms.

"This is the opposite of reassuring," I said. "Tell me what your gut is telling you."

He was quiet for a long moment.

"That it's not safe for you here. That if I want to protect you, we need to leave. But it won't be safe for you then, either."

"Well, that doesn't sound promising."

"No, it does not," he agreed.

"Any idea where your instincts are telling you to go?"

"Home."

I sighed, understanding that he meant his caves.

"It makes sense. You said you lived there for several lifetimes. You'd obviously found a way to keep the hounds at bay."

"Yes. They avoided the light from the crystals."

I pulled back to stare at him.

"The crystals are their kryptonite? Then we go there and grab the crystals."

He shook his head and held up his wrist so I could look at the crystal tied there.

"Their light fades after a few days on the surface."

I understood what that meant. We couldn't move the crystals. We could only use them where they were. Which meant living underground…forever. But was that really any different than my thoughts of a bunker the night before? Only, they'd been able to survive down there without starving for thousands of years. If they could do that, then we could do that too.

"Okay," I said. "Then we start plans to evacuate everyone and move them to your old home. How long will that take?"

He slowly shook his head. "Not everyone."

"Why not? Do you think we can't all make it?"

He frowned and stared at the water running down the wall for a moment.

"I have no answer. I only know we will all die if we all leave.

If some leave, we have a chance to save everyone. And you need to be with me."

"You need to work on your gut premonitions," I said, patting his chiseled abs. "They're a little too vague yet for my tastes."

He grunted and began washing me. I let him do his thing, knowing it was soothing him just as much as it soothed me. When he finished, he turned off the water and took some time to dry me.

I stroked a finger over the crease in his brow.

"Don't worry. We'll figure out what we need to do together. If your instincts are saying we have a chance, then I'm not worried. There's hope. Okay?"

He grunted and kissed me gently before letting me tug the towel from his hands.

"Go get dressed. I'll walk you to work and check with the doctor again before I come back and take a nap."

When we left the house, the late morning sky was clear, and the streets were filled with people walking around. I nodded to a group of women I knew strolling with several fey.

"Doesn't look like the wall's going to progress much today," I said.

Molev grunted, watching the activity around us before a fey jogged over.

"Good morning," I said. "What's going on?"

"Ryan readied another ten homes. Those of us not working on the wall will run over to Unity with the women who wish to move."

"That is good," Molev said. "I will join you. I wish to see Unity with my own eyes."

He glanced at me with a question in his gaze.

"I'll stay here. That way, your arms are free to help carry

whoever or whatever needs to go over there. Hurry back, okay?" I stood on my toes and tugged him down to kiss his cheek.

He watched me with a hungry glint in his gaze.

"The faster you leave, the sooner you can come find me again."

He kissed me once, hard, on the mouth, then left with the fey. Smiling to myself, I walked to Eitri's house. He opened the door before I reached it.

"Do you ever get any sleep, Eitri?" I asked as I entered.

"Yes."

"Are you getting enough though? I know I saw you on the wall last night."

"You need to take care of yourself, Eitri," an older woman said from the living room. Her short hair wreathed her smiling face in a pouf of white. She was the first elderly person I'd seen in months. I wasn't sure if it was that or how she reminded me of my grandma that brought a dangerous warmth to my eyes, but I had to swallow and clear my throat before I could talk.

"Hi. I'm Andie."

"I'm Mary. James, my husband, is in the bathroom. Hurry up, James!" she yelled.

"Woman, you can't rush this," a man yelled back from the closed bathroom door.

"You should have let me help you," she called.

"I slept, Andie," Eitri said softly, reminding me that I'd asked before they'd started yelling. "I promise."

"I can't do it," the man in the bathroom yelled.

"Yes, you can," the woman said, sounding irritated. "This is our chance to be useful. And stop acting like it's your first time. Remember that night in Vegas? You had no problem then."

"That was mine, and I was with you."

"Well, you should have let me help. You could have pretended it was yours again."

"What's going on?" I asked Eitri softly while listening to them shout back and forth.

"James volunteered. He tried to drink a cold sample first, but it was too thick and came back up. Mary said to give him a warm, fresh sample. I left it on the sink for him, but he has been in the bathroom for a long time."

I stared at Eitri, unable to speak because, for the first time that I could remember, I had no idea what to say.

Mary, the older woman on the couch, stood and shuffled toward the bathroom door. She slapped the surface twice, annoyance twisting her features.

"What do you like telling me? 'Don't argue. Just swallow.' So either let me feed it to you like a baby bird, or tip it back like a smooth whiskey. You have two minutes before I have Eitri hold you down."

Eitri side-stepped behind me, like he was using me as some kind of shield from Mary.

"Mya says consent is important," he said softly.

I looked over my shoulder at the distressed fey.

"I don't think she actually wants you to hold him down. I think she's just trying to motivate him."

Eitri didn't look convinced. I wasn't entirely sure either until Mary sighed and said, "Fine. You swallow that, and I'll do that thing you like."

"Woman, I know you and your empty promises."

"It's not empty. We both heard the doctor. One shot won't be enough. I'll give you a reason to come back for the next one."

There was silence from the other side of the door. When it opened, an older man stepped out. He held up an empty cup and grinned at Mary.

"Time to pay up. Let's go home."

He took her hand and started our way.

"You must be Andie," he said to me. "You're as pretty as Molev said you were. You both should stop over for dinner soon."

"Not tonight, though," Mary said.

"No," James said, nodding thoughtfully. "Tonight won't work out. Mary's going to be pretty tired."

He handed the cup to Eitri. "You're not drinking enough water, son. Make sure you hydrate before tonight. It'll taste better. We'll find our own way home."

The pair left, and I stared at the shut door for a minute.

"Did you need something, Andie?" Eitri asked.

"Therapy, maybe. I'm still trying to decide."

"Hannah and Emily say the same thing after hearing Mary and James have sex talk. I like the way they speak. But not when Mary wants us to hold James down."

"Does she want that often?" I asked.

Eitri shrugged and looked down at the empty cup. I made a mental note to talk to Emily about James and Mary the next time I saw her.

"I actually stopped by to talk to the doctor," I said. "Is she here?"

"Yes. Downstairs. Can you let her know that James drank it all?"

"I will," I said, already moving toward the stairs.

The doctor was at the same station, this time looking at a different image of something that I couldn't recognize. It looked like a tiny lightning storm in a moving darkness.

"Eitri asked me to tell you that James finished the sample," I said.

She looked away from the screen, surprise on her face.

"He did?" she asked.

"Yep. And James made it sound like he'd return later."

"Excellent. I was surprised he'd volunteered. In my experience, older married men aren't as...open as James."

"Yeah, they both don't strike me as average elderly."

She nodded and looked at me curiously. "Was there something else you needed?"

"Just here for an update if there is one."

She shook her head. "That was James' first dose. Based on the doses the woman in the partner trial consumed, I don't anticipate seeing any change in James' blood work for several days."

Several days...that was too long.

"Molev mentioned something to me. Back in their caves, there were crystals they used to keep the hellhounds at bay. I've noticed the fey all wear a smaller version of them on their wrists. I know the other team was working on a way to stop the hellhounds, but since we might not be able to contact them, I was wondering if your team might want to look into the crystals."

"A crystal kept them away?" she asked.

"The light from the crystals did. The ones on their wrist don't shine anymore. They would need to be recharged in the caves."

"That *is* interesting. The hounds avoid the light up here as well, but the light from the crystals didn't kill them, correct?"

"No. I know I'm grasping at straws, but anything to buy us some more time, right?"

She nodded, already glancing at her screen.

"Yes. Time is what we need the most."

"Do you want me to see if Eitri would be willing to give you his crystal?"

"Please do. Is there anything else?"

Understanding that she wanted to get back to work, I shook my head and left.

Eitri was upstairs in the kitchen, making sandwiches.

"Would it be alright if the researchers took a look at your crystal?" I asked. "Molev said the ones in the caves kept the hounds at bay, so I'm hoping the doctor might discover something useful."

He looked down at his wrist, and I could see the hesitation in his gaze.

"What's wrong?"

"We never take them off," he said. "Since the beginning, we have always known…we needed them. When Olem removed his crystal, he did not return."

"Wait, are you saying that you'll die without the crystal?"

He shook his head slightly and looked up at me.

"We do not resurrect on the surface like we do in the caves. Even if I am wearing the crystal and die here, I will not return. That was why we took Uan to the caves when he was close to death. When he died there, he was reborn in the pools so he could return to Nancy."

Molev had explained that they died and were reborn from the resurrection pools. And he'd explained how the crystals played a key role in their lives. But he'd never explained the connection between their rebirths and the crystal.

Eitri took a knife and cut the leather cords holding the crystal to his wrist. It fell free into his hand, and he tossed the crystal to me. I caught it, looking at the opaque shard swirled with white and grey. It was almost identical to every other crystal I'd noted that the fey wore. Nothing about it screamed special rock, but if it was the key to bringing them back to life, it could also be the key to their deaths. And that was something I did not want.

Yet, I thought back to everything Molev had told me about their origin. Things Mya had learned after touching their source crystal. Magic. Their cursed lives. The evolution of the hounds in those caves. It all came back to these crystals.

No…it all came back to their source crystal. These crystals were only extensions of the source. A source that existed in a place where nothing truly died.

"I'll be right back," I said.

I jogged down the stairs and found the doctor right where I'd left her.

"Can you check this for those vibrations?" I asked.

She looked up from her work and frowned at me, then at the crystal I was holding out.

"Why?"

"I'm not sure how much Waurlyn shared with you, so try to suspend your disbelief for a few minutes. The fey as they are weren't born; they were created by a curse placed on them thousands of years ago. Yeah, magic. Hard to believe, right? But I've seen the hellhounds' eyes. That otherworldly glowing red. And I've felt that unnatural pulse of power that comes from their hearts.

"Now, hear me out. They weren't born like that either. According to Molev, they started out as deer, and each time they were killed, they evolved into something darker until, eventually, they were the hounds we've seen. They evolved in the caves. Just like the fey. But different.

"In order for the fey to resurrect after death in these caves, they needed to be wearing these crystals. The hounds didn't. They just came back. In order to kill them here, the fey have to crush their hardened hearts. What if the hounds' hearts are their crystals? I don't understand how they can't die up here while the fey can, but I think this crystal might hold the answer to how to kill them."

She took it from me, turning it over in my hand. Doubt filled her expression.

"I'll take a look."

When I didn't move, she added, "It'll take some time."

"Okay. I'll be back in an hour. And that's Eitri's crystal. He wants it back when you're done."

I left her to work, told Eitri I would return, and hurried to Mya's house. Drav answered on my second impatient knock.

"I need to talk to Mya," I said.

"She's sleeping."

"Which room," I said, already walking farther into the house. Drav didn't try to stop me when I turned on their bedroom light.

"Mya, I need you to tell me about the source." She didn't move. I shook her shoulder. "Mya."

She groaned, rolled over, and tried to focus on me.

"What?"

"I need you to tell me about the source crystal. It's important."

CHAPTER TWENTY

Her eyes drifted closed again, and I looked back at Drav.

"Help her up. She'll wake up faster if she's standing."

Drav frowned at me and glanced at Mya.

"Drav, Molev said we're running out of time. Please. She can nap after."

He grunted and carefully withdrew Mya from her warm nest. She scowled and swatted at his hands as he stood her up, but when she saw me, she stopped.

"What's going on?" she asked.

"The hounds and the fey were both made in those caves, right? The hounds don't die here or down there. The fey can die up here and have to wear their crystals in order to be reborn down there. I think that's the line that differentiates the magic that made them both. Molev told me what you said you saw when you touched the source crystal. That the crystal was a source of magic here when their magic was dying in their homeland. You told him they cursed them. With what magic though if theirs was fading? I think they used the source crystal's magic to create the curse, and I think that's why Molev's gut is telling him we need to go back to the caves. But I need to hear it from you. What did you see when you touched the crystal? More importantly, what did you feel?"

Her now alert gaze held mine for a moment.

"I think you're right. About them using the crystal's magic. After they left their home because their magic was dying, they couldn't sense any anywhere but in those caves. They said once they lost their power, they would become just like humans. I don't think they had the power to create a curse without using the crystal. They put their hands on the ground and called up the power from the earth, but the only source was the crystal.

"I remember feeling sick to my stomach when I touched it. I only touched it for a few seconds, but I saw so much. And when it released me, I felt even sicker. Like I could have thrown up."

I nodded, understanding what she meant.

"I was close to Molev when he removed a hound's heart. It emanated an energy that felt wrong somehow. Would you describe the crystal like that?"

She shook her head.

"No. I got the feeling that it was glad to see me. Actually, relieved is a better way to describe how it felt. Like it had been waiting for me to tell me everything that had happened to them." She threaded her fingers through Drav's. "I think his people used the crystal's power in a way that the crystal disagreed with but had no way to stop."

"You think it's alive?" I asked with a sinking despair.

"Yes and no. It's not like us. It didn't have those kinds of thoughts and feelings, but it could show me the past and in a way that influenced my thoughts and feelings. Clips of events, like it knew exactly what to show me."

I glanced at the crystal tied to Drav's wrist. "I think the

source is why we can't kill the hellhounds without crushing their hearts."

"You think we need to destroy the crystal?" she asked intuitively.

"Why else would Molev's instincts be telling him to return to the caves?"

Drav turned Mya toward him suddenly and kissed her forehead.

"Stay with Andie. I will return."

We stood alone in the room a second later. She shook her head.

"We might as well move to the living room. I'm sure we'll have company soon." She yawned as she walked out the door.

"Sorry for interrupting your nap."

She waved away my apology and settled on the couch. I took the chair.

"I'm tired all the time lately. Mom says it's a normal part of pregnancy. It probably is for some, but I'm not so sure that's why I'm sleeping so much."

I remembered the way she'd greeted Molev.

"Growing a baby while trying to keep everyone alive is more stress than I'd want to deal with," I said.

"Yeah, I'm cracking around the edges a little. The lingering headaches aren't helping. We really need to find a way to swing things in our favor. Even just a little." She sighed. "No matter how it looked to you, I've never believed the wall the fey built was some kind of impenetrable fortress. I do believe this is the safest place in the world for us, but only because the fey are here. That doesn't mean I think we're safe, though. The infected have already breached these walls once, proving they aren't as afraid of the fey as we'd like.

"Over the last few weeks, Drav was talking about trying to

kill the infected on a larger scale. Setting traps for them like they set for us. He and Ryan, my brother, were trying to figure out the perfect place. A stadium or something like that."

She rubbed her fingers over her temples. "Can I whine for a moment and just say I really want this to be over? I'm just so tired of it all."

"My brother's a heart surgeon. A pretty good one. Because of that, his name was added to a drawing. He won two tickets to an island sanctuary. One for himself and one for whoever he chose. His wife Rachel told him to take their daughter Nova because she's six and can manage on her own while he worked there, doing what he could to help us fight the infected here and preserve the knowledge he'd gained. Rachel had to watch my brother and niece leave while my four-year-old nephew sobbed in her arms.

"I promised her I would find a way to send him to his father. I signed up for an impossible mission to find a way to end this. When Molev's group came across ours and when we saw for ourselves that he was immune to the infection, my team thought we'd found the answer. Nothing was that simple, though. We didn't get our tickets to freedom we were promised, not without a fight. And Molev's blood didn't contain the answers we needed to stop this.

"My sister-in-law is here with us after sending her son to join her husband and daughter. She has shed her share of tears, but she hasn't whined. Not once. She understands that feeling sorry for herself is a slippery slope. Rather than slide down that mountain, she's still clinging to the sides, waiting for me to figure out a way to climb it because I promised her I would. Because I love her and my brother and my niece and nephew enough to give it everything I have to see them together again.

"We've all been dealt a shit hand, but if we're not willing to do anything about it, we might as well just die now."

She blinked at me like Molev did sometimes.

"You're either shit at motivational speaking or amazing. I'm on the fence."

I smiled a little. "I prefer to think of it as tough love. You should have heard the elderly couple I encountered at Eitri's. I thought that woman was going to beat her husband for not downing a fey-shot."

"Fey-shot?"

"Yeah, the doctor was looking for a male volunteer to drink semen since the results from the test groups showed the method of absorption played a role in successful immunization. The team wanted to verify it wasn't just successful with women, though. I'm not sure what the man's wife promised him, but he said no visitors until tomorrow because she'd be too worn out today."

Mya chuckled. "That would be James and Mary. They hold a special place in my heart. They were the first humans to embrace the fey for who they are. No fear. No hesitation. Just acceptance. They look like the sweetest grandparents you could ever want, but boy are they open. About everything. I heard that Mary lets the fey use their bathroom to shower and washes their clothes so she can peek at the goods.

"The fey love them. They go over to visit all the time, asking all sorts of things I'd never ask my grandparents. But they know that any advice they get from Mary is a little extra and tend to verify it with Angel before taking it to heart."

"Advice?"

"You haven't figured out their single-minded focus yet?"

"Yeah, they want the white-picket-fence package."

"Ha! Nope. That's too nice. They want a woman they can adore, who will adore them in return, and lots and lots of sex. All the sex. All the time. That takes up about ninety percent of their thought process during the day." She smirked at me. "I can see you doubt it. That means Molev did a pretty good job playing it cool with you.

"When I first met Drav, he didn't know what to make of me. Once he figured out what my fun zone was for though, it changed their world. And I say *their* and not *his* because they share everything. Hope you weren't attached to any form of privacy."

"Not really," I said. "Molev already let me know that they can hear everything even through the walls."

Mya nodded. "They were sex-obsessed when they thought it was just a good time. Now that they know we can make babies?" She shook her head. "That's all they think about. Not how hard it will be to keep them alive."

"I don't think all this napping is helping you," I said, hearing how the conversation had wrapped back around to her fears. "Sleep is just another way to hide from the truth. Use your energy to change what you can to build the future you want. It might not be perfect, but at least you did something, right?"

"Do you really think I'm doing nothing?"

"No. But I think you need a break from the mediating, babysitting, and decision-making. Do something with your hands for a while."

"Tried that. My baking is average. My sewing subpar. And because I'm pregnant, they don't want me climbing the walls."

"That's stupid. If the infected get in here, are you going to levitate to safety?"

Mya grinned at me. "You're a lot like Hannah. You pull back just enough to be nice, though."

The door opened, and Drav walked in followed by Molev. I hadn't been expecting to see him yet. It had only been a few hours since he said he was going to help bring people to Unity.

His gaze locked on me, and I could see the warning in them.

"I'm not sure what that look's for," I said. "I'm not the one who interrupted your workday. Did Drav catch you up on why I interrupted Mya's nap?"

"Yes. You think the crystal needs to be destroyed."

"I know you thought that it might be the key to Mya's immunity, but the fact that the other women are immune should be enough proof that it's not, right? And you said something is telling you to go home. I think this is why."

He continued to frown at me.

"I can't read minds, Molev. Body language, yes, which is how I know you're upset, but not minds. So just tell me what's upsetting you. We don't have time to waste playing guessing games."

He closed the distance between us and grabbed the back of my head.

"You're retreating again."

That was the last thing I'd expected him to say.

"How did I retreat?" He hadn't really expected me to run into his arms the moment he walked through the door, had he? Although, come to think of it, I showed him lots of affection in the bedroom but tended to forget outside the bedroom. I blamed circumstances on that though, not me.

"Just now I heard the cold, detached Andie telling Mya to stop hiding from the truth. To risk more of herself instead of staying where she and the baby are safe. Not every female hates the idea of having children."

He had me questioning if I'd been detached until he said that last part. I closed my mouth, which had been preparing an apology for Mya, and stared at the man who I had mistakenly begun to believe understood me better than anyone else.

A bitter smile pulled at my mouth.

"And there it is," I said, hating that he'd waited until now to admit how much he resented my stance on kids. "You could have saved us both time and energy by acknowledging how you really felt from the start. And, for the record, I've never pretended to be anything I'm not, Molev. Saying what I think isn't retreating; it's just speaking my mind." I pushed away his hand. "And so you don't confuse this again, this isn't me retreating either. This is me leaving."

I made it two steps toward the door before I was flipped over his shoulder. I didn't fight it; I seethed and waited for him to jog to our house.

Once we were inside, he stripped my jacket from me and hauled me to the bedroom. His beautiful eyes were filled with an angry fire as if he was somehow the wronged party.

He grabbed my chin and tried kissing me. Well, he didn't try to kiss me. He did kiss me. What he tried to do was get me to kiss back. To fight him. To give him anything to go off of.

I gave nothing. I'd already given enough.

So he kissed me, and when I didn't respond, he started pulling off my shirt.

"I don't consent to this," I said, not fighting him.

He stopped what he was doing and stared at me, his anger growing with each passing second.

"You are mine, Andie," he growled.

"What exactly is it that you think I am? Your puppet? The female puzzle piece you needed to complete your picture of perfect domestic bliss?"

Some of the heat left his gaze, and this time, when his hand touched the back of my head, it wasn't the authoritative grab he so often used. It was a gentle caress. A palm sliding over my hair.

"You are my heart, Andie. My reason to live in this world that has given me nothing but pain and loneliness. Please. Do not retreat from me."

"I wasn't retreating. I'm still not. There's nothing for me to retreat from. Any relationship I thought we'd been building on mutual understanding was just a lie. Because you don't really understand why I don't want kids. You listened as if you did. You told me it didn't matter, as if it truly didn't. But now we both know the truth. You do want kids, Molev, and you are not okay with the fact that I don't."

I straightened my shirt and sat up. He retreated just enough to allow it but continued to glare at me, his fingers twitching at his sides.

"And if you would have paid any attention at all when I had to say goodbye to Zion, you would know I don't hate kids. Not at all."

I stood, and his hands locked onto my shoulders.

"We both know I can't leave unless you allow it, but keeping me here won't resolve our non-relationship; it'll only jeopardize finding a way to save the women who are willing to have your babies. We're running out of time, which you already know."

He looked like he was two seconds from snapping as he inhaled deeply then exhaled. Seeing that barely-contained rage did things to me—things I didn't like or want to acknowledge anymore.

"I need to check with the doctor again," I said. "Since your discussion with Mya was cut short, you should head back there and discuss destroying the crystal."

"We are not done, Andie," he said when I started for the door.

I paused. "With what exactly?"

"Us."

"You're focusing on the wrong thing. If we don't find a way to stop what's coming, whether or not there is an 'us' won't even matter."

He didn't try to stop me a second time, and I grabbed my jacket on the way out the door.

Rather than walking to Eitri's, I jogged. It helped calm my mind and keep my thoughts centered on the problem of living, instead of the problem of loving. Because no matter how hard I'd tried not to acknowledge it, I'd fallen hard for Molev, which only made the pain of his betrayal that much worse.

Forcing the hurt and anger aside, I concentrated on what lay ahead. Molev's instinct said that time was running out. How many days did we have to get to the underground crystal and destroy it before this place was overrun by infected and hounds?

I'd studied the map and knew that we could reach Irving, Texas, the opening to the crater and the gateway to Molev's world, in a day if we drove straight through and didn't have to worry about traps or daylight. But the likelihood of that wasn't high, which meant two days minimum, and who knew how much longer to reach the crystal's location.

If we were going, we couldn't delay.

I knocked on Eitri's door and saw he wasn't wearing his crystal when he answered.

"Any word from the doctor?" I asked.

"Yes. She said she needed more crystals and has been whispering into her radio that she hides in the back corner of the basement."

I paused on my way to the steps and looked at him. "How do you know she's using a radio?"

"I can hear the squeal when she turns it on."

"What does she say?"

He shook his head. "She turns on the machine that hums when she uses the radio so I cannot hear her words."

I considered what that meant for a moment.

"I need you to do something for me. Can you kneel? You're too tall for me to demonstrate." He knelt, and I showed him how to grab the front of a shirt to pick someone up. "The person will feel threatened, but they won't get hurt. Try it on me really quick."

His expression was filled with reluctance as he stood and glanced at my chest.

"I wouldn't ask you to do this if it wasn't vitally important, Eitri."

He grunted and had me up in the air before I could blink. I grinned at him.

"Nothing hurts," I said. "Okay. Put me down." He did. "If the doctor doesn't answer my questions and I look at you, I want you to do that to her, but don't let her down until I say so. No matter what she says, you can't let her down, okay?"

He nodded slowly.

"I promise you won't hurt her."

He followed me down the stairs. The doctor's usual station was on, but she was absent. The researchers were all present at their stations, though, running various machines. The nearest one noticed me and straightened from her computer. Her under eyes were dark with the need for sleep.

"She's resting," the woman said. "She said her eyes wouldn't focus anymore and she just needed twenty minutes."

"If she's trying to rest, shouldn't you turn that off?" I asked, pointing to the machine humming rather loudly.

The woman shook her head. "That's her timer. Once the test is done running, she wants to look at the results."

Either the woman didn't know about the radio, or she was good at lying because I couldn't see any tells.

Nodding that I'd heard her, I veered toward the curtained-off area.

"Wait!" the woman called.

I knew then that she knew. Not stopping, I cleared the curtain as the doctor straightened from where she'd been kneeling by the bed.

"Did you need something?" she asked, frowning.

"Yeah. Information. Are the infected and hounds still on the coast, or have they already started back this way?"

The doctor opened her mouth, and I could see by her expression she was going to continue trying to deny it.

I looked at Eitri, who was only a step behind me.

He nodded and had the doctor in the air by the front of her shirt before she knew what was happening.

Her eyes rounded and her mouth opened and closed a few times without sound.

"Think before you speak," I said, moving around them to reach under her bed. I pulled out the case and found a satellite radio.

Leaving it open, I placed the whole thing on the bed.

"Is Waurlyn still alive? How many did we lose? Are the infected and the hounds still attacking the coast? If not, where are they headed now?"

The doctor looked at Eitri. "I can't breathe. Please. Let me down."

"If you couldn't breathe, you wouldn't be able to speak.

You're here to help find a cure and a way to stop what's happening out there. If you're no longer willing to cooperate with those goals, you have no place here. Put her down, Eitri." He did. "You have one hour to pack your equipment and leave. Good luck out there. You're going to need it."

I turned and started walking away.

"You can't kick us out," she said.

"Molev was very clear that he only wanted people here who would improve the relationships between fey and humans. Keeping secrets from one side while communicating with the other isn't for the purpose of building a better future between our two races, and you know it. The only reason to keep secrets is because you plan to do something Molev and his people won't like. And since they're pretty open and accepting about everything, I can guess what you're keeping secret. We don't need a way to kill the fey. We need a way to kill the infected and the hounds." I turned to Eitri. "Don't let them leave with any samples of anything. Especially from Daisy."

Eitri's expression no longer looked hesitant. He nodded while glaring at the doctor.

"I'm going to find a few other fey to help you keep an eye on the packing," I said.

"Wait," the doctor called as I started toward the screen. "It's not what you think."

"Then what is it?" I asked, showing impatience I wasn't actually feeling. The panicked tension radiating from the woman told me that I'd already won.

"I've been communicating with the other team. Providing updates on our research here and receiving updates on their research there."

"And?"

"There's a commonality in the sample from Adam and the hound."

"The vibrations?"

"Correct. But based on the information you provided during the Loveland expedition and what I witnessed during the attack on our way here, we're speculating that those vibrations might actually be frequencies that the hounds and some infected are using to locate one another."

"Some infected?"

"Yes. Tests confirmed that newly turned infected don't have these vibrations. Only those that have been infected at least a few weeks."

"You believe you've discovered how the hounds and the infected are communicating and wanted to keep that from us? Why?"

She hesitated to answer, and I shook my head.

"I'm just following orders, Andie," she said with desperation. "There are a lot of people who believe we won't be saving the world for ourselves if we end the plague."

"What's that supposed to mean?"

She let out a breath, glancing at Eitri. "No one was fooled by his request for women. They weren't needed to keep the peace; they were needed to breed. Why would they need to multiply their numbers?"

I wanted to roll my eyes that we were back to this level of thinking.

"Waurlyn saw past that kind of pointless fear-mongering a long time ago. Who are you talking to and what are your orders?"

"I'm communicating with the other research team. They've passed on two sets of orders. Waurlyn's and the ones from the people running the sanctuary."

"What are Waulryn's orders?"

"Find a cure and do whatever we can to assist you in stopping the infected."

"And the sanctuary's?" I asked.

"Make sure the cure kills everything."

CHAPTER TWENTY-ONE

HUMANS WEREN'T INHERENTLY BAD OR GOOD. WE WERE SIMPLY survivalists, doing whatever was necessary to stay alive or spare whoever we cared about. So, although the continued mistrust from whoever was on the other end of the doctor's radio frustrated me to no end, I understood it.

"Did they even think that through? They're asking you to create a cure to administer to humans that would somehow magically kill the infected, hounds, and fey without killing us. All while we still don't even know how to kill any of them successfully without some form of artillery."

The doctor gave me a helpless look. "People never want to hear what we can't do; only what we can."

"Why don't you tell me both, then?" I said.

She started talking fast.

"Based on our trials, we should be able to have a working vaccine that will prevent infection in a few weeks. As you've already guessed, having a vaccine that kills everything else without affecting us once we're immune will be harder. Orders are to proceed at all costs. Although it hasn't been said, I think the other team also understands the implied message in those orders—that those safely tucked away at sanctuary won't care if we're all wiped out in the process."

"Why would they?" I said. "With all the supplies I saw shipping to the evac because of Molev's efforts, they've probably prepared for that scenario. Since Plan A is no longer an option, we'll need to focus on Plan B."

I left the back area with her close on my heels. "Keep your research focused on a cure only. Eitri, please stay with the researchers until backup comes."

I took the stairs two at a time and asked a random fey outside to point me to Cassie and Kerr's house.

They were home, but each one had a kid in their arms.

"Uh, I need your help," I said, staring at the toddler Kerr held.

"Lilly's help?" Kerr asked.

"No. Actually, yours and Cassie's. But I didn't realize you had kids."

Cassie chuckled. "Having kids with all these built-in sitters waiting for a turn isn't a problem. What do you need?"

"I need you both to keep an eye on the researchers. They've been ordered to work on a way to kill everything that came out of that crater."

Cassie's humor vanished.

"You're more likely to understand what they're doing than anyone else," I added to explain why I was there.

"We already know what the cure is. Why let them continue researching?" she asked.

"She's reporting her findings to the second team, and they are updating her on theirs. If she stops updating, we stop learning how far the other team is in achieving their goals."

"All right," Cassie said.

She went to the door and yelled out a few names. Fey jogged toward the house.

"Eitri's keeping an eye on them. I need to check in with Molev and Drav."

She waved me away while she handed off her kids to the fey who'd appeared. Kerr was running with her seconds later. The fey now holding the toddler nodded at me and closed the door. Just like that, the kids were passed off. And by the looks of things, they were pretty excited about it too. The little girl was already asking for new braids.

My gaze scanned the fey idly wandering around the neighborhood as I jogged toward Drav's house. How could anyone think that these people were multiplying to create an army? Anyone with eyes could see why they wanted women, and it wasn't just so they could make babies. These men were lonely. Maybe even beyond lonely. I couldn't imagine spending lifetimes without someone else to love.

It hit me, then, how much I hadn't understood Molev's viewpoint. While I'd avoided serious relationships due to the hot mess my parents had called a relationship, I'd always had the love of my brother, sister-in-law, and their kids. They'd filled the need for having a family of my own.

But what if I didn't have them? I tried to imagine what it would have been like to spend thousands of years without anyone to love.

While I knew Molev had his brothers and the love he felt for them was certainly real, it wasn't the same kind of love a person could share with their partner or child. And that's all these fey really craved. A deeper connection with the people around them…a connection they saw in families and spouses—the very thing my messed-up childhood had programmed me to avoid.

My thoughts turned to each reluctant step I'd conceded to

Molev in our relationship. Did he really resent the fact I didn't want kids or did he resent that I was inherently unwilling to give anything?

Shaking my head at the turn my thoughts had taken, I approached Drav's house and reestablished my priorities. First, I needed to let them know what the research team was up to. Then we needed to decide the next steps. Once I knew if we were all going to live or die, I'd address my issues with relationships.

Drav answered on the first knock and stepped back to let me in.

My gaze swept the room, noting Mya on the couch with a blanket over her lap before I saw Molev. He stood near Mya. Frustrated defeat radiated off of him as he stared at me.

I'd done that. Me, a small human who possessed zero strength in comparison–I had come close to doing what so many humans on the west coast had wanted to do. But I'd never intended to break his spirit. I'd only wanted to be me and have the freedom to make my own choices.

Priorities vanished as I entered, my gaze locked with his.

"Drav and I will give you a few minutes to talk," Mya said, standing.

Molev nodded to her without looking away from me as they left the room.

"You were right," he said quietly.

"About what?"

His lips twitched at the corners. "About many things. I shouldn't have treated you as I did, taking you from here and trying to…" He shook his head. "I don't understand you, Andie, but I want to. I want that more than I want anything else in this world. I want to understand you so I will never again give you a reason to want to leave me."

I considered him for a long moment. "I want to understand you too. I'm sorry for not trying harder to see things from your point of view."

He slowly closed the distance between us. "Does that mean you will stay with me and continue to allow me to try?"

"Yes."

His hand captured the back of my head.

"Tell me you want me to kiss you as badly as I want it."

I rested my hands against his chest and tipped my chin up in invitation.

"I want it more," I said.

He kissed me tenderly, pouring his regret and love into it, and I trembled against him, feeling vulnerable and afraid.

"I'm sorry I hurt you," he said when he pulled away and wrapped me in his arms.

"I'm sorry too," I said, hugging him back.

My stomach growled then. He grunted and led me to the kitchen where Mya was eating some crackers.

"Everything good?" she asked.

"Andie is hungry." He started going through their cupboards like it was no big deal. And apparently, to Mya and Drav, it wasn't.

She gestured to the table as he opened a can of something.

"Were you serious about going back to the caves to destroy the crystal?" Mya asked. "Do you really think the crystal is what's keeping the hounds alive up here?"

"I do. The fey came to this land, looking for magic, right? A magic they found in the crystal. One you witnessed when you touched the crystal and it showed you their past. And what did it show you? How their own people abandoned them and how it brought the animals who lived within the caves back to life."

"If the crystal's keeping the hounds alive, then—" Her gaze shifted to Drav.

"Before the curse, everything in those caves just resurrected, right? After the curse, in order to resurrect, the fey had to be wearing the crystal shards they received, right?"

Mya nodded.

"The hounds didn't get a crystal but were obviously part of the curse because they mutated more with each death when the other animals didn't."

"Not their deaths," Drav said. "They mutated when we consumed them."

"Yeah, that was definitely part of the curse," Mya said. "Their people thought the idea of endless resources was unnatural."

"So they made it unnatural in truth," I said. "Those hounds didn't just come back mutated and angry at the fey. They came back with their own crystals that retain their magic when they're on the surface." I looked at Molev and Drav. "You've had their hearts in your hands. You've felt their energy. That negative darkness that pulses from them. Isn't it like the crystal in the caves? I think they're still linked to the crystal."

Mya's mouth dropped open a little. "Oh my God."

Molev slid a bowl of heated soup in front of me.

"That's not all. The doctor found a link between the older, smarter infected and the hounds. Their blood samples both have these vibrations that the fey and the immune women don't have. She tested Eitri's crystal. It didn't vibrate, but I think it might have when it was in the caves."

Drav looked at Molev, and I took a quick spoonful of soup.

"What are you thinking?" Mya asked, watching them just like I was.

"The crystal is large. It will not be easy to destroy."

"Dad and Ryan were talking about using bombs to blow up stadiums. I'm pretty sure they'll have something that'll work."

Molev didn't look relieved. If anything, he looked more worried.

"What is it?" I asked.

"I'm not sure. Something feels..." He shook his head slowly. "...wrong."

"I think there's a good reason for that. The doctor has a satellite radio she's been using to communicate with the other research team. Through them, she's received orders from the people in charge of the sanctuary to create a vaccine that will kill anything not human. That includes the infected, hounds, and fey. I've asked Cassie to keep an eye on what they're doing, but I wouldn't trust anything they come up with at this point.

"She either wouldn't or couldn't answer when I asked if the wave of infected was already heading our way. Any chance Matt's heard anything from anyone?" I asked.

"The radio here's been quiet," Mya said.

"So we have no idea if the urgency or wrongness Molev feels is because of the doctor's orders, the wave of infected, or something else entirely," I said. "That makes it a little hard to know what to do."

"I already know what we must do," Molev said. "Returning to the caves feels right."

That settled our next move in all of our minds.

The four of us talked for the next hour, planning our trip to the caves. Since no one knew what destroying the crystal would do to the fey's home, Drav asked that Molev also retrieve what he could first. Mostly seeds and plants they used as medicine so they could hopefully grow the same things on the surface. That meant taking more people with us to carry out what they could. But Molev didn't like the idea of taking more than ten fey away from the communities with so many infected headed their way.

We tossed around the idea of using the satellite radio to find out more about the infected movement but ultimately agreed we wouldn't be able to trust anything we were told.

"Then we take humans," I said. "You already said I need to go with you, so what are a few more? And it means fewer humans to protect here and more hands to carry things. With the roads fairly clear and a ten-fey escort, there's no reason we can't take vehicles. It frees your hands on the way there and back to kill more infected. And the only thing you'll need to worry about once we reach the caves is running the goods from your home to the top while we gather everything for you."

Molev gave a reluctant nod.

"Do your dad and brother have any explosives on hand?" I asked.

"I'll find out," Mya said. "And if they don't?"

"Then we'll need to find another way to destroy the crystal." Molev looked at Drav. "I will tell the others I am looking for nine volunteers and speak to the soldiers. The fueler needs to be full by first light."

That fast? I thought.

"How long will it take to reach the crystal once we're in the caves?" I asked.

"It will take a day to reach the caves and a night of traveling the caverns with rest periods to reach the city. We will need a few hours to gather what we need. While the rest leave the caves with the supplies, you and I will go to the crystal." He looked at Mya. "How long were you in the caves before you began to feel the sickness?"

"I'm guessing one or two days." She looked at me. "It's harder to tell time down there because there's no actual daylight. The light of the crystals comes and goes at random intervals in different sections of the caves. But I didn't start feeling any kind of sickness until after I touched the crystal."

"Got it. So don't touch the crystals, and everything will be fine."

Molev didn't look convinced.

"Roni, Katie, Roland, Sid, Brandon, Steve, and I all have experience with the vehicles and working with you to stay alive. Seven humans to ten fey. Does that ratio work for you?"

Molev hesitated before he nodded, and I knew he was listening to his gut again.

"All right," I said, standing. "I'll let the team know and will have us ready to head out at first light."

"And we'll talk to Dad and Ryan," Mya said. "We'll make sure you have something you can use."

Molev left the house with me and caught my hand when I would have walked away.

"Can we go together?" he asked.

"Sure, but don't you need to recruit some volunteers?"

"My brothers likely already know what will happen at first light."

I looked around the neighborhood, seeing all the shadows moving between the houses in the twilight, and nodded.

"Okay. Then let's start with Steve and Brandon."

"May I carry you?"

The overly polite way Molev asked spoke volumes toward how far we'd both messed up.

"Only if you do that thing where you knock me off my feet," I said.

His lips twitched, and I was in his arms a second later. I turned my head toward his chest and breathed in his scent as he ran with me. The ride was over too soon. He held me just a little closer for a second before setting me down.

I knocked on the door and asked the woman who answered to get Steve and Brandon.

"This is a surprise," Steve said when he saw us. They both listened to what we wanted to do and agreed to help.

"Let us take care of the rations we'll need," Steve said. "We know what'll move well."

"It's all you, then. Pack for four days, but we should be back on the third."

The next stop took a little longer since Katie was once again locked in her room, and we had to go in to talk to all three of them at once.

"I'm in," Sid said.

"Me too," Roland said. "A little fresh air would be a welcome change."

"Are you actually saying you miss going out?" I asked.

He glanced at Ben who hadn't taken his gaze from Katie since she emerged.

I shook my head at the pair of them. Katie noticed and gave me a desperate look.

"I'll go too," she said.

As soon as Ben heard that, he volunteered to go, too. Katie shot Molev a panicked look when he agreed.

"We'll be traveling inside the vehicles while the fey keep the road clear," I said.

After they promised to meet us by the wall at first light, we headed to Roni's place. A few fey stopped us along the way to offer their help, proving Molev was right about word spreading. Some he welcomed. Some he asked to stay and watch over the people here.

I trusted him to choose his team wisely.

The living room lights were on when we knocked on Roni's door.

Brog answered, looking just as harried as he had the last time I'd visited.

"She still hasn't settled down?" I asked.

"She still hasn't gotten laid!" Roni yelled from inside the house.

Brog stepped aside and gestured for us to enter.

I found Roni once again wearing a thong and a crop top as she made dinner.

"Judge all you want," she said. "At least, I'm not suffering alone this way."

"I think you're taking 'misery loves company' to a whole new level," I said.

She smirked and nodded. "You two staying for dinner?"

"No," Molev said before I could answer.

"We're actually here to recruit you and give Brog a break. Wanna blow up something big?"

She paused what she was doing. "I was going to tell you he didn't deserve a break, but you've intrigued me. What are we blowing up?"

Roni's interest increased once she heard everything.

"Hell yes, I'm in. This place is way more boring than I was promised."

I caught the glance Molev gave Brog.

"I will go, too," Brog said.

Roni snorted. "I guess that's your bad decision to make. I'm going to be carrying, and the source of my sexual frustration will be a running target. Your ass is pretty cute, but your face has been pissing me off. You've been warned."

"No shooting fey, Roni," Molev said, his words laced with serious warning.

"Hey, accidents happen to the best of us," she said with a shrug. "Even you make mistakes. Remember how you said Brog would be perfect for me?"

"We'll see you at the wall in the morning. Come early," I said.

IT WAS STILL DARK when Molev and I left the house the next morning. I was well-rested physically, but not sure where I stood emotionally.

After returning home the night before, Molev hadn't pounced on me like he usually did. He'd made me dinner, and we'd talked about the caves and what we both thought would happen the next day. We washed dishes together then snuggled and watched a movie. Something we'd never really done at Irwin. It was nice. Very domestic but in a good way.

And when we'd gone to bed, he'd just held me until I'd drifted off.

It had reminded me of why I'd let Molev in in the first place. With him, I felt safe. Completely, and totally safe.

I laced my fingers through his as we walked.

"What's your gut telling you now?" I asked.

"To be wary," he said. "Danger is everywhere."

I believed him even though I didn't see any evidence of it. I saw the lights shining from the extra tall wall and the stars twinkling in the night sky. Fey walked the neighborhood, dark sentinels, to protect against whatever might lurk beyond the walls. Everything felt serene and not even a little threatening. And that was the worst kind of dangerous environment. The kind where people let their guards down.

"Did you warn everyone?" I asked.

"Yes," he said.

I spotted Drav and Mya near the wall. She was bundled up in a thick jacket even though it wasn't as cold as it had been. It felt like spring was just around the corner.

"The fueler is full," Drav said. "And the supplies are packed. The others are already waiting."

Molev grunted in acknowledgment.

"Be careful out there," Mya said after hugging me. "Make sure it doesn't take three months for him to return this time."

"I'll do my best," I said.

Drav hugged Molev, thumping his back twice before releasing him.

"We will protect what you have worked hard to obtain," Drav said. "I swear it."

Molev nodded and picked me up just as Brog appeared with Roni.

"Let's get this show on the road," she called as they cleared the wall. We were seconds behind them.

Three vehicles waited. An MRAP, a Stryker, and the fueler. Sid and Brandon took the Stryker, and Steve and Roland took the fueler, leaving me, Katie, and Roni for the MRAP. We had a small supply of food, water, and spears. The rustic weapons weren't something I'd seen before.

"I'll watch our tail," Katie said as we got in.

"I'll drive," I said.

Roni settled in to navigate, and it felt like old times as I started the engine. I had that same sense of determination and anticipation tempered by the reality of what we were about to try.

"Well, this is different," Roni said, looking out the window as the Stryker then fueler started out.

I glanced at the fey escorting us. They were spaced out

evenly between the three vehicles with two in front, two behind us, and three on each side.

Katie snorted. "How is this different? He's right on the other side of a door just like he's been since I got here."

Roni and I shared a glance.

"Sex is supposed to be an amazing stress reducer," Roni said. "You should try it. I bet he'd be willing."

"Sex creates problems," Katie said. "It doesn't fix them."

"Says you," Roni mumbled, moving in her seat. She growled and pressed her middle finger against her window. "Do you know what he did to me this morning? He ate me. But not all the way. Just enough to give us both a taste of how amazing it would be. Then he proceeded to tell me to behave and not take any unnecessary risks. If I do that, he'll eat me all the way when we're done."

She removed her hand. "I want to punch him in the dick for making me blue ball like this."

"I should have rode with Sid," Katie said.

"You know the rules," Roni said. "If I'm suffering, everybody suffers."

I laughed. I shouldn't have. It was the worst timing for finding my funny bone. But it was pretty funny.

Roni gave me a disbelieving look. "Are you laughing at my misery?"

"A little–but a little at mine too," I said.

"What do you have to be miserable about?" Katie asked, sounding both sad and curious.

"Did I tell you that the researchers had a satellite phone with them? They've been using it to coordinate with the team we left behind. Only they aren't using it to find a cure to save humanity as much as they're using it to find a cure that will destroy the hounds, infected, and fey."

Roni made a choked sound. "Hell, no. I haven't even had a chance to dance on Brog's maypole."

Katie said something about Jesus under her breath.

"You really need to think of something other than sex," she said loud enough for us to hear. "A hobby. Overeating. Something."

The next hour continued with the same level of banter. Roni bemoaned her born-again virgin status. Katie complained about Ben's constant attention. And I just drove and listened to it all while waiting for the first road block.

"Can we just acknowledge what we're trying not to?" I asked.

"Where the fuck are all the infected? It wasn't this quiet on the way there," Roni said.

"Thank you," I said.

CHAPTER TWENTY-TWO

The fey jogging alongside my door said something. I couldn't hear it, but I saw his lips move.

A few moments later, Molev appeared. He jumped onto the vehicle, holding onto the side so he could talk to me through the window.

"Scouts ran ahead last night, clearing many of the infected while they searched for fuel. We will see them soon. Be ready."

Those ominous words turned out to be an understatement about ten minutes later.

The first road block wasn't the half-assed attempt that we'd seen on the way but a full-blown blockade across the road with hundreds of infected around the cars.

Our radio crackled to life.

"We're pushing through it. Keep a steady speed, and don't stop," Sid said.

I could hear them hit the cars a minute later. Infected swarmed as we made our way through. The fueler took out a fair number, which splattered my windshield. Having learned from previous experience, I waited to use my wipers until the last moment, just in case any decided to jump on the vehicle. I didn't need to worry, though. Our fey escort removed any that managed to gain a handhold.

"Three fey are falling behind to deal with the runners," Katie said.

"Which is just about all of them," Roni said.

I glanced in my mirror, noting the same thing.

Were there no newly turned infected because they'd gotten them all in this area or because there weren't as many infected around to find the humans still hiding?

I hoped it was the latter and not the former.

We saw more roadblocks and infected after that, but none of those were quite as large of a grouping. When we stopped to refuel, we switched up who was driving. Navigating wasn't so much navigating as it was just watching for infected traps. Even then, it wasn't much work with our escort.

Katie passed out MREs before my stomach even had a chance to growl.

"Bored?" I asked.

"Hungry," she mumbled, retreating to the back to eat hers. But not before I saw the way her eyes welled.

All the pieces clicked into place.

"Katie," I said, twisting to look back at her. "Are you pregnant?"

She burst into silent tears as she shot me a panicked look and held her finger to her lips.

"What?" Roni asked. "What's she saying?"

"Eyes on the road, Roni," I said, giving her a don't-ask-questions look.

Her eyes rounded. Then she looked out her window, shook her head, and waved at the fey there like it was all a big joke.

"I'm sorry for picking on you for eating," I said, keeping my head turned to look at Katie. That's how I saw Ben's head suddenly pop into view through the back window. I ignored his wide-eyed shock. "You're right. It's better to eat when it's quiet than to get hungry and not be able to eat later."

I blinked at her twice. She paused opening her MRE to stare at me.

"What did you pick?" I asked, glancing down at mine.

"I didn't look. I just grabbed."

I met her gaze. "Sometimes, it's better not to look." She nodded that she understood. "I got tuna," I added.

She ducked her head and focused on her food. I faced forward and did the same, feeding Roni hers between bites of my own.

Fate was a cruel thing. It had taken Katie so long to give in to Ted, and he'd been taken shortly after. And now to have a baby from that brief encounter?

"Head in the game, Andie," Roni said softly.

"It is. I'm just thinking about how much I don't like the game anymore."

"Same."

"I don't like it either, but I'm not ready to be done playing," Katie said, sounding more like herself. "We just need to do the best we can with what we've got."

Roni and I shared a look.

"Fine. You're right," Roni said. "I'll stop complaining about Brog not giving up the goods and focus on what's important."

"Staying alive," Katie said with resolution. "I'm looking forward to seeing their caves. Ben told me a little bit about them."

"You actually talked to him?" I asked, glancing back.

His face wasn't in the back window anymore, so I nodded to

Katie that she was safe. She stood and went to look out the window again.

"Not really. He told me about it through the door. I think he heard me crying the first night. It sounds like a pretty place, minus the hounds, of course."

"Of course," Roni agreed with barely any sarcasm.

"He did warn me that we should stay away from the pools of water when we first get in there. Some of the pools have fish that will try to bite your face off. Mya almost learned that the hard way when she went there. Ben says they have homes in their trees. They're that big."

"I wonder if they compare to our redwoods," I said.

The hours dragged on even when Molev pushed for us to drive as fast as possible. Whatever danger he was feeling had to be increasing. Yet, from our standpoint, nothing seemed any more dangerous than it had before.

We primarily stuck to Interstate 35 until we neared Oklahoma City. Knowing that the bombs would have destroyed most of the road, we skirted around it. We still ran into a fair number of infected. However, unlike Loveland, I didn't see any burned undead. Just the fast ones that ran after us for too long.

The backroads around the city slowed us down a little, due to the turns and backtracking, but once we found our way to the highway again, we made up for it.

Near dusk, we reached the outskirts of the northern Dallas area. The bombs had turned the suburbs into impassable rubble.

Molev signaled for us to stop just before we reached it.

Roni, Katie, and I quietly geared up and got out to distribute the light bags and spears to the rest. Two of the fey stayed with the vehicles while the remainder went with us. The fey didn't balk at carrying any of the men. And for my team's part, they didn't bat an eye at the ride either. We moved quickly and quietly toward the apex of what had started the downfall of our world.

There was barely any light left when we reached the crater. Molev put me down but kept a hand on my shoulder to keep me close as he looked around the area and at the gaping black hole.

"They said they left the ropes," Molev said.

"Here," another fey said, kneeling to pull up a rope. He paused then leaned in to sniff it. "Blood."

"It may be Uan's," another said.

"It's not," Molev said.

"That doesn't sound good," Steve said.

Molev grunted. "Brog, Nero, Ben. Go down first. Once it is safe, I will send half the team."

Roni snorted. "He means the women."

The three fey went down. After a few minutes, one reappeared.

"There is nothing waiting for us."

Molev looked even more troubled by the news but nodded to Brog and Ben.

Brog went to Roni. "It is more than one hundred feet. You are strong enough to climb it, but you may want to conserve your strength for whatever comes next."

"What are you saying? That you're going to carry me down?"

He turned his back to her and got down on one knee.

"Hold on," he said over his shoulder.

She grinned like a crazy person, adjusted her firearms, and climbed onto his back.

"Not exactly the way I wanted to ride you, but I'll take it," she said before licking the edge of his ear.

Ben was kneeling in front of Katie a second later.

She gave me a helpless look then resolutely climbed on. His expression was pure joy as he straightened.

"I like the way your breasts feel against my back when you hold me tightly," he said.

She flung herself backward, but he counterbalanced with his hold on her legs, and she hit his back with a thump.

"Are you all right?" he asked. "I swear I will not let go."

She gave me a desperate look.

"Stay focused," I said. "One hundred feet to the bottom." I looked at the fey. "Less talking."

He nodded and headed for the rope as Brog swung himself and Roni over the side.

I looked at Molev. He waved another fey forward and kissed my forehead before telling me to go with the other guy.

"I will follow you."

The bottom of the cavern would have been pitch black if not for Roni's penlight. We waited as the fey brought down the guys next. Molev descended last. Watching him hand over hand that rope did things to my insides and made me regret a night of just holding each other.

One of the fey led the way. Molev walked beside me, keeping a steady hand on my back as I carefully placed each step on the uneven path. No matter how many times Roni shone her light forward, there was no end to the sloping tunnel. The air warmed by degrees until I started to sweat. I saw Steve wipe his forehead and knew I wasn't the only one feeling the change.

The slope bottomed out, and the lead fey disappeared between one step and the next.

"Uh…" Roni stopped walking and aimed her penlight at where he'd been.

"It is the magic of the caverns," Molev said from behind me. "It is safe."

Another fey walked through, disappearing for a few seconds before only his head reappeared. He flashed a smile at Roni then retreated.

"Scaredy cat," Steve murmured as he passed Roni.

Brog caught her by the back of the collar before she could bolt forward.

They walked through together, followed by Katie and Ben.

Crossing through whatever it was felt like a small electrical charge running under my skin, and my ears popped painfully. But the view on the other side had me ignoring the discomfort.

The cavern we stood in was huge, stretching farther than I could see. Soft blue and green light illuminated the rock formations rising up from the cavern floor, courtesy of some kind of algae-type plant that dangled from the ceiling. Underneath the strings to our right, a still pool of water reflected the beautiful glow.

"Is that the pool where Mya almost died?" Roni asked.

"Yes." Brog reeled her closer to his side.

I looked back at the opening we'd come through. Rock, shaped like a series of frozen waterfalls, bordered a gaping blackness where the light didn't reach.

"Come," Molev said. "We should not linger here."

He swept me up into his arms.

"Damn. Some warning next time," Steve said.

I looked and saw every human was being carried like I was. Roni was smirking at Steve.

"Don't lie," she said. "You like it."

Steve flipped her off, and her laughter rang out behind her until Brog leaned in and said something I couldn't hear.

She nodded and quieted but threw one more eyebrow

wiggle in Steve's direction before the fey started jogging out of the area.

They ran between massive rock formations in the cavern. Some looked like pillars reaching up to the glowing algae on the cavern ceiling. Others resembled clusters of misshapen, upside-down ice cream cones. The bits of glowing moss on the tips made them seem like distant snowy mountains. The paths between the rocks crowded so closely at times that it felt more like we were running through a large tunnel, rather than a cavern.

After a few minutes of running, a space between rocks began to open enough that I could see an opening ahead. A warmer breeze drifted from that dimly lit space, and I was surprised when we crossed through into an even larger cavern than the one before. Its massive roof rose three times as high, making it at least six stories overhead.

Embedded in the ceiling, jagged glowing crystals illuminated the area in a soft blue light. Four giant columns rose up near the far end of the space, the only large rock formations. Fernlike vegetation, interspersed with white, stunted skeletal trees, filled the rest of the cavern, like a ghostly orchard.

From those skeletal trees, small brown globes hung from thin branches. A sheen of blue light reflected off their almost opalescent dark skin.

"Is this where the stepmom came for her apples?" Katie asked.

Ben shushed her, and the fey rustled the blue-green fronds with their passing. I reached out for one of the weird apples. Molev shook his head but nodded to another fey, who picked a few and put them in the bag he was wearing. We all had mostly empty bags to collect whatever needed collecting, and I hoped those apples were something we could grow on the surface. They were too unique to abandon.

The fey veered when we reached the end of the orchard, and I spotted another opening. This one glowed more brightly, and I had to squint against the light when we entered it. Because of that, I didn't get to see much before we passed into another cavern. The sudden darkness sent a shiver through me, and Molev held me a little closer. No one made any unnecessary sound, but not by some pre-discussed agreement. The threat of danger hung in the air.

Cavern after cavern, we made our way deeper into the fey's world. I began to see Molev's life in a new light. While there was an undeniable beauty here, there was also a starkness that left me feeling sad for the man holding me. No light. No sounds. Constant darkness and danger. And how many thousands of years had they spent like that?

I rested my head against his chest and smoothed my hand over his shirt. He held me a little closer for a moment, his version of a hug on the run.

When they finally slowed in a well-lit cavern, the backs of my knees were sore, and my feet were tingling.

"We will rest here," Molev said softly. "Try not to make noise."

I nodded and carefully withdrew the canteen from my bag. Molev watched me take a few sips then accepted it from me. We didn't eat. Just hydrated, stretched, then got back to running.

Katie started to yawn first. I only noticed because Ben slowed and looked down at her with concern. Then, I started yawning. Despite knowing that the fey had more stamina than a human, I worried about Molev and his brothers if we were tired just from being carried.

At the next stop, I questioned the pace.

"I know you're feeling driven to get there quickly, but exhausting yourselves won't help us get back. Is there time for a quick nap?"

Molev looked at Katie, who was passed out in Ben's arms.

"We're fine," I said. "It's all of you I'm worried about."

"We can sleep here for a short time."

Although we spoke very softly, the men around us heard. The fey who'd been carrying someone immediately started to bed down in the tall grass. The others took up positions around us, watching outward.

"We cannot stay long," Molev said, wrapping his arms around me and bringing me to the ground. "An infected is following us."

I slowly turned in his arms to look at him.

"What? Why are we letting it follow us?"

The way he studied my face indicated he was trying to put what he was thinking into words that would make sense to me. Apparently, he couldn't because he ended up shrugging.

"It's okay. I trust you."

He leaned in to kiss my head.

"Thank you."

He closed his eyes, and his breathing evened out almost immediately. I knew I should sleep, too, but I tried to puzzle out why his instincts were telling him to let the infected live instead. It didn't make sense. Why let one of them monitor what we were doing? Unless it was to monitor them?

Them.

I thought back to the blood on the rope and how the infected had watched us at Vance, testing our defenses before striking on a larger scale.

That was what the infected was doing. Watching. Waiting to test. But why would we want to appear oblivious and weaker?

Maybe it was a smaller group of infected. By appearing weaker, they might attack altogether versus hiding and lying in wait for a human to get close.

Suddenly, the long grass around us didn't feel as safe anymore.

Thankfully, the break was truly short. After twenty minutes, the fey on guard started waking everyone.

As soon as I sat up, so did Molev. He didn't speak; he simply lifted me into his arms and started jogging again. When I rested my head on his shoulder, I pretended to close my eyes and watched behind us. I could see it then, the infected trailing us at a healthy distance.

It wasn't alone.

Three others trailed it.

As I watched, one of them broke off and ran in another direction and disappeared into another cavern's dark opening.

I lifted my head and looked at Molev.

"How much longer until we get there?" I asked.

He picked up the pace without answering. That was answer enough, though. No matter how long it was, it wasn't soon enough.

Infected came and went as we moved through the caves. The group's tension increased, proving I wasn't the only one noticing their movements. Exhaustion won at some point, and I slept in Molev's arms until we stopped again in a lit cave. We took another very short break there before our group was running again.

Molev had said that it would take a day to reach the caverns and a night to reach the city, but it felt like it was taking much longer. I checked my watch and saw it was almost five in the morning.

I glanced at Molev. His jaw tensed with his effort. Running

all day beside the vehicles and carrying me all night with only two twenty-minute naps?

I didn't like it.

The thought had barely formed when he nodded toward something ahead of us. I followed his gaze and saw another cavern opening. This one opened into a vast space that easily stretched for miles. Crystals twinkled like distant stars on the towering ceiling.

In the distance, another larger crystal looked like a full moon on a clear night. The group ran noiselessly across the barren cavern floor, and I was once again struck by the stark beauty of Molev's world. Cool silence and dim light. Down here, both felt comforting, not like on the surface.

As we drew closer and that orb grew larger, I could see a stone wall ahead. It stretched in both directions in front of us. Carved out of existing stone, or made from magic, the wall seamlessly rose out of the cave's floor. The soft light from above played on veins of white running through the grey and black stone.

"Our home," Molev said softly.

Two of the fey sprinted ahead. One slowed as the other neared the wall. I watched as the first one stopped at the base and the other started sprinting again. The first one bent in the knees and caught the other's foot as he jumped, launching him even higher in the air.

"The base of the wall is smooth so the hounds could find no footholds."

"Which means you can't either," I said, understanding.

The fey landed on top of the wall and ran along the top to a pile of something. He threw it over the side. A rope with loops. Our group started to slow.

"Will you be able to climb?" Molev asked.

I nodded and shook out my legs as soon as I stood on my own two feet. Two of the fey went up first, followed by Steve then Katie. We moved fast, but I could tell by the way the fey kept watching the darkness that they were impatient with the progress.

Rather than try to spot an infected, I ran my hand over the deep furrows scoring the wall. Hound claw marks. If they'd been down here for lifetimes, how had they not clawed their way through?

I looked at the line of light cast from the orb above and then the shadow in which we stood. It was the perfect dark pocket for the hounds to hide from the wall's light.

Molev nudged me, and I hurried toward the rope, climbing until I pulled myself onto the top of the wall.

What I saw beyond robbed me of thought for a moment. The bleak landscape outside the wall had misled me into thinking inside the wall would be the same. But it wasn't.

Neatly planted fields spread out in front of me. The thick flowering vegetation in the fields was lit by countless crystal lanterns suspended at the top of long poles. In the distance beyond the fields to the right, I saw a grove filled with vast, towering trees.

"Welcome to Ernisi," Molev said beside me. Then he picked me up and jumped down. Instead of running again, he released me.

I looked around in wonder.

"What is all of this?"

"Our fields. It was safer to grow what we needed within these walls once the hounds hunted us than it was to forage for what we needed. And the caves provided everything."

He reached out and ran his hand over a thick green leaf.

"Medicines. Food. It's all here." He held out his hand to me. "Come. Everything we need is in our stores."

We moved through the field, meeting up with a dirt trail that wound its way toward the grove. I could see Katie's wide-eyed amazement as she looked at everything. Steve and Brandon too, although they were more subtle about it. Roni didn't look too impressed, and I was pretty sure Sid and Roland saw this place through the same lens I did.

It was something out of another world…and we were going to destroy it to save ourselves.

That didn't sit well with me.

"Something doesn't make sense to me," I said softly. "Why would the hounds try to kill you down here but not care about you on the surface?"

Molev's fingers tightened around mine, and he drew me a little closer to his side. When I glanced at him, I saw movement in the fields just beyond.

"I know," he said softly. "There are more ahead."

I faced forward. Katie and Ben led the way. She was still making soft sounds and reaching out to touch the flowers we passed. The only one of us still relaxed. The decoy.

Leaves of the taller plants in the next field swayed gently even though there was no breeze. So much movement. So many infected hiding. Waiting to pounce.

Molev had said that infected were drawn to humans and essentially ignored the fey. Then why would the infected hide where no humans lived? I couldn't think of any reason other than they were somehow waiting for us. But could they have known we were coming? Even if the doctor's speculations were right that the hounds and infected could communicate, I hadn't known we would be here until the night before we left.

Step by step, we drew closer, and I understood why the fey

weren't picking us up and bolting. If we moved now, the infected would know that they were spotted and swarm before we reached them, forcing us to retreat. And based on the movement I saw to the side, there were more waiting in that direction too.

In front of us, beyond the hiding infected was the grove. Molev obviously thought the trees were our safest option now.

"It's pretty here," I said softly. "Was that crystal always there?" I pointed up.

We were almost to the infected-filled field.

Molev glanced at the crystal above. "Yes. This cave is one of the largest. We had seeds with us that we had no memory of. But something told me they needed room to grow. So we planted them here." He nodded toward the grove as Katie reached the field. "Those are the trees from seeds we carried with us."

"They remind me of our redwoods. I'll need to take you there someday."

He grunted.

The leaves to our right rustled notably.

An infected moaned, and hell opened its front door.

CHAPTER TWENTY-THREE

MOLEV HAD ME IN HIS ARMS AND WAS RUNNING AS THE CALL rang out.

The infected erupted from the field around us. Dozens of them. Molev jumped over some and spun out to kick others back. But it wasn't enough. I could feel hands brush my legs.

Gunfire filled the air.

"Run!" someone yelled.

Who wasn't?

I looked ahead and saw Katie and Roni. Ben carried Katie like me. Brog wore Roni like a backward backpack. She had a handgun in both hands and was firing over his shoulders as he hauled ass.

I couldn't look back to see how the others were faring or to help cover them. So I held still and trusted Molev to do his thing and watched as the distance closed between us and the trees. More infected ran from the side fields, trying to cut us off before we could reach the grove. The fey sprinted faster, over and around obstacles.

We passed the first tree. Then the second.

I wasn't sure why until I finally spotted a tree with nubby indents slowly spiraling up its massive trunk. Ben was up that tree without slowing. Brog was right behind him. I wasn't squeamish about heights, but the gravity-defying way they climbed had me closing my eyes when Molev jumped.

Seconds later, he exhaled heavily and dropped my legs to crush me against his chest.

"I'm okay," I said, patting him. "I'm fine. We're fine."

His heavy breathing slowed, and his hold loosened enough for me to look at the others.

"Was anyone bitten? Katie? Roni? Guys?" I asked.

Everyone shook their heads even as they patted themselves down.

Katie slowly collapsed to her knees, shaking hard.

"Keep it together, Katie," I said. "You're in a tree surrounded by infected. You don't want to fall off."

She nodded and closed her eyes, focusing on her breathing to pull herself together while Ben squatted beside her and rubbed her back.

"I won't let her fall," he said to me.

Another fey walked out onto a smaller branch. Smaller was a relative term. It was still as wide and flat as a sidewalk at its center.

He leaned out and looked down.

"They cannot climb it," he said.

"Are we stuck up here until they leave?" Steve asked.

"No," Molev said. "We cannot wait for that. Go to the storage huts on this tree and the next and gather what you can."

The storage huts he referred to were a combination of burl growths on the main branch that had been hollowed out and actual huts woven together from the smaller branch limbs. The time and patience it had to have taken to create those and wait for them to grow together astounded me. I couldn't even imagine.

And that wasn't the only branch with huts. There were many. And they intersected between trees, creating a highway. Not always a stable highway but still a way for us to cross from one tree to the next without having to go to the ground.

Molev led me into a hut filled with leathers and baskets. He folded a few of the thicker leathers and packed them in my bag. It weighed more than I cared to admit after that. Then he took a pouch off the hook on the wall.

"These are the seeds from our home trees," he said. "Along with a few other kinds."

"I really hope they grow on the surface. The idea of destroying this forever isn't okay." I shook my head.

"If it saves you, I will give anything. Endure anything."

He kissed my forehead and added the seeds to the bag.

Infected calls echoed around us as we made our way back to where we started.

"Now what?" Roni asked. "They've spread out enough that it won't take them long to spot us even if we go down another tree."

Molev walked out onto one of the thinner branches. I followed, wanting to see for myself. However, I didn't have the courage to lean forward and look until I found an offshoot I could hold onto. What I saw below us wasn't good.

Thousands of infected milled around below. And as Roni said, they weren't all grouped together. A hundred or so wandered between the bases of the nearby trees. Another few hundred were stealthily hiding in the fields. And more were disappearing off in the other direction.

"What's that way?" I asked softly.

"The place where we train, the resurrection pool, and our water source," he said absently.

"Are you thinking of jumping down there and thinning their numbers?" I asked.

He shook his head. "There are many here but more may be in the caves, coming this way now. If we fight these, the others in the caves may decide to wait until we are more vulnerable."

"You mean until the humans with you are more vulnerable," I said.

He grunted.

"So then we bait them all here," I said.

His frown deepened, and he nodded after a moment.

"Talk, Molev. What are you thinking?"

"I knew there would be dangers here. Just as I knew there would be dangers on the surface if you remained. If we stay here any longer, more infected will come, and those we left behind in Tolerance, Unity, and Tenacity will die. We need to go to the crystal while the rest stay here to distract the infected."

I looked back at the people with us. Although Molev spoke quietly so the infected below wouldn't hear, the fey had. One by one, they nodded to Molev. Brog and Ben were the last to do so, each looking at the female who stood near them.

"After all our weeks together, I know that's not your happy face, Andie," Steve said.

I left the branch and went to Sid, removing my backpack and offering it to him.

"We need to switch," I said. "And don't worry. I know not to drop yours."

Sid slowly handed over his bag filled with the explosives then pulled me in for a spontaneous hug.

"I don't like this," he said softly. "It should be me."

"Trust Molev. He knows what he's doing. The world will be a different place when we see each other again topside."

Sid released me, and I looked at Roland.

"Everyone has a role," Roland said. "You have yours. Do it well."

"Go kick some ass," Roni said. Katie nodded beside her.

"We'll see you topside," Brandon said.

"We'll keep count and let you know who has the top score," Steve said with a smile that didn't quite reach his eyes.

I nodded and stepped back toward Molev.

"We will move quickly," Molev said. "As soon as you can, leave. We will not wait."

The other fey grunted, and Molev picked me up. I didn't look over his shoulder as he sprinted away on the branch. Not even when Roni started howling with laughter, yelling, "I got one! Did you see that shit?"

Molev quietly raced from branch to branch, staying away from the edges so we wouldn't be spotted. I hugged the backpack I wore and thought about Zion and Nova. It'd been months since I'd seen either of them. At their ages, they had to be growing like crazy. Would they even recognize me the next time they saw me?

I tried not to think about the possibility that we would never see each other again. That I would die trying to make the world a safer place for them.

Molev ducked his head and whispered, "Shh," a second before he jumped. My stomach flipped at how far we fell. There was no way he'd land without noise. And I was right. The jarring thump rattled my brain.

I looked up at him as he straightened and caught the wince on his face. All I could do was offer him a silent pat on his chest. He nodded and began moving through the grass without a sound. A section of wall nearby had footholds that he scaled easily. Then we both landed flat at the top of the wall while he listened to the darkness on the other side.

A scuff of noise reached my ears a few minutes later. Molev's hand brushed my ankle, tapping it twice. I waited. The noise sounded farther away the next time. Molev's hand wrapped around my ankle and tugged gently. I took that as a sign to move and eased into a crouch. He picked me up and jumped over to the dark side.

I couldn't hear a hint of sound as he ran away from the wall, staying to the shadows cast by rock formations. When he reached a dark opening, he paused again, pressing me into the rock as he listened. Once more, his intuition saved us as an infected walked through a patch of light not too far away. I watched it move, each quiet step fluid. It lifted its head and looked around. Thankfully, not in our direction. Then, it paused, turning its back on us to stare at the grove, now barely a speck in the distance.

Carrying me, Molev slipped quickly into the tunnel while it was distracted.

I couldn't see a thing in the next cavern and hoped that meant the infected couldn't either. Molev moved swiftly and without hesitation, his vision obviously better than my own.

Another opening glowed as we neared it, but Molev veered away from it and chose another darkened cave. He ran like that for more than an hour before he stopped in the shadow of a pillar. He pressed his finger to my lips as soon as I stood on my own. I nodded in understanding and watched him ease into a seated position. Quietly, I removed the canteen from the bag and offered it to him. He drank and leaned his head back. I ran my fingers over his hair and stood beside him as he rested for a bit.

We didn't stay like that for more than a few minutes though. He stood and took one more drink. After I put the canteen away, he picked me up again. I rested my head against his chest over his heart, listening to its steady rhythm.

What would be the end of this journey?

A magic crystal and a bomb?

Death?

With nothing else to do, I closed my eyes and held onto Molev, regretting that our time together had been filled with so much danger and not enough of the simple stuff. Late mornings with breakfast in bed. Early nights snuggled together on the couch. Just the simple task of making meals together. I barely knew anything about him. Did he like to dance and listen to music? Did he like coffee? Was he an early riser or a night owl? That one was hard to tell given our current circumstances. Did he prefer sunsets or sunrises? What was his favorite season? What would he look like as we grew old together? What his kids would have looked like…

Those thoughts swam in my head, and I wished more than anything I had something else to do other than think. Molev had made a place for himself in my life, growing closer to me than even my brother and his family had. And the idea of losing him now hurt. It was a vulnerability I'd tried so hard to avoid. Yet, I'd fallen for it. For him.

I turned my head and pressed a kiss to his shirt over his heart. He held me just a little tighter for a moment, acknowledging what I'd done.

Time stretched. The caves we passed through were mostly dark with a few dimly lit ones. I began to understand why he chose the dark caves. If there were infected in them, I never heard them. The dimly lit caves were another story.

In those, the infected lingered in the shadows at the edge of the light, the place where they could likely see the best. They rarely made any noise, standing still and just watching everything.

We had so many close calls that I lost count. Moments where Molev paused and listened only to change his mind at the last moment and backtrack. He moved quickly, darting from shadow to shadow to avoid being spotted.

He put endless effort into evading detection after ignoring the infected that had followed us on the way in. It gave me something else to think about when we were in the dark caves, and I couldn't help watching for infected. I'd seen him disappear under a wave of infected and come out just fine. He had to be worried about being swarmed by them and unable to protect me.

Why bring me with then? Did he think the rest of the group at the tree wouldn't make it out?

I saw a distant speck of light ahead and glanced up at Molev. His gaze was scanning everything around us as he paused in a shadow. Instead of looking for the next shadowed spot away from the light, he was focused on it.

I scanned the darkness with him, looking for infected and spotted one ahead to the left. Molev nodded at the light tap on his left shoulder but didn't stop scanning the path ahead.

The infected turned away slightly, watching in the other direction. Molev sprinted forward toward the next shadowed hiding place.

Another infected appeared in front of us, walking by gracefully without looking at where Molev had us pressed against the rock. I barely breathed and waited until it passed, hiding my face against Molev's chest.

It wasn't out of fear. Molev's grey skin helped him blend

with the shadows. My clothes and gloves were dark, blending just as well, but not my pale face.

He sprinted forward again then stopped. I kept my face hidden and waited. Something scraped nearby. How many were there? How close were they?

His hold tightened on me, and he lurched forward.

An infected called out.

And another.

I lifted my head and looked behind Molev as he ran.

Infected emerged from the darkness. Maybe a dozen. Nothing horrible that he couldn't handle on his own.

They chased after us, growing more visible in the increasing light.

I turned to look at the next cave opening, not far away now, and blinked against the blindness.

"Go to the source," Molev said. "I will guard the entrance."

He released me and spun around. I ran for the light on unstable legs and entered a much smaller cavern. Ferns, grass, trees, and other strange vegetation grew in a dense tangle around an odd formation of crystals in the center of the space.

The massive cluster of crystals extended down from the ceiling and up from the floor, creating an hour-glass shape. A white-blue crystal connecting the two, pulsated with life and power.

The source.

I ran forward as I unzipped my bag. The bomb was simple enough. It was the effectiveness I questioned. Richard and Ryan had been worried about it going off too quickly and causing a cave-in that we wouldn't be able to escape. So they'd rigged something that had some hand grenades in the middle of it. I only hoped it would be enough to destroy the glowing rock ahead.

Panting, I stopped in front of the crystal and pulled out the rope I'd need to tie the bag in place.

A scrape of noise behind me had me spinning with my arm up. Why I hadn't thought it might be Molev, I couldn't say. But my fast reaction blocked the infected as it grabbed my shoulders and tried to bite my cheek.

I heaved to the side in an attempt to throw him off and win some space so I could pull my knife. The infected's red gaze held mine as it pulled me along.

We both fell into the crystal. His cheek connected with the glowing stone at the same time as my knuckles.

The cave around me faded, and I saw the world through a different lens.

The darkness wasn't dark anymore, and I felt a hunger and a hate I'd never known before. The earth trembled, and I howled my rage when I felt two of the cursed ones leave.

They were not meant for this world. The surface and all it held was forbidden to them. We needed to destroy it. Destroy everything. End the cursed ones' hope forever.

We poured out onto the surface, ravaging everything. We watched our need to destroy spread.

With a single bite, the humans understood why they needed to die. They understood the cursed ones would forever be alone and trapped as they were meant to be if they could not breed with them.

The humans were weak and slow, but we continued regardless, understanding our evolution had taken time. Theirs would too.

We warned them to avoid the fey and focus on the humans. They couldn't hear us. Many fell to the fey, but many remained to replace them.

The older ones grew smarter. They began to hear us and avoid the fey. However, they still died easily. The lingering hint of fey in their bloodlines kept many of their hearts from crystalizing like ours. It kept them from connecting to the crystal's power and life source for a very long time.

And then we felt it. The connection of the first one with eyes like ours. More connected to us.

It was our time.

We gathered many and sought out the lingering pockets of humans hidden away.

Devastation consumed the world. We saw it all.

Camps in different countries torn apart. People crying out in languages we couldn't understand and didn't want to understand. We reveled in the destruction of everything.

We were close.

So close.

Very few humans remained now.

Soon, all hope would be gone and the cursed ones would once again be trapped in darkness for their sin of wanting what was not theirs to possess.

I EXHALED...

THE HATE AND RAGE VANISHED. Power filled me. Life.

I saw the crystal as it was. Not an entity, exactly, but a source of something. It echoed the emotions of the things tied to it.

I saw how it had given pieces of itself when the fey had asked for its help.

I asked for help.

And I saw a shard drive into the skull of the infected pressed against the surface.

. . .

I INHALED...

INFORMATION FLOODED MY MIND. *All the things that had come before. Details I'd heard from Mya and Molev and more I hadn't.*

I saw the endless suffering of the fey.

I saw Molev sitting beside the source, admitting his weariness.

I felt the source's message.

Life.

Choose life.

I STUMBLED back from the source as the shard broke off and the infected fell to the side. It blinked at me, not dead, but not standing. It couldn't die. Not with a headshot anymore. Its heart had hardened like a hound's, powered by the crystal.

Molev's angry cry echoed from the mouth of the cave.

I hurried to finish setting the bomb. As soon as I had the fuse laid out, I lit it and sprinted toward the mouth of the cave where Molev was still fighting.

"We need to run!"

CHAPTER TWENTY-FOUR

MOLEV'S SAVAGERY REACHED A WHOLE NEW LEVEL AT THE SOUND of my voice. He ripped heads off and threw them far. I saw why when one of the headless infected went stumbling after it.

He removed the last one and turned in time to catch me up in his arms.

He ran hard, dodging oncoming infected.

One caught my ankle, and Molev almost lost his grip on me because his arms and hands were slick with blood. But I held onto his shirt with cramping fingers and kicked out with my other foot. The infected lost its hold without Molev slowing.

It wasn't enough.

We hadn't yet reached the cavern's opening when the explosion rocked the ground beneath us. The boom filled my ears, and I looked behind us. The infected chasing us fell in their tracks. Debris rained down from above as the cave continued to rumble.

I wrapped my arms around Molev and held on.

"I love you," I said. "No matter what happens, I love you."

He ran faster, swerving around falling obstacles.

We reached the next cave just as the ceiling above collapsed in the previous cave.

The dust from it flooded the new cave. Molev didn't stop, staying just ahead of the mess. The next cave was better and lit. We saw the infected bodies lying where they'd fallen.

One still walked around but aimlessly. When it saw us, it ran after Molev for a bit until it lost sight and returned to shambling without direction.

Molev's steps slowed, and I saw a collapsed opening ahead. He veered in another direction, taking a different route. We found another blocked passage there too.

The dust was growing thicker, and the rumbling from above hadn't stopped.

"Wait. Put me down for a second," I said.

He hesitated.

"We can't keep going like this." I coughed, and he finally put me down and watched me strip out of my shirt. Once I had my layers on again, I tore the clean shirt in half and tied the pieces around our faces.

"It'll help a little."

He picked me up again and ran with me for almost another hour before we found a miracle. A cave that ended in light.

Molev leapt from boulder to boulder, making his way upward until he had to put me down and we climbed together.

Fresh air and sunlight greeted us at the top.

I collapsed on the grass and tore my shirt away from my face as I stared up at the sky. Molev's uncovered face blocked my view a second later.

He pressed his forehead to mine and closed his eyes.

I tipped my head up and kissed him lightly.

"We did it," I said.

He pulled back to look down at me.

"But was it enough?"

I reached up and cupped his cheek in my hand.

"It was. I promise. I saw it when I touched the crystal. The hounds and the infected with the red eyes were connected to the crystal in a way that prevented them from dying but also kept them going. Without the crystal, they fell where they stood. The ones not connected to it are still around, though."

He grunted and pulled me to my feet. "We should keep moving then."

I looked around the grassy slope and spotted a road in the distance.

"Let's head for that," I said.

We walked for a bit before Molev spotted a mailbox on the road. He opened it and handed me the paper.

"Does it say where we are?" he asked.

"It's a Morehead Kentucky paper," I said. "Let's check the house and see if we can find any supplies."

We found infected, which Molev killed, and an already cleaned out house. However, we were able to wash up and change clothes.

The next house had been cleaned out as well, but we found keys to the car in the driveway. It didn't have much gas in it, but that turned out not to be a problem. About ten miles down the road, we came across a cluster of abandoned cars. One had gas cans and a siphon tube in it. The decaying bodies around it and the infected inside of it told the tale.

Molev killed the infected and filled our tank. We continued on, weaving our way along, checking homes and cars until we had food and a map. Near sunset, we found a house with heat and running water.

"Go shower," I said. "You still have stuff in your hair. I'll have something warm to eat when you're done."

He looked around the house and eventually nodded.

"Keep the door open if you're worried," I called.

I wasn't worried. Not that I had Molev's instincts or anything. I just knew what the crystal had shown me. The world had once again undergone a major change. Without the crystal's power, the hounds were dead. I was sure of that after seeing the way the evolved infected had dropped. And even though there were still a lot of unevolved infected out there, I was confident we could deal with them if we were smart.

The soup was steaming on the stove when Molev wrapped his arms around me from behind and kissed the side of my neck.

"You eat," I said. "It's my turn to shower. I feel like I have dust everywhere."

He let me go, and I basked in a lukewarm shower.

When I emerged, he was waiting for me with a mug of still-steaming soup. A mattress and a dresser blocked the hallways.

His gaze swept over me, and I glimpsed his worry.

"Do you think they made it out?" I asked softly.

He threaded his fingers through mine and led me to the bedroom.

"I have no answer for that," he said as he sat on the bed.

I sipped my soup, studying him. He was tired. For the first time, I saw circles under his eyes.

"We're on the second floor. You've blocked the hallway. How about you get some sleep? You look like you need it."

He plucked the cup from my fingers and set it aside before falling back with me sprawled on top of him.

I looked down at him and saw his plea. He needed me. It wasn't only a physical need but a balm to help him forget.

Straddling him, I removed my shirt then leaned down to

kiss him gently. His hands settled on my hips as he kissed me back.

Hours later, I lay next to him, studying his sleep-relaxed face.

The last several months didn't seem real. Hellhounds, fey, infected, my part in everything that had happened to save the people I loved. But most of all, it was Molev who didn't seem real. A man who might not understand every decision I made, but one who would love me no matter what.

I snuggled closer and listened to the sounds outside.

Everything was quiet. No howls. No moans.

Just Molev's soft breathing.

MOLEV'S FINGERS toyed with my bare nipple, and I hummed my approval as I woke up.

"Sounds like rain," I said, threading my fingers through his hair when his mouth closed over me.

He grunted and scraped his teeth against my sensitive skin.

"We can stay here and finish what you started, or we can get up and head out so we're in our own bed tonight."

He growled lightly and drew hard on my nipple before releasing it with a pop.

I smoothed my hand along his jaw and touched his frown line.

"You know everyone back home is going to be worried until we show up and tell them what happened."

He sighed, rolled away, and sat on the edge of the bed.

I got to my knees and wrapped my arms around his neck from behind.

"Once we're home and everything's settled, we can lock

ourselves in our house for a week so you can have your way with me without interruption,"I said. Then for good measure, I lightly bit his earlobe.

He groaned, and I grinned.

"I'll bite other things too when we're back. I promise."

He had me pinned to the mattress and entered me with a single thrust that made my eyes roll back even as I winced.

"Just right," I breathed when he didn't immediately move.

He took his time, loving me twice, then helped me shower.

It was close to ten by the time we finally headed out. No infected had found their way into the house overnight, but a few lingered in the yard. Rather than take the car, we moved everything over to a truck so Molev could ride in the back.

He cleared any roadblocks we encountered and killed the infected.

Some of them still showed signs of intelligence that I didn't like, but none of them had red eyes, supporting my theory that those were the ones that had died.

The detours around the larger cities ate up the daylight, and I was starting to worry that we'd need to find another house until I saw the sign for St. Louis. I pulled over near an abandoned car on the highway and took out the maps I'd collected throughout the drive. While Molev siphoned the gas, I planned the next leg of our journey home.

"What do you think?" I asked when he returned. "Should we push through or find somewhere for the night after St. Louis?"

"Push through," he said. "We're close."

Once daylight faded, his eyes saw farther than the headlights. He tapped on the roof a few times for me to stop so he could deal with whatever was blocking the road. An infected came out of nowhere one of those times and tried my door, but I'd locked it, thankfully.

That infected lost its head quickly.

We turned onto Tolerance's road well after dark, and that was a good thing. The night kept me from seeing every gory detail in the sea of undead surrounding the place or the fey who walked among them, picking up the bodies and loading them into the back of trucks like the one I drove.

I did a Y turn where I was and backed in as close as I could.

When I stopped, Molev hopped down and opened the door. He waved over the closest fey as I looked over the fields of dead. Most of them were headless. Some lay where they fell, their heads still on.

"Did the others return?" he asked the fey.

The man nodded, looking extremely tired. "At midday. They are helping clear the remaining infected."

Relief coursed through me as someone called the fey's name. He nodded toward Molev and jogged away to climb into a waiting truck.

"Looks like our passionate night together will need to wait," I said.

He grunted and kissed my forehead. "I will take you inside and return to help."

A few of the fey called out half-hearted greetings when they saw him running with me but continued picking up bodies and carrying them to the trucks. We passed one with its head still attached, and it stood suddenly.

Another fey quickly ran over and beheaded it.

"Some are still alive," he said. "I'll go with you."

He ran as an escort until Molev cleared the wall.

Inside, the streets were stained with more blood, and I felt a twinge of guilt for stopping the night before.

"Molev!" a woman called. She ran toward us, her blonde curls bouncing. "God, am I glad to see you."

She didn't wait for him to put me down but hugged us both. "Can you please talk to Merdon? He's at Cassie's and won't stay down." She sounded angry, but I could see the extra sheen in her eyes.

"How about I help with that?" I asked. "It looks like the guys outside could really use Molev."

She nodded, and Molev put me down.

"Send some of those men inside to wash up and rest," I said. "I know there are still infected out there, but your brothers aren't doing anyone any favors by working until they collapse."

"Finally, a voice of reason," the woman said.

Molev grunted, kissed my forehead, and jumped over the wall again.

"I'm Hannah," the blonde said, hooking her arm through mine.

"Andie."

"I kind of figured, considering who you showed up with."

"How bad is it here?" I asked.

She exhaled heavily. "It could have been worse. They came out of nowhere. A sea of infected just like you and Molev had warned. If we wouldn't have added to the wall, they would have gotten in here within seconds. It saved us. The infected hit the wall and fell under the infected behind them, building up at the base, while more infected climbed over them. We all knew it was only a matter of time.

"Then the howling started. It sounded like it was coming from everywhere, all at once.

"Angel and I came up with a 'when shit hits the fan' plan. We had ladders ready by a few houses. They were meetup spots. When one of the fey used the airhorn we found, we all ran for the ladders. We climbed to the roofs and pulled the ladders up with us. So we had a perfect view of how the infected flooded over the wall with the hounds. The fey fought hard. Heads flew everywhere. The hounds clawed at the siding, climbing it." She pointed at a house that had shredded siding.

"Then I saw a headless body pick up a head and stick it back on."

She looked at me, tears gathering in her eyes.

"We were fucked. They were piling up around the houses like they had the wall. Then suddenly, over half of the infected just...dropped. So did every single hound."

She shook her head and cleared her throat. "It was still a fight. There were so many infected left. We stayed on the roofs last night, listening to the fey behead them. The fey managed to give the all-clear just before first light. A few of us came down and helped double-check the houses.

"Then we worked together to clean up the bodies. We finished in here just before dinner."

"How many did we lose?" I asked.

"A few were too slow to reach the ladders," she said. "And the hounds did a number on the fey. There isn't a single one of them who isn't sporting some stitches. That doctor you brought and her team came in handy. She knew how to patch them up and send them back out."

We turned up a blood-stained sidewalk to Cassie's house, and Hannah let herself in without knocking.

A low murmur of voices came from the back of the house before one rose above the rest.

"If you wake the kids, Kerr will knock you out," a woman said.

"Cassie hasn't slept yet–like most of us," Hannah said softly, leading the way through the house.

Cassie stood in a room, one hand on the stitched-up fey's chest to pin the surly owner of said chest to the bed.

"Hey, Cassie," I said. "Heard you're exhausted and could use some sleep."

"Yes," she said without taking her eyes off the patient.

The fey looked at me, his gaze mostly unfocused. He blinked several times.

"Molev?" he asked.

"If you can't see I'm a human woman, you have no right to get out of that bed."

"I see who you are. Molev's female, Andie. Is he back?"

"He is. Why do you keep trying to get out of bed?"

"My brothers need help."

"How far do you think you'll make it before you inconvenience them by passing out and making them carry you back in here?"

He blinked at me again.

"Help us by staying in that bed," I said. "And stop wasting everyone's time by being stubborn. You've done your part while we sat on the sides, unable to do anything. It's our turn now. Rest."

He grunted and closed his eyes.

"Hannah will be back to check on you in two hours," I said. "No getting out of that bed until then."

"If you need to pee, use the bottle," Cassie said, turning and leaving the room.

Hannah kissed his forehead.

"Sleep, baby. The faster you heal, the faster you can get out there again."

We left the room and let ourselves out of the house.

"I like your level of tough love," Hannah said as I looked around the quiet houses.

"Thanks. What's everyone doing to help?" I asked.

"The humans who know how to shoot are helping watch the wall. The fey who are able are loading up bodies and hauling them away. Ryan found a gravel pit they're using as a dumping ground."

"Okay," I said. "Let's round up some drivers. We can drive the trucks back and forth so the fey don't have to."

We knocked on the doors of the immune women, including Mya, to ask for help so the fey could rest. We pitched in and worked through the night in shifts, doing our part to help to clean up the thousands of bodies around Tolerance.

By the end of the third clean-up day, the gravel pit was overflowing, but all three communities were clear of the deceased. Ryan and Richard pushed dirt and gravel over the body pile that night. I heard from Mya that June in Tenacity had buried her ex-boyfriend in a separate grave between our two settlements and planted one of the Ernisi tree seeds.

We all finally had a chance to grieve everyone and everything we'd lost since the quakes.

The next morning, a torrent of rain started. It marked the first day Molev and I didn't need to hurry out of bed for some reason.

I lay in Molev's arms, sweating and tired from our sex-a-thon, and listened to the rain drum against the roof.

"It's a weird combination of feeling like it's finally over and that things are just starting," I said.

"Explain," he said, running his fingers through my hair.

"The bodies are cleaned up, and the immediate danger is gone. It's time to start thinking about what's next. What we want our future to look like. We don't have to worry about the hounds anymore, and the infected that remain aren't as smart or as organized. They're still a threat, but not to the same degree they were."

He grunted in agreement.

"So, what's next for us? And I don't mean me and you; I mean humanity."

"We find out how many are left," he said.

I sighed heavily and nodded.

Since we'd returned with news that destroying the crystal had killed the hounds, the doctor had been trying to contact the other research team. No one had answered yet. However, we had heard from other survivors. Families and small groups here and there who reached out after hearing all the hounds were dead.

Matt and June had met with a few of them to provide supplies and information. The last meetup had been ambushed. It hadn't gone well for the ambushers. The poor family had been a little shocked by the sudden appearance of fey.

The fey, including Merdon, were doing well and healing quickly. All the stitches had gained them extra attention and care. Unity had more couples in it than Tolerance now.

"I'm not so sure there will be many volunteers to go out and find more survivors," I said. "Your brothers won't have any reason to leave soon."

"Won't they?" Molev asked. "We do not know if there are still humans out there, trying to find a way to kill us. We need to protect the future children my brothers may have."

His words poked at my heart.

"I *am* sorry," I said softly. "My choice was never to hurt you."

He kissed my forehead.

"I know. It was to spare yourself the fear and worry you already feel for your brother and his children. How is Rachel?"

"A mess," I said. "Neither of us imagined not being able to contact them eventually."

"Matt said there's fuel left at Whiteman. They were using a small plane to look for me when I didn't return. We can use it to reestablish bases. We will build a network of communities like these here, where humans and fey co-exist, until we reach the coast and can send a message to your brother."

I ran my fingers over Molev's chest.

"I like that idea. I have another one you might like."

I kissed his chest then an inch lower, slowly working my way down his abs.

His fingers threaded through my hair, adding that kick of dominance I craved from him.

"I like this idea too," he said.

CHAPTER TWENTY-FIVE

Spent and shaking, I collapsed on top of Molev. He kissed my head and picked me up as he stood with me still impaled. Instead of heading toward the shower, he pinned me to a wall and started thrusting into me. I panted as I met each one with growing fervor.

He bathed my insides yet again after a few minutes, detonating another orgasm for me. I moaned and fell against him, sweaty and weak.

"The sun will be setting soon," I panted. "The others will come for us if we are late."

With the hell of the last few days past us, Emily had organized a get-together. Our invitation had come via Fallor. He'd politely waited outside the house until after my first O then let himself inside and called out to Molev while I caught my breath.

Life in Tolerance would take some getting used to that way. I'd need to get used to Molev's insatiable sex drive too.

After our invite, there hadn't been any interruptions, and Molev had gotten his day with me, just like he'd wanted. I had to admit, it was pretty magical getting his undivided attention like I had. However, I wasn't sure I could survive 365 days of it. The man needed distractions, or I'd never leave the bedroom.

So, Emily's party was a welcome reprieve…if I could walk.

Molev chuckled at the way I spasmed when he finally removed me from his still-hard cock in the shower. I insisted on washing myself so we didn't start anything and smirked at the hint of disgruntlement in his expression.

The hunger in his eyes when he watched me dress had me hurrying. We left earlier than we needed to, but that was okay.

He held the umbrella over us as we walked down the street together. The rain was already working miracles, erasing the horror of what had happened, and I inhaled deeply, smelling spring.

"A new season is starting," I said. "We should talk about where else we want to plant those seeds."

Molev grunted and looked at the high wall surrounding Tolerance.

"The wall hides your trees. If our trees grow here, they would be seen for miles."

"Is that a good thing or a bad thing?" I asked.

"That is not something I can answer now," he said.

I nodded. "Until we know what's left out there, it's hard to say if a giant tree at our doorstep would be a good thing or a bad thing. Although, those trees will take time to grow to the size they were in the caves." I glanced at him. "I think we should plant one in the open field here, no matter what. Something to mark that this is your home too."

He looked down at me, love showing in his gaze, and I smiled.

"Aw! Look at you two being all cute and coupley," Roni called from behind us.

I turned and watched her jog our way, a hood up to protect her from the rain.

"Where's Brog?" I asked.

She shrugged, looking way too innocent.

I stopped walking. "What did you do?"

"Nothing he didn't have coming. I'm sure he'll catch up with us soon." She hooked her arm through mine.

"How's the sex been?" she asked. "Off the charts as usual?"

"Is he still not giving up the goods?" I asked.

"Not yet. But he's close to snapping. I can feel it." Her grin was a little crazed.

"So, Mya mentioned supplies are getting low," I said, changing the subject. "I think a group is heading out in the morning. I was thinking of going with to find out what level of infected we're dealing with now."

"Count me in," she said. "I heard through the fey-vine that there are still a lot of them out there. That's why Matt and June get a heavier escort when they go, not because the fey are just looking for new vag-vaults to crack.

"Speaking of vag-vaults, have you seen Katie around?" she asked.

I chuckled and shook my head. "I saw her yesterday. Ben caught her trying to get someone else to take her over the wall when she was done driving to the pit."

"Bet that was fun to watch. Sucks I missed it."

"I'm sure we'll see her tonight."

Roni rubbed her hands together. "Good. I need some distraction."

She speculated where the group would be going for supplies the next day as we made our way to Emily's place. Hannah opened the door on the first knock.

"Welcome and come on in," she said, waving us inside while Molev shook out the umbrella.

I saw Katie was already there, talking to James and Mary. Mya was by the food set out on the table, sampling with Angel. Shax held fey court with baby Daisy in the kitchen. All those men gathered around that tiny baby was admittedly adorable.

"Can I get you anything to drink?" Emily asked.

"I'm fine. Thanks," I said.

"Got any whiskey?" Roni asked. "I'd kill for an actual drink."

James perked up at that and waved her over. I watched him slip a flask from his jacket and pass it to her.

"Having a hard time, dear?" Mary asked.

"I'd like to have a harder time, but Brog still isn't cooperating," Roni said.

Katie cringed, and Mary hooted her laughter.

"There is not enough therapy chocolate in the world for what's coming," Hannah said. "I wish I still drank."

"Hannah." Merdon, who'd been ogling the baby with the rest of them, stared at Hannah with warning in his eyes.

"I said, 'I wish,' not that I will." She rolled her eyes and took my arm, steering me to the table. "I'm seriously considering jumping on the baby wagon just so he stops helicoptering me."

Emily snorted. "Like that would change anything. There are too many hands waiting to hold babies. Now, if you wait a few years, you might get your wish."

"What's going to change in a few years?" she asked.

"Fewer infected, and people will start feeling safer," I said.

"Pregnancy will be more appealing when a girl isn't imagining sprinting for her life while waddling," Angel said. Daisy started to fuss then, and twin spots appeared on Angel's shirt. She looked down and sighed. Shax hurried over with Daisy.

"I'm sorry, my Angel."

"Pfft. You're doing all the laundry. I'm sorry I keep doing this. Whoever goes out tomorrow needs to find me reusable nursing pads. Please."

"I like washing your clothes," Shax said, handing the baby over and watching as Angel started to nurse standing where she was.

"If they can't find you any, I think one of the ladies over in Unity can make you some," Emily said. "She's amazing with the sewing machine."

"Sounds good to me." Angel glanced at Mya. "Chip me."

Mya grinned and fed her a chip.

The house continued to fill with people. Steve and Roland showed up before Sid and Brandon. They chatted with the fey about the upcoming supply run and relocating some of the herd to Unity since it had more pasture space.

"You really don't want all those animals here much longer," Brandon said. "The smell will sneak up on you fast."

Julie, Mya's mom, talked about building raised beds, and Angel jumped in, talking about building a greenhouse so the community could have fresh produce all year round.

"Terri has a green thumb and would love to have one," she said. "The bigger the better. Here and in the other communities."

"I think we could make that happen," Richard said. "Especially if we can reclaim some of that space in that empty lot."

"June knows something about hydroponics too," Mya said. "We should add that to the project plans for this year."

"Are June and Matt coming over?" Julie asked.

Emily shook her head. "No, they're having a gathering over there to celebrate too."

As I listened, I felt a bittersweet sense of peace. The world hadn't magically reverted to the one we'd known, but that didn't mean we were doomed. It just meant we needed to find a new way to live. To survive.

And in that regard, I guessed nothing had really changed. People everywhere had struggled to survive before the earthquakes too. Just in different ways. No one was worrying about paying the bills now. Or building a career that meant something.

Our worries were simpler in a lot of ways. We just needed to worry about putting food on the table and not dying when we left the community. But I understood now that those worries would lessen as time passed. We'd work together to ensure we didn't starve. And the fey and people like my team would do their part to continue to reduce the number of infected.

"All right," Angel said. "Who wants Daisy?"

Drav moved incredibly fast, scooping the baby from Angel's breast before Shax could. Mya pouted when she realized she hadn't even stood a chance, and Angel laughed as she reclasped her nursing bra.

"See?" she said to Mya. "This is why I'm fine with having another one right away. I'm going to eat up all the willing help while the rest of you dither."

"The only thing you're going to eat up is all the food," Hannah said. "And dither? When did my grandma get here."

"I heard that," Mary called.

Everyone was still laughing when a tween girl I hadn't yet met burst through the door.

"We need help!"

Daisy was in Mya's arms, and the fey were out the door

before I could blink. Roni and I were right on their heels. She passed me a handgun from one of her many holsters as we ran.

Then we heard it.

A long, mournful howl.

It was familiar and not a sound I ever thought I'd hear again.

"Fuck," Roni breathed. "It's a dog."

We both ran faster, making it to the section of the wall where a young woman and a woman in a wheelchair waited.

"Is it crazy that I was starting to believe they were really all gone?" the older woman asked when she heard us.

"No," I said.

"We were on the way to the party when we heard it, and Mom didn't want Uan to attempt it on his own."

"That man already went through hell, wrestling a hound," the older woman said. "I have no idea what a scared dog will do to him. I'm Nancy, by the way. This is my daughter Brenna."

"Nice to meet you. I'm Andie. This is Roni."

"I really hope they can get it before it runs off," Brenna said.

Another long, lone howl rang out.

"Doesn't sound like it's going anywhere," Roni said, stealing her firearm back.

"Uan said it ran from him," Nancy said.

"It'd probably go faster if one of us went out there," Roni said.

Brog materialized out of the darkness.

"I will take you," he said, tossing Roni over his shoulder in the way I personally hated.

She seemed to as well. "How is this the best way to take me over the wall?" She slapped his back. He slapped her ass. She stilled and hissed out a breath. "Okay. Fine. I'll give you that one. But you hit me that hard again without immediately rubbing it, I'm dick slapping you while you sleep."

He ran up the wall without answering her.

"Uh, are they together?" Brennaa asked.

"I'm not really sure," I said. "But it's not from lack of trying on her part."

Nancy chuckled. "She's got fire, grit, and is able to use both. He'll figure out how to handle that eventually."

High-pitched yipping and whining broke out.

"Sounds like someone's ripping its legs off," Brenna said.

A second later, Brog appeared at the top of the wall with Roni. He held her in his arms while she struggled to hold a thrashing dog in hers.

"Get us down there," she yelled.

Brog stepped off the edge. They fell. She swore. When they landed, she released the dog.

"It peed on me," she said, holding out her arms in disgust. "Take me home to wash me, Brog, or I'm going to be very not okay in about two seconds."

He quickly left with her, and I laughed and watched the dog zoom around Nancy and Brenna, leaping and licking and wagging its tail like crazy. Its fur was a mess, and it smelled horrible.

"You need some love, don't you?" Nancy crooned, trying to pet it. "I know just the girl to take care of you."

"Not it," Brenna said quickly.

Nancy chuckled until the fey who'd run to help came raining down from the wall, which sent the dog leaping into her lap.

"Not today, my friend," Brenna said, quickly scooping up the large dog. "Uan, get Mom so this thing can't jump on her again." One of the fey carefully picked Nancy up.

"I will take her home," Uan said.

"We're right behind you," Brenna said, easing the dog down. It immediately tried crawling back into her arms. A stern-looking fey moved up behind her.

"Sit." The command was spoken softly, without a hint of anger or volume. Yet, the dog immediately responded. It sat and whined as it wiggled in place.

"Thallirin, I think you're a dog whisperer," she said.

"It probably understands I will not tolerate it hurting you," Thallirin said.

Brenna smiled up at him and patted the dog's head before looking at me.

"Would you mind sending Tasha home and letting everyone know we probably won't make it tonight?" she asked.

"You do know that the party's probably just going to move to your house because of that," I said, nodding toward the dog.

"Not my house," she said quickly. "Tell everyone it's Tasha's, and they need to go to Uan and Nancy's."

"Got it."

I left her to deal with the dog and found Tasha and the rest of the party-goers well-guarded by Steve, Brandon, Sid, and Roland.

"Well?" Steve asked. "Was it a dog or a hound? It sounded like a dog to me."

"A dog," I confirmed. "One that needs a bath, something to eat, and a face to lick for at least an hour."

Tasha squealed and clapped her hands in excitement.

"Brenna said you should go home. Sounds like they were taking the dog there."

"I will walk you," one of the fey who'd followed me said.

Several left with her, including Steve, who wanted to look at the dog.

"Where there's one, there's bound to be more," Julie said. "Better start gathering the dog food up."

Mya laughed at the face Drav made. "Don't worry. We'll feed them the dry stuff, and you can keep eating the canned stuff."

Molev wrapped his arms around me from behind.

"I will find you one," he said softly.

I twisted to look up at him in question, and he kissed my nose.

"I saw the longing in your eyes when you looked at it," he said.

"My niece and nephew had a dog. It's them I'm longing for, not the dog."

His arms tightened around me, and he hugged me close.

"I know it's been hard to focus on anything else with all the clean-up," Emily said, overhearing, "But that doesn't mean anyone is giving up on finding more survivors."

"Matt's been working with the pilots to run fuel calculations for those locations you gave him," Mya said. "There are a lot of promising ones. Plus, there are general airports we can hit up. We'll make contact with that island sanctuary even if we have to fly there ourselves."

MONTHS LATER, the sound of a plane overhead drew me out of the house. Shielding my eyes, I looked up and watched it fly toward Whiteman. The base, once abandoned, was once again secured against infected as were half a dozen more in the central states. Hopefully, the people arriving would have news of more.

"Hey, Andie," Katie called. "I was just about to come see if you wanted to go shopping with me."

Katie's airy summer dress molded to her large baby bump in the light breeze as she navigated the sidewalk in front of my house. Almost every square on this block had a chalk design on it, courtesy of Lil and Timmy.

"Shopping? Where are you going shopping?"

"Warrensburg. Ben said that it's clear enough that they're taking buses in for non-essentials."

Essentials had been cleared out the weeks following the fall of the hounds. Those with a knack for repurposing had been begging to take another trip in.

"Thanks, but I think I'm going to hang out here for news," I said.

She nodded. "I understand. I'll see if Roni's interested."

"If you see Rachel, tell her I'm headed to Unity tomorrow and to clear her schedule."

"Will do," she said with a wave, making her way to the wall.

Leaving the front door open to let the breeze in, I walked to Drav and Mya's house. Fey nodded to me as I passed. Most of them looked at my legs and chest. I tried not to grin. Until recently, they'd had no idea how much skin would be exposed in the hot summer months and absolutely loved August…and bikinis.

Fey lounged on Mya's neatly mowed front lawn in the shade of the single tree and said hello as I walked to her house. It was a pretty familiar sight these days.

Since the front door was open, I called a hello through the screen.

"Come on in," she called back. "I'm just feeding Ricky."

She was sitting on the couch, nursing her newborn son, who

was a replica of his father in every way but the eyes. Those were just like his mother's.

"Mind if I listen to the radio for a bit?" I asked.

She shook her head. "Figured you'd be here when I heard the plane."

I looked at the map she had framed on the wall above the radio. Pins marked the locations of the reestablished bases. They weren't manned by fey, but welcomed fey, having been reclaimed and continually supplied by them. Steve and Roland were at two of them, heading up the efforts to spread to the west, just as eager to reunite with their loved ones.

"Did you hear that they finished the third greenhouse this morning?" Mya asked.

"That's a lot of planting room," I said, thinking of the large frames the fey had moved from a local nursery.

"We have a lot of mouths to feed. Matt says we should have enough fuel to do monthly drops at all the bases so they can have fresh produce too. And Ryan and Viki think the potato crop is going to stun us. Drav said he'll take us there tomorrow."

"I planned on visiting Rachel tomorrow. But I'll check it out."

She lifted Ricky and set him against her shoulder, not worrying about covering up in front of me. It was the fey she set the boundaries with "for the sake of future shy moms."

"We have an update for all our listeners," a voice said over the radio. "We've officially reached California. Fort Irwin wasn't abandoned and the survivors were glad to see us. Supplies were low and the infected count was high. Their fences have been cleared, and their supplies will be restocked within a day, thanks to the efforts of our fey friends. If you see a big grey guy with pointy ears, remember, guns are a challenge, and a smile is a welcome. I highly suggest not trying to ambush them after a smile, either. It won't end well for you. Stay tuned for the regular update at high noon and dusk. Rebroadcast on all stations."

The person announcing didn't repeat the message. They'd wait to do that for an hour at noon and again at dusk. They'd dedicated the channel and set times like a news station. There were pockets of survivors out there who regularly listened and responded now. It still wasn't safe enough to share locations, but talking was a start.

I turned the volume down on the radio and faced Mya again as she nursed Ricky on the other side.

She smiled excitedly. "Someone there has to know the location."

I nodded, holding onto my hope. "And if not, we still have the location on the coast."

Ricky pulled away from her and squirmed. She sighed and gave me a hopeful look.

"Would you mind?" she asked.

"Not at all."

I put him against my shoulder and inhaled his baby scent as she righted her shirt.

"You any closer to caving?" she asked, watching me.

Shrugging, I smiled slightly. I wasn't as opposed to a baby as I'd been. In the fey's mind, there were no set gender roles when it came to parenting. If I wanted to be a "dad" and sit on the couch while Molev bounced a kid on his hip and made dinner, it was socially acceptable here.

I kissed Ricky's dark head of hair.

"Want a nap?" I asked.

"Would you mind?"

"Not even a little," I said, grabbing the diaper bag that was always ready and by the door. Angel had started the trend so anyone could steal little Daisy whenever they wanted. It was handy because the fey were always wanting to do things with the "tiny humans."

As soon as I walked outside with Ricky and the bag, there was a chorus of groans.

"Sorry, guys, he's mine for a while," I said with a laugh.

I hadn't even reached our house when Molev materialized in front of me. The look he gave me was hungry in so many different ways.

"I stole the baby with Mya's permission," I said. "Want to play Daddy?"

I barely had the words out of my mouth before Ricky was in his arms.

"Your father wishes he was the strongest among us, but you will be stronger," Molev said as he walked inside with the infant.

Grinning, I followed the pair.

"Did you hear the other news?" I asked. "Or did the fey network only tell you how I'd taken off with Mya's baby?"

"They reached Fort Irwin," he said, settling on the couch and patting the spot beside him. "The researcher stopped experiementing after the last injection failed terribly."

"Good. No human-hellhound mutants running around then. Any news on where the sanctuary is?"

When I went to sit, he pulled me into his lap so he was holding me and the baby.

"We will find them soon," he said, sounding very sure.

"You think so?"

"I'm certain."

I let out a long exhale and looked at Ricky sleeping peacefully in Molev's arms.

"You're rarely wrong," I said, thoughtfully. "Which is why I want to ask you something."

He watched me, waiting.

"Will I regret having a baby with you?"

Taking my question seriously, he didn't answer immediately. And I loved him more for it.

"No," he said finally. "And we will have more than one."

I didn't get mad about that statement. Because I knew it would be the truth. Once my IUD was out, there would be very little stopping any pregnancy. After all, sex with Molev was amazing and would be non-stop if I hadn't set some rules, which I heard was common.

"And if you do start feeling anything close to regret, you will tell me immediately so I can change whatever is causing you to feel that way."

My heart swelled for the man holding me.

"Okay," I said. "As soon as you're done holding Ricky, we'll go talk to the doctor and Cassie about removing the IUD."

Molev blinked at me. I could see how torn he was. He didn't want to give up Ricky, but the idea of putting a baby in me had him by the bits.

"This is just a taste of what life will be like. Wanting me but not able to have your way with me because there's a baby that needs taking care of. Are you going to be okay with that?"

He gave me a slow smile with heat and warning in his gaze.

"Very."

EPILOGUE

Five years later...

I LOUNGED on the picnic blanket and watched my brother chase after the kids under the shade of the towering tree. He wasn't the only adult playing tag. Human and fey alike romped around with the horde of preschoolers.

"Drav is it!" Ricky yelled. Kids bolted in every direction, not that they could go far. Those watching them carefully kept them all corralled.

Molev slid in behind me, becoming my personal backrest as he kissed my temple and the side of my neck.

"Roni and Brog stole Tholin and Naomi," Molev said. "I have no baby to hold. When will this one come?" He slid his hands over my giant belly, massaging it.

"No harassing the pregnant lady for the next baby for at least six weeks after birth, Molev," Cassie said, passing by.

I twisted to look up at him. He frowned down at me, and I started laughing.

"I'll do my best to talk this one into coming soon," I said.

His hands drifted up to my breasts, rubbing them carefully. "I can help."

I rolled my eyes and turned to face the playing kids, and he slowly rubbed everywhere until I was a sighing puddle of relaxation.

Although I knew Molev would rock my world if I asked him to, it hadn't been comfortable when we'd attempted it a few days ago. The midwife had checked me after and had silently communicated that I was a little dilated but the plug was still in place. Grateful for her discretion, I'd confidently reported to Molev that everything was fine and I was just closer to giving birth.

Most of the fey husbands went a bit overboard with anticipation when they heard things were dilated. Molev was one of them. Keeping things low-key preserved my sanity.

I set my hands over Molev's when they paused on my stomach to feel the baby kick. If someone would have told twenty-year-old me that I would be doing my part to add to the world's meager population in the decades to come, I would have laughed my ass off. But having babies and being a mom wasn't the hardship I'd thought it would be. And I knew it was because I'd found the right partner. It helped that the earthquakes had ended the stereotypes of the patriarchal society I'd grown up knowing too.

"Waurlyn says that the delegates are asking to renegotiate their terms," Molev said.

"I bet they are," I said with a snort.

When we'd finally made contact with them four years ago, the people in charge of the sanctuary hadn't been so willing to talk. They'd tried demanding the return of the research team like we'd been holding them hostage. It didn't matter that the team members insisted they didn't want to go or that all attempts at a synthetic cure had failed. They hadn't believed a word of it. So, I'd told them to let us know when their supplies were low and they wanted to start kicking people off the island. It'd only taken them a week to get back to us.

My brother and the kids had been on the first aircraft of volunteers. That had been one of the last flights. Everything was by boat now. There were too few people left to warrant producing the fuel needed for flying. It wasn't a lost technology, just a rare one.

"What do they want this time? More jet fuel?"

"Information," Molev said. "They want to know how many hybrids there are."

My gaze swept over the people around us. Almost all of the women had grey patches on their skin somewhere. Were we now considered hybrids?

"And what did you say?"

"Nothing. Waurlyn laughed at them and ended the call."

I grinned. "I'm so glad Waurlyn's on our side. When is she due for a visit?"

"In a few weeks. She's in Canada now, meeting with the leaders there and learning how we can aid their recovery. She's already reported that the survivors are struggling but not due to infected. They are fighting each other."

I made a face. "No way. Canadians are knownfor their niceness."

"Groups migrated there thinking the cold would slow the infected."

"Ah. That makes sense. Not the slow theory. The fact that the people fighting aren't from there.

"Well, let Waurlyn know that once this bun is out of the

oven, I'm willing to volunteer for a three-month peacekeeping tour."

"Liar," Rachel said, sitting down beside us.

She pulled up her shirt and started nursing her youngest while rolling her eyes at me.

"Like you would miss a moment of these rug rats growing up."

I made a face at her and looked at my adorable niece. At six months, she was alert and had the prettiest blue eyes that she used to stare at Molev. Every now and again, she would smile at him. I knew those milky smiles melted him every time. He would take several bullets for any of these people, but especially the kids.

"Fine. You're right. I don't have it in me to leave."

I tipped my head back to look up at the already impressive tree June had planted five years ago.

"Did you ever think it would be like this, this fast?" I asked.

Rachel looked over at me from under her sunhat.

"The tree?" She shook her head and looked up at it. "They're tracking its growth rate and estimating fifty feet a year. I'm really glad we didn't plant it in the open lot like you wanted. Can you imagine if that thing fell over in a windstorm? It would have taken out too many roofs."

"I didn't mean the tree," I said, looking at the expansive branches and the vines already twisting their way up the thick trunk. "I meant sitting out in the open like this."

The last infected sighting in this area had been almost a year ago now. And it had been a lone infected wandering its way north. Our guess based on its worn-out flip-flops and the mission volunteer teeshirt was that it had been someone in South America who called the northern Midwest home.

Other parts of the world weren't as lucky, and people were

still fighting the infected. We did our part by offering what aid we could through supplies and sometimes a small group of fey. But only for short periods since they all had families now.

Little Tholin and Naomi ran up to us then with Roni's two kids and Brog close on their heels. Molev shifted me in his lap, catching both of them before they could pounce on me.

Tholin had his father's hair and eyes, but my skin tone and ears. Based on his current growth rate, he'd take after his father in size. Naomi was all her father and nothing of me except her comparatively petite size. The one in the oven kicked, a reminder that it would soon be three.

"Not in a million years," Rachel said when she looked at me again. "But we earned this peace, don't you think?"

We had.

AUTHOR'S NOTE

I can't tell you how much I appreciate each and every person who fell in love with the Resurrection world. When Becca and I first started this fun idea, we had no idea what it would turn into beyond that trilogy. Honestly, I'd planned to end it after book four, but so many of you were writing me, asking for more that I couldn't say no. I hope it never felt like I dragged out the series. That was never my intention. And I hope the ending was everything you were hoping for.

Some of you wrote in, asking about the humans (Emily, Garrett, Ryan) and wanting stories for them. I'm sorry I couldn't fit them in, but know that they (along with all the new characters and fey) are happily living their lives in the core communities enjoying their hard-won peace.

And for those of you wondering about Katie…I just couldn't kill her. I had her sleep with Ted with big plans of Molev being the first one to find out she was preggers and then not being able to save her. But I couldn't do it. So, fictional Katie eventually will succumb to Ben's charm and live happily ever after with all the foot rubs, back rubs, and boob rubs she could want.

As for Roni, I hope to write some Bonus Content yet this year for how she finally lands Brog. (Watch my Patreon site https://www.patreon.com/MelissaHaag for details!)

I absolutely loved writing about men obsessed with the women of their dreams. And I won't stop with the end of this series. If you're willing to take a leap of faith, check out my Sage Alder books. They're a little different from the zombies in this series, but I promise all the steam you've found in these books will be in those as well.

And if you haven't already checked out my other MJ Haag books, you need to start with the Beastly Tales. They have a darker twist on fairy tales but still deliver a sweet happily ever after. Or if you're after something a little more wolfy and grown up, check out the Melissa Nicole books (read a free sample at https://melissanicoleauthor.com/bb-chapter1)

And finally, be sure to sign up for my newsletter at http://mjhaag.melissahaag.com to watch for future releases and pen names. (I'm going to be writing adult shifter romances soon too!)

Until next time, happy reading!

Melissa

BLOOD AND BONBONS

BY MELISSA NICOLE

Everyone knows werewolves, fey, and goblins are real. No one warned me about vampires.

Everly's dream of becoming a baker almost shatters (along with her tailbone) when she topples into a vampire cave. Offering a tasty treat isn't enough to make amends for waking the surly, tall, and devastatingly handsome vampire. He'd rather have Everly…to help him adapt to the modern world, of course.

After one of her friends disappears, it's Everly's turn to ask Cross for help navigating the Shadow Trade world–a place she never wanted to enter. One misstep around supernatural creatures could cost Everly her life. But she soon finds she'll risk anything to keep the people she cares about safe.

With sugary bribes, questionable artifacts, mysterious tattoos, and extremely sexy supernaturals, Blood and Bonbons is the perfect blend of paranormal romance and cozy mystery.

Check out the first chapter at

https://melissanicoleauthor.com/bb-chapter1

THE RESURRECTION CHRONICLES

Humor, romance, and sexy dark fey!

Book 1: Demon Ember

In a world going to hell, Mya must learn to accept help from her new-found demon protector in order to find her family as a zombie-like plague spreads.

Book 2: Demon Flames

As hellhounds continue to roam and the zombie plague spreads, Drav leads Mya to the source of her troubles—Ernisi, an underground Atlantis and Drav's home. There Mya learns that the shadowy demons, who've helped devastate her world, are not what they seem.

Book 3: Demon Ash

While in Ernisi, cites were been bombed and burned in an attempt to stop the plague. Now, Marauders, hellhounds, and the infected are doing their best to destroy what's left of the world. It's up to Mya and Drav to save it.

Book 4: Demon Escape

While running from zombies, hellhounds, and the people who kept her prisoner, Eden encounters a new creature. He claims he only wants to protect her. Eden must decide who the real devils are between man and demon, and choosing wrong could cost her life.

Book 5: Demon Deception

Grieving from the loss of her husband and youngest child, Cassie lives in fear of losing her remaining daughter. To gain protection, Cassie knows she needs to sleep with one of the dark fey and give him the one thing she isn't sure she can. Her heart.

THE RESURRECTION CHRONICLES

The apocalyptic adventure continues!

Book 6: Demon Night

Angel's growing weaker by the day and needs help. In exchange for food, she agrees to give Shax advice regarding how to win over Hannah. If Angel can help make that happen, just maybe she won't be kicked out when her fellow survivors find out she's pregnant.

Book 7: Demon Dawn

In a post-apocalyptic world, Benna is faced with the choice of trading her body and heart to the dark fey in order to survive the infected.

Book 8: Demon Disgrace

Hannah is drinking away her life to stanch the bleeding pain from past trauma. Merdon, a dark fey with a violent history, relentlessly sets out to show her there's something worth living for.

Book 9: Demon Fall

June never planned to fall in love. She had her eyes on the prize: a career and independence. Too bad the world ended and stole those options from her. Maybe falling in love had been the better choice after all.

The Beastly Tales

Beauty and the Beast with seductively dark twists!

Book 1: Depravity

When impoverished, beautiful Benella is locked inside the dark and magical estate of the beast, she must bargain for her freedom if she wants to see her family again.

Book 2: Deceit

Safely hidden within the estate's enchanted walls, Benella no longer has time to fear her tormentors. She's too preoccupied trying to determine what makes the beast so beastly. In order to gain her freedom, she must find a way to break the curse, but first, she must help him become a better man while protecting her heart.

Book 3: Devastation

Abused and rejected, Benella strives to regain a purpose for her life, and finds herself returning to the last place she ever wanted to see. She must learn when it is right to forgive and when it is time to move on.

Tales of Cinder

Becareful what you wish for...

Prequel: Disowned

In a world where the measure of a person rarely goes beneath the surface, Margaret Thoning refuses to play by its rules. She walks away from everything she's ever known to risk her heart and her life for the people who matter most.

Book 1: Defiant

When the sudden death of Eloise's mother points to forbidden magic, Eloise's life quickly goes from fairy tale to nightmare. Kaven, the prince's manservant, is Eloise's prime suspect. However, when dark magic is used, nothing is as simple as it seems.

Book 2: Disdain

Cursed to silence, Eloise is locked in the tattered remains of her once charming life. The smoldering spark of her anger burns for answers and revenge. However, games of magic can have dire consequences.

Book 3: Damnation

With the reason behind her mother's death revealed, Eloise must prevent her stepsisters from marrying the prince and exact her revenge. However, a secret of the royal court strikes a blow to her plans. Betrayed, Eloise will question how far she's willing to go for revenge.